SHADOWS THROUGH TIME

SHADOWS THROUGH TIME

FROM THE SHADOW COUNCIL ARCHIVES

JAMES PALMER

Charlotte, NC

FALSTAFF
BOOKS

WWW.FALSTAFFBOOKS.COM

This book, as always, is for
Kelley and Gracie

PART I
THE DEPTHS OF TIME

THE MADNESS IN LONDON

But what is most peculiar," said Professor Challenger, "is the recent outbreak of madness all over the city."

Richard Francis Burton stared at the big, bearded man and realized he didn't have a clue what he was talking about. He'd scarcely been back in London for a month, but already he was caught up on what he thought was the important news of the day. That didn't stop Professor George Edward Challenger from bending his ear as soon as the latest meeting of the Royal Geographical Society had adjourned, telling Burton of everything he had missed in the thirty-three months he had been away. Since Challenger held the rather infamous reputation for being a domineering and disagreeable sort, Burton was inclined to just let the man talk as the hall emptied of occupants. Now the place was empty, the hour late, and Burton had no interest in prolonged exposure to the man. Until, of course, he mentioned the madness.

"I've read about it in the papers," said the explorer as he dashed out the remains of a cheroot in a silver ashtray. "But is it really all that peculiar?"

"It is when you consider those afflicted," said Challenger, stroking his thick black beard with sausage-like fingers. "It is only affecting spiritualist mediums."

Burton arched an eyebrow. He hadn't realized the madness was so specific. "That is strange."

"Mediums are already half mad if you ask me," Challenger continued. "Half mad, or charlatans. But isn't it strange that so many of them would be killing themselves or running deranged through the streets?"

"So it would seem," said Burton, glancing at his pocket watch one final time and, spying a way out, said, "but, I'm afraid we must solve the mystery of the madness of the mediums another day. I have a prior engagement."

Professor Challenger stared at Burton wide-eyed, taken aback at being so suddenly dismissed. "Oh, yes. Very well then. It was nice talking to you."

The two rose from their chairs and Challenger offered Burton his hand, the much larger man giving it an almost bone-rending shake.

"And you," said Burton half-heartedly.

He had heard stories about Challenger for years, but had never met the man until now. Challenger had made quite a name for himself while Burton was in Africa searching for the source of the Nile, going on an expedition of his own that caused a stir throughout London. Half the city thought him mad, while the other half thought him a charlatan.

Burton hadn't made up his mind where he fell along that divide. But he had enough to worry about right now, so soon after returning from his explorations, a trip that had almost killed him. This business with his partner on the expedition, John Hanning Speke, who had succumbed to madness on the journey, and who had died in an apparent hunting accident before the two were to debate their findings before this very society, combined with Burton's impending nuptials, had taken up most of Burton's faculties. Now he wanted nothing more than a quiet evening among like-minded friends and plenty of brandy.

As the two men were about to part ways, a small, female voice from the other side of the vast hall said, "Excuse me."

Both men turned at the sound. Across a sea of wooden chairs stood a tall woman in a dowdy, dark green dress of a style no longer in fashion. She stared at the two men nervously, her lace-gloved fingers clutching a large carpetbag.

"I'm sorry, Madam," Challenger boomed. "The meeting ended an hour ago."

"Oh dear," she said. "I'm sorry. I'm terribly late, aren't I?"

"Is there something we can help you with?" offered Burton.

"Yes, there is. I am looking for Captain Richard Francis Burton and Professor George Edward Challenger."

Challenger's eyes widened in surprise, and he ceased stroking his enormous beard.

Burton made a slight bow. "Well, Madam. You are in luck. I am Richard Francis Burton, and this is Professor Challenger."

The woman brightened and closed the distance between them, extending her right hand. "Perhaps my timing wasn't so unfortunate after all. My name is Elizabeth Marsh, and I need your help."

Burton settled himself back into the chair he had occupied while Challenger wagged his gums at him. Challenger did the same. Elizabeth Marsh took one of the small wooden chairs used for the meeting and turned it so she faced them, sitting down and placing her carpet bag by her right side.

Burton observed the woman carefully. Her American accent identified her as a denizen of New England, if he remembered his dialects correctly. A plain woman, yet not unattractive, her sea-green eyes seemed to take everything in, a careful study of her surroundings. Her mouth seemed over large, the lips unnaturally thick, her ears small and almost nonexistent. Her dark brown hair was twisted into a tight bun.

Challenger slouched in his chair beside Burton, unsure of what to make of their latest acquaintance.

"What can we help you with, Miss Marsh?" asked Burton, afraid Challenger would show off some of his trademark bluster and rudeness.

She sat in silence for a long moment, choosing her words. "Perhaps it's best I begin by showing you."

The woman leaned over and reached into her voluminous carpet bag. After rooting around in it for half a minute, she pulled out a small object wrapped in what appeared to be dried seaweed. She unwrapped the little parcel and held it out for Burton and Challenger to see.

"My traveling companion and I discovered this off the coast of Rapa Nui, in the South Seas."

Burton removed it from its seaweed wrapping and stared at it. It was a rather large, flat object composed of some blue-green stone, almost metallic, with a series of strange glyphs worked into it. Burton rubbed the images with his fingers. They had been worn smooth by time and the ocean, but were still very detailed. The subject matter seemed to concern some strange oceanic god Burton wasn't familiar with. Three tiny, supplicating human figures lay prostrate before a grotesque, looming being with the head of a fish and a frog-like body. He'd never seen anything like it, and didn't want to again. He passed it to Challenger, who turned it over in his large hands, studying its every line and texture.

"What do you make of it?" asked Elizabeth Marsh.

"It's very unusual," said Burton.

"Where did you say you found it?" asked Challenger.

"Off the coast of Rapa Nui," said the woman.

Professor Challenger arched one of his vast eyebrows. "You mean underwater?"

"Yes," said the woman, her green eyes glancing back and forth between the two men, as if seeking something.

"Are you a treasure, hunter, Miss Marsh?" asked Challenger.

"No," she said with a grin. "Nothing like that. Merely an explorer, like yourselves."

"What does this have to do with us, Miss Marsh?" asked Burton.

Marsh stared at them for a moment before speaking. "This artifact isn't the only secret the oceans hold. I'm sure you are both aware of the recent bouts of madness occurring in your city among its more...*sensitive* inhabitants."

"The mediums, yes," replied Burton. "The Professor and I were just discussing it before you entered."

"Then you must also know that this plague, if you will, has also been recorded all over the continent of Europe."

"No," said Challenger. "I was not aware of this."

"In fact," Elizabeth Marsh continued, "it has been occurring as far north as Greenland and as far south as..." She took the artifact from Challenger. "Rapa Nui, where this was found."

Challenger grinned and began stroking his beard. "Madam, are you suggesting that this little trinket is somehow the cause of a few so-called mediums falling out of their tree?"

"No. What I am suggesting is that it is the symptom of a greater malady. One that spans the globe."

Professor Challenger bellowed laughter that rocked his barrel chest and threatened to send him out of his chair and onto the floor. Burton kept his response a bit more reserved.

"Miss Marsh, you must understand that it is quite hard to believe that this artifact, found in the South Seas, is tied in any way to mental instability in London, England."

"I understand your reluctance to believe, Captain Burton. I scarcely believe it myself, but there is something else. Something that is happening beneath the ocean even as we speak. Something my traveling companion and I discovered during our explorations of a remote section of the ocean, far from any landmass."

Professor Challenger ceased his laughing. "Oh, I have *got* to hear this!"

When Challenger calmed down, Elizabeth Marsh continued. "There is a great, undersea upheaval at coordinates 49°51'S 128°34'W."

Professor Challenger glared at her, then got up and left the room. Burton and the woman followed him.

The big zoologist was in the Society's map room, selecting a map from a rack set along one wall and spreading it out on a large desk. He bent over it, studying it intently.

"What is it?" asked Burton.

Challenger stood up and looked at Elizabeth. "Those coordinates of yours are in the middle of the ocean between your South Seas islands and Antarctica. There's nothing out there for thousands of miles."

7

"That is correct," said the woman.

"Well," said Challenger. "My question then, Madam, is how could you possibly be aware of some undersea upheaval this far from land? There have been no large sea quakes reported that I know of."

Elizabeth Marsh grinned. "Your curiosity is understandable, gentlemen. But to find out, you must meet me at this address." She handed both men slips of paper with an address scrawled on them. "Be there, tonight at midnight, and your questions shall be answered."

Without another word, Elizabeth Marsh departed. They watched the mysterious woman as she hurried from the map room and, retrieving her carpet bag, moved toward the entrance to the hall and was gone.

"What the devil do you think that was all about?" muttered Challenger.

"I haven't the foggiest," said Burton. "But I really must be going. I'm late for my other engagement."

Burton grabbed his topper and walking stick, leaving the professor to stand there muttering to himself about the strange woman who had just vanished from their lives as quickly as she appeared.

THE CANNIBAL CLUB

Thirty minutes later, Richard Francis Burton exited a horse-drawn carriage in front of a building near Fleet Street. He paid the driver and stood staring up at the familiar edifice as the driver urged his tired old dray into motion. The upper floor windows were suffused with a warm glow, and Burton could see the shadows of figures milling about up there. Burton grinned. The Cannibal Club had been his home away from home for several years, and he couldn't wait to see his friends once more.

"Burton!" Thomas Bendeshye called as Burton entered the upper room and doffed his topcoat and beaver. "About damned time you show up. Where the devil have you been?"

"At the Royal Geographic Society," murmured the explorer. "That zoologist Challenger bent my ear."

"Oh no," Bendeshye said with a chuckle. "He didn't invite you to his museum, did he?"

"No, he was consumed with other news. Where's my brandy?"

Charles Bradlaugh thrust a snifter of the stuff in the explorer's face. The other man's eyes were wide and bloodshot. Burton could tell he had a lot of catching up to do.

Burton selected a wingback chair in the center of the room and sat down in it. In a matching chair directly across from him, his friend, the poet Algernon Charles Swinburne sat cross-legged, his long red hair hanging in his face. "What ho, Richard?" he screeched. "You look positively flummoxed. What's got hold of you?"

"I just had the strangest conversation," said the explorer.

"No doubt," the poet agreed. "You were talking to that blowhard Challenger!"

"No, that's not what I mean. We were discussing the recent bouts of madness among the city's population of spiritualist mediums."

"Yes," said Dr. James Hunt, his voice slurred by the brandy. He was standing behind Swinburne lighting a pipe. "I've been reading about that. They say Bedlam's almost full. Though I believe we're all much better off without those charlatans running rampant."

"True," said Burton. "Still, to affect only them and not the rest of the population? I don't believe in that spiritualist nonsense any more than the rest of you, but even I can't ignore how strange a coincidence it is."

The five of them mused on that for a while as they drank, Burton doing his best to catch up to the level of inebriation of his friends. Only the young poet Swinburne constantly bested them. Their mutual friend and fellow Cannibal, Richard Monkton Milnes, once quipped that Swinburne woke up drunk, but whatever the case, the poet demonstrated a remarkable tolerance for alcohol.

The conversation drifted on to other topics, and Burton contented himself with listening as his friends conversed. Burton needed a stable, stationary point in his life, and the Cannibal Club was it. The group had a steadying, recuperative effect on him that he didn't know he needed until right at that very moment.

He just wished the Cannibal Club's full roster was in attendance—it appeared that Milnes, Sir James Plaisted Wilde, General Studholme John Hodgson, and Charles Duncan Cameron were otherwise engaged. He would have liked to hear their thoughts on the mysterious Elizabeth Marsh and her strange invitation.

Talk soon turned to Speke's death, with everyone keen to hear Burton's take on the matter. The explorer was still angry with Speke and confused by the suddenness of his death, and was, therefore, reticent to speak on the matter. That didn't stop the others from pontificating about it at some length. Burton drank and listened, but kept his own thoughts to himself.

Speke had appeared quite competent before the expedition began. Burton had known him for years, and was confident that there was no one he'd rather travel with to Africa than John Hanning Speke.

However, Speke had some rather strange ideas with regards to ethnology, and seemed intent on pursuing some esoteric line of study during their travels. He kept a journal separate from the one he used to detail their journey, and grew angered when a curious Burton attempted to read it. Burton awoke on several occasions to Speke screaming in his tent, in the throes of some horrible dream, long before both of them succumbed to malaria. What was it he chanted? *Ia! Ia! Cthulhu fhtagn!* Burton had a great talent for languages, and he was damned if he knew what Speke was uttering on those nights. And that particular chant occurred too often to be ascribed to malarial gibberish.

Eventually Burton too had contracted malaria, and had to be carried much of the way by their porters while he warred with his own delusions. To make matters even more strained, Speke, who had recovered from his bout of malaria before Burton, had journeyed north without him from Lake Victoria to Lake Tanganyika and, despite lacking the equipment to survey and study it properly—said equipment having been damaged or stolen—claimed that Lake Tanganyika was indeed the long-sought source of the Nile.

Burton regarded this as poppycock, of course, and was angered at Speke's presumption at arriving in England far ahead of Burton and proudly proclaiming the Nile source debate settled and done.

Then, before Burton had a chance to debate Speke's findings, the old fool went and got himself shot.

Burton could find no logical bridge by which to bring up the matter of the strange woman and her eerie invitation, so he consulted his pocket watch.

Quarter past eleven. Midnight was getting nearer. If he was going to make it in time, he'd best go now.

Should he go? The proposition was silly on the face of it. A mysterious woman shows up and hints at a way of gleaning the secrets buried beneath the limitless waves of the deepest oceans, and asks him for his help. But only if he'll meet her at midnight in an unwholesome part of the city. If anyone met him there at that hour, it would in all likelihood be a cutpurse ready to unburden him of his valuables. No thanks. He had other matters that needed his attention. He was home now, after years of wandering, exploring. And he was going to marry Isabel Arundel, if she would still have him.

But as the evening went on, Burton found himself growing restless. He couldn't get Elizabeth Marsh, and the compelling mystery she represented, out of his mind. He drained his brandy. Thomas Bendyshe came around to refill it; Burton refused. James Hunt barked drunken laughter at one of Swinburne's bawdy lines of verse the poet had composed on the spot. Burton heaved himself up out of the armchair, lest he become permanently affixed to it and, choosing his steps with care, made for the door.

"Leaving so soon, Richard?" said Braidlaugh.

Swinburne stared up at the explorer, combing an errant shock of hair from his face and twitching drunkenly. "You haven't been here long enough to catch up."

"I don't think that's possible, Algy," said Burton. "I must go. I have some important matters that need my attention."

"In the middle of the night?" said Bendeshye.

"So long, gents."

Burton grabbed his coat and hat and left the dining room, putting on his topper and coat on his way down the stairs to street level. After five minutes of waiting, he hailed a hansom and gave him the address Elizabeth Marsh had provided.

He arrived at five minutes to midnight. Though the day had been clear, a fog crept in off the water, transformed by the gaslights that dotted the bank of the Thames into a milky gloom. Burton wasn't surprised to find someone standing in that gloom, recognizing the broad, bearded form of Professor George Edward Challenger.

The big zoologist rocked on his heels. "I'm surprised to see you, Burton. I thought you had done with exploring."

Burton moved next to him. "Nothing wrong with getting a few questions answered before settling down."

The big man smiled, which looked more like a sneer. Burton blew into his hands and rubbed them together. The night had become unusually damp and chill. "What now?" he muttered.

"Now," said Professor Challenger. "we wait."

AN INVITATION

The two men stood in silence for what felt like a long time, the dank waters of the Thames lapping up against the wooden pilings of the wharf. Professor Challenger rocked back and forth on his heels, beefy hands in his pockets, looking like someone out for a leisure stroll through Green Park.

Burton checked his watch by the murky light of a fog-shrouded gaslight. Five past midnight. They had been played for fools. A cheap trinket no doubt found in some Pacific Rim market stall had them standing out in the damp fog like a couple of imbeciles.

"Stand out here if you want," Burton said. "I'm getting home and going to bed."

As he was about to turn away, a loud churning and gurgling came from the water. They ran to the wharf's edge and peered down.

Burton couldn't be sure, due to the late hour and the fog, but it appeared that a large, dark shape was rising up from the water like some great whale. At first, he thought it some huge creature of the sea, traveling up the Thames because it had somehow lost its way. No, the skin was hard, uniform. Metallic.

A portal or hatch opened and out climbed a familiar female form, wearing the same green dress.

"Sorry I'm late," said Elizabeth Marsh, looking up at them. "I am glad both of you are here. My traveling companion said to invite you both, in case one of you declined."

She emerged from the small hatch in the hide of the metallic beast and stood next to the opening. "You asked me earlier how I could find that artifact deep underwater, and how I could know of some undersea upheaval. This is how." She gestured with a gloved hand to the thing she stood on.

Burton looked from the woman to the opening in the top of the contraption and took a step back.

"My dear Miss Marsh," said Professor Challenger. "This might answer one question, but it raises a hundred or so more."

Elizabeth Marsh smiled. "And those questions will be answered, if you are ready. My traveling companion has selected you for a noble purpose. A great, dangerous journey awaits you, full of wonders you couldn't possibly imagine."

"Miss Marsh," said Burton. "I have traveled all over this world. I have seen things few white men will ever see. I've crossed dangerous jungles, treacherous mountains, dealt with ferocious natives. I've almost been killed by malaria more than once. What could you possibly show me that I haven't already seen?"

"With all due respect, Captain Burton," said Elizabeth Marsh, "you have only traveled the earth's surface. What my traveling companion offers you is a glimpse at the remaining two thirds. What I can offer you abides below."

"By Jove," Challenger rumbled. "Count me in!"

"Miss Marsh," said Burton. "I thank you for invitation, but I am done with exploring. I am going to marry and take a diplomatic post and write."

"That is your choice," said Elizabeth Marsh. "I am not asking either of you to make your decision right this minute. My companion knows what an important decision this is. And believe me when I say that history will not think less of you for declining. You have each done enough for a thousand lifetimes. But this is a one-time offer that expires twenty-four hours from now. You have until tomorrow at midnight to make up your minds and prepare for your journey. If you are coming with us, meet me here then."

"My mind is made up," said Challenger. "I will see you on the morrow, Miss Marsh." He bowed and tipped his hat. "What say you, Burton? Are you game for another adventure?"

"I don't know," he murmured, turning his head and looking down the wharf. "I don't know."

When they looked down at the water once more, Elizabeth Marsh and her incredible underwater machine were gone.

HOME AND ISABEL

Burton awoke to late morning light filtering through his window, shaking off the vestiges of strange dreams.

He thought himself back in his tent on the banks of Lake Victoria, still in the grips of malaria. He could almost smell the horses, hear the tent canvas snapping in the hot breeze. It took him a moment to get his bearings, to remember where he was.

"I'm in my bed," muttered the explorer. nIn my home at Gloucester Place."

He squeezed the freshly starched sheets, which solidified his place and time. He felt like he was being pulled in a dozen directions at once. Burton lay there until the sensation passed, then got up and dressed in a loose-fitting white *jubba* before heading down the hall to his study.

Burton entered and, for the first time since returning to London, felt like he was home. He moved passed the elephant foot umbrella stand to the row of bookshelves covering one wall. "Home is where the books are," he said, running his fingers along the spines.

Burton turned from his books to the wall of weapons. Gleaming swords, spears and firearms and other mementos from his travels greeted him. Burton glanced at one rather lethal-looking spear, touching his left cheek, where a similar weapon had left a triangular scar.

A knock on the study door startled Burton from his reminiscences. "Come in."

His landlady and house keeper Miss Angell appeared, carrying a silver tray laden with food. "I thought I heard you up and milling about. Figured you'd want breakfast up here."

"That would be fine, thank you."

Miss Angell moved to Burton's writing desk, which was almost devoid of papers and knick-knacks, and set the tray down and poured him a cup of coffee.

"There you go," she said. "Eat up. You almost withered away on that trip of yours."

Burton smiled. Since his return, it had been Miss Angell's main goal in life to return him to some level of fat respectability. When she left the room, Burton sat down and did just that, tucking into his eggs and sausage with relish. He drank his coffee and stared at his massive bookshelf, starting to feel like his old self once more. He could almost forget the strange events of last evening had happened at all.

Almost.

Burton finished his breakfast and puttered around in his study, a loss as to what to do. He wrote letters and stared at one of his manuscripts without doing anything productive with it. Around noon, he had a visitor.

"Isabel," he said before she had entered the room.

Isabel Arundell. The one thing that had kept him sane throughout his long journey had been thinking of her. She was always there, even when he was in the grips of malarial fever. He never wrote to her the entire time he was gone, save for a few lines of poetry he composed upon leaving the jungle at last and arriving at Zanzibar:

> *To Isabel*
> *That brow which rose before my sight,*
> *As on the palmer's holy shrine;*
> *Those eyes—my life was in their light;*
> *Those lips—my sacramental wine;*

That voice whose flow was wont to seem
The music of an exile's dream.

Burton went to her and kissed her cheek, squeezing her hands in his. She smiled up at him. "I thought I'd surprise you," she said. "How have you been? I heard about that business with Speke."

"I am doing much better now that I've seen you." He turned from her sight and looked out the window, as if seeking something far away.

"What is it, Richard?"

He met her gaze once more. "It's—I've been restless since I returned. I think it's the old explorer in me, wanting to set out on another adventure."

"You will, my love," said Isabel. "When we get to Trieste. You can write and finish your translations. We will be adventurers together."

Burton opened his mouth, closed it. The diplomatic post destined to be the most boring thing the explorer had ever set out to do. He'd told himself that was what he needed for the back half of his life, solace and solitude with which to write. No malaria, no restless, spear-waving natives to menace him.

"I know that look," Isabel said. Her mouth, a perpetual smile, began to quiver.

Burton took a step back. "What look?"

"The wanderlust in your eyes." She took a step back, fidgeting with the bodice of her dark dress. "I thought you'd come back to me ready to settle down and start our lives together."

"It's nothing like that," said Burton. "It's just that…something has come up. An exciting invitation too enticing to turn down. I thought I could, at first, but now…" He let his voice trail off. It would do him no good to say anything further.

Isabel stared at him for a full minute before her mouth creased into a smile. "I should have known better than to think an explorer could just stop exploring. You haven't got it out of your system yet."

"It would appear so," said Burton.

"So where is it this time? Back to Africa? A trek across the Himalayas? Steamy Kathmandu?"

"No, nothing like that. I can't really say. I don't think you'd believe me if I told you. But I can promise that there will be no treacherous jungles and no malaria involved."

"I can thank God for that," Isabel said flatly. "All right, Richard Burton, you old pain in the rump. I've waited three years. I can wait a little more. You can go on your little adventure. I'll be right here when you get back."

She reached up to squeeze his shoulders. "But I'd better not hear you've been visiting brothels with that reprobate Swinburne or the rest of your Cannibal Club lot."

Burton grinned. "I would not sully your good name in such a fashion. I can assure you the Cannibals are in no way involved."

Isabel gave him a stern glance. "Just assure me that you will come home to me. Safe and sound."

She kissed him on the cheek and left. Burton stood there for a long time, staring at his study door, wondering just what he had done. His adventuring was behind him, and now he was going off on another. One in which he had no idea what was going to happen. It was the most excited he had felt in a long time.

BOARDING THE NAUTILUS

Now clear on what he had set out to do, Burton tackled his tasks with much more clarity than he had shown that morning. He dashed off a few quick letters to various members of the Cannibal Club—Swinburne, Dr. James Hunt, Richard Monkton Milnes, and Sir James Plaisted Wilde—asking them to do various things for him while he was away, such as looking in on Ms. Angell and Isabel, as well as one to Sir Roderick Murchison, president of the Royal Geographical Society, regarding his conclusions about the true source of the Nile. Once that was done, Burton set about packing for his strange journey.

The problem was that, for the first time in his life, he didn't know what he would need. He had traveled by ship many times, but he had never voyaged beneath the waves. He settled on filling a worn leather portmanteau suitcase with a few linen shirts, khaki pants, and an extra *jubba*. Next Burton went to his wall of weapons, selecting a pistol and ten rounds of ammunition and an Nepalese khukuri, or Gurkha, knife. The curved, almost boomerang-shaped blade glinted brightly in the late afternoon sun that shone through his study window. He gripped the blade's wooden handle and tested the blade's keen edge on the fine hairs on his left arm and, finding its sharpness satisfactory, sheathed it and placed it atop his portmanteau alongside the holstered revolver.

At midnight, Burton arrived, carrying his portmanteau and armed with pistol and blade. Last night's fog didn't make a return appearance. Burton stepped to the edge of the wharf and looked down at the Thames, the water green where the street lamps touched it, black where it twisted out of their reach. He curled his nose from the stench.

A moment later another horse-drawn hansom clopped to a stop, and a large man alighted and paid his fare. Challenger glanced at Burton and nodded once. He too carried a large bag, but Burton couldn't tell if the huge zoologist was armed.

"Captain Burton," he said as he stepped to the water's edge.

"Challenger."

"Lovely night for an adventure."

"I suppose," said Burton. "If one must have them at night."

Challenger barked laughter. "Let's hope our strange Miss Marsh doesn't keep us waiting, eh?"

They stood in silence a while before Challenger broke it by saying, "I thought you had your fill of exploring."

Burton shrugged, his eyes still on the Thames. "So did I."

Challenger chuckled. They waited some more.

At midnight—on the dot this time—they heard a familiar churning of the water and watched in amazement as a familiar shape arose from the Thames. The hatch opened, and once again Elizabeth Marsh climbed out to meet them, this time in a red dress.

"Professor Challenger," she said, addressing the big man. "Captain Burton. I'm very happy you decided to join us. Please toss your bags down the hatch and climb down. We must hurry, lest we be spotted."

"Who's going to see us out here?" said Challenger. "At this time of night?"

"My traveling companion takes no chances, Professor."

Challenger positioned his bag over the hole and dropped it in. A muffled thump sounded from within. Burton did the same.

"Now," said Marsh, "one of you climb down and through the hatch, moving as far as you can to the rear of the craft." She gestured at the vehicle's farthest end with her left hand. "I'm afraid it's quite cramped."

"We're not going to journey across the ocean in this, are we?" Burton asked.

"No," she said. "This isn't the main craft. The Thames isn't wide enough or deep enough to allow my companion's ship passage."

Not sure how he felt about being in cramped confines underwater, especially with a man-bear like Challenger, Burton waved to the zoologist to go first. The explorer watched as Challenger lumbered down the creaking ladder and stuffed himself through the hole in the top of the craft. He heard a faint echo from within as the larger man moved toward the vehicle's rear as instructed.

"Now you, Captain Burton," said Miss Marsh.

"Please, I'm not a captain anymore. Just Burton."

Miss Marsh nodded. "As you wish." She gestured to the wharf's ladder once more.

Burton twisted around, his feet finding the wet, wooden rungs and bringing him to the top of the bizarre contraption. It looked much smaller than it had from above, and Burton once again had misgivings about climbing into the thing. But Miss Marsh helped him inside, where his feet met with plush, crimson carpeting. A set of lanterns hung above the inner chamber of the tiny vessel, casting wan light about their spartan surroundings.

"Back here," said Challenger, gesturing. He sat on a couch that looked close to buckling beneath his bulk. "I took the liberty of stacking our baggage there," he said, pointing to his right. "I'm glad we packed light."

In a moment Miss Marsh appeared and seated herself at the fore of the vehicle before a panel of instruments and a thick square of glass through which murky water was visible. Burton sat down next to Challenger on the couch—which was quite cramped—and watched as Elizabeth Marsh pulled a lever, causing the open hatch above them to seal.

"We'll be off now, gentlemen. You might want to hang onto something."

She opened a valve, pressed a few more levers forward, and

23

Burton felt the submarine craft submerge as it surged forward. More lights appeared visible on the outside of the craft, illuminating the murky waters of the Thames.

"Miss Marsh," said Burton, his voice echoing in the tiny cabin, "how long will this journey take?"

"Not long," she answered without looking back. "We will rendezvous with the main craft in six minutes."

"We'll reach the Thames Estuary before then," said Challenger thoughtfully, "and pass into the North Sea. Miss Marsh's traveling companion no doubt awaits us there."

"That is correct, Professor," said the woman, keeping her eyes on the controls.

Burton noted the remarkable skill with which she guided the small craft through the dark water. "You seem to be a capable pilot, Miss Marsh."

"Why thank you, Mr. Burton. I could not have had a better teacher than the man who built it."

"What is it called?" asked Challenger.

"I call it *Errand Boy*." She giggled at this and opened up what Burton assumed was some sort of engine throttle, as the craft seemed to pick up speed.

"We have now left the Thames and have entered the North Sea. Hold on."

A moment later Burton could see through the poorly illumined darkness a vast black shape growing larger in the viewing window. Miss Marsh slowed the tiny submarine, and a dull thump indicated they had somehow docked with the much larger craft. Miss Marsh killed the craft's engine.

"What now?" bellowed Challenger.

"We must wait a few more moments."

Burton felt the vibration of churning water on the other side of the vessel's hull, and they heard a loud gurgling. "The water's being pumped out," said Challenger. "Errand Boy must be in some kind of airlock." Marsh nodded to them, moving the lever that opened the hatch. The cabin was suffused with warm light from above.

"Gentlemen," she said, standing and moving beneath the glowing portal, "welcome aboard the *Nautilus*."

This time Burton went first, the fresh air hitting him like an arctic blast.

"Your bags will be brought to your rooms, which I will show you now," he heard Miss Marsh say, but he was too busy taking in his new surroundings to hear what she said. They were in a metal clad, cylinder-shaped room. A man in plain blue coveralls without any military insignia or ornamentation helped Burton out of the hatch and onto a metal gangway that extended over the vessel, which had been winched up into the larger vessel with heavy chains. Seawater ran down the sides to collect in reservoirs in the floor that carried it out of the craft and back into the ocean.

Led down a set of metal steps, Burton waited at the bottom for Challenger and Miss Marsh while he admired the machine they had exited.

An ironclad submersible. Sleek and compact, it could easily pass for a fish to anyone who happened to see it. It was shaped like a shark or a dolphin, right down to metal dorsal fins and a razor-edged tail that held twin propellers. The design was extraordinary, and Burton imagined the vessel sliding through the water with great speed and agility, perhaps matched only by the underwater creatures it was intended to mimic.

"Most impressive, Miss Marsh," said Burton when she and Challenger had both alighted beside him.

"You haven't seen anything yet," she said. "Follow Mr. Murgal through that door there, and he'll escort you to your quarters so you can freshen up."

Burton fell in behind the tall, swarthy man Miss Marsh had designated Mr. Murgal, who said nothing as he led them away from the dripping submarine and into a narrow corridor lined with pumps and other equipment. At the far end stood another door, which Mr. Murgal twisted open with a metal wheel set into its face. The two men followed Mr. Murgal through the doorway and into a corridor more lavish than the finest sailing ships had to offer.

The walls were paneled in ornate wood and fitted out in gleaming brass. The floor was covered in plush red carpeting. Soft lights shone down on them at regular intervals. "Remarkable," murmured Burton.

Challenger nodded in approval as they followed Mr. Murgal through a maze of such corridors before stopping before opposite doors. He motioned to them. Burton took the one on the left, and Challenger the room on the right.

"Breakfast is at seven," said Murgal in heavily accented English.

"And what of our host?" said Challenger.

"You will meet him at that time." Without another word, he walked up the corridor and disappeared through a hatchway.

Burton and Challenger regarded each other for a long moment before the burly zoologist turned and entered his room. Burton was about to turn the brass knob of his own door when he heard someone talking back the way they had come. A young man in a brown tweed suit was coming up the corridor, accompanied by another dark-skinned, blue-uniformed attendant, who ushered him through a door at the far end on the same side as Burton's room. The young man glanced in his direction, nodding once before stepping into what must be his quarters. "Who in the devil is that?" Burton mused aloud. It couldn't be their host. Another adventurer?

Burton found his room to be small, yet much more elegant than he had expected. There was a bed and a large desk, both bolted to the carpeted floor. Other than that necessity aboard a submarine, it could have been a room at one of the finest hotels in London. He sat on the bed, finding his portmanteau sitting on the end of it. Burton found a small closet on the other side of the bed and began emptying the contents of his case into it. He removed his revolver and khukuNri and placed them in a drawer of the desk.

Putting on his *jebba*, Burton climbed into bed. He closed his eyes, but he did not go to sleep for a long time. The strange ship, full of unusual noises no doubt peculiar to this form of transport, occupied his thoughts for a long time. When he at last fell asleep, his last thought was of Isabel.

CAPTAIN NEMO

Burton awoke, dressed, and waited for the knock at his door for breakfast.

A different man than Mr. Murgal met him at the door. "You will accompany me, please," he said in a thick Indian accent. Burton nodded and followed. The man rapped three times on Challenger's door, and it opened to reveal a fully dressed but bleary-eyed zoologist. He joined them, and together they were taken to the far end of the corridor, through a hatchway, and up a set of mahogany stairs to another corridor that opened up into a grand dining room dominated by a long table laden with pickled herring and other food taken from the sea.

Elizabeth Marsh was sitting near the center of the table. Next to her, chatting amicably, was a young man with blond hair, wearing a smart tweed suit. He was clean shaven, and his pale eyes sparkled in the electric light shining from above. Burton realized he was the same man he had spied the night previous.

At the head of the table sat a tall, rigid man of Indian descent. A turban of crimson silk adorned his stolid head, and he wore a crisp blue uniform with golden epaulets that spilled down the shoulders. The medals and symbols of rank adorning the uniform's front was obscured by his thick yet neatly trimmed blue-black beard. The man's intense dark eyes followed Burton and Challenger to the table, where they sat across from Elizabeth Marsh and the mysterious young man.

Miss Marsh addressed them. "Captain Richard Francis Burton, Professor George Edward Challenger, I'd like you to meet your host and the commander of this vessel, Captain Nemo."

Burton arched an eyebrow. Nemo. Latin for "nobody."

"It is a pleasure to make your acquaintances at last," said Nemo in a crisp accent. "News of your exploits has reached even my ears, and I am honored to have you aboard my *Nautilus*."

"The pleasure is ours, Captain," said Burton.

Challenger grunted in the affirmative and skewered a piece of herring with a fork.

"And this," said Marsh, motioning to her companion, "is—"

"I am an inventor," said the young man. "You can call me Herbert."

"What are you an inventor of, Herbert?" said Challenger around a mouthful of herring.

"Oh, many things. Mostly I am a machinist and student of optics."

More interested in their host than to pay any heed to what Challenger and this Herbert lad were discussing, Burton regarded Nemo. The captain of the *Nautilus* projected a regal air. Where did he and his crew hail from, and how did he acquire this remarkable vessel?

Captain Nemo followed his gaze. "You are curious about me."

"Well, uh, yes," said Burton. "I mean no disrespect. This is just—" He waved his hands about the dining room. "Very strange. I'm sure you must appreciate that."

Nemo gave a thin smile. "Of course, forgive me. I do not often have visitors. You are my guests. Ask your questions. If they are pertinent to the matters at hand I will answer them."

"Well, then," said Burton, unsure of where to begin. "This vessel. You built it yourself?"

"I did."

"Do you live in it year round?"

"I do. My crew and I have shunned the land and all it contains, living always beneath the waves. All of our material needs are provided by the sea. We surface only to take on fresh air."

"And you did this without the patronage of any government?"

Nemo nodded. "That is correct. I designed and built the *Nautilus* myself, for no other purpose than to live in it and explore the ocean's depths."

Burton continued studying Nemo while they ate, knowing full well that there was much more to this strange man than he was letting on. He turned his attentions to young Herbert, who devoured his meal with gusto while an attendant came around and poured them wine, a luxury Burton was surprised to find on a submarine vessel. It appeared not everything at Nemo's table came from the sea.

"And what brings you aboard, Herbert?" asked Burton after a sip of the excellent vintage.

Herbert smiled brightly. "Well, I'm afraid seeing is believing. Suffice it to say I have brought something aboard with me that will be of immeasurable use in our adventure." He glanced once at their host before drinking his own wine.

"But more to that point," he added. "I am a student of the future. Our great and glorious future, when mankind has ended all disease and has stopped starting wars with one another. When there are no more social classes, and all of our material needs are taken care of."

"Ho ho," Challenger boomed. "We're trapped aboard with a bleedin' socialist."

"Scoff if you will," said Herbert. "but the time will come when what I've described will be. Mark my words. Just imagine it! An egalitarian society, free of want and social strata."

"My dear young man," said Burton. "Your ideals may be lofty, but I have traveled all over this world. I have seen man only capable of the same dark urgings, the same social shortcomings. The dearest ambition of a slave is not liberty, but to have a slave of his own."

Herbert scowled and finished his breakfast in silence.

"When we are finished," said Elizabeth Marsh, "Captain Nemo has promised you a tour of the *Nautilus*."

The three men nodded and said nothing. Burton continued watching Nemo, wondering what he had gotten himself into.

A MASTERPIECE CONTAINING MASTERPIECES

When everyone had breakfasted to their satisfaction, Nemo rose from the table. "Please join me on a tour of the *Nautilus*. When the tour is concluded I shall explain why I have asked you all aboard. Come."

Burton and the others followed Nemo out the other side of the grand dining room and into a more finely appointed part of the underwater ship than the section containing Burton's quarters. Expensive oil paintings hung in gilded frames from the walls, and plaster busts stood bolted to their pedestals or adorned recessed nooks in the walls. For all his shunning of the surface world, this Captain Nemo certainly brought much of it with him, Burton mused.

"The quality of the light is astonishing," Herbert remarked. "This isn't gaslight."

"No, no," said Nemo. "Gas would prove fatal in such an enclosed space. The lighting is provided by electricity, the same thing that powers the *Nautilus*."

"How is this power produced?" Challenger asked.

"Sodium-mercury batteries," answered Nemo. "The sodium is provided by extraction from seawater. That is also how we produce all drinkable water aboard ship."

"Incredible," said the young man as they continued onward. Nemo showed them a fully stocked library, every shelf bursting with leather bound volumes. But what impressed Burton the most was the enormous pipe organ that dominated the room, both with its size and its incongruity. It stood out as being unusual on a ship that was filled with wonders.

"This version of the *Nautilus* is more than 140 meters long, more than twice the length of its predecessor," said Captain Nemo. "It is a long cylinder with conical ends, like a cigar, which helps it slide effortlessly through the water. Its top speed is fifty knots."

"How does it dive and ascend?" asked Herbert.

"Come, I will show you."

Nemo led them down a short flight of stairs into a more utilitarian part of the vessel, everything a dull gray. A low roar drummed in their ears, the sound of the ship's engines. Nemo nodded to a passing attendant as the little man ducked out of sight through a hatchway, then twisted open another door set near it. He ushered them through.

"Wait," said Challenger. "Where's Miss Marsh?"

"I'd wager she's already had the tour," said Burton, urging the bigger man through before him.

Long rows of pipes ran along the walls, some of them feeding into enormous tanks that crowded the corridor walls from floor to ceiling.

"Ballast tanks," said Herbert.

"Exactly," Nemo replied. "We can control the ship's buoyancy and depth with these tanks. To dive, the pumps suck in water. To surface, the pumps expel the water with great force. But enough of that. You did not come here to marvel at my vessel's engineering."

Captain Nemo led them from the room as Herbert and Challenger barraged him with questions about the *Nautilus*. Burton did not care one wit about the vessel, as fantastic as it was. He cared no more about the *Nautilus* than a tramp steamer bound for Zanzibar. His interest was in the man who built it. What kind of a man would shun not just a particular king and country, but the world entire, to live in the ocean? What must have happened to that man? What could such a man possibly want with him? What was such a man capable of?

Burton considered the true purpose of the *Nautilus*. A perfect weapon of war. A fleet of such submarine vessels could attack and destroy ships of an enemy nation with impunity.

Yet the *Nautilus* did not belong to any government. It was not part of a fleet. And it was built for comfort, not war. That was something, at least. Burton hoped he would find out his purpose for being there soon.

They returned to the more familiar section of the ship, and Nemo ushered them into a large, wood-paneled room. The floor was covered in Persian rugs, the walls adorned with framed displays of preserved sea life, and there were more objects on pedestals displayed throughout the room. This piqued Challenger's interest. He stared into case after case, amazed.

"You have specimens here that are unknown to science," the zoologist declared.

"I am aware of that, Professor," said Nemo.

"But they must be in a museum," said Challenger. "They must be shared with the world."

"They *are* in a museum," Challenger corrected. "As for the rest of the world, if they want to discover them, they had best get past their petty bickering and get on with it."

Before the debate grew more heated, Miss Marsh entered the room, smiling. "I trust you all enjoyed your tour."

Nemo grinned, taking her hands. "They most certainly did. Now to the matter at hand; why you are all here."

THE SHADOW COUNCIL

Burton, Challenger, and Herbert formed a semi-circle in front of Nemo as he moved to a wide flat desk and opened up the carpet bag Burton remembered from his first meeting with Miss Marsh. He reached in and pulled out a stack of newspapers, his eyes glancing over the headlines.

"The first iteration of this vessel," said Nemo, "held a library containing newspapers and magazines from all over the world, dated from when I first shunned the surface to live aboard the *Nautilus*. I read through these for years, feeling no need to have any awareness of current news. Recent events have convinced me I need to stay more up to date. Miss Marsh is kind enough to go ashore and procure these for me from time to time."

He picked up an issue of *The London Gazette*. "You, no doubt, are aware of the recent bouts of madness occurring among spiritualist mediums in your country."

"Yes," said Burton. "Is that why we are here?"

"That is part of it," said Nemo. "This occurrence of madness is just the symptom. I seek the cause."

"Miss Marsh told us of the recent undersea events occurring at a set of remote coordinates," Challenger said. "Now, what is all this about?"

Nemo placed the newspaper down on the stack with the others. "You have been recruited for a great and secret purpose," he said. "Certain cataclysmic events are taking place across the world, which require men and women of a certain fortitude. From time to time, these exceptional men and women assemble, in secret, to battle the darkness that threatens us all. We call ourselves the Shadow Council."

"And what darkness is that?" asked Professor Challenger.

"You already know of the madness in London, among the spiritualists," said Nemo, hands clasped behind his back. "This, so far, is its northernmost point. For now. It goes much farther, down through the coast of France, through the Greek Isles, the southernmost island of Japan, and into the South Seas, though it is much worse down there, near the epicenter."

"Epicenter?" said Challenger. "You speak as if it is the locus of some disease."

"Perhaps it is," said Nemo. "Though a disease of the mind rather than the body. It started with several remote sea quakes too far away from any inhabited land to be felt. But I and my crew felt them."

Nemo came around the desk and went to a long table, where a large map had already been unrolled, the four corners held down by large conch shells. "I am convinced the quakes, and the resultant madness, originated here." He pointed at a spot in the middle of the ocean just above the Antarctic Circle.

"Those are the same coordinates Miss Marsh showed us," Burton observed.

"And there's nothing there," added Challenger. "As I explained to Miss Marsh."

"Above the waves, that is true," said Nemo. "What we seek is underwater. I believe a large landmass is rising. I also believe it has been above the waves before, and its return is causing upheavals not just in the physical world, but on the psychic plane as well. It manifests itself as a general sense of dread or unease, all the way to full-blown madness. I know you have seen evidence of this—perhaps you have even experienced it yourself, or witnessed it in others."

Burton thought of his late friend John Hanning Speke and his lunatic ravings before the malaria took hold of them both. A chill ran up his spine.

"We believe this madness will spread," said Miss Marsh. "First to those unusually sensitive to such things, like mediums, then to the general populace, until the entire world is affected."

"How can you possibly know this?" asked Burton. "And how can you think that these two remarkable events are related?"

"We have found entire islands where the inhabitants were slain," said Nemo. "Like some mass suicide. As we moved toward the continents, this strange behavior was lessened but still present. When questioned, the affected people will say they have a vague sense of doom, like the end is coming, though even they cannot say how or why they feel this way. Miss Marsh has collected newspapers from every port of call between here and the South Sea Islands. They all report the same occurrences. People nervous without cause. Unexplained murders. Suicides."

Burton thought once more of Speke, who died less than two days ago in a hunting accident. Had it really been an accident? Or had the old fool sensed some dread approaching from far away?

"Miss Marsh showed us an artifact," said Challenger, no doubt eager to change the subject to something more tangible.

"Ah, yes." Nemo approached a cabinet full of drawers and opened one, pulling out a familiar lump wrapped in seaweed. He showed them the artifact in all its grotesque novelty. "It is obvious it was made by some intelligence, and is quite ancient, perhaps even older than the pyramids. I believe it predates when man was first believed to have acquired the ability to use tools."

"But that's impossible," boomed Challenger. "Look at those markings. It was made by human hands."

"It was made by *intelligent* hands," Nemo corrected. "We don't know that they were human. I've uncovered similar signs that man is not the first intelligent creature to walk this planet, or swim in its oceans."

He moved to a far corner of his strange museum. "We found this in an antique shop in Arkham, Massachusetts," he said, gesturing to a glass case that housed what appeared to be a large, ornate and strange-proportioned tiara made of some unusual amalgam of gold. Burton, Challenger, and Herbert moved in for a closer inspection, marveling at its grotesque outline. "Who would make such a thing?" muttered Challenger. "And what kind of head would it fit?"

"Wait." Burton looked to Nemo. "You mean to tell me that you have lived beneath the ocean for years engaging in some sort of underwater archaeology? Why? What started you on this track? Forgive me if I offend you, but you don't strike me as the altruistic type."

Miss Marsh made to protest, but Nemo held up a restraining hand, silencing her. "You are correct, Captain Burton," he said. "I began my tenure beneath the sea as a misanthrope, even making war with the surface world for a time. But I have seen the error of my ways, and to atone for that violent past, I have dedicated myself to being mankind's savior, whether they know it or not. There are secrets down here that were invisible even to me, but Miss Marsh here has helped open my eyes to a greater threat than even man himself."

Burton glanced at Miss Marsh, who nodded.

Challenger pointed at the artifact, still in Nemo's hand. "But what does this mean? What is that ghastly thing depicted in the artifact?"

"It is a representation of Dagon," said Captain Nemo. "An ancient deity of most sinister aspect feared by most primitive seafaring peoples of the world."

"You mean worshipped," said Burton.

Nemo's eyes narrowed to slits. "I mean feared. Most of the ritual regarding Dagon involves not paying him obeisance but avoiding his wrath. That, and keeping him asleep, at the bottom of the ocean."

Challenger chuckled. "And I suppose in all your fabulous wanderings you have run across this Dagon? Is he stuffed and mounted somewhere in this undersea museum of yours?"

"I have not, and he is not," said Nemo, glaring at the much larger scientist. "Nevertheless, recent worldwide events have lead me to believe that, as the Bard said, 'There are more things in heaven and earth than are dreamt of in your philosophy.' And I think you of all people, Professor Challenger, should know that more than most."

"And we will find the cause of this mental malady at these coordinates, 49°51′S 128°34′W," said Herbert, pointing to the spot Nemo had indicated on his map.

"Exactly," said the Captain.

"And that's why you procured my services," said Herbert.

"Right again," said Nemo. "We have a long voyage ahead of us, and I have urgent matters that require my full attention. You have the run of the ship. Please, make yourselves at home. You may avail yourselves of my library as you wish. My crewmen will attend to your needs. In ten days' time I have a special activity planned I'm sure you will all enjoy. Herbert, I believe you have some preparations to make. Until then."

The captain of the *Nautilus* exited through a short hatchway at the other end of his curious "museum," letting Burton and the others know in no uncertain terms that this little meeting had adjourned.

Challenger arched a dark, bushy eyebrow at Burton. "His answers only raised more questions."

"He is usually quite taciturn," said Elizabeth Marsh. "He will reveal more of himself in time."

"What of you?" asked Burton. "Nemo said it was you who started him on this strange path."

Marsh grinned. "All in due time, gentlemen. This has been a lot for you to take in." She strode carefully from the room.

Burton looked to where Herbert had been standing near the map, but he too had gone.

"Curiouser and curiouser," said the explorer.

"Indeed," said Challenger. "And what do you make of this impossible ship of wonders? Built without oversight or patronage from any government. This Nemo is a man of perhaps limitless resources."

"So it would appear."

"He'd have to put in for repairs somewhere," mused Challenger. "The *Nautilus* would have to be in dry dock at some point. He said himself that this was a newer model. Who could house such a vehicle *and* keep their mouths shut?"

"I don't know," said Burton. "But I think we have bigger things to worry about just now. Such as what mystery awaits us at coordinates 49°51'S 128°34'W."

HUNTED

Over the next few days Burton availed himself of Nemo's vast library. There were several original Indian texts he found interesting, including a copy of the *Kama Sutra* written in Hindi, but much of the volumes replicated his own, and after three days he lost interest. Instead he wandered the *Nautilus*, hands in his pockets, busying himself with studying the comings and goings of the crew. Burton realized the *Nautilus* had to surface every two or three days to replenish its supply of air, always far from the shipping lanes and, whenever possible, at night. During some of these times Burton came out and smoked while Nemo consulted his sextant and wrote in a little notebook he kept for navigational purposes.

Challenger entertained himself by spending hours in Nemo's museum studying the strange specimens their host had collected in his explorations of the ocean. Most, as Challenger had said, were unknown to science, and the zoologist couldn't resist further study and perhaps even taxonomic cataloging of these plants and animals no other human eye had ever seen.

Burton had seen very little of Herbert, but had come to understand from talk among the crew that he was working on something in the bowels of the *Nautilus*, connecting some contraption of his own invention to the wondrous submarine. He disappeared for days at a time, looking tired and haggard when he finally made himself known, his clothes looking slept in. Sometimes Nemo would join them, and they talked of current world events, which Nemo had a keen interest in. But he rarely spoke more than a few words about where they were going and what they were going to do once they got there. Was this a journey of exploration and discovery, or one of violent action? Burton didn't know and no one seemed willing to tell him.

Elizabeth Marsh had made herself scarce during this time as well. The few times Burton did see her, she was walking arm in arm with Captain Nemo, the two of them conversing in forced whispers.

Burton didn't know whether to be overjoyed at the thought of another exciting adventure, or worried, and he shared his misgivings with Challenger one afternoon in Nemo's museum.

"It's the thrill of the hunt, Burton!" said the burly zoologist.

"Yes," replied Burton, "but what are we hunting?"

On the tenth day of their voyage, Captain Nemo addressed them after breakfast. "I have an activity planned that I think you will all enjoy. A hunting expedition."

"Hunting?" Burton thought they must have surfaced near a remote island plentiful with game. The thought of seeing the sun again thrilled him more than he thought possible. "Hunting where?"

"In a kelp forest," said Nemo. "I told you everything that is consumed upon this vessel is harvested from the ocean. This is how it is done. Come."

Nemo marched up a corridor and down a familiar set of stairs to the rear of the vessel, where a formidable-looking hatch stood, surrounded by a row of lockers fronted by a long wooden bench bolted to the floor. Four large brass helmets sat on the bench, brightly gleaming in the electric light shining from above.

"This entire region is rich in flounder, halibut, grouper, anchovies and cod," said Nemo. "We come here often."

"Are you saying we are going to walk around outside the *Nautilus*?" said Herbert.

"Precisely," said Nemo. "My crew will help outfit you."

As if on command, three blue-garbed men entered the area and opened the lockers, pulling out heavy canvas and oilskin suits and large, heavy-looking boots. Burton hefted one of them and discovered the soles were filled with lead. "To keep from floating away."

"Yes, Captain Burton," said Nemo, as he pulled on his own diving suit with practiced ease.

Removing his jacket, Burton allowed Nemo's men to assist him in shrugging on the thick, heavy suit and watched them as they tightened the complex series of buckles and straps around the arms, ankles, and chest of the rig. Without removing his boots, they helped him push his feet down into the heavy boots, adjusting and tightening more seals.

Burton hoped the ocean water would act to keep him cool, as the suit's heavy material was stifling hot. He looked around at Challenger and Herbert, who were being similarly outfitted. "Where is Miss Marsh?"

"She might join us later." Nemo now stood before them fully dressed save for his helmet. He brandished a lethal-looking harpoon gun in his thick-gloved hands. "Now, I have a few more instructions. Please listen carefully. We will not be able to communicate with one another outside through our helmets. The *Nautilus* will provide exterior lighting for our activities, but it will still be very dark. We will be attached to the *Nautilus* by air hoses, but please, stay close together."

Burton, now gloved, was handed a harpoon gun. He stared at it, trying to become familiar with its workings. Though quite proficient in most classes of weaponry, he had never used such a device. It appeared straightforward enough, but he worried about the water being too murky to hit anything with any real accuracy.

Burton watched as Captain Nemo put on his helmet, his attendants lowering it slowly and over his head and twisting it clockwise until it clicked. A helmet went over Burton's head and was snapped into place. "Remember to breathe normally," said his attendant.

Nemo looked out at them all through a thick circle of glass. He turned heavily in his boots as one of the attendants opened a sealed hatchway, allowing the captain inside.

"Follow the Captain, please," the attendant said, his voice muffled by the thick brass of the helmet.

Burton lurched forward, moving slowly in the heavy boots. Normal breathing was difficult, the suit and helmet hot, confining. He tried a Sufi meditation technique, which seemed to help calm his nerves somewhat, at least for the time being.

"What now?" Burton said.

"Air lock," came Herbert's muffled reply. "We're going into a sealed room. Water will be pumped in. When the pressure equals that of the ocean at this depth, an outer door will open, and we will walk where only Captain Nemo has walked before."

Burton stepped into the small room, and two of Nemo's crew began fiddling with his helmet. Glancing at Challenger's suited form through the thick porthole in his helmet, Burton realized they were being fitting with air hoses. Cool, fresh air flowed into Burton's helmet, relieving some of his claustrophobia.

Once everyone's air hoses were in place, the attendants scrambled from the room and sealed the hatch behind them. Almost immediately, it began filling with cold ocean water. Burton could feel it move over his boots to the legs of the suit. The sensation was strange, like taking a bath with one's clothes on and remaining dry, but not unpleasant. It rose over their heads in seconds.

Burton watched Nemo with great attention. The other man's gaze was fixed on some gauge set into the wall. When the room reached the requisite ocean pressure, Nemo twisted open the outer hatch and opened the door. The pressure was perfectly balanced, keeping them all from being sucked out into the muck surrounding the *Nautilus*, which had set down on the seabed.

Captain Nemo raised his left arm, motioning them forward, and stepped out, followed by Challenger, then Burton and Herbert. Burton's lead-booted feet sank heavily into the mire, but he found he was able to move a bit more easily underwater.

The lights of the *Nautilus* stabbed through the gloom, illuminating a vast kelp forest in the distance. Long vines of the stuff rose up toward the ocean's surface in neat green rows. Wan shafts of sunlight shown down from high above, revealing the occasional shrimp and several specimens of some strange, feathered starfish undulating through the gloom. Captain Nemo held his harpoon gun in a ready position, and Burton aped his movements, keeping a wary eye out for any fish that might be hiding in the thick cluster of vegetation.

They moved slowly toward the forest, their boots churning up the muck. Burton felt something move frantically beneath his right foot and bent downward just in time to see some sort of ray flapping its wing-like fins in its hurry to get away.

The area teemed with life. Tiny crabs moved sidewise through the depths, and stranger creatures swam through the water. A thing that looked like palm fronds writhed in a shaft of light above him, moving toward some distant bundle of kelp, and Burton was struck by how much animals resembled plants and plants resembled animals down here.

Captain Nemo suddenly changed direction. Instead of going straight into the kelp forest, he veered to the right of its boundary, hoisting his harpoon gun to his shoulder as if taking aim to fire. Burton looked, but could see nothing ahead of Nemo but mud-churned darkness. A hand wrapped itself around Burton's helmet and pulled him in close. It banged against someone else's, and he heard a muffled voice say, "Can you hear me?"

"Y-yes," said Burton. "Challenger? But how?"

"The vibration of our voices is conducted through the contact between our helmets. Do you see where Nemo is headed?"

"No."

"You don't see them?"

"No!" said Burton again, annoyed. "See what?"

"The ruins."

Twisting out of Challenger's grasp, Burton peered into the gloom. As his eyes adjusted to the waning light, short columns of square black stones stood along the bottom, jutting from the muck like rotting teeth. Nemo appeared to be inspecting these, though he kept up his guard.

Challenger's helmet barked against Burton's once more.

"I don't think we're on a fishing expedition."

"Nor do I," Burton agreed. "Someone should tell Herbert."

"I will," said Challenger. Burton looked out after Captain Nemo. A second later, Challenger's helmet struck his once more.

"Herbert's gone."

"Where the devil is he?" said Burton. "He couldn't have gotten far."

"Let's follow his air hose." Challenger pushed away from Burton and moved past the explorer in the direction Nemo had gone. He found Herbert's air hose and began following it, bobbing up and down as he moved through the thick muck covering the ocean bottom. Burton trailed him, using his free hand to clear the water before him of debris. A tiny seahorse danced in front of him, oblivious to his presence. The explorer gently swatted the tiny creature away and continued.

Burton's feet, already unsure in the uneven sand, went out from under him, and he scrambled to find his footing again. He missed the gentle slope, clumsy in the heavy boots. Burton wrenched his left knee as he went down hard, face first, into the dank muck.

"Bismillah!" he swore, his voice echoing inside the helmet. With considerable effort, he brought himself to his knees and looked around. He could see Captain Nemo ahead inspecting the strange ruins, but saw no sign of Challenger or Herbert, only the black lengths of their air hoses snaking into the gloom to Burton's right.

Burton attempted to use the harpoon gun as a kind of crutch to help push himself to his feet once more, but it went off in his hand with a muffled hiss, sending the harpoon into the kelp forest. Propping his weight against the weapon, Burton was, at last, able to right himself, and looked around to get his bearings. He had indeed fallen down a slight precipice that Challenger had seen and navigated without calamity. "So kind of him to warn me," Burton thought, as he moved in the general direction the zoologist had gone in search of their companion.

He found Herbert near a strangely glowing obelisk that rose more than ten feet out of the ocean floor. It was encrusted with some phosphorescent sea life. But that isn't what so entranced the young inventor. Dancing there before him, undulating slowly in the water, floated some bizarre apparition. The blue glow coming off the obelisk gave it a ghostly appearance. Blue-green hair stood out from its head. Its white, diaphanous garments writhed in the water, hinting at a nakedness underneath. It's face ensorcelled Burton. The apparition bore Isabel's likeness!

"Isabel," Burton murmured, lifting a heavy boot to take his first lumbering step closer. A powerful arm shot out of the dark, slapping into his chest. Burton's helmet clanked with another impact.

"No," said Challenger. "She is not what she appears."

Burton twisted his torso to his right. Beside him, Challenger was already taking aim at the wraith with his harpoon gun.

"No!" Burton screamed. "Isabel." Then his rational mind took hold. It couldn't be Isabel. It was impossible for anyone to be down here without the survival gear they wore, let alone his beloved Isabel.

Herbert was reaching for her now, getting closer. She placed her long-fingered hands around his helmet, grasping it tightly. Burton and Challenger watched as she twisted it counterclockwise to loosen it.

"Herbert!" Burton cried, feeling useless.

Challenger's harpoon hissed, the missile surging through the water toward the underwater apparition. It hit close to the wraith's right shoulder, shredding her sparse garments before vanishing into the distance. She glanced in their direction, anger marring her otherwise perfect face—Isabel's face.

Then it changed. What had once been a beautiful woman became hideous and fish-like. Its hands stretched into webbed talons, the flowing garments transmogrified into dark green scales. Only its hair remained, sea-green and writhing around its head like a halo of snakes.

It lunged at poor Herbert now, gripping his shoulders and shaking him as the poor fellow reached for his harpoon gun, which had fallen to the sea floor. Challenger bounded toward them, his long strides not getting him far due to his lead-filled boots. Burton took off after him, waving his arms in an attempt to get Nemo's attention.

Challenger had taken his harpoon gun's barrel in his hands to use it like a cudgel against the thing that tore at Herbert's suit, rending the thick fabric and allowing water to get in. It was obvious to Burton that neither he nor Challenger could reach him in time.

Something flashed past Burton from the rear, almost knocking him down. The way it propelled itself through the water reminded him of a fish or dolphin, but its proportions were definitely those of a human. It collided with the vengeful wraith, knocking her off Herbert just as Challenger reached him. The big scientist hauled Herbert off the sea floor almost without effort and touched their helmets together as they watched the strange melee unfold.

The fish-things grappled with each other, spun around, before Herbert's rescuer kicked the apparition in the chest, sending it sprawling away into the gloom. It did not return.

The other being turned and looked at Herbert and Challenger as Burton arrived next to them, panting and sweating inside his diving helmet. Nemo waited standing just off to Burton's left, harpoon gun held down at his side.

The creature looked at each of them in turn, her big-lipped mouth opening and closing, expelling bubbles as she did so. Her scaly, pale green skin was unclothed. Her naked breasts bobbed like pale globes in the water. Burton recognized something strangely familiar about her.

"Miss Marsh?" he muttered.

She kicked hard, rising up and over them, swimming with great speed back toward the *Nautilus*.

ELIZABETH'S STORY

When they had returned to the *Nautilus* and doffed their undersea diving suits, helmets and boots, Burton, Challenger, and a slightly sodden and frightened Herbert met in Nemo's museum, where they sat on a long couch and enjoyed hot coffee. Burton drank the dark, rich, unmistakably Kenyan brew while appraising Nemo and the others. Poor Herbert had changed into dry clothes, but still shivered, more from fright than from the cold ocean depths.

"I believe," said Challenger to Nemo, "you owe us an explanation."

"Indeed, I do." The captain of the *Nautilus* shifted in the wingback chair that sat opposite the couch. "I told you a half truth when I said we were going hunting. This kelp forest is an active hunting spot, but it was the ruins that interested me the most."

"You should have told us," said Burton.

Nemo glanced at him and said nothing.

"That-that woman," said Herbert. "That thing. What was it?"

"That's what I came here to find out," said Nemo. "The ruins tend to bring them up from the depths. It was my intention to capture or kill one."

"She looked like my fiancé," said Burton, "Isabel. How is that possible?"

"They play tricks with the mind," said Nemo. "But do not fall for their treachery."

"What did you see, Herbert?" Burton asked.

"Something," Herbert began. "Someone…impossible. Weena."

"I saw a siren about to rip off your helmet," Challenger offered, draining his cup and getting up to refill it. Burton watched as he did so, taking a small flask from his pocket and pouring some of its contents into the steaming cup. Challenger then returned to his seat at Herbert's side.

"Then there was that other thing," said Challenger. "Or person. And we all know who it was, don't we? Why don't you come clean, Captain?"

"I'd best let Miss Marsh tell you in her own words," said Nemo.

At tha,t Elizabeth Marsh entered the room, dressed in a blue coverall similar to what Nemo's men wore. Her hair was wet, dark ringlets spilling down her back.

"Hello, gentlemen," she said, taking a chair next to Nemo.

"Hello," said Challenger, "whatever you are."

"I-it was you?" said Herbert, wide-eyed.

"It was, indeed," said Miss Marsh. "I am sorry to have kept this from all of you. It's just that it is a lot to take in, and there wasn't a need, at the time, for you to know of my true nature."

"We'd better know now," said Burton.

Elizabeth nodded and began.

"My story is a long one, and I won't bore you with the particulars. Suffice it to say that I am not fully human."

Herbert gasped.

Burton coughed.

Challenger drained his coffee cup and refilled it from his flask.

"H-how is this possible?" said Burton.

"I will try to explain," said Miss Marsh. "But I feel you need further proof. Look."

Miss Marsh stretched forth her right hand, fingers splayed. There was a definite webbing visible between the digits.

"Most extraordinary," said Herbert.

"I hail from a small, seaside town in Massachusetts called Innsmouth, unremarkable save for its abundant fishing. But one year, the fishing dried up, and my father, Captain Obed Marsh, made a deal with a race of undersea beings similar to the one you saw earlier. They caused the fish to return and plied the townsfolk with gold, and certain members of our town had to...mate with them."

Challenger coughed, almost spitting out his valuable whiskey. "What?"

"It's true," she said, head hung low. "I'm not proud of it, but I and my two younger sisters are the result of such a union."

"My God," Herbert said, sinking into the sofa cushions.

"I know you must think this strange, even blasphemous, but to Innsmouth folk, it is normal. As long as we continued, we would experience abundance not just in this life, but the next. For in old age, those of us born to the Deep Ones can walk into the ocean and swim down to Y'hanthlei, there to live with Father Dagon and Mother Hydra forever and ever."

"What is this Y'hanthlei?" asked Burton, saying the word slowly, testing it on his tongue. Even with his considerable facility with languages, he had a hard time saying it, as if the word wasn't meant to be formed by any human lips or tongue, and the whole thing sounded horrid and repellent.

"It is a city where my mother's kind lives," said Miss Marsh. "The Deep Ones."

"There are several such cities located all over the world," said Nemo. "I have been trying to locate them, but they are very deep. Deeper than even my *Nautilus* can go."

"That's why you were inspecting those ruins," said Challenger.

The Captain nodded. "Yes. A recent seaquake unearthed them. I hoped they would give me some clue to the whereabouts of another Deep One nest."

"I daresay you've stirred one up," said Herbert, still shaking. "So there are more of those...things. Down here?" The poor fellow looked around frantically, ready to jump out of his own skin.

"Oh yes," said Nemo.

49

"H-how many?"

"Millions," Miss Marsh answered.

"M-millions?" said Herbert, shrinking even deeper into the couch cushions.

"Here," said Challenger, opening his flask and upturning the remaining contents into Herbert's coffee cup.

Burton looked at Miss Marsh. "You said something else. Something about dwelling in this Y'hanthlei forever and ever."

She nodded. "The Deep Ones are immortal, at least functionally so. I believe they can be killed, but in their present form, if left alone, they will live for eons, never aging, never getting sick, and never dying."

"So, it was a Faustian bargain your father made," said Challenger. "All the fish you can catch, and more gold than King Solomon, but you must forfeit your humanity."

"That is the long and short of it, yes," said Miss Marsh. "But the thought of life eternal here on this Earth was a boon to some. When they grow weary of this world they'll walk into the waters of Plum Island Sound, swim out to Devil's Reef, complete their transformations, and be done with it. Many of them can't pass for human now and live out their lives in secret isolation. I have aunts, uncles, cousins whom I've never seen, residing in one of the fine old houses on Washington Street where the gently bred—including my family—lived."

"These world-weary Innsmouth residents sound much like our host, eh?" bellowed Challenger.

"But what of you?" asked Burton. "Why are you here, instead of back home in Innsmouth?"

Miss Marsh grinned. "I was just getting to that. I said before that I know how awful this must sound to all of you, or to any sane ear for that matter. But grew up thinking it normal. Until I began to see the real toll my father's bargain with the Deep Ones was taking on the town. Not only had Innsmouth declined in social relevance, but people were starting to disappear. My father told me the Deep Ones also required human sacrifice in order to keep herding fish into our waters and giving us gold. Obed didn't want to go along with this, but he knew the consequences of disobeying them."

Elizabeth Marsh poured herself a coffee before continuing. "I was repulsed. By my heritage, by what my father had done, by what the Deep Ones wanted of us. I wanted no further part in it. The time for another sacrifice came, and certain members of the town were rounded up. Father and the town's leadership thought it better to choose who should be sacrificed, rather than the Deep Ones. They gathered up the town's layabouts, outcasts, people whose parents refused to mate with the Deep Ones, and so did not have the requisite Innsmouth look about them, even the occasional outsider. I knew it was just a matter of time before we would run out of such people, and I knew what would happen then. The Deep Ones, my mother's people —my people—would overrun the town, killing everyone they encountered.

"And why stop with Innsmouth? They could take the marsh road to Ipswich, to Rowley, even faraway Arkham. They could overrun the surface world in days. They were preparing for such a time. Though Father tried to keep it from me, I heard about the things being dragged out of the sea at night and hidden away in the houses that line the beach. 'Powerful items' Obed called them. I don't know what they are, maybe weapons. For all I know, they are still there.

"On the night of the next sacrifice, I ran for the shore, doffing my clothes and diving into the cold water. I swam out to Devil's Reef, where my father and his men were forcing people off the boats, herding them like cattle toward their doom. I hovered there in the dark water thinking. What was I going to do? I realized I had no idea. How could I stop something so big, that had been going on for so long?

"I looked around as Father and the others herded the poor souls doomed to be sacrificed off the boats, sometimes with force, and an idea formed in my brain."

"Diving beneath the water I came up underneath one of the boats, emerging beside it and gripping the bow with both hands, rocking it violently. The passengers were frightened by my sudden appearance, and the boat's pilot, my father, was caught off guard, and he fell and toppled into the water, dropping the oar he had been using as a cudgel against his fellow townsfolk.

"'Go!'" I screamed. "'Run! Fight! Get out of here!'"

"They took up the oars themselves and, now free of Father's presence, began to row the boat away from Devil's Reef and toward shore.

"'Elizabeth?'" my father said, sputtering in the water just a few feet away. I ignored him and dived again, grabbing one of his lieutenants and dragging him screaming out of another boat, dashing him into the water beside my father.

"Emboldened by my attempts at heroism, the would-be sacrifices already standing on the Reef began shouting and fighting back against their masters. The fish folk joined in, and received several well-placed blows for their trouble. Whatever happened out on Devil's Reef this night, there would be no human sacrifice.

"While considering my next move, something grabbed my foot and pulled me down, down, into the dark water. I looked down, and saw two of the fish-fiends tugging at me. I kicked one of them in the head, causing him to release me, but I was dragged down even harder by his associate. There was malice in their inhuman eyes. One of their own had betrayed them.

"They were strong and accustomed to the deep water. I thrashed against them, but it was no use. I realized I would never again see the surface world I had fought so hard to protect. They would either kill me or keep me prisoner forever.

"There were five of them on me, then six, all pulling and tugging and pummeling me. Then there came a bright light from underneath us, as bright as the sun. The Deep Ones recoiled from it and let me go. At first, I thought it was a great fish, some giant sea predator that even the Deep Ones feared. But I could see by its hard outline that it was something else. One of the Deep Ones attacked it, swimming toward it like a ram. But it was deflected off the thing's metal hide.

"It turned sharply to the side, very close to me. I reached out, gripping some fin or protrusion, and the thing surged forth at an angle away from the Reef, carrying me with it.

"I found her clinging to the side of the *Nautilus*," said Nemo, "and brought her inside."

Miss Marsh smiled. "We've been together ever since, two exiles searching for answers."

THROUGH TIME AND SPACE WITH
CAPTAIN NEMO

Strange dreams troubled Burton that night.

He was back in his tent, somewhere between Zanzibar and the waters of Lake Victoria. The air baked, hot and dry as a kiln. Sheens of sweat lay over his entire body, racked with malaria. Through this mad, hot haze he saw his partner and colleague, John Hanning Speke, standing over him, his arms raised in a chant.

Ia! Ia! Cthulhu fhtagn!

Burton tried to speak. "What the devil are you rambling about?"

Ph'nglui mglw'nafh Cthulhu R'lyeh wgah'nagl fhtagn!

"Isabel," Burton groaned in his dream. He moved his head with considerable effort toward the tent flap, which snapped in the hot breeze. In the dust outside, he saw many dark feet.

Somalis! The attack! It comes now.

This was wrong, Burton knew, in that part of his mind that understood how strange dreams are. They were not attacked by Somalis during their trek to discover the source of the Nile; that had been back in his army days in Berbera, where he had first met Speke.

"Be ready," he said to Speke. "Take up arms."

John Hanning Speke, his eyes shining pale silver like those of a fish, continued his monstrous chanting, flinging spittle as he made noxious alien sounds that were never meant for human vocal cords.

Cthulhu R'lyeh wgah'nagl fhtagn!

The tent flap opened then, but instead of Burton's fragile refuge filling with angry Somali warriors, there was just one person, his Isabel. She was armed with a spear, which she thrust sidelong into Speke's face. In that inexplicable way dreams had, Speke's side turned red, staining his linen shirt with blood as he collapsed to the ground.

Isabel turned to Burton then, smiling down at him like an angel. He reached for her, and in that brief, feverish second, Richard Francis Burton, who had never believed in angels or gods of any sort, believed his Isabel was an angel come to rescue him.

Her face twisted and changed. It wasn't Isabel, but Elizabeth Marsh. She pulled off her clothes, revealing her true form. Her arms and legs were covered in chitinous scales. Her pale green breasts bobbed as if buoyant. Between her legs a dark mass of undulating kelp promised secrets best left untouched. "In his house at R'lyeh, dead Cthulhu waits dreaming," she said with an adder's hiss.

Burton awoke to his own screams.

At breakfast, Burton could tell that he wasn't the only one troubled by strange dreams. Challenger was tired, haggard, and more cross than usual. Herbert came in quickly, ate, poured coffee down his throat, and was gone, and working on whatever project for which Nemo had recruited him.

"Do you know what's going on with that one?" Burton asked.

Challenger scowled. "I know nothing anymore."

The two of them ate in silence. Neither Captain Nemo nor Miss Marsh put in an appearance, but that wasn't unusual. It seemed everyone had a role to fulfill, but what was his purpose aboard the *Nautilus*?

Burton trod the vessel from stem to stern, restless, the dream he had still foremost in his mind. What did it all mean? His only consolation was that it wasn't just him. He'd heard mutterings among the crew, and watched as Nemo dressed down one poor bosun's mate for nodding off at his post. Was this the madness that Nemo had spoken of? If true, it would be worse in this part of the ocean, so near the event they were on their way to investigate.

Burton caught up with Herbert and watched him for a while, though he didn't have the foggiest idea what the man was doing. Using a set of engineering schematics of the ship, the inventor raced from deck to deck, running wires and cables all over it. He climbed through tiny hatchways and service ports, tangles of wire slung around his breast, a spanner clenched between his teeth. Burton didn't ask for the purpose, and Herbert didn't offer any explanation as he scurried from one end of the *Nautilus* to the other.

Ten days after their ill-fated "hunting" expedition, the *Nautilus* slowed to a stop, and Captain Nemo gathered them together to tell them they had arrived. Burton, Miss Marsh, Challenger and Herbert joined Captain Nemo in his museum.

"Let's go out and see what we're up against," said Challenger.

"We cannot," said Nemo. "The region is undergoing great volcanic upheaval. The sea is filled with noxious gases and oppressive heat— even our Miss Marsh wouldn't likely survive such conditions. But I have prepared for that. Herbert, is it done?"

"It is, Captain," said the inventor, who strode forth into the room, covered in grease and grime. "I am ready to go at your command. Though I must remind you again that I have no idea if this will work."

"Will what work?" said Burton.

"And no more bloody secrets and riddles," Challenger added.

Nemo nodded at the large zoologist. "Very well. But know this: you have come to believe many impossible things on this journey. I require of you one more. Herbert?"

The inventor stepped into the center of Nemo's museum to stand next to the captain. "We live in a world composed of three dimensions: height, length, width. This is common knowledge, yes?"

Burton and Challenger nodded.

"But there is a fourth dimension: duration. Time. Now, what if I told you that it was possible to travel that fourth dimension just as easily as we traverse the other three?"

"But we do travel it, you grimy sot," rumbled Challenger. "We all move forward throughout our lives, from birth to death, at a rate of one second per second."

Herbert held up a finger. "This is true. But what if you could travel forward at an even greater speed? Or backward at a rate so slow you could track the movements of a hummingbird's wing?"

"How do you know this can be done?" said Burton.

"Because I've done it," said Herbert. "I've invented a machine that, using peculiar properties of light, can travel forward or backward through Time itself. Furthermore, I have, I hope, imbued the *Nautilus* with that same ability."

Challenger barked laughter.

"You mock," Herbert said, "but remember those who mocked you for your claims."

"I care little what other people think," said Professor Challenger. "I know what I saw."

"As do I," Herbert replied.

"After everything I've witnessed," said Burton, "I'm willing to take Herbert's word for it. It's no more outrageous than a submarine vessel or a fish woman or a South American plateau inhabited by dinosaurs." He looked at Challenger as he said this last. The big man's eyes narrowed, but he said nothing.

"Splendid," said Herbert. "Let's test it out then. I've wired the *Nautilus* into my Time Machine. It is our hope that this will allow the *Nautilus* to travel into the distant past, there to witness this troublesome landmass the last time it was above the surface of the ocean."

"For what purpose?" asked Challenger.

"To see what we are up against," said Nemo. "To learn the cause of this madness affecting the world. And this vessel." He looked each of them in the eye. "I know we've all had troubled sleep. Whatever is rising up from the bottom of the ocean at these coordinates is the cause. If we know more about it, we might be able to stop it."

"It sounds as if you want to stop nature itself," said Challenger.

"Is it nature that mankind be exterminated?" asked Nemo. "Is it natural to be slaughtered by the Deep Ones?"

Challenger stared down Nemo.

"Gentlemen, please," said Miss Marsh. "This posturing will get us nowhere."

"The proof is in the pudding," Burton added. "Let's see if Herbert's Time Machine works."

Challenger nodded and stepped away from Captain Nemo.

"Very well then," said Herbert. "Follow me."

The Time Machine was stored in a rather small area near what Burton assumed was the engine room. A peculiar instrument consisting of a cushioned, high-backed chair inside a brass frame, behind which sat a large dish suspended vertically. Herbert stepped over to it. "The Time Machine is operated by these two levers," he said, removing two shafts of some crystal from his pocket. "One controls the machine's direction through Time, and the other its speed. I remove them to prevent someone other than the operator from activating the machine."

He carefully screwed them in place, then climbed over the frame and sat down, his hands on the levers.

"I don't have a precise destination in mind," said Nemo. "But I know we must travel hundreds of thousands of years into the past. The four of us will go to the observation deck, which affords an ample ocean view, while Herbert remains here, piloting the time machine. I will communicate with him via the speaking tube positioned just over his head, telling him when to speed up, slow down, or stop."

"The engines have ceased then?" asked Herbert.

"I have ordered full stop an hour ago. Our forward momentum has ceased."

"Excellent," Herbert said. "I'm ready when you are."

Burton, Elizabeth Marsh, and Professor Challenger accompanied Captain Nemo to what he called the forward observation gallery, a grand compartment fitted with padded seats and fronted by a thick pane of glass, through which the limitless ocean could be viewed. The current scene was quite hellish. Streak of molten red zigzagged along the ocean floor, while columns of thick black smoke billowed out. Burton watched, amazed, as tendrils of hot lava oozed out and were instantly cooled by seawater and turned black and semi-hard.

"I have seen islands form in just this very fashion," declared Nemo.

"But what we're witnessing here is not the cause of a great change, merely a symptom. Look."

Nemo pointed, and through the ocean's gloom, he could see some huge shape rising up on columns of molten rock, being lifted off the ocean floor after untold eons.

"Is everyone ready?" came a tinny voice.

Nemo leaned toward a brass pipe rising from the floor next to his seat and spoke into its flared end. "We are ready. You may begin at once."

"Very well," came Herbert's thin reply. "I suggest you hang onto something. The journey can be jarring at times. Here we go."

At first, Burton noticed nothing, though he didn't have the foggiest idea what he should expect. Embarking into new territory, he smiled at the idea of being a chrononaut—and among the world's first.

Then, he noticed something strange about the shifting underwater landforms. The glowing lava tendrils that had had him so transfixed were moving backward. First cooling cinders, then molten worms being pulled back down into the earth. Landmasses swelled and shrank. These processes repeated, over and over, faster and faster. He grew dizzy and steeled himself against his padded seat.

The light shifted with great rapidity, brightening and dimming. He saw schools of fish swimming backward, chasing their predators. The landmass that had been rising up before them fell back down into the ocean depths. Molten scars sealed and subsided.

"Faster, Herbert, if you please," said Captain Nemo.

For a time it seemed as if nothing changed, just that rapid brightening and dimming of the distant surface light. Burton squeezed his eyes shut for a moment to steady himself. When he opened them again, the ocean depths crawled with life.

Challenger gasped. Large beasts sped past the viewing port, moving backwards. Burton watched as a squid as long as the *Nautilus* disgorged a giant fish from its beaked maw, the bloody pieces knitting themselves back together before the now living creature chased the squid backward and out of sight. A multitude of fish and other sea creatures, many of which were unknown to current science, sped past in similar fashion.

Several times, Burton glanced at the carpeted floor to focus on something that wasn't moving. But it was moving nevertheless, he realized. The *Nautilus* was moving backward through Time itself. Just the thought of it took his breath. It wasn't logical. It wasn't possible. But here he was. His friends at the Cannibal Club would not believe a word of this adventure. His thoughts of his friends back home reminded him of poor Speke.

Ph'nglui mglw'nafh Cthulhu R'lyeh wgah'nagl fhtagn!

Speke, who must have been looking for something more than the source of the Nile. Some dark secret out of Time itself.

Ph'nglui mglw'nafh Cthulhu R'lyeh wgah'nagl fhtagn!

"In his house at R'lyeh, dead Cthulhu waits dreaming."

"What?" said Challenger, who sat next to him.

Burton looked at him, startled. He hadn't realized he'd said anything aloud.

"Nothing."

"Faster," ordered Nemo.

The sickening feeling increased. Burton watched as countless sea creatures moved from death to life, rising from where they had fallen and swimming away. Veritable herds of some large, bony-looking insect things scurried about on the bottom. "Trilobites," said Challenger. "Oh, to have a living specimen for my museum!"

Backward they went through Time, the pace quickened now. They watched as once again the molten tumult that was occurring in their own time period returned, launching a vast landmass up and out, the long, slow volcanic processes that had created it taking place for them in a matter of seconds.

"Forward now," ordered Nemo. "We've gone too far back."

The disconcerting backward view slowed and stopped, then started again in reverse. Now they were moving forward, hurtling past geologic ages in an instant. Now Burton could witness birth and death in their proper order, though with the same terrifying swiftness.

"Slow to a stop," said Nemo.

The dizzying quickness of Time slowed and came to a full stop. They were now at one fixed point in Time.

"When are we?" Nemo asked Herbert through the speaking tube.

"An exact year would be meaningless," said Herbert. "But we are in the depths of the Pleistocene Epoch, roughly one hundred and twenty-eight thousand years before our time."

"Well," said Challenger with a sneering grin. "Let's go out and meet the neighbors, shall we?"

R'LYEH

"Herbert, is the Time Machine unharmed?" asked Captain
Nemo.

"It would appear so."

"Excellent. Please join the others on the observation deck."

The captain of the *Nautilus* moved toward the doorway.

"Where are you going?" asked Challenger.

"To the bridge. We need to find a safe place to put into shore,
where we will mount our expedition."

"I'm coming, too," said Challenger.

"As will I," added Burton.

"Fine," said Nemo. "Suit yourselves."

Burton and Challenger followed Nemo to the bridge of the
Nautilus. It took up two levels and was fitted out in brass. The most
utilitarian portion of the ship Burton had yet seen, it was staffed with
uniformed men of almost every conceivable race. A long gangway
stretched across the upper half of the bridge, and Nemo strode across
this confidently—followed by Burton and Challenger—to a standard
ship's steering wheel, which stood before a large, rounded viewing
port.

"Surface three hundred meters," Nemo said, and Burton could feel the ship begin to rise, stopping when it had reached the indicated depth. "I don't want to give away our position to anyone who might be watching," he said to Burton and Challenger. The two men exchanged quizzical glances as he lowered the periscope and looked out at the portion of the mysterious landmass that rose above the waves.

"Yes," he said. "Marvelous."

Pulling away from the periscope, he offered Burton a look.

Burton saw a vast, flat stretch of land that appeared devoid of life. In the hazy distance, he could make out several tall structures, too regular in shape to be natural. One of them appeared to be a pyramid, but bigger than any he'd ever seen in the Valley of Kings in Egypt.

"Bismillah."

Challenger shoved Burton out of the way and jammed his face into the periscope's viewer. "Blimey," he said. "This has South America beat."

The view shifted due to the submarine's movements. Challenger pulled himself away. "Well," he said, "I guess there's just one question."

"Just *one*?" said Burton.

Challenger smiled. "What do we call it? Atlantis? Lemuria? Mu?"

"R'lyeh," said Burton, his voice almost a whisper.

Nemo's eyes narrowed to slits. "How do you know that name? Have you been talking to Miss Marsh?"

"No, uh," said Burton, "I dreamed it. At least I think I did. It might have been a memory." He stared at the periscope in silence.

"Let's worry about the naming of things later," said Captain Nemo. "Gentlemen, prepare for your expedition while I navigate us into a safe, secluded place from which to launch it."

Burton and Challenger could both tell by now when they had been dismissed, so they left Nemo to his preparations.

Feeling a bit more useful now, Burton returned to his room and unpacked his gear. He cleaned, oiled, and loaded his pistol, then sharpened his khukuri blade. Then he donned a white linen shirt, white linen pants and boots. A pith helmet completed the ensemble. Sheathing the knife, he tied it to his back, the handle within easy reach of his right hand.

There was a knock at his door. Herbert and Challen him, likewise similarly outfitted.Only poor Herbert l place, even though he had cleaned up from his exertior the *Nautilus* to his Time Machine.

"Nemo has put in to a bay on the far side of the isle from where we surfaced," explained Challenger. "It should be safe there. Nemo is going to accompany us to shore."

"What about Miss Marsh?" asked Burton.

"He said I should stay behind, where it's safe," said Miss Marsh, gliding up the corridor. The tone of her voice suggested her displeasure over the decision. "Don't worry, boys," she said with a wink. "I'll be keeping my eye on you." With that, she sauntered off.

"Most extraordinary, isn't she?" said Herbert, staring after her.

"That's an understatement," said Challenger with a laugh. "Well, Burton, are you ready to embark on the adventure of the ages?"

"I'm as ready as I am ever likely to be." Burton left his stateroom and closed the door, following Herbert and Challenger up the corridor.

Precisely at noon—if such a man-made designation held any meaning in an age that existed before recorded human time—Captain Richard Francis Burton, Professor George Edward Challenger, and Herbert the Time Traveler stood atop the *Nautilus* with Captain Nemo and surveyed what no human being had ever seen, the mythical landmass Burton's nightmare had dubbed R'lyeh.

The *Nautilus* had put into a little cove. Nemo surveyed the land through a pair of field glasses, studying every line, every rock and tree.

The air was stifling and thick, strange given their proximity to the South Pole. This was a more temperate age, stuck between Ice Ages.

"How do we get ashore?" asked Challenger. "By swimming?"

Nemo waved to one of his attendants, who stood near the submarine's open hatch. He turned and opened a watertight locker attached to the hull and pulled out a tight, heavy-looking bundle. Yanking the cord attached to the side of the bundle, the attendant tossed the whole thing overboard. It grew into a raft as it hit the water.

"Remarkable," rumbled Challenger.

"Another invention of mine," explained Nemo. "It uses compressed air to inflate. It deflates almost as easily and can be used over and over."

"Ingenious," declared Herbert.

The attendant reached into the locker and produced two short oars. He handed one to Burton and one to Challenger as Captain Nemo leapt into the raft, sitting at the head of it, his back to the sinister island.

The two explorers glanced at each other, surprised they were expected to row. Burton shrugged. Such divisions of labor by perceived class were inherently silly. He jumped into the boat and took his place on the left side. Herbert jumped in and straddled the boat in the middle, clearly not used to being at sea.

With considerable effort, the much larger Professor Challenger joined him, taking position on the right. Nemo's silent attendant tossed them the rope and disappeared back into the *Nautilus* with the speed of a rabbit diving into its warren to escape a predator. R'lyeh clearly unnerved the crew. And Burton and the others were headed straight for it.

They rowed. A feeling of sinister unease stole over Burton as they got closer to the mythic landmass. There was something wrong about it. By all rights, it shouldn't exist, and yet here it was. But there was more to his unease than that. There was a pervading sense of cosmic malignancy, of hostility toward man. He got the feeling they were being watched, but he couldn't tell from what corner or by what agency. All he knew was he didn't like anything about any of this, and he longed for London, and Isabel.

"Atlantis," Herbert said, giggling. "Mu. Lemuria. It's true. All of it."

"Herbert, calm down," said Burton.

"Don't you see? It's all true. We thought it based in fable, but it's not."

They put into the shallows, and Captain Nemo jumped from the raft in ankle-deep water. Burton and Challenger followed suit, and the three men towed the raft up onto the sand. Only then did Herbert alight, still giggling and talking to himself, his forehead covered in a sheen of cold sweat.

"Pull yourself together, man!" rumbled Challenger.

"Do you think the raft is safe here?" asked Burton.

"Yes, it will be perfectly safe," Nemo said. "If not, we can always signal the *Nautilus*."

"Where should we head first?" Challenger tromped up the beach, examining the thick, course jungle green that rose up to oppose them. Burton had never seen anything like the vegetation that surrounded the beach: giant ferns and thick, stumpy trees with fronds like those of the familiar palm jutting out the tops of them.

Nemo unsheathed a machete and started hacking at the dense growth. "We need only reach the island's interior," said the captain of the *Nautilus*. "Our starting point makes little difference."

They fell in behind Nemo. With every step they spent several minutes hacking away at the jungle. Herbert took up the rear, drinking from a waterskin made from whale bladder and muttering to himself. "All that we'll accomplish," he said. "All that we'll become, doesn't matter! The Valley of the White Sphinx. The Palace of Green Porcelain. Morlocks. Eloi. All for naught. Weena! Oh, Weena. I shall never again see your beautiful face."

"What the devil is he rambling about?" Challenger asked as he htrashed at a vine as thick as his wrist. "He's bloody well out of his tree."

"He's feeling the effects of this damnable island," said Burton. "Be quiet and keep going!"

"802,701," said the Time Traveler. "Into the future. I've now gone even farther into the past. I should have journeyed to the past first. One must see where we've been in order to learn where we'll end up, hey?" He laughed.

They came into a grove of the stubby, stunted trees. Hot sunlight filtered down on them, and Burton realized he was sweating, and not just from the stifling humidity. There was a cloying miasma of malignancy that lay over the place like a pall. The feeling that they were being watched was now even stronger, and he wondered if the others could sense it as well. He surveyed the others. Nemo looked nervous, his movements furtive. Challenger was more irritable than usual. And

Herbert was a gibbering mess. He sat on the carcass of one of the stubby trees, talking to himself excitedly.

"Weena. Oh, how I wish you were here with me now."

"It looks like we made it through the worst of the foliage," said Nemo. "Let's keep heading inward. If we can keep to this path, the bay containing the *Nautilus* will remain at our backs."

"We should keep a wary eye out for predators," warned Challenger, clutching his Snider-Enfield rifle.

Burton nodded and unsnapped the holster on his hip. Captain Nemo unslung his own rifle, a direct ancestor to the piece Challenger carried, and held it at the ready, moving deeper into the grove of strange trees.

Challenger kicked at Herbert, who rose and followed, wide-eyed and sweating. Burton took the rear.

Burton wondered if there were any predators about. It was fortuitous that they had arrived at a point after the age of reptiles. But his explorer's instincts were on edge just the same.

It took them an hour, but after chopping through one final thick clump of ferns and other brush, they came, at last, to the interior of R'lyeh.

It was flat and had obviously been cleared of trees and jungle some time ago. A vast alien city made of green stone stood in the jungle's wake, scarred by age. On the outskirts, the jungle was encroaching, and it looked as if the place had been abandoned long ago. It was also clear to Richard Francis Burton, who had glimpsed the pyramids of Egypt and the sacred shrines of Mecca, that this city had not been conceived by the mind of man, nor built with his hands. The lines were all wrong, non-Euclidean in their ornamentation, the stairs, platforms and passageways made for something with very different anatomy.

"Fascinating!" Challenger declared. "A pre-human city. But what does it mean?"

"It means we're not the cocks of the walk," gibbered Herbert, his eyes darting from every shadow and rampart of the strange alien city. "We never were. Everything we've accomplished, will accomplish, doesn't matter. It's all a lie. Everything we have become, will become, for good or ill, does not matter. This is their world, not ours."

"Steady, Herbert," said Burton, but the Time Traveler ignored him. He was shaking now, even more so than he did after his brush with one of Miss Marsh's undersea relatives.

Herbert turned toward Burton. "Don't you see? This is their world. Whomever built this city will return." He uttered a nervous laugh.

"We don't know that," said Challenger. "We don't know anything yet. In our time, this place is a mile beneath the ocean."

"And it is returning to the surface," Nemo said. "That is why we are here, to find out what we are up against once R'lyeh rises from the ocean once more."

"This place looks abandoned even now," said Burton. "Look. There's no one here, and it looks as if that has been the case for quite some time."

"Time," said Herbert. "Yes. Time. We can travel up and down its length, but there is no escape. None. I have seen the end. The end of Time, at least for us. And this," he gestured about the city, "is our terrible beginning." He cackled, his voice echoing throughout the strange, fungoid towers of the city.

"Does anyone have any idea what the devil he's muttering about?" Challenger roared.

"I think I do," said Burton. "But that doesn't answer the question at hand. Captain Nemo, we've joined you on this expedition and traveled into the remote past. We've surveyed this island that appears to be once more returning to the surface. Now what do we do? How does knowing this city exists help us back in our time?"

Nemo opened his mouth to say something, but there came a sound of many voices muttering in some incomprehensible, inhuman speech. The party turned and saw a group of vaguely human figures exiting the mouth of an obelisk-shaped building. Raising their rifles, Burton, Challenger, and Nemo watched in fascination as the group moved cautiously closer.

There were three males and one female. They were short and squat, with short yet powerful-looking arms and legs. Their tiny frames rippled with muscles. As they grew nearer, the explorers could make out more of their facial features. The creatures were chinless, and possessed prominent, bony brow ridges.

"Neanderthals!" Challenger whispered.

"What?" said Burton.

Herbert giggled.

"Named after the Neander Valley in Germany, where one of their skulls was discovered," Challenger explained.

"That's all very interesting," said Captain Nemo. "But I'm afraid it is of little help when confronted by the real thing."

"Living fossils," said Herbert with a nervous giggle.

"What shall we do?" asked Burton.

"Nothing yet," said Nemo. "They don't seem intent on harming us."

The little group of Neanderthals came up very close and stared at Captain Nemo and the others, their great nostrils flaring. They spoke to one another in some incomprehensible tongue, pointing and staring. They seemed especially curious about Professor Challenger, whose imposing form was bigger than the others.

"The Neanderthals are adapted to flourish in colder climes," Challenger whispered. "I wonder what the devil they're doing down here."

"Perhaps we can ask them," mused Nemo.

"Morlocks," whispered Herbert, as he fell back to gibbering to himself.

The Neanderthals were sparsely dressed in animal skins. One of them, apparently their leader, carried a long spear. Burton didn't want to shoot them, but his pistol was a comforting presence by his side. They would have the upper hand if things went sour.

After several minutes of both parties gawking at each other, one of the Neanderthals turned toward the city and gave a loud, shrill whistle. Soon more Neanderthals came loping out of every structure, hurrying toward their position. Now Burton felt less sure about their odds.

The Neanderthals crowded in closer, heedless of their weapons, touching skin and clothing and conversing in that liquid tongue.

Herbert slapped one of their hands away, as if the creatures reminded him of some repulsive memory.

"This is getting out of hand." Burton freed his pistol from its holster, aimed it straight up and fired. The retort reverberated around the cluster of alien buildings, and the Neanderthals shouted and scattered, regrouping a few feet away.

When the echo died away, they were greeted by a new sound, that of some eerie piping across a wide range. Burton thought it was some sinister musical instrument, but when he looked toward the city, he saw something that chilled his blood.

It was green and barrel-shaped, standing midway up a short ziggurat-like structure on a series of writhing tentacles. More tentacles sprouted from the top of its blasphemous body where the head should be. It piped at them again.

"What is that?" blurted Challenger.

The presence of the creature seemed to set the Neanderthals into frenzy. They gesticulated and shouted at one another, as unnerved by the creature on the ziggurat as they were Captain Nemo's party. The brutes lashed out at the group, dashing their weapons from their grip and grabbing them roughly.

"Now see here!" Challenger delivered a powerful blow to one of the primitives, who answered in kind, powerful enough to stun the big zoologist.

"I'm afraid we have no choice but to go with them," said Burton as they were dragged toward the nearest grotesque alien structure. "For now."

"Matches!" Herbert snapped, reeling from their touch but otherwise making no effort to escape. They were completely surrounded now. Burton felt a spear poke him in the side and had a painful momentary flashback to the injury he suffered in Berbera. He rubbed his left cheek, feeling the triangular scar there.

Speke had been there, too.

Ph'nglui mglw'nafh Cthulhu R'lyeh wgah'nagl fhtagn!

He struggled briefly with the nearest brute, but they were possessed of a strength that belied their smaller stature. As the strange portal of the building yawned dark and forbidding before them, Burton wondered what would become of them. He thought of the *Nautilus,* so far away it might as well have been waiting for them in the year of their origin 1861, and shuddered.

CAPTURED

Burton, Nemo, Challenger and Herbert were herded into the building and tossed into metal cages. The Neanderthals locked the door and left the room, still communicating in that liquid speech and gesticulating wildly.

Burton tested the door, slamming against it. It held.

"This is not at all what I expected," said Nemo calmly.

Challenger fumed. "Well what *did* you expect? And why the devil didn't you share it with us? Now we're trapped, with no way to signal the *Nautilus*."

"Please, gentlemen," Burton pleaded. "This bickering will get us nowhere."

"Morlocks!" said Herbert.

Burton stared at the Time Machine's inventor before continuing. "Let's think this through, shall we? Challenger, what do you make of this cage?"

Challenger studied it, wrapping his fingers around the bars. "Iron. Crudely fashioned, yet solid and sturdy. It is beyond the kin of those simple, Stone Age brutes."

"Yes," said Burton. "So if they didn't build it, who did? And for what purpose?"

"That *thing* on the ziggurat appeared intelligent," said Nemo, beads of sweat standing out on his high forehead. "Though plant or animal, I can't say what it was."

"It's probably just as curious about us," said Burton. "Perhaps even just as fearful."

Challenger shrugged. "Man and Neanderthal coexisted. Since it knows of one, it is likely it knows of the other."

"Not like us," said Herbert, in a momentary expression of sanity. He tugged against the bars. "Nothing like us has yet walked this Earth. Forget our cage, gentlemen. Look at the room."

The explorers studied their environs beyond the cage in which they were imprisoned. They were in the center of a low-ceilinged room illuminated by shafts of sunlight filtered down from somewhere above. Along the far wall was a row of long tables composed of some dull white metal, shining in the light. Shelves set into the adjoining wall contained what appeared to be clay jars, cracked with age. An oblong leather satchel sat open on one of the tables, filled with wicked-looking metal implements.

"What does this place remind you of?" asked Herbert with a giggle.

"Why," said Challenger, "it's an examination room. They wish to dissect us!"

The burly zoologist gripped the bars and shook them violently. They rattled but didn't budge.

"Calm yourself, Professor," said Nemo. "I assure you we are not going to be dissected by those mindless brutes. They are not the true masters of this city."

"Quite right," said Burton. "That thing on the ziggurat. It told the Neanderthals to capture us. It holds some sway over them, probably through fear. Perhaps we can use that."

"Dissected," Herbert muttered from the far corner of the cage. "That's quite a turn, hey? How many times at University did I cut open a lower animal to study the mechanisms of life? Now we are the lower animals!"

"Calm down, Herbert," said Burton. "No one's getting bloody dissected. We're going to figure a way out of this."

They heard a strange noise then, as if something slick was sliding against the rough-hewn stone floor. A shimmering, globular form loped into view. It resembled an ambulatory oil slick, iridescent and covered in thousands of what looked like eyes that shimmered into existence only to swell and pop in seconds like soap bubbles. Two of the green, barrel-shaped monstrosities flanked it. The pile of slime came right up to the cage, interposing itself between the bars to come inside. Nemo, Challenger and Burton backed up with revulsion. It ignored them, going straight for Herbert. It wrapped itself around him as he screamed.

Challenger lunged at the beast, but Nemo and Burton restrained him. The contact lasted mere seconds. In a moment, the glowing oil slick had released Herbert and exited the cage, the Time Traveler crumpling to the ground in a sobbing heap.

Burton and Nemo went to him while Challenger glared at their jailers. "What have you done to him?"

"Contact successful," said Herbert as he sat up, his eyes blank and staring. "This one shall make an adequate bridge for communication."

"What's he on about now?" demanded Challenger.

"I don't believe he is the one speaking," said Burton, glancing at the blasphemous beings outside the cage.

"You are correct," said Herbert, his vocal cords confiscated by the barrel-shaped creatures resting outside the cage. "We are known by other races as Elder Things."

"What do you want with us?" said Nemo.

"We wish to study you. You are not like the bonehead slaves. You are not even like their cousins, the small brains from the northern continent. Your companion tells us you traveled through Time."

Burton glanced at Herbert, who stared straight ahead, a blank expression on his sweaty face. "They must have ripped this from poor Herbert's mind."

"We wish to know how this was accomplished. Only the Great Race of Yith is capable of such travel. Your companion showed us a machine. Where is it located?"

"You'll never get it out of us," declared Nemo. "What you *will* do is release us at once!"

"You have no power over us. We are the masters of this world."

"Wait," said Burton. "You did not build this city. Why are you here?"

"Our predecessors built it," said the beings through Herbert. "We waited until the Time of Ice ended to return here and reclaim our planet, only to find this world infested."

Challenger barked laughter. "Man, an infestation? Let me out of this cage, and I'll show you how pestilent we can be!"

"It must have been quite a shock for you to realize your planet has new masters," Burton said.

"You are correct, biped. But we are the masters. We made slaves of your cousins for the purposes of rebuilding this city and awakening Cthulhu from his eons-long slumber."

Cthulhu.

The word sent a cold chill fleeing up Burton's spine. It hadn't been a dream. John Hanning Speke really had uttered those words over him in his tent. Whatever had happened here in the dim past, the presence of these entities must be stored in the race memory of mankind, coming to them as disjointed myths and half-remembered nightmares. But it was all true.

"In his house at R'lyeh, dead Cthulhu waits dreaming," Burton said.

The barrel beings quivered, tentacles flailing about in what Burton assumed was surprise.

"That is correct," said Herbert. "It appears Cthulhu's dreams have reached even into your distant future. Perhaps your presence here means we are predestined to fail. More time to evaluate is needed."

The Elder Things made ready to leave, beckoning with their tentacles at the iridescent blob that undulated near the cage door.

"Come," said Herbert, still in contact with them. "Come, shoggoth. Your masters command it."

At last, the thing moved toward them and led the Elder Things back the way they had come.

Herbert fell to his knees, wincing.

"Oh, rot," he said. "That was horrible."

Challenger helped him to his feet, but he insisted upon sitting against the iron bars, his fingers massaging his temples.

"How much did they learn?" asked Nemo.

"Way too much about me, I'm afraid," said Herbert with a giggle. "But I believe I was able to block them from learning too much about us, and my Time Machine. I showed them my own first voyage through Time. I'm sure that will give them much to chew on for a while. If they have mouths."

"Good," Challenger said. "As soon as they learn how we got here, we're bound for those tables yonder to be flayed."

"And the *Nautilus* is doomed," Nemo added.

"What did you learn from them?" asked Burton.

"Very little I could understand," said Herbert. "They are not of this world. They sail the stars with the same ease as we travel across the ocean. They are beyond our reckoning and our kin." He started babbling, giggling like one bound for Bedlam.

"Herbert—" Challenger began, but Burton placed a hand on his shoulder. "Leave him be for now. Let him get his wits about him again. If he can."

Challenger nodded and looked about their cage. "That *thing*—what did Herbert call it? A shoggoth? They seemed to have a bit of trouble controlling it."

Nemo nodded. "I noticed that too. It was almost as if it were defying them. But why?"

"Defying them or testing them," said Burton. "Perhaps the Neanderthals are not the only slaves in R'lyeh."

RESCUED

R ichard Francis Burton awoke with a start to the sound of
gunfire.

He didn't remember falling asleep, but he did remember
his dream. He was hacking away at a thick jungle. As he worked his
way into a clearing, he saw a pristine lake, reflecting the blue sky like
a mirror. He glanced to his left and saw John Hanning Speke staring
back at him. The earth rumbled and shook, causing ripples in the lake.
A vast black shape emerged beneath the water. As it rose up and out,
Burton could see that it was a large green pyramid, water sluicing
down its rough-hewn sides. Grotesque imagery was carved into its
bulk, and Speke chanted at the sight of it, leaping into the water and
swimming toward it.

"No!" Burton dived in after him, only to find many cold hands
grabbing him, pulling him down and down. He looked around and
saw fish faces staring back at him. Deep Ones, pulling him toward the
pyramid's base.

Burton shook the vestiges of his nightmare from his mind as he
raised himself up off the cold, hard floor. The others were also rising,
awakened by the unmistakable sound of gunfire.

"We're being rescued?" Challenger asked, as if the whole idea was preposterous.

Nemo leapt to his feet. "It would appear that Miss Marsh has brought the cavalry."

Burton and Challenger exchanged surprised glances. It was night and dark inside their examination room cage, but clear moonlight filtered in just as the sunlight had, casting everything in a whitish glow.

"You planned for this?" said Challenger.

"I did, indeed," said Nemo. "That is why Miss Marsh stayed behind. If we did not return or signal the *Nautilus* in the allotted time, she was to command a rescue party."

"Bloody brilliant," said Challenger, getting in Nemo's face. "Though you could have bloody well told us."

"If I had," said the captain, giving the bigger man a shove, "then our captors could have gleaned it from their mental contact with the Time Traveler."

"Gentlemen," said Burton before their conversation could escalate further, "how do we alert Miss Marsh of our presence? She has no idea where to look for us."

Nemo shrugged. "Let's bang on the bars."

Challenger rattled the cage while Burton, Nemo, and the Time Traveler took to shouting as loud as they could. After almost a minute of this, they saw something enter the room. The wan moonlight picked out the grotesquely familiar form of a shoggoth.

"It appears we've only succeeded in alerting our jailers," said Herbert with a giggle.

They backed away from the cage as the shoggoth moved toward them. It squeezed its putrid bulk between the bars, growing a stout tentacle and wrapping it around cage's locking mechanism. The acrid smell of burning metal filled the air, and the lock fell away. The creature slithered back, allowing Captain Nemo to push open the cage door. They exited the cage as fast as they could, relieved to be free of their crude prison and no longer bound for the dissecting table.

"Wait," said Herbert, leaning toward the sinister creature who had rescued them. "I think this is the same shoggoth from earlier. Yes. It is. I sense familiarity coming from it."

"Are you still linked to it somehow?" asked Challenger.

Herbert thought about it a moment, then nodded. "Yes, I believe I am. Hello there, my dear, um, fellow."

As if in answer, the shoggoth formed a large bubble atop its quivering, shifting mass, a bubble that partially solidified into an approximation of Herbert's own head. It smiled at them with it, before the whole construct collapsed and fell back into the shoggoth.

"My God," said Challenger. "It's a bloody chameleon."

"It's more than that," said Herbert, fascinated by what they had witnessed. "It's a thing of pure protoplasm. It can be whatever it wants to be. And right now, it wishes to no longer be a slave of the Elder Things. It wants us to follow it. Let's go!"

The three explorers followed the quivering shoggoth out through a dim hallway. In an alcove, they found their weapons, snatching them up easily. Burton, for one, was glad to be reunited with his khukuri blade and pistol.

Seconds later, they arrived at the entrance. The alien city, illumined in moon-glow, was filled with the sounds of gunfire and guttural screams. Challenger wanted to push ahead, but Nemo held him back until they could tell what was going on.

Burton did the same, getting down on one knee, pistol held at the ready, his eyes trying to pick out individuals among the mass of running, dying Neanderthals. Flapping overhead was one of the obscene Elder Things, tentacles writhing.

He took aim and fired, hitting it near the center of its abhorrent body. When he hit it again, the Elder Thing fluttered and fell to the ground with a wet thud.

"What did you do that for?" asked Herbert.

"To prove that those things are mortal," said the explorer. "That means we can kill them."

"Don't wound them too badly," said Challenger. "I want a specimen for my museum."

The four men tumbled into the fray, their shoggoth savior slumping just behind.

"Don't shoot the Neanderthals," said Burton.

"Why the hell not?" said Challenger.

"They are just as much prisoners as we were and slaves just like the shoggoths."

The Neanderthals didn't put up much of a fight, being more interested in running for their lives. Burton even saw signs that they had turned against their masters. Atop the ziggurat, he saw an Elder Thing dangling from a Neanderthal's spear tip. The brute brought the spear down hard on the steps of the ziggurat as the thing tried to fly away, dashing its innards all over the green stone steps.

"Captain Nemo," said a familiar voice, "Captain Burton. I am glad to see you."

Elizabeth Marsh appeared from around the corner of one of the strange buildings, garbed in pith helmet, pants and boots, brandishing a rifle. Right behind her were ten men from the *Nautilus*, all similarly armed.

"Splendid," said Nemo. "You arrived just in time."

Challenger harrumphed. "You and I have very different ideas about timing."

"What are your orders, Captain Nemo?" asked Elizabeth.

"Let's get out of here," said Challenger. "And take one of those dead Elder Things with us."

"No," said Nemo. "We still haven't done what we came here to do, which is to learn the secret of this place."

"You want the secret of this bollocks place?" said Challenger. "It's bonkers!"

"The Elder Thing said something about awakening Cthulhu from his eons-long slumber," said Burton.

Captain Nemo nodded. "They know we traveled here through Time. They think our presence here put some sort of kink in their plans."

"They may try to make good on them, now that they are losing ground to their own slaves," said Challenger.

"We can't let that happen," said Burton.

"In his house at R'lyeh dead Cthulhu waits dreaming," said Herbert with a maniacal giggle.

"What's that?" said Burton, startled at the Time Traveler's utterance of words he thought only he knew.

"The shoggoth told me," said Herbert. He cackled once more, and Burton could see the beginning of madness in his wide, staring bloodshot eyes. He could feel it creeping up on himself too.

"Don't you see?" said the Time Traveler. "Ry'lyeh is the name of this place, this city. Not the landmass. The landmass became Mu. Lemuria. Atlantis. While this decrepit alien city fell into the domain of myth and nightmare. Oh, would that it had stayed there!"

"None of that helps us now," said Captain Nemo.

"Wait," said Challenger. "By Jove! I think I know what the half-mad little blighter is getting at. We can undo it."

"What?" said Nemo. "That's preposterous!"

"No," said Challenger. "Don't you see? Herbert here has created the ultimate weapon, his Time Machine. What gets us all, in the end? Time itself. What erases entire geologic ages from the earth's memory? Time!"

"How can we stop an entire landmass from existing?" said Burton.

Challenger shook his head. "I don't know, but we have to try. These creatures are highly advanced. They must have machines. Where are the machines?"

Every head turned to the shoggoth, who undulated languidly, refracting moonlight like a prism. It extruded a tentacle and pointed to the shadowy outline of a distant building.

"There," said Herbert.

The large group took off in a mass, the marksmen ready for any creature who attempted to cross their path. As they neared the oblong structure, Burton could feel a great rhythmic rumbling through his boots, and a sense of profound cosmic dread stole over him. He tightened his sweaty grip on his pistol and made for the building's entrance, wary of what they would find inside.

PALACE OF THE MACHINE

The large room they entered glowed with its own eerie inner light. Some grand machine rose up through the center of it, consisting primarily of finely milled cylinders composed of some dull white metal. They moved up and down like gigantic pistons in a steam engine, and the group could feel a profound heat coming from below.

"I think these go down deep into the earth," said Herbert, studying the vast contraption. "Perhaps it is powered by the heat created in the furnace beneath the planet's crust. How remarkable."

He shivered, and Burton wondered how he managed to cope, how he was able to defeat his madness to offer glimmers of sanity and insight. The dread he knew they all felt was even stronger here. Nemo's men looked about fearfully, eyes wide in sweat-covered faces. Glyphs on the wall outlined in the light that shone from the machine. Tentacled creatures writhed, and things not even vaguely anthropomorphic held court. Looming over them all was an impossibly tall being, its head like an octopus, a beard of feelers almost undulating. Its great arms were outstretched, and looming over the shoulders were the outlines of what appeared to be furled wings.

Somehow Burton knew that this was the feared Cthulhu, the Dreamer in R'lyeh.

This is what John Hanning Speke had never shut up about, the blot they were now trying to erase from the collective unconscious of this world.

"It's artificial," said Herbert with a mad giggle. "This island. They created it. It's nothing to them. Like building a bookshelf would be for us. Or a Time Machine." He cackled.

"Are you saying this machinery keeps the island aloft?" asked Nemo. "How do you know this?"

"The shoggoth." The Time Traveler pointing to their amorphous companion. "It told me." He descended into laughter. "The pile of ooze told me."

Miss Marsh placed a steadying hand on his shoulder. "Herbert, dear, keep yourself together, please."

The Time Traveler steeled himself. "Yes. Yes. All right."

Burton knew it wasn't easy to maintain one's sanity in such a place. He was having trouble concentrating. He couldn't even look at the glowing, slowly churning components of the machine for very long without his eyes growing cross, and the horrid glyphs etched into the green walls recalled vestiges of half-remembered nightmares. He concluded that this is what a mouse in the clock tower of Westminster must feel, a tiny, terrified mind standing in the midst of something it could never hope to comprehend, a machine created by a higher-order intellect.

Burton closed his eyes for a second and steadied his breathing, putting into practice the old Sufi meditation technique. It seemed to help, but only a little. But he noticed something when he opened his eyes again, a slime green plinth in the midst of the machine, and embossed upon its surface was a familiar object. It stood out for him in this swirling sea of alien irregularity like a blazing sun, and he moved toward it.

"Captain Burton," said Nemo. "What are—"

Burton didn't heed him. He went up to the plinth and studied what had caught his eye. It was the artifact Elizabeth Marsh had shown him back in the meeting place of the Royal Geographic Society scant weeks ago. Or will show them a hundred thousand years from now. *Time travel plays hell with the tenses*, he thought with a laugh. He touched it, tracing its lines, startled by how sharp and fresh and new it looked. The grotesque imagery was crisp and clear, the patina shiny. Burton didn't know why, but he flipped his pistol over in his hands until the grip was facing up. Then he began hitting the artifact, striking it like a cudgel.

"What are you doing?" said Nemo. "Stop."

"No," said Elizabeth Marsh. "He has the right idea. Everyone, smash the machine!"

Everyone went to work, hammering, smashing, and shooting at the machine. They had no idea if it would do any good, but they did it anyway. It made as much as sense as anything else in this place, and it took Burton's mind off the feeling of encroaching dread that threatened to pummel him into insanity.

Their efforts attracted the attention of the Elder Things, who were little match for the guns of Captain Nemo's men. A section of the machine fell with a bone-shaking clang, and everyone redoubled their efforts. Burton kept smashing at the artifact, the brittle green metal cracking slightly. He struck it a final time, and there was a flash of green light as it came off. He caught it with his free hand. It was warm. An electric shock went through him, and he squeezed his eyes shut.

Burton was falling into green depths where thick, swirling things writhed in the gloom. He counted himself lucky that he could not see them fully. He was in a dense, roiling fog, worse than any London pea-souper he had ever experienced. Hideous black shapes heaved up in the distance, inhuman outlines ripe with vague menace. He heard a membranous wing flap, saw a vast tentacle slowly unfurl. A thing made of soap bubbles moved perilously close. A giant pyramid-shaped form shambled past. The fog cleared somewhat, and there, in the distance, atop some grotesque alien throne made of spires of green metal, was the shape he had seen carved into the wall of the Palace of the Machine, vast leathern wings jutting from its back, its head a writhing octopus.

The inhuman god-thing man called Cthulhu glared at Burton with callous, cosmic indifference, filling the explorer with more dread and fear than he had ever felt. He was too afraid to look at it, yet he could not look away. It stared at him as he would an insect, not with cold malice but mild annoyance. Burton understood from the entity's inhuman gaze that it knew he was no threat to it. There was nothing Burton could say or do that would sway the creature from getting what it wanted. The grotesque things moving around it seemed to be making placating gestures with tentacles, webbed claws, and feelers, and Burton realized they were just as frightened of their alien god as he was.

Then the ground shook, and Burton fell once more. He opened his eyes with a start, looking around. Chunks of green stone were falling to the ground, smashing bits of the machine as it, too, started to come apart and plummet to the chamber floor.

"Burton!" Nemo shouted. "We've got to get out of here. Come on!"

Burton looked at his empty left hand. He had been holding something, hadn't he? Yes. He looked down at the artifact. Their vandalizing of the machine had done something. Scowling, the explorer stabbed at the abhorrently sculpted piece of metal with his boot, cracking the brittle metal. Then he holstered his pistol, turned, and ran with the others.

ESCAPE!

T he green city crumpled and fell, walls tumbling in on themselves, blasphemous porticos and oddly-dimensioned ramparts collapsed and turned to dust. Neanderthals uttered liquid screams as they died under the crumbling architecture.

Burton, Elizabeth, Herbert, Challenger, Nemo, and his men made a beeline for the coast, where more boats no doubt waited to return them to the relative safety of the *Nautilus*. The ground fractured around them, dropping stubby cycads into the abyss created. Streaks of glowing red appeared out of the cracks, and Burton's nose cringed at the sulfur and noxious gases that filled the air.

They made it to the beach unmolested, but the very sea thrashed along with the island's death throes, tossing Nemo's wondrous inflatable boats about.

Shouldering their guns, Nemo's men thrust themselves into the churning water to get control of the boats, grabbing their tethers as if trying to calm frightened horses. Nemo jumped into the nearest boat, followed by Elizabeth and Herbert. Burton and Challenger leaped into a nearby boat and helped Nemo's men hold it down so enough of them could get on that they could all depart from this place of nightmares.

Burton didn't remember much of that harrowing ride back to the *Nautilus*. It all happened so fast. When he climbed inside, Burton thought he would never be so glad to see the machine of wonders once again, and he slapped its firm metal hull to reassure himself that he was inside its comforting confines once more.

Herbert curled into a ball in the observation lounge and gibbered himself to sleep. Nemo brought the *Nautilus* out more than a hundred miles from the decaying, collapsing island, and watched the rest of its destruction through his periscope, the ocean waters churning as the nightmare of R'lyeh sank beneath the waves. At daybreak, Challenger kicked Herbert awake and Captain Nemo sent him into the bowels of the submarine to use his Time Machine to take them home.

Burton did not bother to watch as they hurtled through the ages, making the journey in his stateroom, lying on his bed with his eyes squeezed shut. He did not need to witness the slow march of Time unfolding in its proper order. He did not need to see the creatures of the deep being born and dying in an eye blink, or the countless generations that would thrive and wane between the ticks of a second. At some point, he fell asleep and dreamed of groggy green depths where things that were not men pondered man's existence and plotted against him.

He awoke to a knock on the door. Burton got up, knuckling grit from his eyes, and opened it.

"We're back," said Challenger. His eyes were half-mad and watery, and Burton couldn't decide if the boisterous zoologist had always looked like that.

"There's no sign of undersea upheaval," Challenger continued. "The sea floor is as calm as a mill pond. Whatever we did, we stopped R'lyeh from returning to the surface in our own time."

Burton nodded. "Or we just postponed its arrival," he murmured.

Challenger started to say something in rebuttal, then thought better of it. "Nemo has already set course for England. "We're going home, old son." He clapped Burton hard on the shoulders with both hands, a devil-may-care grin on his lips, before departing. Burton watched him go—not stopping at his stateroom but continuing onward toward Nemo's amazing museum—and closed the door.

HOME

Burton put on his *jubba* and meditated, then slept. Then meditated some more. He went to the galley for some food, and was offered a shot of whiskey from the secret, and no doubt contraband, flask belonging to Nemo's cook, a French-speaking Chinese man who fixed Burton with a toothless smile as he wandered in.

Everyone, for the most part, kept to themselves on that long, uneventful journey homeward. Burton yearned for home, as much as he had once longed to be anywhere else. He missed Isabel. He tried to write in his journal, but couldn't. He couldn't wrap his mind around everything he had seen and witnessed. No one would believe him anyway, and for some reason, writing about Captain Nemo and his amazing submarine seemed unfair to Nemo and his crew, like telling tales out of school. He was certain that, this adventure aside, Nemo wanted nothing more than to be left alone, and Burton was adamant about letting the man have his wish. He had certainly earned that right.

Herbert was recovering quite well. Burton found him in Nemo's museum on several occasions, pouring over display cases with Professor Challenger or playing cards with Elizabeth Marsh, who he seemed to have taken a shine to. Everyone spoke of mundane things. It was easier than trying to understand what they had just been through together. Challenger dickered with Nemo in an effort to buy off some of the captain's museum specimens. Herbert unhooked the Time Machine from the *Nautilus*.

"I should destroy it when we get back," said the Time Traveler. "It's given me nothing but grief. I used to think too much knowledge was a good thing. Now..." He let his voice trail off.

Burton nodded.

"Maybe I'll send it on ahead through time," Herbert mused, "without a pilot. Just lean over and turn the dial forward. It could hurtle on into futurity, past the Eloi and Morlocks. Past the Palace of Green Porcelain. Past the Earth being swallowed by the Sun, on and on until the very stars grow cold. Until the death of the Universe, the death of Time itself."

Burton thought about that for a long time. He pictured the Time Machine spinning through the endless dark and wondered if Cthulhu and his blasphemous ilk would be there waiting on it. He shivered.

The *Nautilus* made way for England at great speed, and made good time, slowing only to replenish the vessel with fresh air from the surface. Within four weeks' time, they had arrived in the North Sea. It was near dark when they arrived, but Nemo bade them wait until midnight before making the journey up the Thames in the smaller submarine. Everyone said their goodbyes. Herbert remained behind, having a few arrangements to make in removing the Time Machine back to dry land in secret.

Burton and Challenger climbed into the stifling confines of the little submersible, once again piloted by Elizabeth Marsh.

"What for you now?" Challenger asked her as she guided the vehicle up the Thames Estuary.

"I will remain with Captain Nemo," she answered, "at least a while longer. We still need to investigate the undersea ruins left behind by my...people."

"Be careful," said Burton. It seemed absurd once he'd said it, but it was all he could think of to say.

Elizabeth Marsh nodded. "I will, Captain. And you as well. Enjoy your appointment."

Burton looked at Challenger. "What about you?"

"Oh, I'm going back to tending my museum. And, of course, I'll now be on the lookout for one of those Elder Thing rotters to put in it."

Burton chuckled. Same old indefatigable Challenger.

Miss Marsh soon guided the thing to a slow stop, and Burton knew that their strange journey was, at last, at its end. They said hurried goodbyes and climbed up and out of the little submarine, glad to be in the fresh air, though the fog and coal smoke-shrouded air hanging over the stinking Thames could hardly be called fresh. Up the rickety wooden ladder they went, and Burton found himself standing on dry land for the first time in...a hundred and twenty-eight thousand years. In weeks. Yes, weeks.

Burton and Challenger watched as the hatch sealed itself and the whole thing submerged and disappeared into the dank, green-black water, never to be seen by either of them again.

The two men walked together away from the wharf and toward a more hospitable and more populated area of town. They hailed separate hansom cabs and went their separate ways. Burton gave the driver the address of Bartolini's dining rooms, where he knew the Cannibal Club would be convening. It would do him much good to see his old friends again before heading for the silence of his rooms at Gloucester Place. He gritted his teeth at the thought of what awaited him in that silence.

The driver, a slumped, hunchbacked gentleman, his features hidden under a black slouch hat, nodded and goaded his beast of burden into motion.

Richard Francis Burton entered Bartolini's dining rooms and walked upstairs. It would be good to see his friends again after such a long, strange voyage. For the first time in his life, Burton felt like his long journey had ended. He had seen everything there was to see, and he was finally sated. He would marry Isabel. He would take his commission as British consul in Fernando Pó. He would write. He would be happy.

Burton opened the door to the upper room, where Cannibal Club convened. What he saw there chilled his blood.

"My hat, Richard! You're back!" screeched a familiar voice from an armchair near the center of the room. The thing brushed a shock of red hair out of its face with a pale, scaly hand. Looking at him with bulbous, yellow watery eyes and thick, bluish lips was his friend, the poet Algernon Charles Swinburne.

"Come," said Charles Bradlaugh, beckoning to Burton with a claw-like hand from the far corner. His face was covered in green scales, his once familiar eyes now watery and reptilian. "Tell us of your latest adventure."

"Algy?" Burton said, feeling weak in the knees.

"Is something wrong, Richard?" said Sir James Plaisted Wilde. He was bald and fish-belly white, his mouth working like that of a gold-fish. "You didn't start drinking without us, did you?"

They were coming toward him now, those horrid entities who had once been his friends. He thought of Challenger's remarks about being able to change the future by affecting the past, using Time as a weapon. What had they done?

"Why, Richard," said Bradlaugh, "you look positively green around the gills."

Burton backed away from their cold, questing appendages, feeling his knees buckle under him. His mind reeled. He remembered the green, tentacled abyss, and the chanting of John Hanning Speke.

"Ph'nglui mglw'nafh Cthulhu R'lyeh wgah'nagl fhtagn!" Burton murmured.

"Ia! Ia! Cthulhu fhtagn!" his friends in the Cannibal club answered in unison.

Burton's last thought before sanity left him was this: In his house at R'lyeh dead Cthulhu waits dreaming.

PART II
SHADOWS OVER LONDON

"Dream manfully and thy dreams shall be prophets." —Edward Bulwer-Lytton

"Once you have eliminated every possibility, whatever is left, no matter how improbable, is the truth." —Sherlock Holmes

"We all have our time machines, don't we. Those that take us back are memories...And those that carry us forward, are dreams." —H.G. Wells

ISABEL!

R ichard Francis Burton stood in a hallway in Buckingham
Palace, a feeling of existential dread enveloping him like a
funeral shroud. Was he really to be knighted? It felt so
strange, so surreal. And yet it was real.

Wasn't it?

He felt disconnected, like he had forgotten something. He had the
strange sensation that he was supposed to be somewhere else, like he
had a prior engagement, but for the life of him he couldn't remember
what it was.

Everyone had come to see him be knighted. What would they call
him now? Captain Sir Richard Francis Burton? Bismillah, what a
mouthful. Why did the British insist on such long, complicated titles
for themselves? He was Captain Burton if one must, or Dick Burton.
Ruffian Dick, if one had a bone to pick with him. Dick Burton the
explorer. Dick Burton the apostate. But never "gentleman Dick." And
certainly not Sir Dick! The very idea seemed preposterous.

He walked past a line of his friends. To his left: Charles Bradlaugh.
Doctor James Hunt. Richard Monkton Milnes. Sir James Plaisted
Wilde. To his right: General Studholme John Hodgson. Charles
Duncan Cameron.

Down at the end of this procession was the young poet Algernon Charles Swinburne, smiling up at Burton drunkenly, raking an unruly shock of curly red hair out of his face. Burton nodded to these men and continued walking.

Where in the deuce was he going? Part of him wanted to turn and run out the door. He thought he could still feel the blazing heat of a distant desert sun upon his back. His uncomfortable formal clothes itched, and he longed for his loose-fitting *jebba*. He needed to meditate, clear his head.

Where is Isabel? She should be here, by my side.

A face Burton had not expected heaved itself up out of the din and crush of bodies hunched together on either side of him.

"Speke?"

"Hello, Richard," said John Hanning Speke, standing at the end of the long hallway. He wasn't wearing formal attire, but dressed for hunting. But that wasn't the strangest thing. Burton looked down at Speke's right side, which was emblazoned with dark blood.

"What happened?" Burton said, but even as he spoke he remembered. He knew.

A hunting accident, the papers had said. But Burton hadn't believed it. At least not at first.

"That is not dead which can eternal lie," said John Hanning Speke. "And with strange eons even death may die."

"What?" Burton's mouth was dry.

"They're coming, Richard. You did not stop them. You cannot. They will have what is theirs."

John Hanning Speke reached out to touch Burton's shoulder then, and his hand was cold and clammy, the fingers webbed, the skin fish-belly white. A powerful fishy odor assaulted Burton's nostrils. "When the stars are right."

Buron tore from his grasp, spun around. Everyone was staring at him. His friends, his colleagues. They looked on him with glassy, bulbous, watery yellow eyes set in pale, scaly faces. Their mouths opened and closed, opened and closed, an unspoken litany, and they reached for him with sickly green flippers that used to be hands.

Burton screamed.

～

R ichard Francis Burton's eyes snapped open. He felt a cold sweat all over his body. Mid afternoon sun filtered in through his bedroom window. A shadow hovered over him.

"Well bless me," said his housekeeper and landlady Miss Angell. "Your fever's finally broken."

She dabbed his forehead with a washcloth she had just rung out over a basin beside his head.

"Mother Angell?" Burton murmured. "Good. Have to get ready. I have my, uh, coronation."

He tried to rise, but she pushed him back down, chuckling.

"Coronation?" she said with a lopsided grin. "I don't think the Empire is quite ready for *that*. Now get some rest. You've had an awful time of it since your return. And it's no wonder, what with all this galivanting about the globe. I've a mind to nail your feet to the floor. Oh, but who can blame you? After what happened to Ms. Arundel."

She returned the washcloth to the basin.

"Isabel?" said Burton. "What happened?"

The old woman stared down at him, frowning. "Oh, you poor man. You really have been out of it. Don't you remember? She disappeared while you were away. You slipped into this horrible fever when you returned and found out. Up and vanished in Hyde Park a week ago, she did. But there's no use worrying about that now. You just lie back. I'll nurse you back to health. I've worked too hard to get you this far. I won't let you backslide."

"Isabel?"

Burton sat up all the way this time, pushing himself up onto his elbows, fighting against the soggy, tightly tucked bedclothes. Isabel? Missing?

"That can't be right."

Ms. Angell slowly shook her head. "You poor, poor man. That fever really scrambled your brains, it did. Now lie down. You need your rest. The worst has passed, but you still need to get your strength back."

Burton stared at her, his mouth slowly opening and closing. This wasn't right. Was it?

"I don't believe it," he said finally.

"Now, Captain Burton," said the housekeeper. "I'll not go through this again. The sooner you accept it, the better off you'll be."

Burton scowled, pushed himself up fully to lean against the wooden headboard.

His housekeeper wagged a finger at him. "Now the doctor said that you must resume your regular routine as soon as you are able. Looks to me like you're able. I'll bring you some lunch."

"I'll take it in my study," said Burton, not really hungry. He stared out the window as she gathered up the basin and other nursing implements and left the room.

When she was gone, Burton got up, changing into a fresh, clean *jebba*. The white linen gown-like garment billowed about him like a cloud as he pulled it on over his head. He looked at himself briefly in the dressing mirror as he smoothed out the gold brocade running from his neck down the front of the material. It was so much more comfortable than the stodgy tweed suits, neckties, cravats, and corsets worn by his fellow Londoners, and once again Burton felt he was a stranger in his own country. He scowled at his reflection and went down the hall to his study.

There was nothing amiss. And yet something still seemed off about it. He lit a cheroot cigar and smoked it thoughtfully. Isabel. My Isabel. What had happened?

In a flash of memory, he knew. He remembered. He had returned from his trip aboard the *Nautilus*, he and Challenger going their separate ways. Herbert had stayed on board to unload his Time Machine. He went home to a tearful Miss Angell telling him about Isabel's disappearance, showing him the paper that carried the news.

Bismillah! No. That wasn't right. After emerging from the smaller submersible, Burton had hailed a hansom and went to the Cannibal Club, eager to see his friends. But when he arrived at Bartolini's dining rooms, he found that his friends—James Hunt, Thomas Bendeshye, even Algernon Charles Swinburne—had been transmogrified into horrifying entities. After that, he couldn't remember any more before the horrible dream about Speke before waking up in his own bed.

"I must still be suffering ill effects from the journey," he murmured aloud. He sucked on the cheroot and exhaled fragrant smoke that formed a brief halo around his head before dissipating. The eldritch horrors he'd witnessed must have profoundly affected his psyche, causing him to hallucinate. His friends, worried for his safety, brought him home.

Or...

The other memory reasserted itself, like experiencing the *deja vu* of someone else. He remembered coming home to learn about Isabel, and then falling into some sort of madness or stupor to awaken as he had minutes ago. Both memories were as real, as strong, but only one of them could possibly be real, and Burton knew which one that was.

Burton sensed movement from the corner of his eye, as if someone was standing just over his left shoulder. He spun around in his chair, finding his study empty.

Burton tossed the blackened stump of his cheroot into the fireplace and tried to meditate but couldn't achieve the level of mental peace he desired and gave up. More memories—contrary memories—floated into his mind, like objects bobbing up in a murky mill pond.

Burton wandered to his writing desk and glanced at a newspaper sitting there. It was dated the day he left, but the headline he had half-expected to find was no longer there. The headline was supposed to read:

Madness Grips City's Spiritualists

But instead it read:

Royal Geographic Society to Host Debate on 'Hollow Earth' Theory

"What the devil is going on here?" Burton said aloud. He sat down behind the writing desk and pondered the paper until Miss Angel brought his lunch, a plate of cold cuts and pickles, with a snifter of brandy. Ignoring the food, Burton looked up at her from his chair. Seeking his words carefully, he said, "Do you remember the trouble a few months ago, before I left? The madness among the city's spiritualists?"

Miss Angell shook her head, perplexed. "What? No, sir. I don't remember anything like that. Those spiritualist mediums are pretty well near mad enough for my liking."

Burton stared down at the paper on the desk in front of him. "This newspaper. It's..." *Changed? But how?*

"If you don't mind my saying, Captain Burton," said Ms. Angell with an air of motherly authority. "I think you should go out and get some fresh air. It would do you some good."

Burton nodded and poured himself a brandy. He looked up from his troubled thoughts, half expecting to see Mother Angell still standing there doting over him, but she had disappeared. He scowled at the newspaper, then got up and wandered over to the window. It was a rare bright, sunny day over Gloucester Place, though gray storm clouds threatened from the east.

Isabel was gone. Just like that. Snatched away from him in Hyde Park. While he was gone on another one of his blasted adventures. Just one more jaunt to cure him of his wanderlust. And what a jaunt it was. He had boarded a submarine vessel and traveled backward through Time to confront alien horrors. He had returned with his sanity barely intact. He had hallucinated. He had fallen ill.

No.

Burton caught movement from the corner of his eye once more and searched behind him. No one was here. And yet he thought he saw something, a shadowy some*one*, lurking in the periphery of his vision.

"Bismillah," he muttered. He drained his brandy, poured another and emptied it down his throat.

Something had changed. Their journey through Time had altered something. Perhaps several somethings. Maybe Isabel's disappearance included. And Burton was the only one who had noticed.

No. Challenger. Herbert. They had gone on this strange voyage with him. They would notice anything that was changed as well. He had to speak to them.

Burton ran to his bedroom and hurriedly dressed. He shouted to Miss Angell that he was going out as he bounded down the stairs.

THE TIME TRAVELER

Burton walked up Gloucester Place toward Baker Street, rational thought setting in, slowing his steps. He stopped, looked around before realizing he had no idea where either man hung his hat. He supposed finding Professor Challenger would be easy enough. A short conversation with one of the members of the Royal Geographical Society would be enough to locate him. But what of Herbert? He didn't even know the Time Traveler's surname.

Burton tapped his walking stick on the pavement in thought. He recalled from a conversation he'd had with Herbert aboard the *Nautilus* that he resided near Kew Gardens. It wasn't as specific as Burton would like, but it would have to be enough.

Kew Gardens was in Richmond, in south-west London. It would be mid-afternoon before he arrived, and he didn't know how long it would take to narrow down the Time Traveler's address. He decided to locate Herbert first, then worry about Challenger's current whereabouts later.

Burton hailed a hansom and began his journey.

Lulled by the clop of the horses' hooves on the cobblestones, he let his mind drift, allowing the conflicting memories that filled his mind to bob up to the surface once more, both alien and familiar. He could not reconcile them. He wanted to choose one set of occurrences over the other, but he was increasingly finding it more and more difficult. The memories that had felt so wrong and out of place earlier—those involving Isabel's mysterious disappearance—were now beginning to seem as if they were the right ones. And yet that other nagging notion—that Isabel was still safe and sound—felt out of place. He thought of himself as two Burtons, both fighting for supremacy of one body, one reality. And he was starting to feel crowded.

Using a Sufi meditation technique, Burton banished the feeling from his mind, at least for the time being. When he opened his eyes again, he was staring out at the entrance to Kew Gardens, the hansom having come to a stop in front of it.

Burton paid the driver and got out. As the driver and his horse clopped away, the explorer looked left, then right, considering his options. "Eeny, meeny, miney, moe," muttered Burton and started off to his right. Just up the street was a cluster of buildings containing various shops. He introduced himself and started asking if anyone knew a young inventive chap with a passion for optics. A half hour later, Burton had Herbert's address, after describing the Time Traveler to a kindly, withered old chemist who had delivered a tincture of what he called "nervous medicine" to the home in question that very morning. Burton thanked him and moved on.

It was a lovely day, and the home, the chemist told him, was nearby, so Burton had no qualms about walking. He had traveled on foot greater distances—and through much harsher conditions—than this, and it felt good to stretch his legs. He had been in bed too long, and still felt weak from the ordeal. The human body, he decided on the spot, had no place for lethargy.

Forty-five minutes later, Burton strode up the front walk of the Time Traveler's house. He knocked on the door with the knob of his walking stick. After almost a full minute, an older, harried-looking woman appeared, wearing a crisp housekeeper's apron. "Can I help you?" she said.

"Good afternoon. I am Richard Francis Burton, and I was hoping to call on the master of the house."

"I'm sorry," she said. "The master doesn't feel well. You'll have to come back another time."

"Please," said Burton. "It will only take a moment. He and I recently traveled together, and—"

"You did, did you?" said the housekeeper. "Well, I suppose you are to blame for his sorry state. Did you know he's been wandering around here half mad since he returned? He's saying the strangest things you've ever heard. Some rot about shoggoths and other things I can't even pronounce. Strange, guttural things that no human mouth has any business sayin', if you ask me. Why, it's worse than the last time."

"Last time?"

"Yes sir. No doubt he told you about it. He tells everyone else. Can't shut up about it. And I had just gotten him back on the straight and narrow. Now this."

"Can I talk to him, please?" asked Burton. "I think I can help."

"Well," said the housekeeper, eying Burton suspiciously. "I suppose you can't make him any worse. He's down in his basement laboratory, tinkerin' with that bleedin' contraption of his."

"Tinkering?" said Burton, a dark thought crossing his mind. The memory of a brief conversation he and the Time Traveler shared during their return to England.

I should destroy it when I get back. It's given me nothing but grief.

Burton reached up and pushed open the door, Herbert's words echoing in his mind. "No!" He barreled past the protesting housekeeper and glanced around. In a moment he heard the sounds of banging coming from what must be the basement, and he ran down the narrow wooden steps as fast as he could.

In the middle of a dusty workshop stood the Time Machine, looking just as it had aboard Nemo's submarine. Its brass fittings glittered in the late morning sunlight that filtered in through a set of glass doors on the basement's far end. An ornate saddle sat in its center, fronted by a brass and wood inlaid console from which the twin crystalline control rods glittered. Behind this was the large dish that spun when the Time Machine was in operation, its polished surface studded with clockwork emblems. Its presence had a strange solidity, and it set the disparate memories warring for supremacy of Burton's head once more.

Looming over the machine was the Time Traveler himself, standing there in his nightclothes, his face a mask of sweat and pain. He had a long pipe wrench raised over his head, which he was about to bring it down on the contraption with all the strength his frail form could muster.

"Herbert, no!" The explorer lunged at him just as he brought the wrench down toward the machine with great force, tackling him. The heavy wrench clattered to the floor.

"Hey!" shouted the housekeeper from behind them. "Get off him. He's out of his tree."

Burton rose to allow Herbert to get up. The Time Traveler stared at him with contempt, and Burton could tell by the set of his eyes that he didn't even recognize the explorer. "You'll not stop me from destroying that infernal machine, Morlock! I will not let you get your fungoid hands on it. You'll not drag it down into your tunnels. You will never get access to all of Time."

"Herbert, it's me. Captain Burton. Don't you remember?"

Herbert stared at him, trying to recall. A spark of recognition appeared on his face. "Shoggoths," he said.

"Yes," said Burton. "The shoggoths. R'lyeh. Nemo. Ms. Marsh."

"Elizabeth," said Herbert slowly, smiling. "Weena. My Weena."

"If you say so," said Burton. "I really must hear that story sometime. But you cannot destroy the Time Machine."

"Why not?" Herbert said, scowling.

"Because we still need it." Burton glanced self-consciously at the housekeeper before proceeding. "Something has happened. Something terrible. We have to go back."

Herbert appeared to consider this, stroking his chin in thought. Then his eyes narrowed. "You lie, Morlock. You only want to steal the machine from me."

Herbert closed the short distance between them and swung a weak right hook that Burton easily dodged. Even in his weakened state, Herbert was an inventor by trade and an academic by inclination. He was clearly no fighter.

"Please," murmured Burton. "I don't want to hurt you."

Herbert roared as he closed in on Burton once more, reaching for the explorer's throat. Burton grappled with him, pulling his arms down easily before jabbing him as hard as he dared on the chin. The Time Traveler collapsed in an unconscious heap.

Burton turned toward the Time Machine, remembering something Herbert had told him aboard the *Nautilus* about its operation. He reached for the twin control levers, unscrewed them, and put them in his coat pocket. Then he glanced at the housekeeper. "Help me."

Together, he and the housekeeper—whose name, he discovered, was Mrs.Watchett—helped Herbert up the stairs to his bedroom, where Burton laid him on his bed. "Is there a key to the basement?"

"Yes," said Mrs. Watchett.

"Good. Lock the door and hide the key. Don't let him back in there until you've heard from me."

"Just what in blazes is going on here?" asked Mrs. Watchett.

Burton considered her for a moment before answering. "I wish I could tell you. You wouldn't understand half of it, and you would scarcely believe any of it. Suffice it to say that he must not further tamper with the Time Machine. Is that understood?"

The old woman nodded quickly, fearfully.

"Good," said Burton. "I must go, but I will return as soon as I can to check on him. Do not let him near that contraption."

Without another word, the explorer left the Time Traveler's bedroom and bounded back down the stairs to see himself out.

THE DIOGENES CLUB

Burton hailed a passing coach and returned to London proper, giving the driver the address of Bartolini's dining rooms on Fleet Street. It was unlikely anyone from the Cannibal Club would be around at this time of day, but it gave Burton a sense of purpose to his movements that he found somewhat soothing. And if anyone was there, he could ask if they knew the present whereabouts of Professor Challenger, as well as get more confirmation as to which set of his memories was true.

Given his current state, it was obvious the Time Traveler would be of little use, and Burton feared for the poor man's sanity. But there was nothing to be done about it now except check in on him later. He still had no idea exactly what he was going to do, only that he would need the Time Machine intact to do it.

Once again, those conflicting memories of recent events began the battle for his mind. The coach turned onto Fleet Street, and Burton rapped on the roof of the conveyance with his walking stick and instructed the driver to let him out. He paid the man and disembarked, deciding it would be best for his continued sanity if he walked to clear his head.

Fleet Street was alive with people and crowded. Burton pushed his way through the press of bodies. The crowd thinned as he continued moving east. He could see the building containing Bartolini's in the distance, and stopped briefly to catch his breath and adjust his top hat.

He had the vague feeling of being watched. From the corner of his eye, he noticed a man moving quickly behind him, stopping when Burton did. But he did not continue onward as he would have if he were merely trying to avoid a collision and then be about his merry way. He stopped and waited for Burton to move on, as if he wanted to keep himself firmly behind the explorer.

Burton continued walking, though keenly aware of the other man. He moved deliberately, then glanced behind him to see if the stranger did the same. He did.

Grinning now, Burton quickened his pace, intrigued that the man did the same. He was definitely being followed. But by whom? And for what purpose?

Burton walked faster now, threading his away in among a group of three women and one man, then on beyond them. He shrank into a narrow alley on his right and waited.

A scant span of moments later, the man appeared, looking around frantically, no doubt wondering how he lost his quarry. Burton stepped from the alley, jamming the knob of his walking stick hard into the man's solar plexus. The man doubled over and sputtered.

"Who are you?" demanded Burton. "And why are you following me?"

The man sputtered again, squinting at Burton dumbfounded. He tried to speak, but nothing came out but a wheeze.

"Who are you?" Burton said again.

The man held up his right index finger, his left hand reaching into his coat, producing a shiny metal object. He stuck it out for Burton to see. It was a police inspector's badge.

"I'm very sorry," said Burton. "But I don't take kindly to being followed."

The man shook his head. "No...my fault." He wheezed some more before recovering his breath.

"Chief...Inspector...Frederick George...Abberline...Metropolitan Police...at your service."

He finally stood upright. "I've been looking all over the city for you, Captain Burton."

"Well," said the explorer, "whatever for?"

He looked around quickly. "Not...here. Out on the street."

"Let's go to my club," Burton said. "It's just up the street there." He pointed with his stick, and the policeman nodded.

"After you, Captain," said Abberline cordially, and Burton stepped out of the alley and continued on his original course.

Old Bartolini was surprised to see him but greeted him warmly enough. He allowed Burton and Abberline entry, the latter following Burton up the stairs to the upper room where the Cannibal Club held their weekly debaucheries.

Burton was surprised to find the room already had an occupant. A skinny young man with long red hair sat hunched over the table, fiercely writing something. He turned as they entered.

"Algy?" said Burton.

"Richard! My hat, but you still look a fright. Your housekeeper is falling behind on her duty to fatten you up, what?"

"I just got out of bed this morning," said Burton, removing his topper and hanging it on the coat tree by the door. Abberline did the same with his bowler. "What are you working on there?"

Swinburne shook slightly, involuntarily, quivering with a nervous electricity that never ceased to fascinate the older explorer. "Oh, just some new lines of poetry." He recited, "Time turns the old days to derision, Our loves into corpses or wives; And marriage and death and division make barren our lives."

"A bit morbid," said Burton. "But I like it."

Swinburne shook. "Oh, it needs a spot more polishing."

"That's all right." To Abberline he said, "Is this private enough for you? I can ask Algy to leave."

"No, no," said the Scotland Yard man. "That won't be necessary."

"And right so," added Swinburne. "For wild horses could not drag me away."

Burton scowled at his young friend. "Inspector Abberline, meet Algernon Charles Swinburne. Algy, meet Chief Inspector Frederick George Abberline."

The two hastily shook hands before Burton offered Abberline a seat. He regarded the man now for the first time. Of average height and build, a simple brown tweed suit covering his lean frame. He wore furry muttonchops that curved into a thick mustache, and had a high forehead made all the more prominent due to his receding brown hair.

"May I get you a brandy?" asked Burton. "It's the least I can do for assaulting you."

"No, no," said Abberline, dismissing the notion with a wave. "That won't be necessary. And anyway, I'm on duty. But not on official Metropolitan Police business."

"Oh?" said Swinburne, swinging a wooden chair around backward and straddling it. "Do tell."

Burton shot Swinburne a warning look before taking a wingback chair opposite Abberline.

"I've been following you all morning," said Abberline. "I was sent to retrieve you by a man named Mycroft Holmes. Do you know that name?"

"Should I?" Burton countered.

"He's rather well known in British intelligence circles. Perhaps you've heard of his more famous younger brother, the consulting detective Sherlock Holmes."

"Yes, I believe I have," said Burton.

"My Aunt Flora's pretty pink bonnet," blurted Swinburne. "What intrigue."

"Mr. Holmes," said Abberline, "that is, the elder Mr. Holmes, requests your presence for a very important—and discreet—matter. I am to escort you to meet him immediately."

Burton nodded. "And where is this meeting place?"

"The Diogenes Club," said Abberline.

Swinburne quivered in his seat, making a noise like he was going to say something, then fell silent. Burton considered the inspector's words. He had heard of the Diogenes Club, but so much was still shrouded in mystery. It was a gentleman's club not unlike his own Cannibal Club, yet one open only to intellectual elitists and misanthropes. Burton had once heard a rumor that no talking was allowed at all within its walls. To violate this sacred law was grounds for immediate expulsion from the club.

Burton nodded finally. "I must say, Inspector, you have aroused my interest. I will accompany you to meet with Mr. Holmes."

"Excellent," said Abberline, rising from his seat. "He is expecting us."

"Well, that's settled," said Swinburne. "You must go at once. And I must have another drink and tackle my verse." He glanced at the grandmother clock in the corner. "My hat! I'm due for the lash in a bit. What ho what ho!"

Swinburne jumped from his chair and returned to the table where his lines of verse awaited him.

"Let's get going then," said Abberline, and the two men, taking up their hats and Burton his gentleman's stick, left the room.

"My," said Abberline when they emerged back onto the street once more. "If you don't mind me saying so, your friend Swinburne is a bit of an odd duck, isn't he?"

Burton chuckled. "You have no idea."

"Did he say he was due for a lashing?"

Burton nodded once. "Yes. Algy has a rare condition that apparently causes his body to sense pain as pleasure."

"Remarkable," said the policeman.

"Indeed. There's not another one like Algy. He also possesses a keen intellect for one so young, and he can drink ten men under the table."

"Extraordinary," said Abberline. "But we have bigger fish to fry. I'd best get you to Mycroft Holmes."

Abberline hailed a hansom and gave the driver the address for the Diogenes Club. Burton sat back and pondered this new situation he found himself in, the mystery keeping his dueling memories at bay for the moment. He turned his stick in his hands and looked out the window at the hustle and bustle of London. The sky above, a cloudless blue when they entered Bartolini's dining rooms, was now a dirty gray, as bruise-colored clouds rolled through to shroud the sun.

The Diogenes Club loomed over them frolm a nondescript, somber gray building on Piccadilly Circus, though Burton didn't recall that being the infamous club's original location. They got out, Abberline paid the fare, and they went up to the door. He glanced at Burton sternly. "There is to be no talking except for in the room where we are meeting Mr. Holmes."

"I am familiar with this bizarre protocol," said Burton. "Proceed."

The policeman knocked three times slowly, and the door opened. A taciturn butler in the finest livery greeted them with a frown Burton took to be the man's natural state, and they entered quietly.

Abberline stepped inside and Burton followed. The butler disappeared.

Burton's boots sank into a dense pile of lush, lurid red carpeting. Every wall was covered in fine oil paintings and Italian frescoes. There wasn't a speck of dust in evidence, and every stick of furniture was of the finest manufacture. It reminded Burton of Isabel's parents' home, formal and decadent and not the least bit inviting.

He choked up. *No. Must not think of her now.*

Here and there a few men sat, all well dressed, most of them scowling into a book or reading a newspaper, careful not to rustle the pages. In one room off to Burton's right was a great fireplace with a huge boar's head hanging upon it. Near the fireplace two men sat opposite an ornate marble chessboard, each of them staring down at their hand-carved armies of enormous marble chessmen as if frozen, like one of the paintings on the walls. Neither of them made a move in the time it took Burton and Abberline to cross their path and out of sight.

Abberline stepped up to a formidable-looking oaken door. A placard set in it proclaimed it the Stranger's Room. Burton had heard that name uttered among his friends in hushed tones. This was the Diogenes Club's inner sanctum. Abberline tapped on it three times, leaned his head toward the wood, listening, then opened it. Burton followed him inside.

A large man, Mycroft Holmes sat in a green wingback chair that faced the entrance to the Stranger's Room, his right elbow resting on an ornate wood and marble side table upon which sat a cup and saucer. He wore a crisp suit obviously tailor-made for him, and he projected a haughty, self-assured air that was almost palpable. This,

Burton knew, was a formidable fellow. One who was used to being obeyed.

Abberline closed the door and breathed a heavy sigh, as if relieved to speak again. "Mr. Holmes, sir. I present Captain Richard Francis Burton."

Mycroft made no move to get up or shake Burton's hand.

"Please have a seat, Captain Burton. We have much to discuss."

Burton took a similar chair across from Holmes, while Abberline leaned against the wall next to the side table and crossed his arms.

"You are a very interesting fellow," said Mycroft Holmes. "You are a soldier, ethnologist, spy, writer, the first white man to journey to Mecca, and one of the finest swordsmen the Empire has ever produced."

"I try," said Burton, glib.

Holmes ignored his quip and continued. "But what is more interesting, to me, is that some weeks ago you departed England with one George Edward Challenger and a young inventor from Kew and returned almost four weeks later. How you left England is a mystery. You did not book passage on any passenger or cargo ship, nor did you leave the city over land by any route or mode of transport. In fact, you seem to have just up and vanished, traveling on some mode of conveyance unknown to current science."

"You are quite well informed," said Burton. "Am I to take it that you have had me under some sort of surveillance?"

"Not at all," said Mycroft Holmes. "Just a bit of deduction on my part. I am skilled at taking many disparate, seemingly unrelated details and putting them together to form one broad, clear picture of an event."

"I see," said Burton.

"After I learned of the mysterious circumstances of your departure, I recalled an odd item from a few years ago." He tapped a sheaf of yellowed papers on the table next to him. "It seems several years ago that a French marine biologist named Professor Pierre Arronax joined a unique expedition to track down an unknown sea creature that was believed to be attacking several ships."

"I recall reading about that," said Burton.

"Monsieur Arronax was tossed overboard in an encounter with the beast, along with a harpooner named Ned Land. Several weeks later, they were discovered on a small island off the Norwegian coast and had a very strange story, which has been recorded in these pages and kept under lock and key by me. Arronax claimed that the sea creature they were tracking was nothing of the sort, but was, in fact, a large submarine vessel piloted by an enigmatic captain who called himself Nemo. I believe this is the self-same vessel in which you, Professor Challenger, and the inventor departed London."

Mycroft went silent, keen eyes staring into Burton's. The explorer considered him for a time, wondering how much he should tell him. After all they had been through together, he respected Captain Nemo's privacy. But the proverbial cat was already out of the bag. Mycroft Holmes knew about Nemo and his fabulous underwater vessel. And what could he do to Nemo anyway? The man was untouchable. No one on Earth could find him, let alone match the power and agility of the *Nautilus*.

"It's true," Burton said at last, and told the tale of his strange journey across oceans and Time with Captain Nemo. He held nothing back, even adding the strange circumstances that led to his departure, the spiritualist madness that had so piqued the curiosity of Professor Challenger, as well as the trouble brewing in the South Seas that led Captain Nemo and the American woman Elizabeth Marsh to seek Burton's and Challenger's help.

"Good Lord," said Abberline when Burton had finished. "I need a drink."

Mycroft Holmes looked at Burton appraisingly.

"You don't believe me," he said.

"On the contrary," said Mycroft. "Under the circumstances, I have no choice but to believe you. As my brother is fond of saying, once you have eliminated every possibility, whatever is left, no matter how improbable, is the truth. Now, what of this Herbert?"

"He's mad," said Burton. "He tried to kill me this morning because he thought I was something called a Morlock. Of course, seven days ago I thought my fellow Cannibal Club members had all been transmogrified into the creatures we encountered on our voyage aboard the *Nautilus*."

"And I take it these Morlocks were not present during your adventure," said Mycroft.

"No. They were something he encountered the first time he activated his Time Machine, on a journey into far futurity."

Mycroft nodded. "I see. Is he the only one who can operate the machine?"

Burton stroked his beard, staring off into space. "Well, no. I don't think so. He explained its operations before our journey back through time aboard Nemo's submarine. It seemed simple enough. The controls are composed of only two levers made of crystal. One controls the motion—forward or backward—through Time. The other controls the speed." Burton returned his gaze to Mycroft Holmes.

"Why did you visit him this morning?"

"I wanted to know if his memories surrounding our return to London are the same as mine." Burton told them of his conflicting memories, and the differing events that took place before he left. "I needed to see if Herbert had the same recollections. If so, it would point to..." He let his voice trail off. Chief Inspector Abberline stared down at him as if he had just sprouted a second head. Mycroft appeared more understanding.

"This spiritualist madness sounds interesting," he said. "I do not recall any such incidents. But let's table this for now. I'd like you to forget about the Time Traveler as well for the time being, for we have more pressing concerns. And I think you are just the man for the job."

"Why me?" said Burton. "Why not Challenger?"

"You know what a difficult man Challenger can be," said Mycroft Holmes. "I have sent him several invitations to meet me here at the Diogenes Club; he has denied them all. I have sent messengers around with an official summons, and he has thrown them out bodily, sometimes violently. Besides, he is much too boisterous. What I need requires tact and subtlety."

Burton nodded. "Neither a quality the good professor possesses in abundance."

"Exactly," said Mycroft.

"But there's more to it than that, isn't there?" asked Burton. "I'm not here just because I boarded a secret submarine."

"Your brother recommended you," said Mycroft.

"Edward? You know Edward?"

Mycroft nodded once. "As you well know, your brother Edward Burton holds a vaunted position within the British government, as do I. He thinks you are just the man I need, and after careful investigation, so do I."

"And what of your famous younger brother?" asked Burton. "Why not the illustrious Sherlock Holmes?"

"He is otherwise engaged. Like yourself, my brother is a member of the Shadow Council."

Burton leaned back in surprise. "You know of it?"

"I know everything I need to know," said Mycroft Holmes. "If it happens anywhere in the British Empire, you can be assured I either know of it or had a hand in orchestrating it."

"Well," said Burton. "Be that as it may, I am no longer a member of this mysterious group. I did what was asked of me when I stepped aboard the *Nautilus*, and that's that."

"The appointment," said Mycroft, "is for life. It is not a commission one can decline. I assume you were given the chance to do so before you left on your little jaunt?"

Burton nodded. He disliked where this was headed.

"Well then," said Mycroft Holmes, steepling his fingers. "As a fellow member of the Shadow Council, would you like to know why I have brought you here?"

"I would indeed," said Burton. *So I can get back to my life. So I can fix whatever damage I've done to Time. So I can save my Isabel.*

"What I'm about to tell you cannot leave this room."

Burton nodded. Abberline simply looked bored. He had obviously heard Mycroft's spiel before.

"We have evidence of a weird cult operating in the East End," said Mycroft. "They call themselves the Esoteric Order of Dagon, and they are growing in numbers. They are engaging in strange occult rites, including, we believe, ritual human sacrifice."

A chill fled up Burton's spine at the mention of the cult's all too-familiar name. Mycroft saw the spark of recognition on his face.

"You know of this cult?"

"I have heard of it," said Burton warily. "There was an American woman traveling with Nemo who hailed from a seaport town called Innsmouth, its history tangled in this dark cult."

Burton didn't tell Mycroft and Abberline the story of her experiences with the cult, but decided it best to keep some things to himself. He didn't not fully trust this Mycroft Holmes. Not yet.

Mycroft smiled briefly. "Well then, it appears I have chosen wisely. You are just the man to look into this cult and stamp it out before it spreads to the rest of London."

"What? Stamp it out? And how am I supposed to do that?"

"You're resourceful. I have confidence you'll figure something out. I'm sure I don't have to tell you how important this is."

"I know all too well the power and the danger this Esoteric Order of Dagon represents," said Burton flatly.

"Good. Then you will act with the utmost haste to see this mission to its only acceptable conclusion."

"Mission? Am I to take it I'm to be a foot soldier in some sort of war?"

"We are already at war, Captain Burton," said Mycroft, rising to his feet. He moved to the far corner of the room, which was crowded by a small table and a set of chairs. Sitting atop the table was a wooden box Burton hadn't noticed when he and Abberline had entered the Stranger's Room.

"At first," said Mycroft, "the actions of this cult were little different from the normal crimes in the Cauldron. Disappearances, murders. The usual rot and ruin. Until this turned up."

Burton rose from his seat to join Mycroft beside the box. Only Abberline stayed put where he was. Mycroft lifted the lid, and what Burton saw inside chilled his blood.

It was a tall, elaborate tiara, worked in a strangely tinged gold and covered in images of marine life. Burton took an involuntary step back from it.

"You've seen this before," said Mycroft Holmes, regarding him expectantly.

"One very similar," said Burton. "Aboard Captain Nemo's submarine. I had hoped to never see another one. Where did you get this?"

"In a pawn shop on the edge of the Cauldron," said Mycroft Holmes. "The gold itself is of a peculiar quality. I've had experts from all over Europe and the United States examine it, and none of them have ever seen its like. The only thing we know for sure is that the gold used to create it was not mined anywhere on Earth."

"Nowhere overland," Burton corrected.

"What?" said Mycroft.

"When did you first become aware of this cult?" asked Burton.

"Some three weeks ago, during your absence. And through a most bizarre contact. A criminal, the self-described arch-enemy of my brother, one Professor Moriarty."

"He's been running most of the East End gangs for many years," added Abberline. "If it's dirty and in the Cauldron, Moriarty's got his grubby hands all over it."

"He came to my brother shortly after you departed London," said Mycroft, "filled with a most uncustomary fear. He told Sherlock of strange things taking place in the East End, of people going missing, numerous drownings, and large objects being heaved up out of the Thames late at night and stored in buildings along the wharf. There have also been reports of strange creatures, including fish-like entities and amorphous, iridescent blobs, like an oil slick, but that are said to move as if guided by a cold intelligence. My brother, being too preoccupied with another important matter, told me of his encounter with Moriarty, and I began putting my great intellect toward the problem. The police have scoured the Cauldron but returned with more questions than answers. Chief Inspector Abberline here has been most helpful toward that end."

Abberline nodded. "This Esoteric Order of Dagon is growing in strength and numbers. Folks in the Cauldron have always been reluctant to talk to the police, but they are afraid to speak a word against anyone part of that cult. I think the ones not in it are afraid of the ones who are. And one of my men saw one of them blobs Mr.

Holmes spoke about. And another man hasn't been seen since Tuesday last."

"The day I returned," said Burton absently.

"You must root out the organizers of this cult," said Moriarty. Because it is spreading. I fear that soon the whole city will be caught up in this madness."

"I will do what I can," said Burton. "If the trouble has just started, perhaps it's not too late."

"What do you mean?"

"I've heard a similar story from the American woman I met on my journey. If what happened there is taking place here, we must move quickly to contain it."

"What happened there?" asked Mycroft.

Burton considered his words carefully. "Let's just say the entire town slipped into a state from which it will probably never recover."

"Sounds like you *are* the man we need," said Mycroft Holmes. "Just as I surmised."

"I'm flattered, but it's going to take a lot more than just me."

Mycroft motioned toward the policeman. "Inspector Abberline is at your disposal. You are welcome to recruit anyone else you need for this venture. Discreetly, of course."

Burton couldn't think of anyone else he disliked enough to want to drag them into this madness, so he changed the subject. "And how exactly am I to root out the founding members of this cult?"

Mycroft reached into a pocket of his coat, producing a scrap of paper. "Moriarty gave my brother this."

Burton took the proffered scrap and unfolded it. Scrawled on it was a strange yet simplistic design he had never seen before. It appeared to be a stylized pentagram with a horizontal oval in its center. In the center of the oval was a kind of flourish that put Burton in mind of either the pupil of an eye or, more likely, a burning campfire. "I've never seen this before."

"Nor have I," said Mycroft. "And I can't find it in any occult text. But this emblem is popping up all over the East End, scrawled on buildings, in alley ways. And there is a pup in the East End called the Elder Sign. This insignia hangs above it from a wooden placard. I want you to go there with Chief Inspector Abberline and get to the bottom of this Dagon cult."

"I don't see as we have any other choice," said Burton to Abberline. "This is our only lead. We'll need to go in disguise, of course."

"I'll leave you two to manage the particulars," said Mycroft Holmes. "It's settled then. God speed you on your journey."

"There's just one more thing," said Burton.

Mycroft Holmes arched an eyebrow. "Oh?"

"My fiancée Isabel is missing. She was last seen in Hyde Park. I'd like you to put your considerable intellect and resources toward finding her."

The large man heaved a sigh. After a beat, he said, "Consider it done."

THE ELDER SIGN

Burton followed Chief Inspector Abberline out of the Diogenes Club and back out onto the street. It was late afternoon, with the sky now obscured by dirty gray clouds, all evidence of the beautiful morning erased.

"Sorry to get you roped into all this, old boy," said Abberline. "I'm afraid Mr. Holmes can be quite persuasive. My superiors have more or less assigned me to his service for the foreseeable future."

Burton arched an eyebrow in surprise. "He is quite formidable, isn't he? Well, I suppose there is nothing for it but to go along. We should probably make our plans for this evening. Not a wise time to go venturing into the Cauldron, but a perfect opportunity to ferret out this weird cult. Though I'm not precisely sure what Mr. Holmes wants us to do about it. I've never even heard of such a thing."

"It grew to prominence while you were away. There has been some speculation about it in the papers. Speaking of which, those strange incidents you mentioned…"

"The spiritualist madness," said Burton.

"Yes. You seem to have a very good memory of it, but I don't have any recollection of it at all. Nor did Mycroft Holmes."

"Yes," said Burton with a nod, "that is one of my main concerns, and the reason I called on the, um, Time Traveler. I read several news-papers discussing it before I left. One of them was still on my writing desk when I returned home, only now it has a completely different front page headline and story."

"What? But how is that possible?"

Burton pulled a cheroot from the pocket of his coat, struck a lucifer and lit the tip. He puffed on it thoughtfully before continuing. "There are only two possibilities. Either I am completely mad, or my journey through Time has inadvertently changed some small, minute detail that somehow led to this new turn of events, and this cult.

And Isabel's disappearance, he thought.

Abberline nodded. "The problem with that is, how can you prove it? It's your word against…well…the whole of London's."

Burton watched a passing hansom, the smelly dray pulling it clop-ping on the cobblestones. "Exactly. Everyone will simply think I'm mad, which, as I just pointed out, I very well could be."

"Well," said Abberline, "if the story you told us in there is true, they'll need to lock me up in Bedlam right beside you. But I can tell you one thing, this cult is real enough. I don't know exactly what they're up to in the East End, but I don't like it."

"We'll get to the bottom of it," said Burton with a smile. "Of that you can be certain. Now, let's go to my rooms at Gloucester Place."

Abberline scowled. "For what?"

"To try on disguises."

"Blimey. This day just gets stranger and stranger. Scotland Yard is going to owe me double time for this."

~

It was approaching midnight when two ne're-do-wells stepped into a decrepit pub called the Elder Sign. Both men were tall, but one man was several years older than the other, and had a very pronounced Y-shaped scar on his left cheek, no doubt a memento from some long ago scrape in which he obviously emerged the victor. He wore a long, ragged coat, threadbare and one size too large for him. The top of his head was stuffed into a dirty, misshapen bowler.

His companion was thin, with graying whiskers. He wore a brown tweed suit that had definitely seen better days, and a worn slouch hat perched at a jaunty angle on his head, casting his features in semi-shadow.

"I look ridiculous," said this man to his companion.

"What matters," said his compatriot, "is that you don't look like a policeman. And you'd best not act like one either, or we're both in for it."

Chief Inspector Frederick George Abberline stared at his companion Captain Richard Francis Burton, seeing the man beyond the petty disguise, and took a deep breath, steeling himself. He nodded to the older man. There was a lot he could learn from the explorer, he told himself. After all, the man journeyed to Mecca—a place forbidden to the white man—and no one was the wiser. If he could blend in with the Mohammedans, he could bloody well fit in with the degenerate denizens of some dodgy East End pub. All Abberline had to do was follow his lead.

The two men looked around the dingy pub, which was packed despite the late hour.

"Do you have a plan?" asked Abberline.

"Yes," said Burton, "don't get found out."

"Capital," said Abberline, and the two men ordered pints—which arrived in chipped, dirty glasses—and waded into the thick of it.

For the first hour, the two gentlemen in disguise got nothing for their time and trouble save a repertoire of bawdy limericks. Then they noticed a man in the back corner of the place, having a spirited yet secretive discussion with a trio of men Abberline identified as well-known cutpurses.

Burton leaned into the bartender, a tall, swarthy man with a thick red beard, cleaning a glass with a dirty rag.

"Who is that man?"

The bartender looked where Burton pointed and scowled. "That's John Gingham. He showed up in here one night about two weeks ago, talkin' all crazy. Says he knows where anyone can get all the money they want, just by askin."

The barkeep shook his head and went back to making the glasses appear less dirty.

Burton shot Abberline a sidelong glance, and the two men threaded their way toward the table of John Gingham.

"These strange events all seem to have started while I was away," said Burton. "There must be some connection."

The stepped up to the table John Gingham occupied and listened.

"That's right, gents. No more silly prayers and all that genuflectin' to a god that does nothin' fer you. I know some gods that'll give ya whatever ya want, whatever ya need. I know some gods that will actually do ya some good in yer lives. Real gods ye can see, that'll swim up to ya outta the deeps, all nice and proper like."

A chill fled up Abberline's spine. He looked at Burton, who returned the policeman's gaze. The look in Burton's eyes told Abberline all he needed to know. The inspector had been seeking some indication that John Gingham was insane, but everything about Burton's face said the man was telling the absolute truth.

John Gingham was an older man, probably around Burton's age, though he could pass for far older. He had little if any facial hair and, despite all his talk of wealth and prosperity, appeared as if he had slept in his clothes for ages. A tattered and dirty slouch hat was stuffed over his misshapen head, and his skin had a pale, scaly pallor. The smell of fish was strong in his vicinity, which mingled unpleasantly with the other smells of sour alcohol and sweat coming from all the unwashed bodies crowded around them.

A few of the men stepped away, laughing, giving Burton and Abberline room to shove in and replace them. A couple other men behind Gingham followed suit.

"Don't believe me?" said Gingham. "Fine. But you'll see. Afore this is over, everyone will see. The whole of Londontown will get what's comin', what those of us in the Esoteric Order of Dagon have known all along. Prosperity not only in this life, but in the next. Why, I'll be drinkin' to my health over yer dried up bones." He uttered a throaty cackle, revealing a mouthful of rotted teeth that reminded Abberline of broken tombstones. Still more people moved away, shaking their heads or cursing Gingham for a drunken fool.

"We'd like to know more," said Abberline.

Gingham looked up at them, studying their faces intently. "You're serious," he said at last.

"Of course," said Abberline.

"Good!" said Gingham, looking around furtively. Seeing that no one was still engaged in the conversation, he reached into a pocket and pulled out a small leather sack. Opening it, he reached inside and produced two oddly shaped and strangely colored ingots. Abberline recognized them immediately as being made from the same gold as the grotesque tiara in Mycroft Holmes' possession. Abberline and Burton took the proffered ingots and quickly secreted them away.

"Wise gents," said John Gingham. "These fools wouldn't believe me, but they'd waylay me fer sure if they knew about those."

"What is this?" asked Abberline.

"Consider it a payment, gents," said Gingham. "For work not yet completed."

"You have a job for us then?" asked Burton.

"In a manner of speakin'," said Gingham, returning the sack to his coat pocket. He clapped both of them mightily on the shoulder. "Yer job is to listen and pay attention. And your take will be a hunnerd times what you just received. What I gave I give freely, because it was freely given. Unnerstand?"

"No," said Abberline.

Gingham fixed them with a tombstone grin. "You don't have to struggle in the dark anymore, gents. Jus' imagine it. No more sufferin', no more want. And you can have it right here on Earth, right now. How does that sound to ya?"

"It sounds wonderful," Burton said, though Abberline detected the faintest edge of fear and caution in his voice.

"That settles it then, gents. Ya need to join the Esoteric Order a' Dagon. Let them gods I spoke about show ya what they can do."

"What do we have to do?" asked Abberline.

"Be at the big church what burned two year ago in one hour. Show them this." He produced two cards imprinted with the now-familiar elder sign. Gingham then clapped their shoulders again, squeezing hard as he did so. "Brothers," he said before loping out of the pub.

"These cultists certainly keep some late hours," said Abberline when Gingham vanished from sight.

"If you don't want a lot of prying eyes," said Burton, "the later the better. Do you know this church of his?"

Abberline nodded. I think so. But it's in a very dangerous part of the Cauldron."

"More dangerous than this?"

"Afraid so. You want to turn back?"

"No. Not when we're so close. Lead the way."

THE ESOTERIC ORDER OF DAGON

I t was dark as they threaded their way through the narrow, unpaved streets, and the moon was obscured by pale clouds. The only light they had spilled from a small lantern that Burton had brought. The noxious smells of boiling tripe, slaughterhouses, back yard cows and pigs, and "night soil"—human excrement collected and used as fertilizer—hung cloying and disorienting, and several times Inspector Abberline had to stop to get his bearings before continuing onward. Once he produced a handkerchief from his pocket and clamped it to his nose.

"Please," said Burton. "Endure it if you can. You're going to mark us as outsiders."

"What?" said the policeman, his eyes watering from the stench that assaulted their nostrils. "How?"

"East Enders are no doubt used to the smell."

They worked their way toward the river wharf, twisting through streets that could barely be called such. Burton saw few street signs or other markers. To navigate the Cauldron, he reasoned, one must get by on familiarity and dead reckoning, and he was glad the Inspector was as familiar with it as he was.

As the full moon appeared from her shroud of gray clouds, Abberline pointed to a large dark shape hulking up ahead. "That's it," he whispered.

Burton nodded. Their destination loomed. A large burned-out Catholic church, its spires had crumbled to near dust, its many gambreled roof caved in in places. But lamp and candlelight sputtered from within, and Burton and Abberline could hear inside its walls a low chanting.

They stepped up the crumbling steps and through the ruined doorway. A large man wearing a hooded white robe loomed in the shadows. Burton and Abberline showed him the cards emblazoned with the elder sign that Gingham had given them. Saying nothing, he gestured with his outstretched right arm toward the interior of the ruined church.

They could smell burnt wood and warm candle wax as they moved cautiously toward the nave, where a cluster of white-robed figures hunched on half-burnt, rotting pews. Beyond them, in the right-hand corner, stood the baptismal font, which had been turned into a source of warmth. Burton watched as a robed attendant tossed moldering hymnals and bits of splintered wood into the growing pyre that had been made there.

What was left of the ruined tabernacle was completely covered in glowing candles, sputtering furtively. Trails of many-colored wax ran down its length, transforming it into a lurid work of art.

Suspended from wires above hung a grotesque sculpture carved crudely from a block of maple wood. Burton and Abberline stared up at the blasphemous visage of some abhorrent entity that seemed to be part fish, part frog. A thing of bulbous, staring eyes and a long, thin mouth. Front appendages ended in stumpy webbed, claw like hands. And it chilled Richard Francis Burton to his marrow.

Another robed figure, this one a woman, gestured for Burton and Abberline to take a seat in the last pew on the left side of the nave. Behind the woman sat John Gingham, also in a white robe. Burton and Abberline sat on the creaking wood and watched as a figure emerged from somewhere behind the hideous sculpture. He was garbed in a yellow robe decorated with all manner of crude sigils, including the now familiar elder sign. He lifted his hood and smiled at the small audience, his face ghastly in the candlelight, for it was covered with a grotesque wooden mask, the irregular angles of which were cast in weird shadows by the candlelight.

"Who on earth is that?" whispered Abberline.

"That's the King in Yellow," said the woman. "Now shhhh!"

"Welcome, brothers and sisters," said the King in Yellow, his voice echoing strangely off the burned brick walls of the decimated church. "You come here tonight a member of the great unwashed, having failed in your pursuit of the almighty dollar. But you will leave here as kings and queens of the Earth."

The huge open space filled with the echo of a multitude of excited whispers which the man before the tabernacle silenced with a look before continuing. "Up to now you have lived in filth and squalor. But those days are no more. Those that live in the deeps will end your suffering. You will become masters of men, and live in the House of Dagon forever and ever."

This last remark created more excited whispers from the audience. Burton stared at the man, thinking he should know him from some-where. Some of the phrases he used, "the great unwashed," "the pursuit of the almighty dollar," sounded strangely familiar.

"This bloke is completely mad," whispered Abberline.

"Perhaps. But we need to know what his plans are."

The chatter amongst the small crowd had just started to die down when Burton and Abberline felt a familiar strong, cold grip on their shoulders.

"Excuse me, brothers and sisters," John Gingham shouted above the din. "We have some folks here who should not be. I heard them call you mad, sire."

"Now see here," said Abberline before Burton silenced him with his gaze.

"Who dares interrupt these holy proceedings?" asked the King in Yellow.

"I do, sir. John Gingham. I invited these two here, but they may be imposters." As if testing his hypothesis, Gingham yanked on the fake beard appliance Abberline was wearing. "Ow!" he cried as it tore away from his face.

"See? They ain't who they claim to be!"

"Run, Fred," said Burton.

"What?"

The explorer jumped to his feet, twisted around and punched John Gingham hard in the mouth in one smooth motion. "Run!"

The police inspector proved faster than he looked. He bounded over a crumbling pew and beyond the reaching arms of some angry, confused cultists in seconds.

"What is the meaning of this?" said the King in Yellow. "I will have order in the house of Dagon!"

"Oh, stuff your sea-god rot," Abberline shouted as he punched a robed figure who got too close for his liking. Three more cultists grabbed the police inspector from behind, subduing him.

Burton dove in, fists flying, knocking cultists out of the way. They were just poor people. Some of them cutthroats to be sure, but none expecting a scuffle this night. Burton managed to fight his way into the aisle between the two rows of pews. Standing in front of the tabernacle was a seething King in Yellow, hands clenched into fists though he clearly had no idea what he should do next. He didn't have to do anything, as his followers, stirred into action at last, pounced upon Burton, pummeling him with their fists and limiting his movement.

"You're through, whoever you are," said the explorer as he grappled with them. "Whatever this is, it ends tonight. The police are on their way."

The masked, robed figure laughed. "You're bluffing, sir. You two fools have no idea what you've stumbled onto this night. But I am sorry, gentlemen. I can't let you alert the authorities."

Abberline thrashed in the cultists' grip. Burton watched helplessly as one of the biggest men he had ever seen came toward him with a raised pitchfork.

CHALLENGER

Burton tried to break free and bolt, but there were too many of them, and he wished he had brought a gun.

Fool! Not going heeled into the Cauldron.

Abberline continued to writhe in the grasp of the masked man's followers, but it was no use.

"You should not have come here," said the man called the King in Yellow. "Instead of acolytes, you will become sacrifices. Tonight you shall be offered to Father Dagon and Mother Hydra."

"Not so fast, you yellow blighter."

Burton, Abberline, and everyone else turned at the sound. A large, bearded man in poorly fitting cult robes stood brandishing a pair of pistols.

"Challenger!" Burton smiled.

The big zoologist raised a pistol into the air and fired, the loud report sending cultists scurrying in every direction. The men holding Burton and Abberline released them, and Burton gave a fleeing cultist a solid punch in the mouth for good measure.

Abberline chased one of them around the flaming baptismal font as Challenger fired more shots, this time into the crowd.

"Stop it!" said Burton, ducking behind a crumbling pew. "You'll hit their leader, whoever he is. We need him alive."

The King in Yellow screamed as the first shot went off and ran up onto the tabernacle, pushing one of his cult members and knocking him into two more. The three robed degenerates fell in a crimson heap.

Challenger joined Burton, a playful sneer on his bearded face. His twin barrels smoked, the acrid smell of gunpowder stinging.

"He's getting away," said Challenger. "Let's go."

Burton and Challenger moved toward the tabernacle.

"Frederick," Burton called to the policeman. "Don't let him get away."

The inspector nodded, looking around behind the abhorrent statue rocking back and forth overhead.

One of the cult members came up behind Abberline, a heavy wooden post raised over his head like a cudgel.

"Fred, look out!" Burton called.

Abberline turned just as Challenger squeezed off another shot, hitting the man dead center in his chest. He stumbled backward, dropping his weapon and falling onto the burning baptismal font, flames alighting his loose-fitting robes. His weight pushed the thing over, sending burning kindling into the pews, which quickly turned the entire space into one vast pyre.

"Where the hell is he?" said Challenger.

Burton peered through the growing smoke. "There," he pointed. "There's a passage behind this damned tabernacle."

The three men watched as the yellow-robed figure disappeared behind a panel in the wall.

"Go!" said Challenger.

Their way was blocked by more fleeing cult members, who somehow had the presence of mind to protect their master's escape. Fortunately, none of them seemed to be armed. Burton punched his way through them, and Challenger used his guns as twin cudgels when they were empty of ammunition. Abberline did his part in spectacular fashion. Burton watched, amazed, as the inspector felled one of the cultists with a throat chop, then kicked another in the groin.

"Bismillah!" cried Burton as they reached the no longer secret passage.

"It's called Bartitsu," said Abberline. "The art of gentlemanly combat."

Burton arched an eyebrow. "You must show me sometime."

"Later, gentlemen," said Challenger as he opened the thin wooden door. "Our prey is escaping."

Abberline slid into the passage, followed by Burton and Challenger.

The passage was little more than a tunnel, low-ceilinged and rough hewn. They all ducked to move through it, which made for slow progress. Burton fumbled with their lantern, getting it lit and passing it up to Abberline.

The tunnel ran straight, and after ten minutes of painful crouching, they reached a wall with a similar crude door. Abberline pushed on it, and the trio emerged in a darkened tenement.

The place was dank and foul-smelling. They heard the faint scurry of rats, and vermin bulged behind the crumbling, faded wallpaper.

"Where is he?" said Burton.

"We should search this building," said Abberline.

Challenger winced as he stretched, his back creaking loudly. He doffed his cult robes and tossed them to the floor.

"I'm glad to see you," said Burton to the zoologist. "Now what are you doing here?"

"Mycroft Holmes' invitation did not fall on deaf ears," said Challenger as he followed Burton and Abberline from room to room in their search for the mysterious King in Yellow. "I just wanted the pretentious fop to think I was ignoring him."

Abberline went up a set of rickety stairs to check the upper floors.

"I must admit my curiosity got the better of me," Challenger continued. "I thought investigating this weird cult would explain the changes I've witnessed since our return. Changes no one else seems to register."

"Like the madness of the mediums never occurring?" said Burton.

Challenger nodded. "That was one thing, yes. But my wife is also... different. Less understanding of my...idiosyncrasies."

Burton turned his head to conceal a grin.

"I know I am not the easiest man to get along with, but she acts as if this is somehow new to her. It's as if I came home to a stranger. Until I realized it is I who is the stranger to her."

"We changed something when we went back through Time," said Burton. "My fiancée Isabel is…gone. Disappeared in Hyde Park shortly before I returned. I have no clear memory of this. Except…" His mouth tried to say something else but failed.

"I remember returning home to the news, but I also remember going to my club as soon as we disembarked, and finding my friends and colleagues transmogrified into hideous creatures. A hallucination obviously, but…"

"I know what you mean," said Challenger. "I have had similar experiences. Almost like *deja vu*."

Burton nodded. The pain of her disappearance was once again gnawing at his breast.

Challenger placed a hand on his shoulder. "I am glad our paths have crossed once more."

"No one up there," said Abberline, bounding down the stairs. He stopped next to Burton, staring up at the large man who had rescued them.

"Well? Aren't you going to introduce me?"

"Fred, Professor Challenger. Professor, Chief Inspector Frederick George Abberline."

Challenger gave the policeman a hateful sneer of a smile. "So you're Mycroft's lap dog, hey?"

"Nice to meet you, too," said the policeman. "I've read about your South American expedition in the papers."

"And what did you think?" asked Challenger.

"I think you're a con artist," said Abberline. "Or bollocks."

Challenger stared down at him for a long moment before bellowing laughter. He clapped both men on the shoulder, and in another moment Burton and Abberline were laughing too, even though they had no idea why. It wasn't an appropriate response after what they had just been through, but at this moment it felt like the most appropriate response in the world.

MORIARTY

"You still haven't explained how you infiltrated the cult," Burton said when the laughter died.

"Same as you," said Challenger. "And I had to listen to such blinking rot once I got in."

"Give us the short version," said Burton.

"What's he planning?" asked Abberline

"This King in Yellow chap is in league with the Deep Ones," said the zoologist. "I've seen them."

"What's a Deep One?" said Abberline.

"You don't want to know," said Burton.

"He also has shoggoths doing his dirtier business. Anyone who won't pay him tribute gets a visit from them."

"Human sacrifice," said Burton.

Challenger raked a hand through his beard. "For starters. Some of his 'great unwashed' have already started mating with those undersea devils. It's Innsmouth all over again."

"Innsmouth?" Abberline looked from Burton to Challenger and back again. "The place you told Mr. Holmes about?"

Burton nodded. "They have already gone through what we are

now up against, and if this King in Yellow succeeds..." He didn't dare finish the sentence.

"London isn't some quiet sea village," said Challenger. "If that mad blighter succeeds, it'll mean the end of the British Empire."

They heard a low noise, as of something oily and slick were sliding toward them. It was an all too familiar sound to Burton, one he had hoped he would never hear again.

"Shoggoth," Challenger whispered.

Burton nodded. His mouth had gone dry, his tongue sticking to the roof of his mouth.

"What's a shoggoth?" asked Abberline.

"That," Professor Challenger said, pointing behind the policeman, iIs a shoggoth."

The three men turned as a slimy, bulbous glob of iridescent goo congealed up the narrow hallway toward them. Burton's lantern light illuminated a multitude of undulating pustules that blistered and popped along its heaving, jelly-like bulk. In the dim light Burton saw the skeletal remains of rats and other vermin suspended within the shoggoth's mass. He had no interest in joining the poor creatures.

"Bloody hell," swore Abberline.

"Run," Challenger advised.

They ran.

Discovering a door, Abberline pushed through it and into the darkness outside. Burton came next, leading them with his lantern, moving away from the crumbling tenement as fast as their legs would carry them. Burton could feel the shoggoth behind them, closing fast.

They turned a corner and darted to the right, caring little for where they ended up. Their priority was to put as much distance between themselves and the protoplasmic thing as they could.

"Where are we?" Challenger heaved.

"Not sure," said Abberline. Few, if any, gaslights, coupled with a lack of street signs made everything look the same. Black tenement houses leaned over the narrow cobblestone streets, threatening to topple over at the slightest provocation. The lantern bounced in Burton's hand as he ran, sending strange shadows fleeing into the distance.

"We must...slow down," Challenger panted. "My heart...will get me...before that...thing does."

They rounded another corner, moved to the left, and then stopped, Burton shining the lantern in the direction they had come.

"Maybe...we lost it," Abberline said, gasping.

In a moment they heard the telltale sliding sound, as the thing moved over the rough cobbles.

"No," said Burton. "We did not. Move."

Challenger spun around, raising both pistols from their holsters and firing into the dark.

"Professor," said Burton. "It's no use. Come on."

Challenger snarled at the amorphous blob and joined them in their flight up the street.

"There's a gaslight flickering up ahead," said Abberline, pointing. "We can get our bearings at least."

They ran toward the comforting light, the sounds of the shoggoth growing closer.

If we can just get to where there are people, Burton thought. From somewhere in the distance they heard a harlot's laughter.

"Look," said Challenger, pointing to the gaslight. Quivering in its glow was another shoggoth.

"There are two of them?" said Abberline.

"Come," said Burton. "Up this alley. Move your feet, gentlemen."

Burton led them up an alley so narrow they had to walk sideways to traverse it. At the other end was a rotting wooden fence that stymied their efforts to climb over it, so Challenger began kicking the impediment to smithereens. When this was done, they twisted right, then left, then emerged onto another street. But that feeling of being followed, being hunted, did not go away.

Burton glanced to the left or right at intervals, always with the feeling that there was something there following them from the shadows.

"They're getting closer," said Abberline. "This way!"

They passed a cross street, turned a corner and found themselves in the mouth of a blind alley.

"Bismillah, we're trapped," said Burton.

"They've been herding us," said Challenger.

The three men turned and watched as the two shoggoths slithered into view and slid closer.

"Bloody hell" Abberline swore again, panic cracking his voice.

They heard the clop and neigh of horses as a pantechnicon—a carriage designed for moving furniture, only this one was black and heavily armored—moved across the mouth of the alley from a side street, pulled by two hulking drays stomping nervously. The black-garbed driver cast a wary eye toward the shoggoths, his gloved hands holding tightly to the reins. A panel in the side of the carriage slid open, and a voice cried, "Get on!"

Burton leapt onto the side of the strangely outfitted carriage, grabbing a brass handle bolted to the side, his feet finding narrow purchase on the ridges between sections of armor plate. Abberline and Challenger joined him, and in a moment the carriage rattled up a wide lane at great speed. Burton looked back to see the amorphous blobs of the shoggoths receding into the distance.

The carriage continued on for some time, and twice Burton almost fell off as it bounced along the cobbles. Finally a door opened in the contraption's side, and Abberline—who was closest to the portal—climbed in, followed by Challenger and Burton.

They found themselves in a plush, dark enclosure, richly appointed, that smelled of rich pipe tobacco. A wan lantern hung from a hook to their savior's left, sputtering fitfully.

"Please, gentlemen," said a man sitting across from them. "Have a seat."

They sat on a padded bench opposite their host, who stared at them with a cool malevolence. Dressed in the latest fashion, he looked set for a night out at one of the shows along the Strand. He wore a black top hat and held a polished walking stick across his lap. He was devoid of facial hair save for a thin, neatly groomed goatee.

"Blimey," said Abberline. "I know you. You're..."

"Professor Moriarty," the man finished for him with a tip of his hat. "At your service. I am flattered you know me by sight, Chief Inspector. There are few among the police who have ever seen me and lived to tell the tale."

"You're the one who alerted Mycroft Holmes about the cult," said Burton.

Moriarty nodded once. "I am."

"What are you going to do with us?" asked Abberline.

Moriarty gave them a bemused grin. "Well, I'm not going to kill you, if that's what you're intimating. If I wanted you dead, I would have left you for the shoggoths. But I didn't want to see Mycroft's precious assets murdered."

"Assets?" said Challenger. "Bah!"

"How did you find us?" Abberline asked.

"I have eyes everywhere," said Moriarty. "I heard about the commotion you caused at the old church and thought you might need some assistance."

"Why are you helping us?" asked Burton.

"Because the enemy of my enemy is my friend," said Professor Moriarty. "This damned cult must be stopped. It's eating into my trade."

"You mean your opium trade," Abberline said.

Moriarty smiled. "Yes. Among other things. The buildings along the wharf have been overtaken by the cult. I do not know what they are storing there. My attempts to ascertain this information was met with...violence. All I know is that large objects are being heaved up out of the Thames and stored in those buildings. Whatever this group is up to, you will find it there. But I will give you a fair word of warning: I have suspended my activities along the wharf. Do not look for a link back to me. You will not find it. Not even my nemesis Sherlock Holmes could sniff out such a connection."

"So you want us to do your dirty work for you, is that it?" said Challenger.

Moriarty shrugged. "You are already doing Mycroft's dirty work. I just thought I'd do you a favor and point you in the right direction. That and save your lives."

They rode in silence for a time, the pantechnicon never once slowing, taking dangerous turns as it moved toward its mysterious destination.

At last the large wagon slowed to a stop. "This is where you gentlemen get off."

The door of the pantechnicon flew open as if controlled by a hidden spring, and Burton recognized his home at Gloucester Place.

"How did you know where I live?"

"Oh, I know a great many things about the three of you," said Moriarty. "You should be flattered that one such as I has taken an interest in you. Now begone. I have other business this night."

"Now see here!" Challenger said, but Burton silenced him with a shove out the door.

No sooner had they alighted onto the pavement than the door of the pantechnicon sealed itself shut and the strange vehicle's black-clad driver urged his two drays into motion once more. The three men watched, perplexed, as the thing rolled out of sight.

"Blimey, that was strange," said the policeman.

Challenger shook his fist in the direction of the retreating carriage. "Damn it all. This Moriarty character is more of an effete snob than Mycroft Holmes!"

"He may indeed be snobbish," said Burton. "But I wouldn't go so far as to call him effete. He is far from ineffectual. In fact, he just saved our lives."

"He's also a criminal, and a dangerous one at that," Abberline added. "My superiors will have my badge if they learn that I was that close to the infamous Professor Moriarty and did not make an arrest."

Burton patted Abberline's shoulder. "Yours is a different assignment, Frederick, and we have bigger concerns. Besides, Moriarty was right: the enemy of my enemy is my friend."

Challenger barked laughter. "Quite right, Burton. Though to cast our lot with a fiend such as that. . ."

"I don't like it any more than either of you do. But what else can we do?"

"I must report to Mr. Holmes," said Abberline. "He needs to know what happened tonight."

"Won't you come inside?" asked Burton. "Have a drink first?"

"No. I'm still on duty. Good evening to you, gentlemen." He tipped his hat and marched up the street and disappeared into the thick fog that began roiling in from the East.

"I'll have a drink with you, if you don't mind," said Challenger. "I have no one to go home to, not really anyway. Not anymore."

"Yes," said Burton. "Come in. No doubt you and I have much to discuss."

The night was already late, but Burton and Challenger sat up for the next hour in Burton's study, drinking brandy and talking over recent events, as well as their thoughts about their journey aboard Captain Nemo's incredible *Nautilus*.

Burton got Challenger up to speed on his own experiences since returning home, including his bout of madness that began after his hallucinations at the Cannibal Club. He even revisited his shock and confusion at learning Isabel had disappeared in broad daylight from Hyde Park, and his conflicting memories of recent events. Challenger nodded politely through all of this, smoking one of Burton's finest cheroots and drinking his brandy. When Burton had finished his tale, he asked, "What do we do now?"

"In the morning I want to call on Herbert," said the explorer. "He was not well when I checked on him this morning and seemed to be suffering under the same sort of delusion that felled me. He was trying to destroy his Time Machine."

"And you believe his madness has passed?"

"I hope it has," said Burton. "For all our sakes. I fear the only way to correct what has happened is by making a return journey through Time."

"And how do you know he won't try to destroy it again? Or make some journey on his own?"

"I have little control over the former," said Burton. "But I do over the latter." He reached into his pocket and pulled out the control levers he had taken from the Time Machine that morning.

"Ah." Challenger nodded appraisingly. "Perhaps this will be enough to sway him from destroying it as well. I want to go with you. Perhaps together we can snap him back into coherence, and he can once again be of use to us."

"That would be much appreciated. Thank you. But the hour grows late. For us to be effective we should probably both get some sleep. I have a spare bedroom if you'd like."

"Sounds splendid," said Challenger. "I thank you for your hospitality, my good sir."

Burton put on his *jebba* and climbed into bed, using a Sufi meditation technique to help him relax. His body was bone tired, but his mind whirled with recalled events and memories of that other Burton's life their jaunt through Time had inadvertently created. Finally, he drifted off, the distant drone of Challenger's snoring lulling him to sleep. He dreamed of tentacles in the darkness and a strange sliding sound coming from behind.

THE TIME MACHINE

It was eleven in the morning before Burton or Challenger awoke and, after explaining to Miss Angell why she suddenly had a new house guest, he and Challenger were treated to a sumptuous brunch of eggs and sausage.

"I must say," said Challenger after taking a sip of coffee, "there's nothing like a hearty breakfast to make one feel like himself again. I could almost believe the events of last night happened to someone else."

"As could I," Burton agreed. "But we must hurry, for we have much work to do."

Burton heard a distant knock at the door and listened. Miss Angell answered it, and in a moment Frederick Abberline was lumbering up the stairs, a tired look on his face.

"Inspector!" said Burton. "Come, sit down and break your fast."

"No thank you," said Abberline. "I ate this morning. I would love some coffee, if it isn't too much trouble. Two sugars."

Wiping his mouth, Burton got up and poured the policeman a cup.

"What did our mutual employer have to say about the events of last evening?" said Challenger with a sneer.

"He was pleased that we broke up the cult's ritual but was dismayed that we were not able to catch their leader."

"That is your job, is it not?" asked Challenger.

Burton handed the steaming cup to Abberline, who took a testing sip. "It is. But we have no idea who he is under that damned robe and mask. He could be anyone for all we know."

Challenger scowled at this and impaled another sausage with his fork before jamming it into his mouth.

"He's no doubt lying low," said Burton, returning to his seat. "But even with his features obscured, I think we can figure out who he is. Some things he said sounded very familiar to me for some reason."

"He's a man of breeding," said Abberline. "The way he spoke and comported himself."

"The way he ran when the shooting started," added Challenger around a mouthful of eggs.

"He's not from the East End, that's for sure," said Abberline. "He's obviously educated. A royal perhaps? Maybe a count or a duke? There was a Marquess of Waterford that caused some trouble a few years ago. A right scoundrel as I recall."

"He'll show himself again," said Burton. "Whoever he is. He'll have to."

"Mr. Holmes was also irritated that you chose to investigate on your own," said Abberline to Challenger.

"It's a good thing I had," said the zoologist. "Or you two would be dead right now, your bones floating in the protoplasm of a shoggoth."

"That was very nearly our fate even with your intervention," said Burton.

Challenger glared at the explorer for a long moment before returning his attentions to his plate of food.

"I also told him about Moriarty's assistance last night," said Abberline. "He did not seem perturbed, or surprised. I sometimes wonder if the man can predict the bloody future."

Abberline took another sip of coffee before sitting the cup down on the edge of the table. "I'm to head back to that ruined church in the East End. About thirty detectives will be going over every inch that's left. The fire we inadvertently started finished it off pretty good. Took the East London volunteers the rest of the night to put it out. Anyway, I'd like both of you to accompany me."

"Of course," said Burton. "But first we have a stop to make."

Abberline arched an eyebrow. "Where?"

"Kew Gardens."

~

An hour and a half later they arrived by policeman's carriage at the home of the Time Traveler, only to find it surrounded by police. A group of uniformed patrolmen were streaming out the front door of the home, their arms laden with boxes containing stacks of papers, while Herbert's thoroughly perplexed housekeeper looked on.

"Bismillah," said Burton, alighting from the carriage. "What is going on?"

"Excuse me," said Abberline. "What is happening here, Lieutenant?"

"Confiscation of material deemed to be a threat to the British Empire," said a broad-shouldered, uniformed Sikh in a blue turban.

"What utter poppycock," said Burton.

"On whose authority?" demanded Abberline.

"Mycroft Holmes, sir," said the policeman. "Under the orders of Prime Minister Disraeli."

"Disraeli," said Burton. "I might have known."

"I work closely with Mr. Holmes," said Abberline, "and I was not informed of this."

The Sikh shrugged. "I don't know what to tell you, sir. My orders were to quarantine the house and confiscate any and all notes and materials inside."

"There was a device in the basement," said Burton. "Most unusual-looking. Is it still on the premises.?"

The policeman eyed him suspiciously.

"He is an agent of Mr. Holmes as well," said Abberline. "Answer his question."

"Uh, no sir. It was taken as well. Those were our orders."

"And where was it taken?" demanded Burton.

"I don't know, sir. Some government chaps loaded it up a little while ago. We were ordered to gather up any and all notes that might have anything to do with its creation or operation."

"Is the master of this house still here?"

The Sikh nodded. "He is, sir. Right inside there." He pointed toward the open front door.

"Thank you, Lieutenant," said Abberline, and the big man went back to overseeing the placement of heaps of paper into carriages.

"This is most peculiar," said Abberline. "I've never even heard of such a thing."

"My guess is neither has anyone else," said Challenger.

As they followed Abberline into the house, Challenger said, "This is why I did not take Mycroft Holmes up on his dubious honor of service to the Crown."

"You didn't trust him," Burton said.

"Aye. I still don't."

"I'm starting to wish I hadn't," said the explorer.

They entered the home, past the housekeeper Mrs. Watchett, who eyed Burton cruelly, as if this was somehow his fault. He was starting to feel that it was.

Herbert sat in a high-backed chair, still in his pajamas, his head in his hands while two policemen hovered over him asking questions while a third yanked books off his numerous shelves, thumbing through them for loose bits of paper before tossing them to the floor.

"Herbert," said Burton.

The Time Traveler looked up at the sound, lines of worry marring his young, handsome face. "You! Here again. What is happening? These ruffians barged in an hour ago. I had scarcely recovered my wits when they started tearing the place apart!"

"I don't know what is going on either. We only just found out ourselves."

"And Challenger! How good to see you, old boy."

"Hello again, Herbert," said the zoologist. "I'm glad to see you as well, though I detest the circumstances of our reunion."

"And who is this?" asked the Time Traveler, staring up at their companion.

"Chief Inspector Frederick George Abberline, at your service, sir."

"You did this!" Herbert said, lunging from his chair. "Where's my Time Machine?"

Burton held him at bay while Abberline took a step back. The other policemen in the room moved to intervene, but Abberline waved them off.

"Oh, rot!" Herbert slumped back into his chair. "What does it matter now? This is all your fault, Captain Burton. I was going to destroy the infernal thing. But now they have it."

"I'm sorry, Herbert," said Burton. "That's what I came to talk to you about." He stared at the other policemen warily.

"May we have the room, please?" said Abberline.

The others, nodding, left. Mrs. Watchett slammed the front door closed when they were gone.

"I couldn't let you destroy the Time Machine because we need it," said Burton. "Something went wrong. Things have changed. And we have to change them back."

"What are you talking about?" said Herbert, staring at Burton with bloodshot eyes. "Everything is exactly as we left it."

"No, it isn't," said Burton. "There was no madness among the mediums, and my fiancée Isabel is missing, taken in broad daylight from Hyde Park."

"My wife no longer knows me," said Challenger.

"I have memories of this other time," said Burton. "Memories that conflict with what we know to be true."

Herbert stared up at Burton, blinking. "I, too, have had these memories. I'm remembering things I know could not possibly have happened. I thought I was going mad. I dreamed I was being stalked by shoggoths, and that the Morlocks had come to take my Time Machine." He gaped at Burton open-mouthed.

"You. You were here. Yesterday morning. You stopped me from..." He touched his cheek, wincing as if stung.

"Yes," said Burton. "I'm sorry about that. You were out of control. I had to stop you from destroying the Time Machine before we used it for one last jaunt."

The Time Traveler cradled his head in his hands once more. "Oh.

147

My dear fellow. I almost brained you with a wrench, didn't I? I am extremely sorry."

"No harm done," said Burton. "I'm just glad you're over your, um, spell."

"I am, for the most part," said Herbert. "Those awful police certainly snapped me out of it. What the devil do they want with my Time Machine, and how did they find out about it in the first place?"

Burton's head dipped toward the floor. "I'm afraid that is my fault. "I was brought before a gentleman named Mycroft Holmes yesterday, who knew of our little adventure. He said he was also a member of the Shadow Council and recruited me for another endeavor. He asked me several questions about your Time Machine, and I answered them. I figured he knew so much about us already, what could it hurt? Now I am afraid I have been played the fool."

"Mr. Holmes must have had a good reason for taking it," said Abberline. "I can't imagine he would use it for evil ends."

"He may not have evil intentions for its use," said Challenger, but its use clearly causes more problems than it solves, hence our current predicament. I told you before, Captain Burton, that Time would make for the ultimate weapon. And now Mycroft Holmes has it. What can't the Empire do that can strangle the despot in his cradle, or stop an enemy invasion before it is contemplated?"

"Good heavens!" said the Time Traveler. "Trying to untangle such events before they happened would cause a paradox."

"How so?" said Challenger.

"Well," said Herbert, rubbing his stubbled chin. "Suppose you went back in Time to kill your grandfather before he met your grandmother and conceived your father. Well then, you never existed."

"And if you never existed, how did you go back in Time and kill your grandfather?" finished Challenger.

"Exactly," said Herbert. "We must have done something similar to alter our familiar course of events."

"Bismillah," said Burton. "We've got to get the Time Machine back."

"Does this Micron Holmes fellow know how to activate and use the machine?" asked Herbert.

"My*croft*," Burton corrected. "And yes, he does. But fortunately for us, he does not have the means to do so."

Burton reached into his coat pocket and produced the two crystalline control rods he had removed from the Time Machine the previous morning.

Herbert gasped. "You remembered what I told you, then. About the machine's operation."

"Yes," said the explorer, handing the rods to Herbert. "Without those, your Time Machine goes nowhere. Uh, no *when*."

"He can't substitute them in some way?" asked Abberline.

"No," said Herbert. "The crystals in these control rods are essential to the machine's operation. No other material will do. But by careful reading of my notes, he'll be able to fabricate new ones. My notes! That loathsome devil took everything."

"Now see here," said Abberline. "Mycroft Holmes has done more for the Empire than you will ever know. I grant that he took your property without due course of law, but you will not disparage him."

Burton placed a hand on the Chief Inspector's shoulder. "My dear Frederick, I understand and respect your loyalty, but even you must admit that there is something strange afoot. Are you saying that, after all this, you still fully trust your employer?"

Abberline stared at Burton wide-eyed. His mouth opened, closed. Opened again. At last he said, "I must. Honor and duty require it. But in deference and respect to you, after all we went through last night, I will demand a full explanation from him right this very afternoon."

"Good enough," said Burton. "I must also ask that you do not breathe a word about these control rods to Mycroft Holmes."

Abberline considered this, then nodded slowly in agreement.

"I should like a word with this Mycroft Holmes as well," said Herbert, standing up. "If you will allow me to get dressed, I will accompany you."

"Certainly," said Burton. "We just have one more stop to make. It appears you are once more a member of the Shadow Council."

Burton handed the rods to Herbert. They clinked together softly in his palm.

Herbert nodded. "This time I had best learn the secret handshake. Make yourselves comfortable. I shan't be a moment. Mrs. Watchett?"

The poor housekeeper moved from where she had stood, silently quivering in the corner by the door, to follow her master up the stairs.

The front door opened, and the policemen who had been ransacking the place earlier entered to resume their vandalism.

"You're done here," said Abberline. "Pack up and move out."

The three officers exchanged dumbfounded looks before the highest ranking-policeman and departed.

Burton and Challenger gave him surprised looks.

"Well," said Abberline. "I think the poor fellow's been through enough, don't you?"

FATHER DAGON

The four of them crammed into the police carriage en route to the Cauldron, Herbert fidgeting, crossing one leg over the other, then switching, all the while making perturbed noises.

This rankled Professor Challenger to no end, but to his credit he held his peace, and before long they were moving through the grimy streets of the East End, dirty street toughs glaring bleary-eyed at them as they rolled past.

The carriage trundled through the labyrinthine streets until at last coming to a stop before the still smoking skeleton of the church Burton, Challenger and Abberline had barely escaped with their lives hours earlier. They hopped from the carriage to join a group of police officers who were busy gathering whatever paltry evidence to be found and scaring away looters.

"By Jove," said the Time Traveler while Abberline had a word with the ranking officer. "Did you gentlemen do this?"

"In a manner of speaking," said Burton. "Not that we're proud of it."

"Speak for yourself," declared Challenger, leaning over to yank a wet, filthy cultist robe from under a singed wooden beam, only to toss it away a moment later in disgust.

Herbert studied the damage in silence. They had filled him in on what happened on the way over, but he still looked unable to come to grips with it. Or maybe he just worried about the fate of his Time Machine. Burton couldn't tell which.

Abberline turned to them when he was done conversing with the leading duty officer. "Only one body found. That bloke you shot, Professor Challenger. Burned to a crisp, of course. No way to identify him. It seems everyone else got out."

"What about the tunnel?" asked Burton.

"Some men followed it back to the old house," said Abberline. "No one there but some street urchins what bolted as soon as they saw the coppers come through that hidey-hole. No signs of any regular occupants, and no trace of this King in Yellow."

"There's no such thing as ghosts," Burton said irritably.

"He's still around somewhere," said Challenger, his dark eyes scanning the surrounding buildings. "Probably watching us right now, laughing at us."

"But where?" asked Abberline. "How?"

"Remember Professor Moriarty's carriage?" asked Burton. All eyes turned to him.

"Something struck me about it this morning. It was designed for not only security, but comfort. Like Captain Nemo's Nautilus."

"Odd's Bodikins!" declared Challenger. "The blackguard *lives* in it."

"Perhaps," said Burton. "At least some of the time. Maybe our King in Yellow has a similar setup. He'll want to stay mobile yet remain close to his operations here in the East End."

"And he no doubt has a small legion of people helping him," said Abberline. "Keeping him hidden. And we'll never be able to pry his whereabouts from them."

The four of them thought on this for a while.

"Ho!" the Time Traveler called from amid the blackened rubble. "What's this?"

Burton, Challenger and Abberline stepped carefully through the ruins toward their companion.

"What is it?" said Abberline.

Herbert pointed to the blackened shape resting on the ground. Burton still recognized it as the blasphemous carved visage hanging above the tabernacle.

"That is a rendition of Dagon," said Burton.

Herbert's knees buckled, and he placed his hands on his hips to steady himself. "No. It can't be. It's happening here, in London, isn't it?"

"I'm afraid so," said Burton.

"We didn't stop it at all, did we?" asked Herbert. "Our jaunt through Time did nothing. Nothing."

"We stopped that damnable island from returning to the surface," said Challenger.

"We may have done more damage than anything," Burton murmured.

"We have to stop this," said Herbert.

"I admire your zeal, my friend," said Burton. "But what else can we do? We've destroyed the cult's meeting place and sent their leader into hiding. It's a matter for the police now."

"I'm afraid he's right," said Abberline.

The Time Traveler appeared to consider this for a moment, then shook his head. "This is bigger than the police. Bigger than all of us. We need Captain Nemo."

"And how do you propose we contact him?" said Challenger. "He could be anywhere in the seven bloody seas."

"I might have a way," said Herbert. "But it requires my Time Machine."

"All right, then," said Burton. "Let's pay Mycroft Holmes a visit."

"Of course," replied Abberline.

The four men returned to the carriage, where Abberline gave the driver the address for the Diogenes Club.

As the carriage moved away from the ruins of the church, Burton noticed a large group of people watching them, their dirty, wretched faces filled with anger. Someone hurled a large rock, striking the carriage's driver. He fell from his box with a heavy thud, the horses slowing to a halt at the loss of their driver.

153

"Stop that, you wretches!" called Abberline.

The policemen who had been inspecting the ruins ran over to chase off the ruffian rock-thrower, but the crowd was quite vocal, and some had picked up burned pieces of wood and other implements to use as makeshift weapons.

"Help him, Frederick," said Burton, indicating the carriage's driver. "I'll drive us out of here."

Abberline nodded and exited the carriage from the side facing away from the crowd and went to assist the fallen police officer.

Burton hurried out of the carriage and up onto the driver's box, picking up the reins and giving them a strong tug. The horses obeyed, pulling the carriage a foot or so forward.

Burton glanced down at Abberline who, along with two other policemen, were helping the driver to his feet.

"He's all right," said Abberline. "Just got the wind knocked out of him."

"Get back I say!" said one of the policemen.

"This crowd is getting full of themselves," Challenger called from inside the carriage. "And they have us outnumbered. A hasty retreat would be in our best interest."

"We'll take care of them, sir," one of the officers assured Abberline. He blew into a whistle hanging round his neck, calling for more men. Abberline returned to the carriage and Burton started the horses off at a fast trot.

"You're not wanted here!" a member of the crowd shouted.

Something else was thrown, but it went in a high arc over Burton's head and was gone. He had never seen Londoners act this way. It had to be this abysmal cult, he reasoned. He and his group were being attacked on purpose. The Dagon cult would not let them leave the East End alive.

Other objects flew past Burton's head, much too close for his liking. More police came running, but more people joined in the revolt, and it was a mob the officers greeted. Burton lashed the horses into moving at their top speed, Challenger shouting something from the carriage, no doubt a barrage of profanity at their attackers.

Burton drove the carriage west as fast as the gray beasts would carry it, his eyes ever wary for another assault. Suspicious eyes looked out at them from darkened doorways and partially boarded-up windows. An old woman made the sign of the evil eye at them as they passed.

Burton heard a gunshot and felt something hot fly much too close past his left ear. The gunshot was met with an answering volley of gunfire from the carriage below, Professor Challenger brandishing his revolver in the general direction of where the shot had come from. Burton spurred the horses onward and did not slow them until they reached the relative safety and congested traffic of Tower Bridge.

Burton went a few blocks more, then slowed the beasts to a stop and climbed down from the driver's box. He opened the left-hand carriage door and peered in at Challenger, Herbert, Abberline, and the carriage's poor police driver, who introduced himself as Murphy. They all looked thoroughly jostled.

"Is everyone all right?" asked Burton.

Challenger holstered his revolver and glared at Burton. "Those fiends! Take me back there. I'll burn them all out."

"Calm down, Professor," said Burton. "You may yet get your chance. But they have us at an advantage right now, I'd say."

"Good heavens," declared Herbert. "That was quite a ride. Let's never do it again, shall we?"

"Agreed," said Abberline. "I wish I could go back to rounding up pickpockets."

Everyone climbed out of the carriage, Officer Murphy reclaiming his rightful place atop the driver's box. He appeared a bit dazed, and had a small cut on his temple, but he insisted he was in fine fettle.

"What do we do now?" said Challenger.

"I need to make sure our lads back there have enough help to deal with that angry mob," said Abberline. "I also need to check in with Mr. Holmes."

"Let's go and call on our mutual employer," said Burton. "Not only does he have Herbert's property, but I think he knows more about this cult business than he previously let on."

Abberline conversed briefly with the driver, then they all climbed back into the police carriage.

"Off to the infamous Diogenes Club again?" asked Burton.

"Not this time," said Abberline. "Mr. Holmes is at his office, in the Tower of London."

THE TOWER OF LONDON

An hour and a half later the policeman's carriage pulled up to the gray, imposing walls of the Tower of London. After a quick word with an attendant, the driver guided the horses in through Traitor's Gate, the banks of the Thames on Burton's left. He had never been to the Tower before, and the great edifice managed to look no less imposing up close than it did from a distance.

The driver guided the carriage into a roundabout, stopping before a yawning entrance atop a formidable set of wide stone steps.

Everyone alighted and looked up at it.

"I feel like a bloody tourist," said Challenger to Abberline. "Are you sure Holmes is here?"

"Oh yes," said Abberline. "The British Intelligence Ministry has its offices here."

Burton thanked their driver Murphy, urging him to go home and rest, then looked to Abberline. "Lead the way, Frederick."

Abberline nodded, and everyone followed him up the steps and through two heavy oaken doors set in the wide stone archway.

Men in tweed suits moved about inside, carrying bundles of paperwork, seemingly in a hurry to go absolutely nowhere. They walked up a narrow hallway, past rooms that had been turned into makeshift offices, but yet still held the effects of their previous purpose. Burton watched as a man stamped papers atop an ancient wine rack that still held a few dusty bottles. Another leaned against a creaking lectern, holding a monocle and reading something from a heavy bound volume.

"His office is in the White Tower," said Abberline, veering to the right. "This way."

They went through a labyrinth of hallways and corridors, past a veritable warren of rooms, many of them dark and empty and piled high with old, dusty furniture, until they came into a vast open space surrounded by curving stone columns. This was St. John's Chapel, its original religious purpose giving way to the needs of the Intelligence Ministry. Desks took up the center of the chapel, where clerks sat busily copying things from one ledger into another, sorting paperwork, or consulting strange-looking charts and muttering to themselves.

"This way," Abberline said again, and they moved on from the chapel into another maze of hallways. At the far end of one was a black wooden door. Abberline knocked three times and opened it.

Mycroft Holmes hunched like an enormous toad behind a wide wooden desk in a windowless room. His look told Burton that he was not in the least surprised to see them.

"Where's my Time Machine?" said Herbert.

"What a pleasure, gentlemen," said Mycroft Holmes in mock sincerity. "Would you care for something to drink?"

"Sod off," said Challenger.

"What have you done with Herbert's property?" said Burton. "And what else do you know about the King in Yellow?"

The elder Holmes glared up at them from behind his massive desk. "Are we so full of questions that we have forgotten our manners? How sad." He steepled his sausage-like fingers and heaved a sigh of exasperation.

"Damn your civility," said Burton. "We demand answers."

"You are in no position to demand anything, Captain Burton. What I do, I do for the good of the Empire."

"But sir," said Abberline, squeezing between Burton and Challenger. "Even you have to see this is highly irregular."

"These are irregular times," said Holmes. "They call for irregular measures."

Burton glanced at the wall to their left. Tacked upon it were a series of engineering diagrams. The largest appeared to be Holmes' best guess as to the dimensions of the Nautilus, and he was not far off. The other drawings were all of Herbert's Time Machine, showing the machine from different angles in precise details.

"It's a remarkable machine," said Holmes to the Time Traveler. "I'm sure you are proud of it. My best engineers have been practically frothing at the mouth wanting to take it apart to see how it works. I told them to hold off until I had spoken with you. There is an element missing, isn't there?"

"What do you want with it?" asked Burton.

"Such an invention could be put to great use for the good of the British Empire," said Holmes. "It is much too powerful to be in the hands of one man."

"You're wrong," said Herbert. "Better it be in the hands of one rational man than that of a hundred fools!"

"I assure you I am no fool," said Mycroft Holmes, an edge of anger seeping into his voice. "And I see many noble uses for your Time Machine. And the *Nautilus* as well, once we capture and reverse engineer it. Imagine, a whole fleet of such submarine vessels plying the seas. The greatest Navy in the world would become even better, unstoppable. None could stand against us."

"You sound as if you are preparing for war," said Burton.

"No," said Holmes. "I am preparing to prevent one, and to make war itself obsolete."

"What war?" said the Time Traveler. "We're not at war."

"Not yet," said Holmes. "But we will be. It is years hence, but it is coming. The signs of its coming are as clear as the scar on Captain Burton's face. You have no doubt seen glimpses of it during your first journey forward through Time."

Herbert's mouth fell open.

Mycroft Holmes smiled. "I've been reading your copious notes.

Yes, a rational, forward-thinking fellow such as yourself could not resist using your new invention to travel into the future, to see if your naïve ideas about the glories of mankind were true. I suspect you returned disappointed. I intend to change all that."

"You're a fool!" declared Challenger. "Your attempts to change one thing will inadvertently alter another. Tell him, Burton."

"He's telling you the truth," said Burton. "Our journey back through time changed something. This current world is not the same one I remember leaving. In that original world, my Isabel was safe and sound, and spiritualist mediums were going mad all over the city. Something changed, just by going into the deep past."

"We won't be flying blind," said Mycroft Holmes. "The same guides who told us that war is coming will help us build a new tomorrow, one in which the British Empire will shine forever."

"What the blazes are you talking about?" said Challenger, his face turning red, hands clenched into fists.

Mycroft Holmes placed his hands flat on his desk. "You are aware of the recent interest in esoteric knowledge? The Akashic Record and the legend of Agartha?"

"Bismillah," said Burton. "You're one of those hollow earthers, aren't you?"

"I am," said Mycroft Holmes evenly. "And I'd watch that tone if I were you. I have seen and heard things you could scarcely fathom."

"Or believe, I'd wager," said Burton, his eyes locked with Mycroft's.

"These esoteric sources only confirm what an astute observer such as myself can glean from history," said Mycroft Holmes. "They tell us that a great war is coming that will overtake the entire globe. Every nation will take sides in the conflict. It is my duty to make sure that the British Empire emerges the victor, so that we may fashion a new world order. An order in which war is no longer necessary."

"You're mad!" said Herbert.

"I'm a visionary," said Mycroft Holmes. "War is always inevitable. It is a release valve for man's innate hostility. The pressure comes to a head, and then..."

He balled his hands into fists, then spread them out again, an implied explosion.

"The only difference is, now we know when it is coming, and with your Time Machine, my dear Herbert, we will know the how."

"You will change whatever you attempt to observe," said Herbert. "We learned this the hard way. The war you witness by skipping ahead will not be the same one that engulfs you."

Mycroft blinked, saying nothing.

"That's not all, is it?" said Burton.

Mycroft slowly shook his head.

"The Dagon cult," said Challenger. "An irritant, certainly. A wild card. But something more."

Mycroft Holmes nodded.

"The docks," said Burton. "Whatever the cult has stored there, you think it's a cache of esoteric weapons. Weapons you can use to build this new world order of yours."

"I knew I had chosen you gentlemen wisely," said Mycroft Holmes. "You are worthy of the Shadow Council."

"I don't know what sort of fellow your brother is," said Challenger. "But his sibling is blinking mad."

"Careful," said Mycroft Holmes. "You have been of great assistance to me, but I will not cotton any disobedience. I can have you arrested for treason."

"On whose authority?" said Burton.

"On mine!" shouted the elder Holmes, smacking his palms on the desk. "Detective Abberline, get these men out of my sight before I lose my temper."

"With all due respect, sir," said Abberline. "Sod off! I'm resigning my commission effective immediately and returning to my rightful place in the police force. If you want them to leave you can damn well give them the heave-ho yourself."

Mycroft Holmes glared at them each in turn for a long moment.

"Where's my Time Machine?" Herbert said again.

"Safe," said Mycroft Holmes. "Where it can be put to good use. Once we have the control rods. I know one of you has them in his possession. In fact...guards!"

Within moments three very large men came rushing into the small office.

"Search Mr. Herbert there," ordered Mycroft Holmes.

Two of the guards brandished pistols, aiming them directly at Challenger's and Burton's head, while the third grabbed the Time Traveler and patted him down, finding the lumps in his left coat pocket that indicated the presence of the Time Machine's control levers. He reached in and fished them out. Burton backed away a step, but the guard held his gun steady. One wrong move, and Burton wouldn't survive the encounter. Challenger glared at the man holding him at gunpoint, but did nothing.

"Here you are, sir," said the man who had searched Herbert, handing the crystalline levers across the desk to Mycroft Holmes.

"Thank you," he said.

"How did you know?" asked Burton.

"It was simple to deduce," said Mycroft Holmes. "The police interrogated Herbert's housekeeper, a Mrs. Whatsit. She said you paid our friend the Time Traveler a visit yesterday morning. I surmised it was you who must have the control levers, though I can't imagine why you would want to take another jaunt through time. It was another simple logical leap to surmise that you returned them to the one you deemed their rightful owner, our friend the Time Traveler."

"What are you going to do with my machine?" said Herbert, on the verge of tears.

"We're going to learn how it functions," Mycroft said calmly. "Then we are going to mass produce it, and send spies into the future to see just what awaits us and, depending on the nature of these wonders, either figure out how to stop their occurrence or ensure that they happen."

"You're out of your tree," said Challenger. "You have the ultimate weapon in your hands and you have no idea what to do with it."

"Gorblimey," added Abberline.

Mycroft scowled at Challenger and said, "You three may go now. Your commissions are hereby dissolved. Go home. If I see any of you again I shall have you arrested on the spot and tried for treason. Is that understood? As for you, Chief Inspector Abberline, I shall have words with your superiors."

"Fine by me," the policeman snapped. "They shall hear my side of it first."

The four of them turned and walked out, shoving past the brutes Mycroft Holmes employed as guards, who followed them through the maze of rooms and out the nearest exit.

"Well that's that," said Challenger, stopping to produce a cigar from his coat and light it with a lucifer. He offered one to Burton, who readily accepted, and the four of them stood in a loose circle, thick smoke billowing around their heads.

"What are we going to do now?" said the Time Traveler, almost whining. "That scoundrel has my Time Machine! I should have destroyed it when I had the chance."

"Herbert," said Burton. "Can you reproduce the Time Machine's control levers?"

The young inventor nodded. "Of course, I have more of the materials on hand, hidden where the police didn't find them."

"How long will that take?"

He shrugged. "A couple of hours. Why?"

"Do it," said Burton. "Then meet me back here. We're going to get your Time Machine back."

"I can't be a party to this," said Abberline. "What Mr. Holmes did was illegal. What you're talking about is—"

"Treason?" said Challenger with a grin. "Count me in."

"I'm sorry, Professor," said Burton. "You'll stick out like a sore thumb. I need you to help me track down this abysmal King in Yellow before he does any more damage."

"And how do you propose we do that?" asked Challenger.

Burton grinned. "Simple deductive logic. I think I know who this yellow fellow is, and where to find him."

"I will see if I can find out what Holmes is planning," said Abberline. "Maybe I can give you gents a heads up."

Burton nodded. "Splendid. Now let's go. We may not have much time."

"Not yet, anyway," Herbert quipped.

"If only there was a way to get a warning to Captain Nemo," said Burton, ignoring his manic friend's little joke. "Besides, we could really use his help. We need to destroy whatever is in those buildings along the docks before Mycroft Holmes gets his hands on it."

"As I stated earlier, I might know a way," said Herbert. "But for it to work, I need my Time Machine."

"Let's go then," said Burton, and the four men left the grounds of the Tower of London at a slow jog.

THE KING IN YELLOW

The Lyric Theatre's large auditorium was dark when Burton and Challenger entered it. Once their eyes adjusted to the gloom, they found seats in the last row, to the left of the rear exit.

The room was vast, but only a few dozen people were in attendance. The only light came from sputtering gas lamps set into the walls at intervals. A yellow robed figure stepped onto the stage from the wings, a grotesque mask fashioned in the likeness of the Deep Ones covered the figure's face.

"How do you know this King in Yellow chap will put in an appearance here?" grumbled Challenger.

"Simple deductive reasoning," said Burton with a smile. "Provided I am right about the gentleman's identity."

Challenger scoffed at Burton's mockery of Mycroft Holmes and scanned the room.

Suddenly the heavy velvet curtains concealing the stage began to undulate and pull back—Burton could hear the drone of the building's hydraulic pumps that used water from the Thames to move the thick drapery—and a familiar robed and masked figure appeared.

"The King in Yellow," Burton whispered.

"Brothers and sisters," the King in Yellow intoned when the curtains had fully parted, his arms spread wide. "We are at the threshold of a higher state of being. The stars are right. The time of man's reign upon this earth is over. But we do not have to suffer man's fate. We can ascend."

He trod the boards like an orator, his voice rising and falling. The audience swayed to the sound of his voice, as if mesmerized.

"We will reside in the house of Father Dagon and Mother Hydra forever and ever," he said.

The crowd clapped loudly and stomped their feet, but the King in Yellow waved his hand, silencing them.

"The way is dark, my brothers. The goal is not without challenge, my sisters. Sacrifices must be made. They will come for us, but we must not waver, we must not falter. Ours is the kingdom of Dagon!"

"Beneath the waves," the audience droned.

"Ia Ia," said the King in Yellow.

"Cthulhu fhtagn!" the crowd answered.

A chill fled up Burton's spine.

"But the time for hiding in the shadows, behind masks, is over."

The King in Yellow reached up and removed his mask, lowering his hood.

"Bismillah!" muttered Burton. "I knew it! I thought his words sounded familiar."

"Who?" Challenger whispered.

"Edward George Earle Lytton Bulwer-Lytton, 1st Baron Lytton," said Burton.

"Blimey, what a mouthful," said Challenger. "Isn't he a famous writer?"

"Among other things," said Burton.

"How did you know he is the King in Yellow?"

"I recognized certain phrases he used the other night," said the explorer. "'The great unwashed,' and so forth. These phrases were famously written by Bulwer-Lytton. Combine that with his well-known interest in esoteric subjects, and…"

"This goes far beyond mere interest," muttered Challenger. "I guess he finally snapped, eh?"

"I wish he *was* mad," said Burton. "Don't you remember Miss Marsh's story? This is exactly like Innsmouth."

"I know some of you are shocked to see me here," said the Baron, removing his robes and tossing everything in a heap in the left wing of the stage. Beneath them he wore a dark, expensive suit befitting his high status. "But my years of searching for ultimate, secret knowledge are over. I have found what I sought in the pages of an ancient text called the *Necronomicon*. And that knowledge will imbue us with life eternal. Think of it! A world free of disease and want and class. All we have to do is take the first step."

"I do not withdraw my original summation," said Challenger. "He's blinking mad. He'd give up his humanity for a few trinkets and an empty promise."

"So it would appear," whispered Burton. "But what shall we do about it?"

"I'll show you what we'll do," said the professor. "We'll shove these fiends into the light."

The huge bear of a man stood and, cupping his hands over his mouth yelled, "Bollocks! Baron Lytton is a scoundrel of the first order! A right treasonous sot that ought to be hanged."

Burton shook his head and stood, ready to bolt as things went sour.

"Who is that?" said Bulwer-Lytton. "Who dares speak such things to me?"

His eyes squinted up into the darkness.

"Yes. I know you. From the other night. I know both of you. Stop them! Don't let them escape again!"

The audience rose and turned an angry eye toward the last row. Men and women came toward them in a wave.

"We can't fight all of them," said Burton, making his way toward the rear entrance.

"We don't have to," said Challenger, who produced a whistle from his pocket and blew hard into it. The shrill, piercing sound signaled, a moment later, the arrival of more than a dozen police.

"I alerted Abberline to your plan," said Challenger. "He let me borrow his police whistle, and had some men stationed at every entrance."

"Good man, that Abberline," said Burton, grinning. He glanced toward the stage. "Bulwer-Lytton is gone!"

"They'll find him," said Challenger.

The big zoologist socked one fleeing cultist in the mouth as he tried to run past. The police rounded up as many as they could as they headed toward the exits. These were not East End roustabouts, but well-to-do members of London society. Followers of the Baron's esoteric philosophy.

"We need to head back to the Tower of London," said Burton.

"Good," said Challenger as they headed for the door. "I'm tired of doing that scoundrel Holmes' job for him."

Abberline greeted them on the other side of the door. "Hallo gents," he said with a smile.

Challenger gave him back his whistle.

"Where's Bulwer-Lytton?" asked Burton.

"Who?"

Burton revealed to Abberline the King in Yellow's identity.

"I don't know. If he didn't slip out, he's in our custody."

Burton looked at Challenger. "I don't think we're lucky enough for him to be in custody."

"He'll plan his attack on the city ahead of schedule," said Challenger.

"Tonight," added Burton. "We must warn Mycroft Holmes."

"Attack?" asked Abberline. "What attack?"

"Just get us to the Tower," said Burton. "As quickly as you can. I'll explain, as best I can, on the way."

A SHADOW OVER LONDON

It was early evening by the time Burton, Challenger and Abberline returned to the Tower of London, and a dense fog rolled in off the Thames, full of black flecks of coal that stung Burton's eyes and made his nose run. They waited by the Traitor's Gate for Herbert, who arrived a few minutes later. He held out an oilskin-wrapped bundle for Burton.

"The control rods," said the Time Traveler. "As commissioned."

"Good. Hang onto them. You're going to get your Time Machine out of here and get a warning to Captain Nemo."

"How on earth are you going to do that?" asked Abberline. "Does your Time Machine float as well?"

Herbert opened his mouth to explain, but Burton silenced him. "The particulars aren't important right now. We need to warn Mycroft Holmes of the Dagon cult's impending attack."

"I can help with one of those items," said Abberline. "The Time Machine is in a storage room on the first level. I spoke with one of my men, who helped transport it here. A dreadfully heavy thing. I think they only put it where they did to save their backs. I can show you once we're inside."

They walked through the gate and up the path toward the large wooden doors they had entered through earlier. Light flickered faintly through the fog from high windows.

The place was just as busy as it had been earlier, and the four men managed to make their way unmolested as the navigated the veritable maze of corridors.

Abberline halted them before a set of stairs. "You'll find it in a room down there," said the policeman to the Time Traveler. "There's a set of doors used for loading in supplies. If you've got a strong back, you can drag it out that way."

"Thank you," said Herbert, nodding. "Though that is hardly necessary. I intend to travel to a time in which the Tower no longer exists. Then I shall drag it to what is in our time open air. I can be back in a pip."

"You must not let Mycroft get his hands on it again, Herbert," said Burton. "Take it out of here and dismantle it."

The Time Traveler looked at him, nodding once. "I wish that I had done so already."

"Don't forget to warn Nemo," added Challenger.

Herbert gave the burly zoologist a half-hearted salute. "All taken care of. Good luck, my friends."

They watched as the young inventor darted down the narrow stairs and was gone.

"Captain Burton," said a loud voice from behind them.

The three of them turned to see Mycroft Holmes standing there. Beside him stood two black-garbed attendants.

"Go see about the Time Traveler," he told one of the men bookending him, and he ran down the stairs.

"I told you I'd have you all arrested for treason if you showed your faces around here," said the elder Holmes. "Arrest them. Chief Inspector Abberline too."

"Now wait a minute," said Challenger. "We came to warn you."

"Warn me?" said Mycroft Holmes. "Of what?"

"An attack on the city," said Burton. "The King in Yellow is Edward Bulwer-Lytton. His cult is planning an attack on the city. Tonight."

"We arrested most of his cult earlier this evening," said Abberline.

"With the help of Captain Burton and Professor Challenger. But Baron Lytton escaped."

Mycroft nodded appraisingly. "No matter. We know who the scoundrel is now, and we can round him up. But you three are still guilty of treason."

"Bismillah!" said Burton. "It is the Baron Lytton who is guilty of treason."

The attendant came back up the stairs, panting. "He's gone, sir."

"And your friend the Time Traveler is guilty of stealing government property," Mycroft added. "Arrest these men at once!"

Challenger raised his beefy fists as the other attendant got too close, while Burton pulled away from the man who had come from the stairwell.

There was a resounding boom Burton felt more than heard, shaking the ground as it set his back teeth to vibrating. Plaster dust sifted down onto them like coal dust from the fog.

"What in blazes was that?" said Mycroft Holmes.

"I warned you," said Burton. "Bulwer-Lytton has received esoteric weaponry from the Deep Ones. And now he's going to use it to destroy the city."

Mycroft stammered as another puff of plaster dust rained upon them, his jowls vibrating.

"You've got to help stop them," he said. "As members of the Shadow Council."

"I thought we were no longer in your Shadow Council," said Burton.

"I thought we were traitors," said Challenger.

"Quite so," said Burton. "Perhaps we should all just clap ourselves in irons and save you the trouble."

"All right, all right," Mycroft Holmes bellowed. "Have it your way. You are upstanding members of the Shadow Council once more, and you are no longer under arrest for treason. Now do something!"

Everyone scrambled as the room shook once more, and Burton realized that the Tower of London itself wasn't under attack, but somewhere nearby.

"Get somewhere safe," said Burton. "And contact the army and the London police. You'll need all of them."

"What are you going to do?" inquired Mycroft Holmes.

"Run," said Burton in answer, and he, Challenger and Abberline jogged down the stairs and through the now open loading doors Abberline had described.

"Blimey," said Abberline. "I couldn't have stayed in there another minute! I felt as if the whole place was coming down round my ears."

"It's formidable, but ancient," said Burton. "It might not survive a direct assault from whatever Bulwer-Lytton has pointed at us, but it should hold for now. I just hope we fair better."

They stood in the fog-shrouded night, with a sound like thunder in their ears. They saw flashes of what looked like lightning, only not coming from the sky, but from the ground.

Burton had that feeling again of someone, something, standing just behind him, over his shoulder. It looked as if it was trying to speak. When he turned, there was no one there.

Burton shivered, but not from cold. Dark, sinister, non-humanoid shapes moved in the fog, chilling him to the bone with fear. The sound of police whistles and human screams filled the night.

The three men ran away from the Tower of London, through the Traitor's Gate. They heard splashing from the Thames off to their right, as if many large forms were emerging from the dark depths, shaking water from their broad backs. The sound of wet footsteps slapped toward them. They broke into a run, Abberline huffing and puffing behind Burton and Challenger. Burton hoped they could lose their inhuman assailants in the fog.

In the distance there was a flash of yellow that burned through the fog for a moment. A building was on fire. Burton heard the clang of a fireman's bell. People shouting. Behind them, more gurgling, hopping, slapping sounds, accompanied by the greasy sliding of the shoggoths.

Burton glanced at Abberline, his face pale in the firelight. The poor man looked like he wanted to scream, and Burton wouldn't blame him one bit if he did. He almost felt like screaming himself, but did not want to give away their position in the fog to those fiends he just knew were behind them in the fog-shrouded dark.

They grew near to the fire now, could feel the heat from it. There was another peel of bone-shaking thunder, another sinister curl of pinkish lightning that stabbed the London skyline like an accusatory finger. Burton smelled burnt things and fish-stink and fear, the latter his own.

There were more people milling about in the dense fog now, most of them running, panicked. The three slowed to a brisk walk, feeling the heat from the flames now. Behind them the Tower of London was little more than a vague outline, gaslights burning in its highest windows like baleful eyes.

Burton was thankful for the fog. For he knew no one in the city of London could stand the full knowledge of what was coming for them. Just a glimpse was enough to drive everyone in the city stark raving mad. It was a small mercy, to be denied the face of death as it descended upon them.

"What are we going to do?" Burton heard himself say, his mouth dry, his tongue like sandpaper. The voice he heard come out of his mouth was not his voice, but that of a sad, frightened madman, and it terrified him.

"I don't know," said the shadow that stalked Captain Richard Francis Burton. "I don't know."

THE LADY OF THE EYE

W
e need weapons," said Professor Challenger, the building's flames flashing in his dark eyes. "Guns. Ammunition."

"Follow me," said Abberline.

Burton glanced quickly behind him, looking for the owner of that strange, ethereal voice he knew to be his own. All he saw were flames and fleeing people. He blinked the burning sting of the flames from his eyes and glanced around, practicing a Sufi meditation to help settle his nerves. He glanced around, getting his bearings before moving east, after Abberline and Challenger and toward the epicenter of the conflict. The sky above the East End was full of strange shadows dancing in a crimson mist, evidence of more fires in the Cauldron itself.

"This way," said Abberline, and the men threaded their way through the crowd of volunteer firemen, police, and fearful men and women who had stopped in their running to gawk at the flames.

A policeman's carriage stood unattended, and Abberline wasted no time climbing atop the driver's box. "Hop in, gents."

Burton and Challenger climbed inside, and Abberline tugged the reins, spurring the horses into a brisk trot.

"Hey!" a voice shouted from behind them, but they paid it no heed.

The streets were crowded with fleeing horses and frightened onlookers, eyes darting toward the East End, where strange vibrations echoed and blasphemous visions flashed intermittently before being once again obscured by flame and fog.

"Police!" Abberline shouted. "Out of the way!"

Burton dabbed his watery eyes with a handkerchief and stared at Challenger who sat across from him, his face marked by flame and soot, his enormous, blue-black beard melding with the shadows inside the carriage.

"Where are we going?" said Burton.

"To find weapons," said Challenger, arching a bushy eyebrow. "You all right?"

Burton didn't know the answer, so instead settled into the carriage cushions and said nothing.

After speeding through several blocks, Abberline at last pulled the carriage to a halt in front of a nondescript building with police milling around out front.

"What is this place?" said Challenger as he and Burton climbed out of the carriage.

"Police storage facility," said Abberline, hopping to the ground. "Weapons and ammunition, as requested."

"Good show," said Burton. "We'll—"

A movement in the corner of his right eye startled him. He again had the sense that he was being followed, though more intense this time. He watched from the periphery of his vision, knowing that if he spun around, the apparition would be gone.

"What is it?" Challenger asked.

"Is there anyone behind me?" asked Burton. "Following me?"

Challenger examined the section of street directly across from them. "No. No one here but us and the coppers. Why?"

"I've had the strangest feeling that I'm being followed," said Burton. "It's been happening ever since I recovered from my fever."

Burton watched the figure from his periphery, getting the impression that it went into the shop across the street.

Burton succumbed to his curiosity and turned his head to the

175

right. No one was there. The shop had a sign hanging above the door depicting a luridly painted eye along with the words Psychic Medium. Tarot. Fortunes.

Burton didn't know why, but he had the sudden urge to go inside.

"Where the devil are you going?" said Challenger.

Burton turned and looked toward his friends, surprised to discover he was halfway across the street.

"Humor me, please," he said. "I think this is important."

Abberline and Challenger exchanged glances before joining Burton at the door of the shop.

Burton raised his fist to knock, but the door opened before he could do so.

An old woman stood looking at him, wearing Gypsy garb. She gave him a thin smile.

"Come in," she said, stepping away from the door. Burton stepped through the portal, followed by Abberline and Challenger.

The place was lit only by hundreds of candles. The smell of incense filled the air, sandalwood and something more exotic Burton couldn't quite place.

"Go," said the woman. "Sit. Rest yourselves. This is no night to be running about. I am Lady Helena."

"Uh, thank you," said Burton. "I don't really know what I'm doing here. I don't believe in this..." He waved his hands about, at a loss for words. Lady Helena fixed him with a thin smile.

"You are not the first to say that. Have a seat. Let's see if we can figure it out together."

The three men sat around a small oval table in the center of the room. Atop it sat a deck of ancient, yellowed Tarot cards and other accoutrements of Lady Helena's questionable trade. The incense made Burton woozy.

"This is a dark night," said Lady Helena, taking a seat opposite Burton. "You are running toward the trouble, not away from it."

"You don't have to be psychic to know that," Challenger barked.

"Yes," said Burton, ignoring him. "We are. We seek a way to stop it. But..." His voice trailed off, seeking the words he needed to continue.

"Someone has been following me."

Lady Helena grabbed Burton's hands and flipped them over, examining his palms. Then she let them go and stared into his eyes.

"Yes," she said. "You have been haunted."

"Haunted?" said Abberline.

"Yes. Places can be haunted, of course, but so can people, from time to time. This is the Dweller on the Threshold."

"What in hell's name is that?" said Challenger. "Are you honestly humoring this, Captain?"

"What choice do I have?" asked Burton. To Lady Helena, he said, "Tell me, what is this Dweller on the Threshold?"

"A thing of the spirit realm that attaches itself to a human being," said Lady Helena. "A discarded astral double of a person from a previous life."

"Previous life?" Burton murmured.

"This apparition you see from the corner of your eye is you from a previous life," said Lady Helena. "It has attached itself to you due to your affinity for one another. It is you, and at the same time, not you."

"How do I get rid of it?"

"You must face it head on," said Lady Helena. "It needs to know, in no uncertain terms, that it is no more, and that yours is the only soul bound to this world."

Challenger snorted laughter. Abberline groaned.

"Gentlemen, please," said Burton, shifting in his seat.

"Lady Helena, how can I possibly face it, when I can't even see it? It exists always in the corner of my vision."

"You can face it directly on the astral plane," said Lady Helena. "But the astral plane is in great turmoil this night. The conflagration that plagues the city exists both in this world and the next."

"How do I get there?" asked Burton.

"The way is dangerous for those who have never traveled as the spirits do."

"How do I get there?" Burton said again, more forcefully this time.

The medium acquiesced. "Very well. I can see you are determined. Perhaps you are strong-willed enough to survive the journey. Come."

The old woman gestured to a low couch. "Lie down."

Burton rose from his seat and laid himself upon the couch.

"Captain," said Challenger. "We're losing valuable time."

"I have to see this through, Professor. I believe it is connected to the chaos outside, to Bulwer-Lytton's cult, to everything."

Lady Helena gasped. "Baron Lytton is behind this?"

Burton nodded. "Yes. He made contact with abysmal entities that live at the bottom of the sea."

Lady Helena shook her head. "I have heard him speak. He is very knowledgeable in the area of Theosophy, and the Dweller on the Threshold is his coinage. But he seeks only knowledge obtained from the spirit world and ignores the wisdom and patience that comes from the material realm."

"Help us stop him," said Burton. "Help me confront my double and put an end to this madness."

The medium nodded. "Very well. But I must warn you, the astral plane is no place for a novice."

"Understood," said Burton. "Now what do I do?"

"Close your eyes," said Lady Helena, and he did so.

"Clear your mind. Concentrate on your body, how it feels. Flex your muscles, loosen them. Start with your toes and move up your body. Make sure every muscle is completely relaxed."

Burton did as instructed. *This is similar to many meditation techniques*, he thought.

"Breathe deeply," Lady Helena intoned.

Burton felt something hard rest on his forehead.

"This is a quartz crystal," said Lady Helena. "It will help control your vibrations and protect you while on the astral plane. Continue to breathe. Focus on your breathing."

Burton continued to follow her instructions, slipping into a familiar hypnotic state. Everything and everyone around him felt very far away and inconsequential.

"Now concentrate on moving your toes, your fingers, your arms. But not your physical body, your mental one. Your spiritual one."

Burton felt his fingers flex independently of his actual fingers. A warm vibration spread out through his body, starting from the quartz crystal resting on his forehead and radiating downward. It was quite pleasant.

Burton began to feel light, like a balloon. He bobbed up and out, twisting around to see his body lying on the couch, Lady Helena, Challenger and Abberline kneeling beside him.

His astral form grinned, and he turned and rose up through the ceiling and straight into a dark abyss.

THE DWELLER ON THE THRESHOLD

Captain Richard Francis Burton stared into the abyss, and the abyss also stared into him. The blackness was vast, without light or heat. The nothingness went on forever.

He felt the presence of someone behind him. Burton turned, afraid the apparition would depart like all the other times. But this time, instead of fleeing to the periphery of his vision, it held still.

Burton regarded the figure carefully, his heart pounding, his throat tightening. It was him. The Other Burton. The feeling was like that of looking in a mirror, save for the permanent scowl on Other Burton's face.

"You killed me," said Other Burton, and Burton didn't recognize his own voice, realizing that we all must sound different to ourselves. He was hearing himself for the first time as others heard him, and it was disconcerting.

"I did not mean to," said Burton. "I am sorry, for you have lost so much. We both have."

"Only one of us can prevail," said Other Burton. "We cannot both exist. One of us is the lie; the other is the truth."

"Agreed," Burton said to his double, nodding. "But how do we decide which one?"

The Other Burton was silent for a long moment before raising a hand that now held a sword. He gave a cry of rage before lunging toward Burton, who moved out of his way just in time to miss the blade's stinging arc as Other Burton attempted to embed the weapon in his right shoulder.

"Bismillah!" said Burton. "Wait. I am unarmed."

"Only if you want to be," said Other Burton as he lunged once more. This one Burton parried, surprised to find an identical sword in his hand.

"So that's how it works on the astral plane," said Burton as he counterattacked.

They danced back and forth for a couple of minutes, swords clashing, but neither Burton got the upper hand. Each version anticipated what the other was going to do.

"This isn't going to work," said Burton panting. He pulled back, tossing his blade aside. They had the same training and were equally matched.

The Other Burton regarded him. "We must duel to the death."

"Why?"

"It is the only way to resolve the rupture in Time. The rupture that allowed their incursion into this world." He gestured, and Burton felt a cold presence surrounding them, watching them. He looked, but just as with the Other Burton, he could only discern them indirectly, over his shoulder, behind him.

He felt naked and afraid, as if he were a microbe being examined under a microscope by intellects vast and cruel and unsympathetic.

"They were going to come anyway," said Burton. "They were here before."

Other Burton shook his head. "They came because of you. Isabel went missing because of you."

"No," said Burton. "What I did had nothing to do with her. I—"

He stopped. Could the Other Burton be right? It was something they had changed that caused Time to run along this deadly new course, a course in which Isabel had been in Hyde Park that day and had been snatched from his life. A course in which no mediums went mad. A course in which Edward Bulwer-Lytton started a Dagon cult and was now at war with London.

"I am sorry," said Burton. "We have both lost so much. Isabel—"

"*My* Isabel!" Other Burton shouted. "Yours yet lives, in some other version of Time. In killing you, I will take your place, the time streams will merge, and I will have her back. And the world, *my* world, will no longer be filled with monsters."

Burton could see the madness in his bloodshot eyes. How many sleepless nights had he endured? How many evenings did he spend stalking Hyde Park in search of *his* Isabel? The toll it must have taken on him. This poor man wasn't the doppelganger. Burton was.

"Bismillah!" Burton swore.

He looked in the direction the stygian entities' presence was strongest.

"Bismillah!" he swore again, raising his fists. Somewhere in the distance thunder echoed.

"You may be right about me," said Burton. "But you cannot possibly know how the time streams, as you call them, will merge. Time may indeed be a river, but plotting its course is not like locating the source of the Nile. There will be ripples, eddies. Something else will change. Something you didn't intend."

Other Burton held his sword down at his side, pondering his words. "My fight is not with you. It is these otherworldly entities that caused this. They are the reason we traveled through time. They are the reason history is bifurcated."

Burton regarded his double. "You said there was a rupture that allowed their return to this world. What did you mean?"

"Can't you feel it?" said Other Burton. "It's all around us now, growing in strength. The mediums felt it first, because they are sensitive to ethereal vibrations. Bismillah! I sound like one of them. There was a time I thought them mad. Now, I doubt my own sanity."

"I know what you mean," said Burton. "So this tear in Time is what has given rise to all this madness? Bulwer-Lytton's cult, this sudden interest in the occult?"

"Yes, I think so," said Other Burton. "It makes as much sense as anything else. I just want my time stream back, before we made a mess of it."

Burton nodded.

"It was the artifact that did it, you know," said Other Burton. "The object Miss Marsh showed us was the same one that was part of R'lyeh's control mechanism. We smashed it."

"Of course," said Burton. "Smashing it in the past meant we could not have possibly seen it in the present. How could I have been such a fool?"

"How could *we* have been such fools," Other Burton corrected. "It was the unresolved paradox that created the rupture. It is the rupture that gives power to Bulwer-Lytton's infernal weaponry."

"If we close the rupture," said Burton, "we will stop Bulwer-Lytton. We'll stop them all."

"But what about Isabel?" said Other Burton.

"It might bring her back," Burton offered.

"Perhaps."

Burton watched in horror as the blackness around them resolved itself into chaotic indigo mists through which strange, not even remotely humanoid shapes toiled.

"They are here now," said Other Burton. "On the astral plane. They intend to finish us. Punishment for not doing their bidding."

"How do you know this?"

"They shout at my mind through the crimson mists," said Other Burton. "Our previous contact with the shoggoth in R'lyeh primed our minds for them, and them for us. Can't you feel them?"

Burton didn't know what he felt. An eerie feeling of something wet pawing on the back of his neck.

"What do we do?" he said. "Can we die here?"

Other Burton shrugged. "I suppose I don't truly exist, and you are merely the spirit form of your body back on Lady Helena's couch. What have we got to lose?"

Burton took up his sword from where he had tossed it and grinned a savage grin that made him worthy of his nickname, Ruffian Dick.

"To heal the rupture, one of us must cease to exist."

"You mean die," Burton corrected.

Other Burton raked a hand through his beard. "I'm already dead. I am nothing but unused potential. I mean cease to exist."

Other Burton spun around, confronting a large thing covered in lamprey mouths and indigo tentacles. He sliced at it with his sword, sinking the blade deep into one of its mouths.

"Go." said Other Burton. "Now!"

Burton moved to help his doppelganger, but he felt a tug from behind. He looked over his shoulder and saw the thin white thread of energy that trailed off his back and into darkness. It was pulled taught, vibrating softly.

Other Burton lost his sword down the blasphemous maw of an amorphous spheroid entity. Burton tossed him his as he felt himself being lifted off the ground and pulled gently backward, away from Other Burton and the abhorrent entities that surrounded him.

Down and down he went, through colorless night. He had the impression that his eyes were shut, so he opened them.

Abberline and Professor Challenger were hovering over him, worried looks on their faces.

"Well?" Challenger barked. "What did you see?"

"Are you all right, Captain Burton?" said Abberline, helping the explorer to a sitting position.

"Yes, yes. I'm fine. "Stop fussing over me."

"Did you find the Dweller on the Threshold?" asked Lady Helena, leaning in close. "Did you face him?"

"I did," said Burton. He slid his legs over the edge of the couch and planted his booted feet firmly on the parquet floor. It felt firm and solid and real. "And it wasn't some bloody astral spirit. It was me. The other me, from the time stream we changed. The one who's Isabel disappeared in Hyde Park."

"What the deuce?" said Challenger.

"It's true. He told me how we altered the time streams. The artifact in the machine on R'lyeh. It was the same one Miss Marsh and Nemo found in the South Pacific. By destroying it in the past, I made sure that they never found it here in the present."

"Bugger me," said Abberline. "I need a drink."

"Aren't you on duty?" inquired Challenger.

"Yes, but what of it?"

"Help yourself," said Lady Helena, gesturing to a sideboard in the corner.

They watched as the Chief Inspector got up and poured himself a brandy.

"You may all partake if you wish," said Lady Helena to Burton. "You have been on quite a journey."

"So what happened up there with the other Burton?" asked Challenger.

"It's hard to explain," said Burton, taking a proffered glass of brandy from Abberline and downing it in one gulp. "Our change created a rupture, a wound in Time itself. This rupture somehow empowered these entities to try and return, and powered the Deep Ones' weaponry. The Other Burton sacrificed himself to the entities on the astral plane so that there would be only one Burton, me. Thus repairing the damage."

"And what of Isabel?" Challenger asked softly.

Burton stared at the floor. "Gone. With the rest of that now nonexistent time stream. Oh, how I wish Herbert were here. He could make sense of this, if anyone could."

"Where the devil is he, anyway?" asked Abberline. "A Time Traveler should have returned to the precise moment he left, should he not?"

"Perhaps he is smarter than all of us," said Challenger. "If you had a bloody Time Machine, would you come back to this insanity?"

While Abberline mused on this, Burton got up and refilled his glass. "It's quiet outside," he said after taking a sip.

Lady Helena returned to her table, her eyes closed. "Yes. The ethereal vibrations have calmed. The astral plane is no longer a place of strife and turmoil."

"That's wonderful news for those on the astral plane," said Challenger. "But what does that mean for us here in jolly old England?"

"It means the tide has turned," said Burton. "The rupture in the time stream was what was powering Bulwer-Lytton's esoteric

185

weapons. Now, if he wants to burn this city to the ground, he had best do it the good old-fashioned way."

"By Jove!" said Abberline. "We've got him now. We'll send his army of fish demons back where they came from."

"Let's finish this, then," said Challenger, his eyes seeking Burton's. "What say you?"

Burton downed his brandy. "I say we've come this far. Let's see it through to the end."

IT WAS A DARK AND STORMY NIGHT

The East End was in Chaos.

People ran screaming, running from things that were not people. The smell of fish was overpowering, and twice Burton reeled in horror as one of the Deep Ones emerged briefly from the fog, brandishing some sort of lethal-looking trident made from that strange gold they had in great supply.

The weapons Abberline procured from the police storage facility evened the odds somewhat, and there were no more blasts of ethereal lightning from the esoteric weapons Bulwer-Lytton's cult had received from the Deep Ones as advanced payment for their souls.

Challenger, handy at the trigger, blasted into the crowd that came at them through the fog with much relish. Burton was more deliberate with his shots, wary of hitting anyone human. Bulwer-Lytton's cultists had scarcely had time to begin mating rituals with the Deep Ones. For that, Burton counted his lucky stars.

By the time they entered the Cauldron the army had arrived, pushing people back and cordoning off the most dangerous areas, containing the cultists to the East End.

"We've got to push them back all the way to the docks," said Challenger.

Burton nodded. "I think the army has the same idea."

They moved along through the fog. It was rough going, but they were pushing the enemy back deeper and deeper into the East End.

They fought for over an hour, adrenaline the only thing keeping Burton going. At last they neared the London Docklands. Inhuman screams filled Burton's ears, and he cringed at the sound. People were running everywhere, defenders and assailants alike. Bullets zipped all around their heads, and Burton and his companions took refuge behind an overturned cart, where Abberline assisted with reloading while Challenger hefted twin pistols, firing blind into the darkness. Hunched beside him, Burton caught a flash of yellow in the fog-shrouded, moonlit gloom. It darted into a wooden structure straddling the wharf.

"Cover me," Burton shouted.

"What?" said Challenger.

Burton jabbed him in the ribs, pointing in the direction the yellow robed figure had gone. "Bulwer-Lytton."

Challenger nodded and set about covering Burton's path with copious amounts of lead.

Burton hunched down and ran after the figure, opening the door and following him inside.

The place was dark, safe for shafts of moonlight stabbing through slits in the rough-hewn planks that made up the structure. He heard water lapping at wooden pilings not far beneath him. Around him were dim outlines of barrels, boxes, and old fishnets strung about like immense spiderwebs. Burton caught an eerie glow coming from a stack of large crates and followed it.

Edward George Bulwer-Lytton, 1st Baron Lytton stood glaring at Burton, his dirty yellow robes flowing about him. He held a peculiar object in his hand, brandishing it like a pistol. It was a strange copper color, with a clamshell-shaped node that glowed with an eerie green light. That light made Burton's guts go to water and his stomach seize.

"I don't want to hurt you, Burton," said the Baron. "But I will."

"I don't want to fight you, Baron," said Burton. "But this madness has to end. Those fish-fiends are killing people. Your people."

"Everyone must make way for the new and glorious coming," said

Bulwer-Lytton, adjusting his grip on the pistol-thing. His hands were sweaty. *This is good*, Burton thought. The man was unsure of himself. He could insight people to great violence, but he was no killer. Burton edged closer.

"Those Deep Ones are not your friends." "They only wish to claim the surface world as their own. This deal you made with them is a deal with the devil."

"Nonsense," said Bulwer-Lytton. "They will make us more than we are. The children we have together will live forever and ever."

"But not as humans," said Burton. "They will have to go beneath the waves and live as their fellow fish-folk. They will lose their humanity. What kind of life is that? Immortal or otherwise?"

"You do not know what you are talking about. I have seen our future. It will be glorious."

"Yes, you seem to know a great deal about the future, don't you? This esoteric knowledge, how was it gleaned?"

Bulwer-Lytton put his free hand to his face, shook his head.

"You don't know, do you?" said Burton. "Some insight told you of the Deep Ones' existence, but the rest was all your doing. "You made contact with them, somehow. They offered you some of their strange gold in exchange for your allegiance. By then it was too late. They demanded sacrifices."

"Yes, yes," said Bulwer-Lytton. "Gods yes! It was simple at first. The East End is full of scoundrels and layabouts. Cut-throats and dollymops. We gave the Deep Ones their sacrifices while ridding the streets of the worst of its criminals. The great unwashed became the key to humanity's salvation."

"What salvation?" said Burton, taking another furtive step closer. "The Deep Ones and shoggoths are slaughtering innocents!"

"I know," said the Baron. "It is true, I did not foresee it ending this way, but who am I to argue with progress? The Deep Ones will help us rise to a deeper spiritual understanding of ourselves and our place in the universe."

"Bismillah! They care not a whit for your spiritualist claptrap. They want to rule. This planet belonged to them once, them and their cosmic ilk. They want it back. And if they take it mankind is doomed!"

"I don't believe you," said the Baron, leveling the pistol-thing at Burton's head. It gave off a strange vibration that made Burton's back teeth ache.

"I've seen it!" said Burton, inching closer. "I've traveled through Time. I've seen the hell they made of the Earth in the distant past. This is man's time now, and maybe we'll make a mess of things, maybe we won't. But we won't get the chance to find out if the Deep Ones take London. Don't be a traitor to your entire species, man! Help me put an end to this nonsense tonight."

Bulwer-Lytton seemed to consider this, but still held the weird pistol at the ready, his hand shaking. Burton didn't know what the weapon could do, or if he could duck out of the way in time, so he just stayed where he was. He hoped Abberline and Challenger would reach him soon, and the distraction of their arrival would give him a chance to overpower the Baron. A slim and dangerous chance, but it was the only way he could see to end this madness.

"You're too late, Captain Burton," said Bulwer-Lytton. "The cogs of war already turn. There is nothing anyone can do. Even if I wanted to. This was predicted by the spirits. They...were talking to me. But now they've fallen silent. No doubt because I've done their will."

"You fool," said Burton, inching closer. "Those weren't spirits. They were potential lifetimes from other time streams. My last journey through Time caused a paradox, creating a rupture in Time. I was haunted by one of these spirits, what you would call a Dweller on the Threshold, that was actually myself from another of these time streams."

"Rift?" said Bulwer-Lytton. "What do you mean?"

"I'm not really sure myself," said the explorer, taking another step. "But nearest I can reason, the rupture was caused by the two of us co-existing. The other Burton sacrificed himself so that only one Burton would remain, me. Thereby closing the rift. That spiritualist chatter you think you heard was actually temporal noise coming from the wound in Time."

"No," said Bulwer-Lytton. "The spirit world is real. Just as real as this one. You're just another doubter. Your apostasy is well-known, Burton."

"Be that as it may, I'm telling you the truth. I don't know if there is a spirit world. Bismillah, after all the things I've seen, you may be right. But I do know that this isn't the way to find out. People are dying, Baron. Dying for a cause you gleaned from an Ouija board."

There was a loud concussion, and the entire structure shook, almost knocking Burton to his knees.

Bulwer-Lytton fell against one of the wooden crates, dropping his eerie weapon. It dropped to the floor with a heavy thud and slid in between two planks to fall into the churning waters of the Thames below. Burton could see its eerie glow ebb as it was subsumed by the dank waters.

"Blast it!" said the Baron. "What is going on?"

Another concussion drowned out his words, and sawdust and cobwebs rained down on them as the pilings shook once more.

"The docks are under attack," shouted Burton. "It's over, Baron. We must get out of here."

"No!" said Bulwer-Lytton. "This isn't over."

The building rocked again, this time dislodging one of the pilings.

Bulwer-Lytton held onto one of the crates. "But I was so close. The things in these crates. You should see them, Burton."

"I don't want to see them," said Burton as the building shook again. Floorboards groaned and separated as the rear wall splintered into dust. The whole building pitched backward toward the water. Bulwer-Lytton was tossed out, falling into the dark, frothing waters. Beside him a great, spherical shell heaved up, water running down its black iron hide. Covered in lights, long black tubes protruded from it at regular intervals. In the center of the strange sphere was a thick porthole, illuminated from within. Staring through it was the bearded face of Captain Nemo, giving Burton a quick salute.

Burton watched for a moment as the strange craft submerged, dragging Bulwer-Lytton down with it. He couldn't be sure, but he thought he saw two fish-like forms grabbing the Baron, pulling him down into a watery hell of his own making.

The building rocked back and forth and Burton, fearful of being pitched into the sea like the Baron, turned and ran toward what remained of the shaky structure's entrance, gravity slowing his progress. With a final leap he cleared the building before the whole thing toppled into the water. Burton turned to look at the destruction. There were fires all over the docks. Shrill whistles pierced the night as police and firemen ran forward to tackle the blaze. He saw several people in the distance get driven into the water, along with a few things that clearly were not people.

"It's over," Burton murmured.

"Captain Burton!" shouted Abberline as he and Challenger ran up to join Burton by what was left of the pier. "Are you all right? Blimey, I thought you'd gone down with the bloody building."

"No, I'm all right," said Burton.

"What of Bulwer-Lytton?" asked Challenger.

"He went down with the ship, as it were," said Burton.

"How?" asked Abberline.

"Our friend Captain Nemo. He bombed these buildings containing the Deep Ones' weaponry."

"By Jove," said Challenger. "Herbert got a message to him after all. I shall buy that little rotter a drink when I see him."

They might never see him again. Burton couldn't blame him if he never returned. With Mycroft Holmes threatening to take his wondrous machine, and with all of Time itself at his fingertips, Burton decided that if he were in Herbert's shoes he wouldn't return either.

The three men watched the fires in silence for a time, until the distant horizon flickered with the arrival of the sun.

ISABEL AND THE TIME MACHINE

Dawn broke over a smoldering East End. Black, noxious smoke filled an early morning sky tinted pink with the promise of a new day. Richard Francis Burton, Chief Inspector Abberline, and Professor Challenger surveyed the damage near the docks.

Burton was bone-weary, his face covered in soot. Edward Bulwer-Lytton was dead, pulled underwater by some contraption built by a man who should not exist. The things that had attacked the city had all hopped, loped or crawled back into the water, hopefully never to be seen again.

Mycroft Holmes appeared, flanked by attendants, an angry scowl marring his features. In his hand he held a crumpled piece of paper.

"I demand to know the meaning of this," he snapped, tossing the paper onto the charred ground.

Burton bent and picked up the paper, unfolding it to read.

 Dear Mycroft Holmes,
   While I am flattered that you are impressed with my Nautilus, and I admire your dedication to the British Empire, I must regretfully decline your dubious

193

"invitation." Herbert told me everything. The Nautilus is not a child's toy for you to take apart and guess as to its operation. Nor does the world need an entire fleet of such vessels traversing the globe making trouble.

However, I am a friend to mankind, and will always provide what assistance I can to the noble cause of humanity's survival. In that regard, I hope my specially designed torpedo machine stopped the latest incursion by our mutual enemies, the Deep Ones.

Yr. Faithful Servant,
Captain Nemo

Burton laughed and passed the letter to Challenger, who started reading it.

"It arrived this afternoon, but I only just now discovered it," said Mycroft Holmes. "I demand an explanation. Where is the Time Traveler? And how did he get a message to Captain Nemo aboard his *Nautilus?*"

"You'll have to ask him yourself," said Burton.

Mycroft paused, considering this. Then he reached into his coat pocket and produced another piece of paper. "This arrived a short while ago."

Burton took it and read it. "Meet me in Hyde Park near Alexandra Gate, 2am. Herbert."

"Hyde Park?" said Abberline. "What in blazes is he doing all the way out there?"

"We shall find out soon enough, said Mycroft Holmes. "For the hour is almost two. I've provided transportation for all of us. Let's be off."

Burton's heart raced along with the fast-thumping hooves of the horses that carried them through London's night time streets. Tired now, the rush of adrenaline from all that had transpired was starting to ebb. He intended to sleep for a week when this was all over.

When they arrived at the appointed place, Mycroft's men spread out, scanning every inch of Alexandra Gate for any signs of movement.

A furtive movement to Burton's right caught his attention, and he looked just in time to see the Time Machine flickering into existence. It was soundless as it grew into solidity, and Burton saw someone with Herbert, sitting awkwardly across his lap.

"Oof!" the figure said. "Calamitous contraption! Don't think for a second I'm getting back on that thing."

"I'm very sorry, my lady," said the Time Traveler. "I never considered building it for two."

The group ran toward the Time Machine, Burton taking the lead. The person with him was so familiar...

Burton stopped in his tracks as she spun around.

"Isabel?" murmured the explorer. "Isabel!"

He rushed up to wrap her tightly in a warm embrace. She returned it, holding it for a long moment before pulling back. "Richard! But you look positively dreadful. Have you been visiting brothels with that Swinburne sot?"

"No, my dear," said Burton. "Just..." He searched his friends' faces for an answer and, finding none, settled on, "Saving the world?"

Challenger bellowed laughter that boomed throughout the park, setting a distant dog to barking.

"Who are all these people?" said Isabel. "Why is it night? And where is that burning smell coming from?"

"I think I should explain," said Herbert, coming forward to stand beside Isabel. "I rescued Lady Arundell here and brought her back with me, to my own time."

"Your own time?" said Isabel. "What the devil are you talking about?"

"It's a long, complex story, my dear," said Burton. "If you will just suspend your disbelief for a moment, our friend here will try to explain."

"He had better," said Mycroft Holmes, glaring at the Time Traveler.

"Yes, well," said Herbert. "I was afraid of creating more paradoxes, you see. I remembered what Captain Burton had told me about Lady

Arundel's disappearance. She went missing October fourth, last seen in Hyde Park near Alexandra Gate."

"But it *is* August fourth," Isabel protested.

I'm sorry, my dear," said Burton, taking her hand. "But it is October twenty-third."

"What?" Isabel's face grew deathly pale.

"After I took back my Time Machine," Herbert continued. "I went far into the future, when the walls of the Tower of London had long since crumbled to dust, and moved the machine to a spot where it would no longer be within the Tower's confines once I returned to the past, er, present."

"What on earth is he talking about, Richard?" asked Isabel.

"Darling, please," Burton soothed. "Just listen."

"It was tough going," said Herbert. "I really should have put wheels on the confounded thing. Anyway, once that was done I hopped back on the Time Machine and went back through Time, to a point shortly after we returned from our undersea voyage."

"How did you get a message to Nemo?" asked Mycroft Holmes.

"I'm getting to that," said the Time Traveler. "I went to the telegraph office and dashed off—pun intended—a few missives to English language newspapers in or around the South Seas, even the southern coast of Africa. There I placed ads in each of those papers, worded so that the details would only make sense to Miss Marsh and Captain Nemo."

"Telling them to arrive here by this night and time," said Burton. "Thereby avoiding further paradoxes."

"Exactly," said Herbert, who was grinning from ear to ear at his own ingenuity.

"What about Isabel?" said Burton. "How did you bring her back to me?"

Herbert held up a finger. "That took some doing. As you know the Time Machine travels perfectly well through Time, but does not move in similar fashion through Space. After securing the advertisements, I had to hire a pair of large men with strong backs and a pantechnicon to move the thing out here to Hyde Park. I had to pay extra so that they would keep their mouths shut. Then I went back further still, to the day of Lady Arundell's disappearance."

"I was just taking a stroll through the park while visiting the city," Isabel said to Burton. "I missed you, you big oaf. I neglected to bring along a chaperone. I was minding my own business when this, this ruffian accosted me. He told me he was a friend of yours and that I was in terrible danger. He practically dragged me to that queer gizmo of his, and made me sit on his lap! Before I could climb off the blasted thing, we were here, with all of you, and it was suddenly night. Would someone please tell me what is going on?"

"He just did, my dear," said Burton, trying hard not to laugh. "You, Isabel Arundell, have just become the first Englishwoman to travel through Time."

Challenger laughed. Herbert giggled. Mycroft Holmes uttered a snort of derision.

"Oh," said Isabel. "I see. I've simply gone mad."

"No, my dear," said Burton, kissing her hand. "You have not gone mad. It was I who was mad with worry as to what had become of you. Now I know it was just Herbert mucking about through Time."

"Yes, it appears I was the cause of her disappearance all along," said Herbert. "I'm sorry about that, but if I hadn't abducted her, or returned to an earlier point to tell you she was safe and sound, I would have created yet another awful paradox. I had to fix the damage we caused during our first jaunt, without causing any more."

"I understand, Herbert," said Burton. "And I thank you. You have brought my Isabel home safe to me. That is all that matters." The explorer and the Time Traveler shook hands.

"All right," said Mycroft Holmes. "Enough chatter. The Time Machine is property of the government. I want it under lock and key."

Mycroft's men moved to surround the Time Machine.

"Now wait just a minute," said Herbert, but Burton pulled him back.

"No," said the explorer. "He is right, my friend. This is too much power for one individual to command. It should be used for the good of the Empire. We should give Mr. Holmes the control rods for safe-keeping. Here."

Burton leaned over the Time Machine, gripping the crystalline control levers. Instead of unscrewing them, however, he pulled both of them forward and backed quickly out of the way as the Time Machine's dish spun into furious motion and the device became intangible as it hurled itself into futurity.

"Burton!" said Mycroft Holmes. "Do you have any blasted idea what you have done?"

"Yes, I do," said Burton with a leering smile. "As I stated, the Time Machine is too much power for one individual."

"I shall arrest you for theft of government property," said Mycroft Holmes.

"You'll do nothing of the kind, for I have stolen nothing. Merely placed it out of your reach. Now if you'll excuse me, the Lady Arundel and I have some catching up to do."

He took Isabel's hand and turned to leave the park.

"Oh, and there will be no arrests of any of my colleagues," said Burton. "Unless you want the whole of London to know exactly what transpired here tonight."

Mycroft's eyes narrowed to slits. "Have it your way, Burton. For now."

Challenger laughed, clapping Burton hard on the back as he passed, arm in arm with Isabel.

"You're a force to be reckoned with, Burton," said the burly zoologist. "I shall drink to you tonight."

Burton didn't care about being the subject of any toasts. He only wanted to hold Isabel's hand and walk with her in the early light of dawn. He didn't know how he was going to explain her disappearance and sudden reappearance to Isabel's parents. The truth of that, like what almost happened to the city, was best kept secret. But that was a problem for tomorrow. The past no longer existed. The future wasn't here yet. All that mattered was the glorious golden Now. And Richard Francis Burton intended to hold onto that as long as he could.

PART III
THE DREAM KEY

Do what thy manhood bids thee do, from none but self expect applause;

He noblest lives and noblest dies who makes and keeps his self-made laws.

All other Life is living Death, a world where none but Phantoms dwell,

A breath, a wind, a sound, a voice, a tinkling of the camel-bell.

— -SIR RICHARD FRANCIS BURTON, *THE KASIDAH OF HAJI ABDU EL-YEZDI*

"At the door of life, by the gate of breath, There are worse things waiting for men than death."

— —ALGERNON CHARLES SWINBURNE

"No death, no doom, no anguish can arouse the surpassing despair which flows from a loss of identity. Merging with nothingness is peaceful oblivion; but to be aware of existence and yet to know that one is no longer a definite being distinguished from other beings—that one no longer has a self —that is the nameless summit of agony and dread."

— —H.P. LOVECRAFT, *THROUGH THE GATES OF THE SILVER KEY*

SWINBURNE

C aptain Sir Richard Francis Burton awoke from a comforting dream of desert sands and exotic spices, goaded by his land-lady and housekeeper, Miss Angell. In his dream, he rode horseback, a solid Arabian, the folds of his white, loose-fitting garments flowing in the warm breeze that shifted the ever-changing dunes which surrounded him. By his side on a similar horse was his wife, Isabel, wearing similar garb, their faces tanned by the Persian sun. Burton had never felt happier—until Miss Angell shook him awake.

"Captain Burton," said the old woman.

"Lemme lone," mumbled the explorer. "Araby."

"I'm sorry to disturb your rest, Captain, but someone is here to see you."

Burton's sleeping mind shifted from the sand-shrouded landscape and back into the present day. He felt the cool sheets covering him, his body remembering his comfortable bed in his rooms at Gloucester Place. His first coherent waking thought was that it was Abberline. The policeman had some nerve coming around in the dead of night.

"Tell them to go away," he said, and would have fallen back asleep almost immediately but for his housekeeper's persistent shaking of the bed.

Burton's eyes popped open, his old military training once again coming to the fore. As a soldier he had to get rest when he could, snapping to attention at a moment's notice. He sat up.

Miss Angell knelt by him. A candle sputtered on the bedside table. "What is it?"

"Your friends Mr. Milnes and Mr. Bradlaugh. They have Mr. Swinburne with them...and he's in a bad way. They asked me to wake you. I'm sorry."

Burton knuckled sleep from his eyes. "It's all right. What time is it?"

"Half past three."

Burton stared at her bleary-eyed, a lump forming in his stomach. If his friends were calling on him at this hour, their straits were dire indeed. "All right. Tell them I'm coming."

Miss Angell left the candle and felt her way out of the room while Burton got up and threw on a robe and donned his slippers. He was down the stairs in a flash and found Richard Monckton Milnes, Charles Bradlaugh, and an unconscious Algernon Charles Swinburne, lying prone on the sofa.

"What's the matter with him?" said Burton. "He must really be in his cups for you to bring him here."

"I wish this were the drink," said Bradlaugh, a worried look on his face. "This is something else, Richard."

Burton stared at his unconscious friend and sighed. To Miss Angell he said, "Will you put on some coffee?"

His housekeeper nodded and left the room. Burton took a seat in a chair opposite the sofa on which the poet lay. "Tell me exactly what happened."

"He sold a collection of his poetry, so we took him out to celebrate, explained Bradlaugh. "Long about midnight he had his usual hankerings for the lash, so Charles and I accompanied him."

"Research for a book I'm writing," added Milnes. "Well, in the middle of his, ahem, *session* he collapsed. Fainted dead away. Only we couldn't revive him. Not even smelling salts would arouse him."

"Bismillah!" Burton swore.

"So we got him dressed and brought him here, since you were closer," added Bradlaugh. "We didn't know what else to do. Imagine the scandal if word got out that any of us were at a brothel."

"It's all right, Charles," said Burton. "You did the right thing. How long has he been like this?"

Monckton Milnes and Bradlaugh exchanged questioning glances. "An hour or so," said Bradlaugh.

Burton nodded. "We'll call James Hunt. He'll know what to do and, perhaps more importantly, he'll keep this quiet."

Burton got up, went to the front door, grabbed a lantern, and lit it. Taking a police whistle from a pocket of his robe, he opened the door and blew three quick, short bursts.

"For God's sake man," said Monckton Milnes. "You're summoning the police?"

"Don't be so dramatic," answered the explorer. "I'm calling a messenger. There's a street urchin who sleeps in the alley across the way. He does odd jobs for me from time to time." Burton closed the door.

No sooner had he done so than there was a light knock at the portal. Burton opened it again to find a spindle-thin boy of about twelve years of age standing there expectantly and, despite the late— or rather, early—hour, wide awake. His threadbare clothes were almost one size too small, and he stood shivering in a worn topcoat and fingerless gloves.

"Ah, Master Thomas," said Burton with a smile. "I was afraid you'd not hear my whistle."

"I'm a light sleeper, guv," said the boy. Burton knew little about the boy, except he answered to the name Thomas Malenfant. But he was hardworking and trustworthy, and Burton liked the bright-eyed energy of the youth.

"I have a special task for you this night," said Burton as he handed the boy a shilling. "Go and fetch Dr. James Hunt." He gave the boy the address. "Do it quietly. When you return with him I'll give you another shilling."

"Yessiree, guv!"

"Do so within the hour and I'll give you two shillings."

"Right-o, Cap'n Sir Richard, sir!" he said, taking the lantern from Burton, leaping down the steps, and disappearing into the fog-shrouded gloom.

Burton shut the door with a chuckle and returned to the sitting room, glancing at his friend the poet. "I've never seen him like this. Even when he's three sheets to the bloody wind."

"This isn't the drink," repeated Bradlaugh. "This is something else."

The two men had already helped themselves to Burton's supply of brandy, so Burton shrugged and joined them. There would be no more sleep for him this night, he knew. When Miss Angell brought coffee on a silver serving tray, the three Cannibals added their brandies to the steaming cups and drank deeply while the house-keeper worried and fussed over the prone Swinburne, mopping his forehead with a cool, wet cloth.

They talked nervously, careful to spare Miss Angell the gory details of how Swinburne had fallen into this sorry state. At last, there was a knock at the door.

"Ah, that'll be Hunt." Burton got up from his chair to answer the door.

Dr. James Hunt stood in his nightgown and coat, clutching his medical bag. The boy Thomas Malenfant stood beside him, beaming expectantly for the promised shillings. Burton ushered them inside quickly, paid the boy, and sent him with Miss Angell to the kitchen to fetch him something to eat. He also asked Miss Angell to set up his old army cot in the pantry so Thomas could sleep. He might need the boy's services again, and he wanted him well-rested.

After delivering these instructions, Burton turned his attention to James Hunt, who was examining the unconscious poet. Charles Brad-laugh and Monckton Milnes had already recounted what the three of them had been doing when this mysterious ailment befell Swinburne. When the good doctor finished, he looked up from his patient. "Other than his unconsciousness, I can't find a blasted thing wrong with him. But what's more, his is not the first case I've seen today."

Burton arched an eyebrow. "Oh?"

"The first instance was this morning. A barrister who lives near

Trafalgar Square fell suddenly while on his way to work. His poor wife found him face first in the front garden. And I have heard through my medical contacts of at least four more, all over the city, all at different hours of the day. Swinburne is the last, I hope."

"And are these men all right?" said Burton, a worried edge to his voice.

James Hunt shook his head. "All still unconscious, the last I heard. I just checked on my barrister patient around six o'clock, before heading home. It's all so very strange, and has now hit closer to home than I would like."

Monckton Milnes poured another brandy down his throat. "What can we do?"

"Nothing but wait," said James Hunt. "Make him as comfortable as you can. I'll be around to check on him later in the day. In the meantime, I'd best return home and get some sleep. I have a feeling I'm going to be quite busy upon sunrise."

He took one last look at his patient before turning once more toward Burton. "And I will keep the circumstances of the onset of Swinburne's...ailment a closely guarded secret."

"Thank you," said Burton. He walked with James Hunt to the door and let him out.

Miss Angell stood quivering in the door, a bundle of nervous energy ready to pounce upon the first thing that needed doing. "Young Thomas very nearly ate us out of house and home, but he's tucked away in your cot fast asleep."

"Excellent. Will you get the spare bed ready?"

Miss Angell nodded and disappeared upstairs.

"Let's get him to bed," said Burton, and the three of them carried the unconscious poet carefully up the stairs. Fortunately, the young man wasn't heavy, and within a few minutes they had him tucked into Burton's spare bedroom. Their task completed, they retired to Burton's study just down the hall, where Monckton Milnes and Bradlaugh helped themselves to more brandy while Burton got a fire going, then collapsed into his favorite chair and lit a cigar. Sleep was the furthest thing from his mind. His every thought was on his young friend and the mysterious ailment that had so suddenly befallen him.

BURTON IS SUMMONED

Burton had a dream.

In it, he was probing inky green depths. Around him was the iron shell of the *Nautilus*, though configured differently than he remembered. He caught a glimpse of his reflection in a polished brass surface, and realized he was different too. His beard was wild and unkempt, almost white. He wore a dull blue Naval jacket and a black leather eye patch concealed his right eye. He reached up to pull it back, fearful of what he might find underneath.

"Richard!"

Burton awoke with a start, his head lolling painfully to the right as he sat up with a jerk. He had fallen asleep in his chair, the blackened remains of a cigar still clutched in his fingers. He tossed it into the fireplace, temporarily brightening the dwindling flames. Charles Bradlaugh leaned over him. "You have a visitor."

Burton looked around Bradlaugh, expecting to find Dr. James Hunt standing there, medical bag in hand, ready to give an updated prognosis on Swinburne. Instead, he found Chief Inspector Frederick George Abberline, worrying his bowler hat nervously in his hands.

"I'm sorry to call so early, but you are needed."

Burton scowled, climbing from the chair. He winced at an awful hitch in his back, and he worked to straighten it. "Whatever Mycroft Holmes wants now, it can bloody well wait."

"You'll change your mind when you hear what I have to say," said the policeman. "Miss Angell told me about your friend Swinburne. I'm sorry. But I think my summons and his condition are related."

"Is this the copper you told us about?" said Bradlaugh. He went to Abberline and introduced himself. The two men shook hands. Monckton Milnes had his head down on Burton's writing desk, snoring soundly.

"What's this all about?" said Burton, the vestiges of his dream thoroughly forgotten.

"I was sent here to fetch you regarding this strange sleeping ailment that has befallen several prominent men throughout the city," said Abberline. "Neither Mr. Holmes nor I were aware your poet friend was also affected. When did he take ill?"

"Midnight," said Burton. "I heard there were others, but what does our mutual taskmaster think I can do about it? I'm no bloody physician."

"Well," said Abberline, worrying his poor bowler even further, turning it about in his hands. "It has to do with, um, our uh…" He looked self-consciously at Bradlaugh, who was in the process of rousing Monckton Milnes.

"Go home, Charles, if you please," said Burton. "Take Richard with you."

"Very well, Dick," said Bradlaugh. "You can keep your secrets. We were just leaving." He got Monckton Milnes awake enough to take instruction, and the two of them stumbled out the door of Burton's study and disappeared down the stairs.

"Shadow Council," Abberline finished when they were gone, his voice a stage whisper. "Mr. Holmes thinks that this strange sleeping sickness points to something sinister afoot. Something not of this earth."

"I still don't see how that qualifies me," said Burton. "Now if you'll excuse me, I have a sick friend to take care of."

Burton pushed past Abberline and went to the next room, where Swinburne still lay in bed, as unconscious as he had been when

Monckton Milnes and Bradlaugh had dragged him to Burton's doorstep earlier that morning. For all anyone could tell, the poet was in a deep, peaceful sleep. Burton touched the poet's hand. It was warm to the touch, but not feverish.

"I'm sorry for your friend," said Abberline, following him into the room.

Burton nodded. "How many people are affected?"

"There are six of them so far counting Mr. Swinburne," said Abberline. "The first was stricken yesterday morning."

"The barrister near Trafalgar Square," said Burton.

"Yes. One Nigel Goforth. How did you know?"

"I have my sources too. Who else?"

Abberline pulled a well-worn notebook from his pocket and flipped through its pages. "There's a bookbinder by the name of Nathanial Peacock, a bank clerk called Mortimer Greensmith, William Nash, a clerk from Kensington, and an actor called Oliver Whiteside."

"Nothing connecting them?"

"Not that we can surmise. They are scattered all over the city, and so far as we can tell have never met nor been in contact with one another. Nor would they have any occasion to do so."

Burton turned toward Abberline. "That is indeed strange. But I see nothing of the occult at work here. Tell Holmes to find someone else. I'm busy seeing to my friend."

Abberline stared at him for a long moment, a look of befuddlement on his face. "Very well, Captain. Good day to you, sir. I hope Mr. Swinburne recovers soon."

Burton turned once more toward his friend. "So do I," he murmured as Abberline let himself out.

THE AWAKENED

Burton sat by Swinburne's bedside all morning. He talked to Swinburne, and when young Thomas fetched the morning paper from the vendor around the corner, read to him, pausing to comment on certain topics in which he and the young poet shared a mutual interest. Burton could almost imagine the youth uttering squeals of delight at some bit of literary news, or expressing colorful disdain over some draconian measure being considered by Parliament. But there was no response from the poet. He lay there peacefully, as one dead.

Burton feared for his friend, for he knew that Swinburne couldn't last long in this state. Without nourishment, his body would slowly but inexorably wither away. Miss Angell came in every few minutes to dab his lips with a sopping wet cloth and dote over him. She begged Burton to eat, but he refused.

At midmorning, Dr. James Hunt came around again. "I've got some good news," he said as he checked Swinburne's temperature and blood pressure. "The barrister awoke this morning."

"Splendid."

"Yes. I just came from there. Sat bolt upright, stared at his wife of thirty-two years, and began to utter a bizarre string of gibberish."

"Is he all right?" asked Burton.

James Hunt shrugged. "He seems to be now. From her story, I was convinced he'd had a stroke, but he's alert and eating, though he still seems befuddled, as if he doesn't know who he is or where he is. But I think his memory will come back in time."

Burton scowled. "And this is good news?"

"Yes, of a sort. It means that perhaps this sleeping sickness won't last very long. I also heard through the grapevine that two of the other men have also recovered, all showing similar behavior."

Burton uttered a sigh of relief. "Roughly twenty-four hours since they fell ill. So Algy should recover by sometime tonight."

James Hunt shrugged again, packing up his medical bag where it rested at the foot of the bed. "Makes as much sense as anything else regarding this malady. I've never seen anything like it, Richard. No one has. It has the medical community thoroughly flummoxed."

Burton nodded grimly. "My contact in the government seems to think this sickness has broad, sinister implications for the Empire."

The good doctor laughed. "I wouldn't go that far. But I'd watch Algy's behavior closely once he does regain consciousness. I'll be round again this afternoon to check on him."

He paused in the doorway. "Algy isn't my only patient."

"I know," said Burton. "I appreciate your help and your discretion."

"That's not what I mean," said Hunt. "I was talking about you. Get something to eat. Get some rest. I have a feeling you're going to need it. This thing, whatever it is, isn't over yet."

With that he stepped through the portal and was gone.

Bradlaugh and Monckton Milnes arrived at noon, the former carrying a bundle of afternoon newspapers he plopped unceremoniously onto the sideboard, almost knocking over a bottle of Saltzman's Tincture.

"What the bloody devil?" said Burton.

"The whole city is talking about it," said Milnes. "About them." He pointed at Swinburne, lying in peaceful repose like a ginger cherub.

"What are you talking about?"

"They're calling them the Awakened," said Bradlaugh. "It seems they've all recovered, roughly twenty-four hours from when they first fell ill."

"But they're talking gibberish," added Milnes.

"Yes, I heard as much from James Hunt this morning," said Burton.

"What the bloody hell do you think is going on?" said Bradlaugh.

"I don't know. We'll have to see how Algy behaves once he awakens. At least now we have some glimmer of hope that he will."

Miss Angell came up and shooed everyone out while she worried over Swinburne. Burton, Bradlaugh and Monckton Milnes took the papers into Burton's study and pored over them, scouring every detail they could glean about these so-called Awakened.

The most information came from the barrister, Harrison Goforth, who had been the first to fall ill and hence the first to recover. He was still at home, recuperating, surrounded by family and friends and exhibiting some odd behavior the article did not touch on in any detail. The other cases were similar. Several of the articles detailed the backgrounds of these singular men, but Burton saw no connection whatsoever between them and Swinburne, and couldn't imagine that Algy had ever met these men or interacted with anyone they knew. The only link any of these men had with one another was the strange ailment that befell them.

Burton ate a plate of cold cuts and smoked a cheroot, then wrote a letter to Isabel, who was visiting with her family in the country. Milnes and Bradlaugh had slunk out at some point, so Burton busied himself with working on his translation of *A Thousand Nights and a Night*, but couldn't focus on it. He kept thinking about Swinburne. Nervous energy filled him and he couldn't rest. He didn't want to miss the poet's awakening from this unusual ailment.

When Dr. James Hunt came by, Burton poured him a drink and the two sat in Burton's study and talked of the other patients. The physician was reticent to give many personal details of each patient as he understood them but spoke about their symptoms in a general sense. All the men had, upon waking, spouted a stream of incomprehensible gibberish, and all had behaved as if they had no memory of who they are or where they were. Unusual too was how they seemed ill at ease in their bodies, showing undue fascination toward flexing their fingers and arms and spending a long time examining themselves in a mirror. James Hunt noted with intrigue how he'd watched his patient, the barrister Goforth, stare in revulsion at his reflection, followed by a long session of touching his nose, blinking his eyes, and running his fingers through his bristly salt and pepper beard. None of the men spoke; they communicated by grunting and pointing. Hunt likened it to watching someone revert to a pre-verbal form of intelligence.

Burton feared even more for his friend, and he listened with rapt attention, forgetting to keep track of the hour. At last, the clock in the hall chimed midnight, and he and Dr. James Hunt sprang from their chairs and rushed into the spare bedroom to check on Swinburne.

There was no change at first. The poet lay there as still and peacefully as he had since the previous morning. But Burton noticed a slight facial twitch, and Swinburne opened his mouth in a yawn. His eyes snapped open as he sat bolt upright in the bed, blinking at Burton and the physician. Next, he opened his mouth again, and a stream of inhuman syllables came forth in low-pitched tones Burton thought impossible for the high-pitched Swinburne to produce. Then he closed his mouth and stared at Burton and James Hunt, as if expecting them to say something.

"Algy?" said Burton.

Swinburne's head turned at the sound, curiosity on his face. It seemed as if he not only failed to recognize it as his name but didn't understand that it was a name at all.

"Algy, it's me, Richard. I'm here with James Hunt. Do you remember who you are?"

Swinburne stared at them blankly.

"You're in my home at Gloucester Place. Charles Bradlaugh and Richard Monckton Milnes brought you here last night. Do you remember?"

Swinburne turned his head to the left, toward the room's sole window. It was full dark, the only light coming from lanterns flicking in a distant window. He looked around then, seemingly fascinated at the architecture evident in the walls and ceiling. The lamp Burton had lit moments earlier cast strange shadows about the room.

Swinburne lifted his arms and stared at them, flexing the pale, freckled fingers before finding his face and probing it like a blind man.

"Get him a mirror," said James Hunt, and Burton went for a small shaving mirror Miss Angell had brought up earlier. He held it aloft before Swinburne, and the poet uttered a shriek and cowered from it, pulling the covers over his chin.

"It's all right, Algy," said Burton. "It's you."

The poet quickly recovered, rising and studying his face in the mirror, turning his head this way and that, discovering his ears and tugging them before running his fingers through his unruly tangle of thick red hair.

The doctor rummaged in his medical bag.

"James is going to examine you now," said Burton. He stood back and watched as their mutual friend gave Swinburne a thorough going-over, checking everything from his blood pressure to his reflexes. Swinburne cooperated, showing as much interest in Hunt as Hunt showed in him. When he finished, he stood and looked at Burton.

"He's as healthy as outward appearances would suggest. Again, I can't find a bloody thing wrong with him."

Burton motioned for James Hunt to come closer. "Perhaps the malady goes deeper than we can observe," said the explorer. "There is definitely something off about him, don't you think?"

"There's always been something off about Algy," Hunt replied.

"No, that's not what I mean. Look at him. Absent is his characteristic twitching, his nervous energy."

James Hunt turned toward his patient and stared at him for a long moment; Swinburne busied himself with studying his reflection in the shaving mirror once more. "By Jove! You're right, Richard! I was so used to his spasms I hardly missed them. But yes, they're gone. It's as if…"

"He's someone else," Burton finished.

"Yes, but, that's impossible. He's just suffering from a peculiar form of amnesia."

"Perhaps," said Burton. He glanced at Swinburne, who returned his gaze with anything but confusion or befuddlement. Burton got the feeling the the diminutive poet was only pretending he didn't know what he and James Hunt were saying. "Is it unusual for an amnesiac to cower from their own reflection?"

"I've heard of them not recognizing their own faces," said Hunt, "but no, not that I'm aware of. This is a most singular case."

"Except for the fact that it is not that singular," said Burton. "All over London other men are exhibiting the same symptoms."

"True," said James Hunt. "But there's nothing tying these men together. Perhaps they experienced similar trauma."

"I very much doubt your barrister patient was undergoing the lash," said Burton with a grin. "We need more information."

"We need to closely watch not only Swinburne," said Hunt, "but the others. Now that they're all awake, their behavior will be more informative."

Burton nodded. "I'll keep a close eye on Algy. Please keep me apprised of your barrister and the others."

James Hunt nodded. "Help him to jog his memory. The sooner he recovers, the sooner we'll get back our old friend."

James Hunt turned to Swinburne. "So long, Algy," he said as he left.

"So long, Algy," Swinburne repeated when James Hunt had closed the bedroom door behind him.

"Algy?" said Burton, but the poet just looked at him, a bemused grin on his face.

MYCROFT HOLMES

Burton stayed up with Swinburne most of the night, naming things Swinburne pointed to and helping him when he once fell out of bed, as if he had forgotten how to walk. But he soon discovered his legs—and tottered about like a child taking its first furtive steps. Swinburne wandered into Burton's study, and the explorer followed him, pointing things out to him and keeping Swinburne from touching anything. He seemed most intrigued by Burton's wall of weapons, including various swords and spears from his travels in Africa and Persia. Then, as the first light of dawn crept over the horizon, Swinburne crashed in a heap on his sofa while Burton dozed in his favorite chair. As he dozed, he dreamed.

"Fire!" shouted Burton, and he felt the muffled thud as two torpedoes left the Nautilus *and flew toward their targets. A minute later his First Mate shouted, "Direct hit!" and the bridge of the submarine erupted in cheers. Burton grinned, but held up a steadying hand. The battle was not over yet. They watched through the forward view port as a pair of black basalt towers carved from the surrounding rock into obscene obelisks crumbled and collapsed onto the sea floor, filling the dark ocean water with debris. Debris that would help mask the* Nautilus *from the beings they'd just attacked.*

"Hard about," said Burton, his one good eye peering into the gloom they'd

just created. They needed to move quickly and attack from another angle. He had learned long ago that the best defense was to not be around when your enemy came for you. He had already lost so much; he couldn't bear losing anymore.

Nemo. Isabel. Elizabeth. All had fallen to the Deep Ones. The surface world was under attack as well, but all Burton could do was try and reduce their numbers before they marched onto the land. That, and help ships that ventured too near one of their underwater cities.

"We're coming round again," said the navigator, a big burly Sikh who reminded Burton of the submarine's previous commander.

"Fire!" said Burton.

Burton awoke suddenly, nearly falling out of his chair. *Bismillah*, he thought. *What a strange dream. I wonder what brought that on?*

He realized he had tears in his eyes and wiped them away before standing. Swinburne was nowhere to be seen, but he heard a familiar and excited voice coming from the guest bedroom, and went to investigate.

Swinburne was tucked in bed, grinning while Monckton Milnes read to him from a book of erotic poetry. "I hope you don't mind," said Monckton Milnes. "Your housekeeper let me in. She didn't want to wake you again after the other night."

"That's quite all right," said Burton. "What's going on here?"

"I've taught young Swinburne to read again," said the older man with a smile.

"Don't let Miss Angell see that book, said Burton, "or hear a word of it."

Monckton Milnes grinned and closed the book. "He has been speaking as well. Mostly parroting what I say, but he understands basic concepts. Who am I, Algy?"

Swinburne looked at Monckton Milnes and said, "Richard Monckton Milnes."

"Wonderful!" said Burton.

Swinburne pointed at Burton. "Richard Francis Burton."

"Right again!" said Monckton Milnes. "And where are you?"

Swinburne thought about this for a moment, then said, "Gloucester Place."

"This is a bloody breakthrough!" said Burton.

"Bloody breakthrough," Swinburne repeated. "Richard Francis Gloucester Place Burton. Richard bloody Monckton breakthrough Milnes."

The two men laughed despite themselves, which Swinburne seemed to take for encouragement. He pointed to himself. "Algernon Charles Swinburne."

"Algy," said Burton.

Swinburne turned his attention from the window. "Yes, Richard?"

"Are you back now?"

Swinburne fixed him with a grin. "Yes, Richard."

"It's a bloody miracle," said Monckton Milnes. "His singular physiology must have stood him in good stead."

"Perhaps," murmured the explorer, looking deeply into Swinburne's eyes. What he saw there was not Swinburne. What he saw there was something else, something black and inhuman that flitted away from Burton's scrutiny as Swinburne returned his attention toward the window.

"Algy, look at me please."

The poet returned his gaze, a playful look on his face. Burton reached up and touched the sides of Swinburne's face, his fingers tapping gently against the temples and jawline.

"I want you to look at me. Concentrate on me. Look deeply into my eyes."

Swinburne did as instructed.

"Take slow, deep breaths. Your whole body is relaxed."

Swinburne's body went limp. Burton increased the speed of his taps on the poet's face.

"Listen to me closely. I want to talk to Algy. Talk to me, Algy."

At first, there was no reaction; then Swinburne convulsed. His cheeks puffed outward as if he were about to blow out a candle, then a familiar voice said, "Richard?" The word came out as if unbidden by the speaker, as involuntary as a burp.

"Algy!"

"Richard? Is that you? My hat, everything is ghastly!"

Swinburne collapsed backward, pulling away from him. He fell back onto the bed and shook his head before snapping back upright and staring at Burton with a look of puzzlement. Then he rose from the bed and went to the window to stare out at the fog-shrouded city.

"Gloucester Place," Swinburne said again. He stared out the window like a child seeing the world for the first time.

"Mesmeric touching," said Monckton Milnes. "I've read about the practice but never witnessed it until now. And Algy's reaction!"

"We'll be right back, Algy," Burton told him. The poet turned and smiled before going back to staring out the window at the street below.

Burton tugged Monckton Milnes out into the hallway.

"What's wrong, Richard? What was that about just now?"

"I don't think that is Algy," said the explorer.

"Well, he's not back to full strength yet, that is true. But of course, it's our Algy. Who else would it be?"

"I don't know. But that's exactly what I want to find out."

Monckton Milnes glared at Burton, a look of worry painting his face. "You're frightening me, old friend."

"I know I must sound demented," said Burton. "But look at him. Can you honestly tell me that's Algernon Swinburne? He's not only completely different, but I think he's hiding something. I made real contact with him just then, but there's something else in there too. I don't know how to explain it."

Monckton Milnes nodded. "I suppose you might have a slight point, though I don't know about him hiding something. James Hunt said it would take some time for his wits to return completely."

"James Hunt has never seen anything like this before," Burton added. "No one has. We are treading through wholly unknown territory here. And I'm telling you, there is something bloody off with him!"

"All right, Richard. I'll humor you. I've learned to trust your instincts. What do you want me to do?"

"Help me keep an eye on him. I may require your expertise in parapsychological matters. You are still a member of the Society for Psychical Research?"

Monckton Milnes arched an eyebrow. "Yes, of course. But what does that have to do with poor Algy?"

Burton shrugged. "Nothing, I hope. I must go take care of something. Will you stay here? Watch him close?"

Monckton Milnes patted Burton on the shoulder. "Of course. It is my duty to both of you, as your friend and fellow Cannibal."

"Good man," said Burton as he headed downstairs. Donning his coat and topper, he disappeared out the front door.

Burton moved through the fog-shrouded gloom up Gloucester Place toward Baker Street. It was afternoon, though one couldn't tell by the amount of coal smoke in the sky. The sun was almost completely obscured, existing only as a ruddy disk high over Burton's shoulder as he moved up the crowded sidewalk.

Burton winced at inhuman shapes in the fog and had the terrible sensation that his fellow Londoners had transmogrified into physically abhorrent entities. There a tall, chitinous and many-segmented creature in a long black coat and top hat. There a street vendor with bulbous, watery eyes and a wide, gaping, toothless mouth. Burton shuddered and looked again, but the apparitions were just regular folks going about their business. But something lingered on the periphery of his vision, a feeling there was more to what he was seeing. As if the people he saw were merely facades concealing bizarre shapes beneath coats and corsets. It seemed as if the people he saw contained a vast multitude of different people. "Bismillah," Burton murmured, shaking this feeling away and hailing a hansom. A carriage pulled up, and Burton climbed inside, trying to ignore the driver's wave. For it wasn't a hand that made the gesture, but a black, insect-like feeler.

"The Diogenes Club," Burton called up and settled into the seat with a shiver. The carriage started, the horse clopping on the cobbles as they moved through the thickening fog.

I must be going mad, he thought. *I can't do so just now. Algy needs me.*

Twenty minutes later the hansom deposited Burton in front of the nondescript building that housed the infamous Diogenes Club. The explorer was just about to knock on the solid oak door when it opened, and a familiar figure stepped out.

"Captain Burton!" said Abberline.

"Frederick. Just the man I was coming to see. You and our mutual employer, of course." Burton said this last with a sneer.

Abberline nodded. "I just delivered my report on the Awakened, as the press is calling them. How is your friend Swinburne?"

"Not himself," said Burton. "A condition I'm sure he shares with the others."

Abberline gave him a fearful look and nodded. "You are more right than you know. Come inside. Mr. Holmes will be pleased you have decided to lend your expertise."

Burton followed the detective through the maze of rooms, the Club's assortment of brilliant misanthropes gravely silent as usual. They reached the Stranger's Room without incident and Abberline rapped on the door three times before entering.

Mycroft Holmes was stuffing his jowls with the remains of a bloody T-bone steak. Burton's stomach growled, and he realized with embarrassment he had neglected to eat that day, having been so preoccupied with Swinburne's strange condition.

"I see you've finally decided to join us," said Mycroft Holmes after swallowing a mouthful of meat. "I assume it was your friend Swinburne who persuaded you."

"You assume correctly," said Burton. "Something isn't right about him. I believe some entity has taken his place."

Mycroft nodded, gobbling up the remains of his lunch and dabbing his mouth with a white linen napkin stained pink from his repast before speaking. "All of the Awakened exhibit this unusual behavior. That was Inspector Abberline's assessment as well, after observing them and interviewing close friends and family members. The only question now is what do we do about it?"

"I want to know more about these other Awakened," said Burton. "Who they are, where they live. We need to observe them carefully. Only then will we discover who or what they are and what they want."

Mycroft Holmes nodded and sipped his tea. "I knew you were the perfect man for this. Utilize whatever resources you deem necessary. I consider this matter a threat to the Crown."

Burton arched an eyebrow. "I don't know that I would go that far."

"I don't have the luxury of playing it safe," said Holmes. "Something has commandeered the minds of these men, including your friend Swinburne. As far as I'm concerned, this is tantamount to an invasion."

"But from where?" asked Abberline.

"That is what we must determine," said Mycroft Holmes. "Are you up to the task, Captain Burton?"

Burton pondered the shapes he'd seen in the fog on the way over and shivered inwardly. "Yes."

THE AWAKENED

When Burton returned with Inspector Abberline to Gloucester Place, he found it packed with mutual friends of his and Swinburne's. All the Cannibals were in attendance, as well as some literary acquaintances of Swinburne's. The poet smiled as he spoke with them, but gone was his usual frenetic movement, his characteristic twitching, and he didn't touch a drop of alcohol.

"Frederick," Burton whispered to Abberline. "You met Algy once, some months ago. What is your impression of him now?"

The detective regarded Swinburne for a long moment. Finally, he said, "Although I met him only briefly, I must say that this is not the man I met. People do change, but not that much. They say the eyes are the windows to the soul. Whatever is peering out at us now isn't Mr. Swinburne, at least not as I remember him."

"My sentiments exactly. Ordinarily, Algy would be thoroughly drunk by now, but look at him! He's stone sober. I've never seen him completely sober since I've known him."

"Blimey!" said the inspector. "Never?"

"It's as if he is a completely different person masquerading as the old one, and not very convincingly. I tell you, Frederick, I made contact with something when I put him under a mesmeric trance earlier. There's someone—some*thing*—else in there with him. If the poor man is still in there at all. I'm worried for him."

Abberline looked at Burton. "I'm genuinely sorry for your friend, Captain. After all we've seen and been through together, I've learned to take you at your word, no matter how bizarre that word is. This whole thing certainly has Mycroft Holmes flummoxed. And he doesn't worry easily. He hates not knowing what is going to happen next, and he's as in the dark as any of us."

Burton nodded. "His predictive powers, as vast as they may be, are all for naught this time. I admit the man could stand to learn some humility, but this has me scared as well. Something is happening, or about to happen. And we must know what it is."

"I've put some of my best men on the other Awakened. They'll follow them once they've fully recovered, see what they're up to."

"What if they fall back into their ordinary routines?" Burton asked.

"Then we have nothing to worry about. But if not..." He let the thought fall off as Miss Angell hove into view, carrying a silver tray loaded with cold cuts.

"I hope you are not expecting me to keep feeding your Cannibal Club lot, Captain Burton," she said with a gruff tone.

"No, I most certainly do not," Burton said. "I'll run them out shortly. You have my word."

His housekeeper snorted in derision and sauntered off.

Swinburne came around the corner then, beaming at Burton. "Richard, I want to let you know that I will be returning home tonight. I thank you for your hospitality."

"Are you sure, Algy? You can stay as long as you need."

The poet shook his head. "No, no. I don't want to be any more trouble. I think I will recover better at home."

"Well," said Burton, "if you think that's best."

"I do."

Swinburne stood there as if searching for something else to say before returning to the bedroom full of their fellow Cannibals, where Charles Duncan Cameron was in the midst of an unsuccessful attempt at a ribald joke.

Burton led Abberline into his study and closed the door. Burton smoked while Abberline helped himself to a rare on-duty brandy. When they were done, Burton told everyone it was time to go, promising they would convene that evening at Bartolini's for a regular meeting of the Cannibal Club. When Burton saw the last one out—a drunken Thomas Bendyshe—he turned to see Swinburne standing at the top of the stairs in the clothes he had been wearing when Bradlaugh and Monckton Milnes had brought him to Burton's door two evenings ago. He smiled as he stepped carefully down the stairs, as if still unaccustomed to his legs.

"Leaving so soon?"

"Yes. James Hunt told me I must resume my normal habits if I am to regain all of my memory."

"Do you know the way home? I could accompany you if you wish."

"No thank you, Richard. I know the loci...the address."

Burton opened the door once more and out Swinburne went with nary a look back. They watched him walk calmly down the stairs and turn right toward Baker Street. He disappeared into the afternoon crowd.

"I should put a man on him," said Abberline once Burton closed the door.

"No, let me look after him."

"He'll recognize you."

Burton grinned. "Do you not remember our sojourn into the Caldron? I assure you, he won't recognize me."

"By Jove, you're right. I almost forgot. My own mum wouldn't have recognized me in that dingy getup you had me in that night."

"I'll let Algy get home and settled, then track his movements from there. Will you keep me apprised of what the other Awakened are up to?"

"Of course," said Abberline. "You can count on it. We should meet daily to compare notes. I am to meet with Mr. Holmes every afternoon at three o'clock in the Stranger's Room of the Diogenes Club."

"Then we shall meet daily at one o'clock," said Burton.

The two men shook hands and Abberline bid Burton a good afternoon and departed, leaving the explorer alone at the front door, a bundle of nervous energy. He turned and headed upstairs. He needed to prepare his disguise.

Twenty minutes later a man in dark, soot-stained clothes and boots and a threadbare slouch hat walked downstairs. He was about to place his hand on the doorknob and twist it when something struck him on the head, knocking his hat askew.

"Who are you, ruffian?" shouted Miss Angell as she swatted the man with a broom. "Wait until the master of this house hears of this, you miserable lout!"

"Mother Angell!" Burton shouted, grabbing the broom as it came down for another swat. "It's me!"

Miss Angell's face went from a chalky white to a deep red of shame. "Captain Burton! Oh, I'm so sorry! I had no idea it was you. You scared me half to death!"

"My apologies," said Burton as he handed the broom back to his housekeeper.

"Oh, I am sorry too, Captain. Please accept my apology."

"Your apology is accepted," said Burton with a wry grin. "I'm no worse for wear. I shall remember never to cross you."

Miss Angell blushed even more at that. "Oh pish-tosh. You could never get on my bad side. Now, where are you going in that hideous outfit? No. Never you mind. I don't want to know. Since you've taken on with that government fellow, there's been no end to your clandestine goings on."

"Mother Angell, you have no idea."

"And I'd like to keep it that way, if it's all the same to you, Captain Burton."

"As you wish," said Burton, touching his dingy hat and giving a courtly bow. "Now if you will excuse me." Burton opened the front door and was gone, leaving an embarrassed and befuddled housekeeper staring out after him.

OTHER LONDONS

Burton had inwardly hoped his old friend would quickly return to his old ways, getting reacquainted with his familiar haunts. But upon leaving Grosvenor Place, the new Algernon Charles Swinburne walked purposefully past every pub and shunned every opportunity for female companionship that was available at this hour and instead knocked at the door of the home of the barrister, Harrison Goforth, the first to be afflicted with whatever had befallen Swinburne and the others. At first, Burton was surprised, but soon realized that the young man probably wanted to meet another in his condition to compare notes, as it were. Burton stood watching them from the corner, Swinburne standing on Goforth's top step as the much older man looked him up and down. From this distance, he couldn't tell what they were saying, but the old gentleman seemed to warm up quickly to Swinburne's presence, and they clasped arms in a peculiar handshake, each man grabbing the other's forearm and wrapping their arms around each other in a brisk shake before releasing. This turned into the two pointing at one another's arms and legs and laughing at the seeming absurdity of human construction. Then Goforth reached inside his door, said something to someone inside, and returned with his hat, a gray bowler, in his hand. He slapped it onto his head, and the two men sauntered off as if they were old friends who had known each other for years.

Burton watched for a moment more from his hiding place next to a lamp post and spied a police officer in a dark coat emerge from the alley across the lane and follow at a leisurely pace. This, of course, was the man Abberline had set on Goforth to track his movements. Burton moved off behind him, keeping his distance, careful not to arouse the policeman's suspicions as well as Swinburne's. He would likely have a difficult time explaining to the copper who he was and what he was doing and would lose track of Swinburne in the process.

Swinburne and Goforth made a day of it, moving about the city like a pair of tourists, pointing out the architecture of various buildings, and dining in a restaurant near the Strand. But what astounded Burton the most was when they spent the afternoon at a meeting of the Theosophic Society. Swinburne had never shown the slightest interest in the occult. Like Burton, he had always been a devout unbeliever in anything remotely supernatural. So, Burton was shocked when they disappeared into the Theosophes' regular meeting place. He loitered about for several minutes before consulting his pocket watch and heading off to meet with Abberline at their appointed time and place. He caught a hansom and arrived in front of the Diogenes Club just as Abberline was coming up the sidewalk.

"Captain Burton? Is that you?"

Burton removed his hat. "It is indeed."

"By Jove! I barely recognized you. I'm glad you're on my side."

"I just left from trailing Algy," said the explorer.

"Aye. And what's your friend up to?"

"I'm not sure yet, but I don't like it." Burton described what he had witnessed.

Abberline nodded. "That does indeed sound strange. And you said he's with Goforth?"

"At the Theosophic Society," said Burton. "Algy's never been interested in the occult."

The policeman shrugged. "Perhaps they're looking for an explanation for their mutual condition? After all, medical science doesn't know the answer to what befell them."

Burton shook his head. "I don't think so."

"Well, at any rate, it fits with what we've witnessed of the others' behavior."

"Oh?" Burton raised an eyebrow.

"The rest of the Awakened have all paired off as well. Three groups of two. I figured they had read about each other in the paper and met to see if they could learn more about what happened."

"That was my initial guess as well," said Burton.

"But each of my men has described the same as you, that they met, made introductions, and then went off like they were fast friends. It boggles the mind, it does."

"I saw your man tailing Goforth, by the way," said Burton.

"Yes, Havisham. Good man. Can't shake him off with a stick, that one."

"Yes, well. I made him easily. Next time, each of your men should be in plain clothes. It would not look good should it be discovered that the police are following certain of the citizenry."

Abberline's mouth gaped in surprise. "No, I should think not. Quite right, Captain. I'll let my men know immediately."

He checked his watch. "I'm going in to meet with Mr. Holmes. Are you coming in?"

"No."

"Well, then I'll be around to Gloucester Place this evening to let you know what he says."

"Sounds good."

The two nodded to each other and parted ways. Burton moved up the street, eager to get away from the Diogenes Club. He realized he hadn't had another bout of whatever feeling had plagued him that morning, and wondered if it had been temporary, or if he had merely been so focused on keeping up with Swinburne and his new friend that he hadn't noticed anything was amiss. He looked around cautiously, seeking the faces of his fellow Londoners to see if they held something else.

At first, he saw nothing other than the regular hustle and bustle of men and women going about their daily affairs. A street urchin sold papers on the corner, reminding him of young Thomas Malenfant. An elderly man and woman in swishing finery left an establishment and crossed the street, carefully avoiding a lumbering black pantechnicon pulled by a pair of large drays. This reminded Burton unsettlingly of his encounter with the infamous Professor Moriarty, and he continued onward.

A dense gray fog rolled in, obscuring buildings and sky and leaving only vague outlines of the city's structures. As the sun danced across particulates in the air, Burton swore he saw a massive shape hovering in the distance, like some strange airship. It was held aloft by a huge ovoid mass, like a giant balloon, and had a long gondola suspended underneath. Burton squinted into the fog, eager to make out additional details, but it was gone.

Someone bumped into him, and he realized he had stopped in the middle of the crowded sidewalk. He stared at who had hit him and saw a short fellow with enormous black wings growing from his back. Burton blinked and the wings were gone.

Burton's heart beat rapidly in his chest as the sensation he'd experienced that morning came on stronger than before. He moved through the crowd of people and sought refuge against the dirty brick facade of a building that stood on the corner of Fleet Street and Chancery Lane. Burton gripped the brickwork and stared up the street at a mind-numbing array of people and conveyances transposed over the familiar street traffic he knew. An elephant lumbered up the street, a gilded litter sitting atop its back containing a swarthy, officious-looking man with a thick mustache and decked out in flowing blue silk. An impossibly large turban sat atop his head. A man moved passed Burton wearing a long leather coat with flames embossed upon it. He was tall and thin, with a gray mustache and long beard. A tall stovepipe perched on his head with brass-rimmed goggles wrapped tightly around the brim. In a moment these apparitions faded, leaving behind the usual London scenery.

"Bismillah," Burton murmured. *Pull yourself together!*

The weird tableau was gone, but it once again left Burton with the feeling that each reality he had witnessed existed at once, one on top of the other, like colored plates of glass stacked upon each other. The street vendor selling apples across the street was also a tall, muscled warrior, clad only in sandals and a loincloth, a bronze sword hanging from a leather scabbard upon his broad back. The young woman stepping down from the carriage near where Burton stood was also an Atlantean priestess in a flowing robe of white silk, uttering some mysterious rite in an ancient and long-forgotten tongue. The thought that there were other places, other Londons, somehow co-existing with this one, was pervasive and all-encompassing. It made him sick with terror.

Burton squeezed his eyes shut and gagged, thankful that he hadn't yet eaten. He began muttering a Sufi meditation technique, which helped calm his jangled nerves. When he thought he had a handle on things he reopened his eyes, pleased to find that everything had once again returned to normal.

But for how long?

Burton hailed a carriage and had the driver take him to the meeting place of the Theosophic Society. If he was lucky, he could still catch Swinburne and Goforth as they left the meeting.

A GUN FOR SHOGGOTHS

Burton loitered about the entrance to the Theosophic Society, which met in a white-columned building near Piccadilly Circus. He received wary glances from the doorman and departed, moving to an outdoor cafe across the street. The policeman Abberline had put on Goforth was nowhere to be seen. After half an hour the doors opened, and a group of men and women spewed forth from the open portal. Taking up the rear were Swinburne and Goforth, who looked even more chummy than they had when they had entered. Burton had no idea what sort of discussion they had, but it appeared as if it agreed with them. They laughed and smiled, nodding at some of the others as the throng broke up and everyone went their separate ways, walking or hailing carriages and hansoms, which seemed to suddenly appear at the curb as soon as the doors opened. Swinburne and Goforth eschewed transportation and instead walked east toward Coventry Street, nearing Burton's position. He pretended to be interested in the newspaper someone had left behind on the table as they passed, both talking in a strange language Burton, for all his linguistic skill, couldn't identify.

Burton set the paper down and waited a beat for them to pass by, then got up and followed them through a maze of streets. So intent were they on conversing in that queer tongue of theirs and gawking at the city's architecture that they failed to register Burton's presence.

As Burton listened to them, he picked up on something even more strange. They weren't fully utilizing the peculiar language they spoke to one another, but instead peppered it with English. Burton picked up random words like 'maker', 'building' and 'watch.' It was almost as if Swinburne and this Goforth had developed a bizarre pidgin dialect, and Burton feared he knew why.

The two men turned right and down a narrow lane lined with shops—a candle maker's, a haberdasher's, and, down at the far end, a watchmaker's. Swinburne and Goforth strode purposefully toward this establishment, and Burton stopped to stare into the window of the candle shop, where a tradesman practiced his art with consummate skill, smiling at Burton while hovering over a vat of boiling wax.

Burton waited until the two men had entered the watch shop before turning his attention toward them, moving cautiously to the window of the watchmaker's and peering carefully inside. That was when he heard a noise he had hoped he would never hear again.

It was the unmistakable oily sliding sound of a shoggoth. Burton turned and glanced to his right, down a narrow alley between two shops. The blasphemous blob was gurgling toward him, sliding along the cobbles, its repugnant iridescence catching the light and highlighting the skeletal remains of vermin trapped within its undulating matrix. Gripped by surprise and fear, Burton failed to act before the loathsome entity had excreted from the narrow alley and interposed itself between Burton and the way he had come.

"Bismillah!" Burton swore, and broke into a run, diving into another narrow alley across from the watch shop. Burton huffed, in a panic. He had never seen a shoggoth out in broad daylight. The implications were dire. But he could only worry about that if he lived to tell the tale. Burton ran for his life, emerging at the far end of the narrow passage into a quiet and dingy side street, not a single solitary soul in evidence. He glanced behind him and caught a flash of pulsing ooze as the shoggoth slid easily up the alley, its bulk conforming to every ledge, every cornice, every bit of debris that would slow down a biped held upright by an internal skeleton.

Burton dashed to the right, looking around frantically for anyone who might be able to offer any assistance. He knew there was nowhere he could run that the shoggoth could not catch him. The amorphous blob could slide easily into any crevice or keyhole. But in his panicked mind, he thought his only hope was to find solace in some other, some group. Perhaps if he attracted attention to it, the shoggoth would slink away.

Burton pounded on doors and shouted up at second story windows. But no movement was evident behind the dark glass, and no one opened up to allow him entry. He moved to a brown brick building at the end of the lane, pounding on the solid wooden door there. At his surprise it opened inward, causing Burton to fall into the dim portal beyond. He fell against a large barrel chest and looked up to see a bristly black beard and two wide staring eyes. Familiar eyes.

"Challenger!"

Professor George Edward Challenger stared down at the explorer, a grim expression on his face. His eyes were wide and bloodshot, and he had a quivering energy about him. "Quick! Get inside!"

Challenger gripped Burton by the front of his shirt and hauled him through the doorway, then stepped out past the dazed and startled explorer. Burton saw he had something in his left hand, a long length of curving brass that smelled strongly of kerosene. Burton's eyes widened as he noticed a flame sputtering furtively from the device's far end. Challenger took aim at the shoggoth and pulled a trigger, and the little spark grew into a jet of fire that enveloped the shoggoth. "Go back to hell, you putrescent bastard!" Challenger yelled, uttering a maniacal laugh as the shoggoth writhed in the flames that danced along its bulk. Its many bubble-like eyes puckered and popped along its length, and a noxious sea-stench mixed with burning kerosene assaulted Burton's nostrils. He stood in the doorway as the shoggoth slid away from them, its volume slowly reduced by the destroying flames. It slipped into a storm drain on the opposite side of the street and they saw it no more.

Challenger dowsed his flame and spun toward Burton. "Get inside, damn your eyes! Before they see!" He pushed Burton inside and slammed the door, locking it with a heavy set of bolts made redundant by the sheer number of them. "Come on," blurted Challenger, and Burton followed him up a winding staircase to the topmost floor of the building he occupied.

"Bismillah!" Burton found himself standing in Challenger's infamous museum, where he displayed the unusual array of artifacts he'd collected on his much-publicized trip to South America, a trip cloaked as much in mystery as it was in outlandish blandishments. Burton now believed his story. A small triceratops skull sat across the room upon a broad pedestal, its empty eye sockets staring. A lump formed in Burton's stomach as he realized it wasn't a fossil, but actual *bone*. His eyes darted between display cases filled with similar finds and grainy photographs of Challenger's black porters standing next to titanic creatures that had been shot. Creatures the world at large thought extinct. "This place is amazing."

"Thank you," said Challenger as he moved to a window to look down on the street below. His head moved warily from side to side, and he pulled the shades before turning toward Burton and tossing his strange flame gun onto the floor with a heavy thud. "Welcome to my museum."

"What is that thing?" asked Burton, pointing to the exotic weapon.

"I call it a Shoggoth gun. It's a flame-thrower. Fire is the only thing that seems to kill them."

"You've encountered them recently?"

The burly zoologist stared at him grimly. "Oh yes. I used to hunt them at night in the Cauldron. When it was still safe to go out at night."

"It has never been safe in the Cauldron."

"I mean safe from them." Challenger jerked a thumb at the window. "At first I thought they were a holdover from our adventure stopping Bulwer-Lytton's cult. Now I think they are part of something new and equally sinister. Now the oily blighters hunt me. I saw you running up the lane, and I knew there was only one thing upon this earth that could make Captain Sir Richard Francis Burton run with such obvious terror." He grinned, and it looked for all the world like a sneer. Challenger looked like he hadn't slept.

"What's wrong, old friend?"

"Nothing is what it seems," Challenger said, moving to a mahogany sideboard where he poured himself and Burton a brandy. He handed Burton one with a shaky hand before downing his own and pouring himself another.

"You don't look well," Burton said.

Challenger laughed. "Why should I? I haven't slept in days, and those bloody things are on the march again. Something is stirring, friend Burton. I just don't know what yet."

"Have you read the papers?"

Challenger arched an eyebrow. Burton glanced about the cluttered room, which looked as if he had been sleeping there, and found that morning's edition of *The London Mail*. "Here," he said, shuffling pages until he saw the latest story about the Awakened. Challenger took it and read, pacing the floor slowly.

"Gads! And this is what you were doing?"

"Following my friend, the poet Algernon Swinburne, and a barrister called Harrison Goforth."

Challenger's eyes shifted back and forth, and he ran his sausage fingers through his thick dark beard. "And you think your friend is no longer your friend."

"In a manner of speaking. Yes, I think so."

"See what I meant when I said nothing is as it seems?"

"What do you know about all this?" asked Burton after a beat.

Challenger regarded the floor. "Only that I am losing my mind. I see flashes of things that cannot be. People who are not people, at least temporarily. Things in the sky. Buildings transmogrify, then return to their rightful shapes."

"Buildings?"

"Yes. Yesterday the Westminster clock tower became a pearlescent minaret, gleaming in the morning sun. It wavered, then the familiar clock was back. I haven't been outside since. And the dreams, Burton. Never have I had such dreams. Not since our time with Nemo in that region of the ocean nearest that blasphemous, sunken landmass."

Burton nodded, remembering the sea of bad dreams they had passed through on their way to the Arctic Circle. "I've had those dreams too. Visions, like you're someone else?"

Challenger's eyes bulged. "Yes! You too? Perhaps I am not insane after all."

"They'll have to cart us both off to Bedlam if that is the case," said Burton. "You've been staying here? What of your wife?"

"I thought it would be safest for her out of the city with all these bloody shoggoths about. She is with her mother in Kent. And yes, I have been staying here. No place is safe. I can defend myself up here, like a king in his castle." He laughed at that, and Burton wondered about his sanity.

"I assume you are working on this for Mycroft Holmes?"

Burton nodded. "You assume correctly."

"That man is going to be your ruination."

Burton regarded his friend for a long time. "I need to go. Do you think it's safe?"

Challenger shrugged his broad shoulders. "As safe is it can be. That shoggoth took a great risk showing itself in the daytime. You were following your friend Swinburne when it came upon you?"

"Yes. It must have been protecting them."

"If the shoggoths are in league with them, this can't be good," said Challenger.

"I must go. Can you make more of those shoggoth guns?"

Challenger shot Burton another of his sneering smiles. "Of course. How many did you have in mind?"

"As many as you can."

AN EXTRAORDINARY STONE

Burton returned to Gloucester Place wary and afraid, sticking to public places and availing himself of the city's many carriage drivers until he was deposited safely upon his doorstep. He took one last look around to make sure no eyes—human or inhuman—were on him. Even with Challenger's shoggoth-gun secreted beneath his coat, he felt on edge.

He took an early supper and ate ravenously, then retired upstairs to pen a letter to Isabel, telling her he thought it best if she remained at her family's country estate until he sent for her. He hated to frighten her so, but she knew of his work with the Shadow Council and its often-sinister importance. Besides, his jangled nerves couldn't take it if anything untoward happened to his beloved. Everything would be fine once he got to the bottom of this latest preternatural puzzle.

Burton drank and smoked, scowling as he remembered his promise to meet with his fellow Cannibals that night. He could not risk going out after dark. It wasn't safe, at least for him. Then he thought of poor Professor Challenger, sleeping fitfully on the floor of his museum, his every thought haunted by shoggoths lurking around every corner. At some point, he dozed in his favorite chair—

—And found himself standing in the gondola of an impossible airship hovering over a vast desert, the hot wind making shifting snakes of the countless dunes. He wore a flowing white robe, wielding a spyglass with hands browned by the sun. Beside him in similar garb was his Isabel, her face as tan as the dunes hundreds of feet beneath them. She squinted into the distance, and he followed her gaze to the horizon, where a gargantuan black pyramid stood, gleaming darkly in the sun.

"Bismillah!" Burton heard himself say, but it didn't sound like him. It was a voice made raw by hot desert winds.

"There it is, my love," said this Isabel. She was hard and lean, wearing pants and boots like a man. A thin scimitar hung from her belt, and Burton sensed that this weapon was as lethal in this dream-Isabel's hands as it would be in his own.

"Yes. We've found it. We need to tell El-Yezdi." He pounded his booted foot on the floor of the gondola, and it rang out with a metallic echo. Burton realized then that his dream-self was not standing on a wooden platform suspended beneath the giant pale gasbag of a dirigible, but the familiar metal outline of the *Nautilus*!

"Captain Burton!"

Burton sat up and looking around, bleary-eyed. Someone had called his name. But who? He turned toward the door to spy Miss Angell standing there.

"I'm sorry to wake you, but Inspector Abberline is here to see you."

Burton glanced about, saw the sunlight filtering in through the window behind him. "Of course. Send him up."

Burton checked his pocket watch and was surprised to see it was almost nine o'clock in the morning. He flexed to crack his aching back as Abberline appeared in the doorway, removing his battered brown bowler.

"Sorry to wake you."

"No apologies necessary. It appears I fell asleep in my favorite chair. The bloody thing is fine for sitting but atrocious for sleeping. What can I help you with this morning?"

"Well," said Abberline. "I came round first of all to make sure you were all right. None of the men I put on the Awakened checked in last night."

A cold chill fled up Burton's spine. "Really? I didn't notice the man you put on Goforth yesterday afternoon. I returned to the Theosophic Society to try and catch Swinburne and his new friend leaving their meeting."

"And?" said Abberline.

"I followed them to a watchmaker's shop, where I was run off by a shoggoth."

"Blimey! I hoped never to see one of those bleedin' jelly things again."

"As did I," said Burton. "And if one accosted me, perhaps they waylaid your men. Oh, I'm dreadfully sorry, Frederick."

Abberline looked downcast. "Bloody hell."

"But there was something else you came to see me about?' asked Burton, eager to change the subject.

"Oh, yes. There's been a most unusual robbery," said Abberline.

"Oh? Well, unusual has been my stock and trade as of late. Come have a seat and tell me about it."

Burton moved round to sit behind his writing desk while Abberline took a chair across from him. "I'll get straight to it," he said. "Someone broke into the British Museum last night and stole a meteorite."

"Bismillah, that is strange. But what is even stranger, at least to me, is that our mutual employer thinks this is somehow related to the Awakened."

Abberline gave a small nod. "Aye, that he does."

"And why is that?"

"Because the last people to be seen near the exhibit when the museum closed were Mr. Goforth and Mr. Swinburne."

A knot formed in Burton's stomach. Algernon Charles Swinburne was many things, but a thief was not one of them. Until now. He inwardly cursed whatever entity had Shanghaied the poet's body.

"There's more to it than that, I'm sure," said Burton.

"Yes. The meteorite is said to enhance certain psychic powers."

Burton nodded. "I don't believe I am familiar with this."

"It's called the Wold Cottage meteorite, named for where it fell, way back in 1795."

Miss Angell brought up a tray laden with scrambled eggs and sausage, as well as a carafe of steaming hot coffee. Despite initially declining, the inspector tucked in and ate ravenously before telling Burton the rest of the strange tale.

"The meteorite has been the source of no small amount of unusualness since its installation at the museum," said Abberline after a sip of coffee. "People have reported seeing queer apparitions, and those who claim to be clairvoyant in some way have admitted to seeing visions."

Burton remembered his latest dream and shuddered. "Visions?"

"Yes. As a policeman, you hear them all the time. My Da' used to scare me to sleep with tales from his time on the beat, which included the block where the museum sits. But as I grew older, I never gave much truck to such rubbish. That is, uh, until..."

"You and I met," Burton finished for him, a bemused grin playing on his lips.

"Exactly. It has nothing to do with you, though. I'm just used to the world working in a certain way, you see. I've seen some terrible things in my time as a copper, but there was always a human cause. A footprint, a murder weapon left behind, and that leads us straight to the killer. A human killer."

"And now?"

"Now, I don't know what to think. Maybe there are ghosts. I know for a fact there are monsters. I've seen them. Both the human and the other kind."

Abberline drained his coffee, and Burton could see that his hands were shaking. "Bloody shoggoths," the inspector mumbled.

"It isn't always a spectre or phantasm," said Burton. "Perhaps there is a rational explanation."

"Well, there is more to the tale," said Abberline. "A few years ago, the sightings and visions got so bad the curator traced everything back to when they first installed the meteor, generations before he was born. He had some of his geology boys crack it open, and they found a thick vein of some black, shiny, rocky substance they could never quite identify. All they knew for sure was that they had never seen it before, and that it didn't come from Earth."

"That part should be obvious," said Burton as he poured a little brandy in his coffee and gave it an exploratory taste. "After all, it did fall from the sky."

"Indeed. But the strangest part was, all the eerie activity increased. The curator then had the entire vein removed from the rock—as best they could without further damaging it; there's still some left—and the ghostly visions all but ceased."

"Where is the substance they removed?"

Abberline shrugged. "No one knows. This was done by the current curator's predecessor. He's looking through the museum records now. I don't have to tell you Mycroft Holmes is very interested in getting his hands on that queer dust."

Burton sneered and nodded. "But there was still some left in the meteorite."

"Abberline nodded. "A meteorite which is now missing."

"All right," said Burton, tapping his bottom lip. "Let's put the pieces together, as we know them. A meteorite containing a substance that can amplify psychic powers has been stolen by a group of men who have had their bodies taken over by a group of possibly malevolent entities for some unknown purpose."

"That was my figuring as well," said Abberline. "And the sum doesn't add up to anything good as far as I can tell."

"No, it most certainly does not," said Burton. "But tell me, as an officer of the law, can someone be found guilty if they were not in charge of their faculties?"

"The basic madness plea," said Abberline. "I've seen it work before, but it usually gets the perpetrator a lifetime in Bedlam instead of a prison. And he would have to prove he was not in control at the time of the crime, and not just playacting."

Burton nodded thoughtfully. "Let's go to the museum. I want to see the crime scene firsthand."

"I can arrange that. Come with me."

Thirty minutes later, Burton and Abberline exited a hansom at the steps of the British Museum. The entrance to the geology exhibit was bustling with policemen and a pair of confused museum docents who stammered and stared wide-eyed at the officers who questioned them. After showing their credentials, Burton and Abberline were ushered down a wide corridor lined with rows of pedestals containing every rock and mineral specimen imaginable. The display cases reminded Burton of Challenger's extraordinary museum, as well as the room outfitted for that purpose aboard Nemo's wondrous *Nautilus*. The rocks and crystals, pretty as they were, paled in comparison to those unique specimens. Burton was surprised to find rather large lumps of gold, silver, and platinum among the museum's collection. If anything was stolen, he mused, surely those precious elements would have been pilfered before some plain old meteorite.

The corridor led to a large circular alcove at the far end, at the center of which was an empty pedestal surrounded by a cluster of shattered glass. Smaller displays covered the walls of the alcove, these also containing meteorites of varying sizes and shapes. An older man in a dark suit was speaking gruffly to what appeared to be an elderly, stoop-shouldered security guard employed by the museum.

"My men have been over this place with a fine-toothed comb," said Abberline. "Mr. Holmes even sent for his brother, the famous consulting detective Sherlock Holmes. But he received a bit of bad news this morning."

"Oh?" said Burton.

"Yes. Mr. Sherlock Holmes is dead. He fell from the Reichenbach Falls last night, tangling with that dastardly Moriarty chap. It appears both men fell to their doom."

"Bismillah! That's horrendous."

"Yes. So, it appears we are on our own."

They waited until Abner Donenfeld, the museum's curator, was done berating the poor security guard. Burton knew Donenfeld from the Royal Geographical Society, though the two were hardly friends. He cast a sidelong glance at Burton before dismissing the guard.

"Hold on there," said Abberline, flashing his credentials again. "I am Inspector Abberline, and this is Captain Sir Richard Francis Burton, assisting me on behalf of Mycroft Holmes. We have a few questions."

"Richard?" said Donenfeld. "Working with the police? I thought you'd be halfway to some mosquito-infested diplomatic post on the far side of the world by now."

"Not quite, Abner," said Burton. "I'm here about the meteorite theft. It's part of another case I am assisting Inspector Abberline with. We have a few questions for you and your man."

Abner Donenfeld was tall, with a noble bearing and an aquiline nose. Receding, silver-gray hair topped his head, becoming thick, mutton chop sideburns. He wore an expensive tailored top coat and crisp trousers, and glared at Burton with cold gray eyes.

The guard looked up at Burton, confused. He was a short, stoop-shouldered man who quivered involuntarily. Thin wisps of white hair clung to a tight-skinned, liver-spotted head, and he seemed the very epitome of frailty. "I told the coppers all I know. That bloomin' space rock has been nothin' but trouble since it came here, if you don't mind my sayin' so, Mr. Donenfeld."

"It's all right, Harvey. Tell them whatever they wish to know." He fixed Burton with an officious stare. "Mr. Dunn has been dismissed as of this morning."

"It's all my fault," said the former guard, a tinge of sadness choking him. "But I saw it all. At least, I think I did."

"Good," said Burton. "Tell us everything you can."

There were eight of them, kind of hangin' round near closin'. I didn't pay 'em no mind at first, but when I finished lettin' folks out and lockin' up, I came back here to start my rounds and there they was, all standin' around the pedestal, holdin' hands and chantin' this strange chant, like nothin' I ever heard. Almost inhuman it was, all gutteral like. More like animal sounds than actual words."

Burton reached into his coat pocket and removed a photograph of Swinburne he had brought along for this purpose. "Was this one of the men?"

Harvey Dunn took the photo and studied it closely. "Yessiree. That's one of the blokes all right. "I'd recognize that shock o' flame red hair anywheres."

"Mr. Dunn already identified the rest of the Awakened from portraits provided by their families," Abberline explained.

The old guard nodded. "Aye. That was them all right. They was standin' around like they was in some kinda trance or somethin'. Gave me the willies if you catch my meanin'. There's been lots of queer goings on around that stone. I'm not sorry to see it go." He glanced at Donenfeld as he said this last, expecting a final rebuke. The museum curator regarded him coldly but said nothing.

"After the chanting, what happened?" asked Burton.

"Well, that was the strange part. Things got all fuzzy like, and the scenery changed. The lights flickered, and all of a sudden there were these giant braziers all lit up with fire, like something out of the Egyptian Room here at the museum. Now there's a place that'll give a bloke the willies late at night. All them mummies—."

"Mr. Dunn," said Donenfeld.

"Uh, yes, as I was sayin', everything changed, and the men changed too. They were suddenly wearin' these queer robes, like they was doin' some kinda queer ceremony. You never heard such strange chantin'. I tells 'em to stop and get out, the museum's closed. They just turned and looked at me and kept on chanting. Them some slimy thing, like a clear sack full of eyes, came squeezing through the window yonder." He pointed to a narrow window spaced more than ten feet from the floor of the museum. "It plopped onto the floor and started sliding toward me. I turned and lit out on the double."

"Then what happened?" asked Burton.

"Well, when I turned the corner, I wasn't in the museum no more. I was in this crowded outdoor market, only like nothing anyone has ever seen. People were sellin' this strange sorta fruit, all big and purple, with these pointy bits like spikes stickin' out every which way, and it stank to high heaven. And the people! Lordy, but they weren't people at all. Some of them looked just like you an' me, only with green scales like a lizard. Others were funny shapes, like oblongs covered in quiverin' feelers, and green barrels with starfish heads. I was frightened, but I couldn't go nowhere. Back the way I had come it was more of the same. I wandered around for hours. Nobody could help me. Nobody could even understand me. And when I looked up at the sky! Oh, Lordy! The sky! Pink it was. Pink! And there were two moons up there! And neither of them was our old Moon, with the man in it. No, these was smooth and gray like. An' one of 'em had all these silvery lines goin' across it, like spider-webs and and...as I live an' breathe...there was people up there! Oh Lordy be! I seen 'em! They was flyin' around up there and laughin'. Laughin'!"

Harvey glanced up at Donenfeld. "Oh God! I can't tell no more! Please don't make me tell any more."

The old museum guard was sobbing now, and obviously embarrassed at his behavior. He glanced from Burton and Abberline to Donenfeld and produced a well-used handkerchief to wipe his face.

"The docents found him this morning, just like this," said the curator. "It took him several minutes to realize where he was. He wandered around all night in a daze while an important meteorite specimen was being stolen. It's a wonder nothing else went missing." He glared at the former guard. "You are dismissed, Mr. Dunn. Collect your things and go."

"Yessir," said Harvey Dunn, crestfallen.

"Hold on there, Abner," said Burton. "Mr. Dunn, please go and wait in the security office. I'd like a word with your superior."

Harvey Dunn nodded and sulked away, still wiping tears from his eyes.

"I don't tell you how to traverse the Nile, Dick," said Donenfeld. "Don't tell me how to run my museum."

"Now Abner, I just want you to see things from that poor man's perspective."

"Are you telling me that you believe that poppycock? The old codger has clearly gone mad."

Burton nodded. "That's exactly what I'm telling you. That man is telling the truth, about all of it. Now, don't you think, under these extreme circumstances, he should be allowed another chance?"

"What if he is in league with these miscreants?"

Abberline laughed. "And risk his job? For a meteorite? When there are so many more priceless artifacts in this museum?"

"Two such specimens we passed along this very hall," said Burton. "The gold and silver—"

Donenfeld held up a hand. "Yes, yes, I know about the gold and silver specimens. I am familiar with every item in this museum, including its estimated worth."

"Then you also know that we are dealing with forces beyond our current understanding," said Burton.

"Bah!" Donenfeld spat. "You sound like those Theosophes who used to come pray and sway and chant before that bloody rock until I had the whole lot kicked out. What is really going on here, Dick?"

Burton gave a slight shrug. "I wish I knew. But I know this incident is so out of the ordinary that I believe you should give your man a reprieve, as it were."

Donenfeld chewed his bottom lip. At last he said, "Oh, all right. But if he is a second late from now on…"

"You are well within your rights to do with him as you see fit," said Burton. "Now, we've taken up enough of your time. I'm sorry this happened, Abner, but I assure you I am doing everything within my power to get to the bottom of it and ensure the safe return of the Wold-Newton meteorite."

"Well, uh, see that you do. I don't know what is going on here, Dick Burton, or why you're up to your lapels in it, but I don't like it." With that he stomped off back up the corridor, presumably to tell Harvey Dunn that the old man still had a job.

"That was a nice thing you did for Mr. Dunn," said Abberline.

"Well, none of it was his fault. No one could have stopped the Awakened from taking the meteorite."

"So, you believe his story?"

"Oh yes."

"What about all that rot about wandering around an outdoor market? The pink sky? Two moons?"

"Every word."

"Are you going to tell me why?"

Burton looked at Abberline. "For the sake of your sanity, my friend, no."

THE DREAM KEY

"W"e've got them red-handed, but we can't do a bloody thing," said Abberline as they sat in Burton's study later that afternoon. "Mr. Holmes wants us to wait and see what they do next."

Burton puffed on a cheroot and nodded. "That is probably wise. We need to know exactly with whom or what we are dealing."

"I don't like it," said Abberline. "All this waiting for them to make the next move, and us with plenty of cause to arrest them. It's maddening."

"I know what you mean, Frederick. But I'm afraid Mycroft Holmes is correct in this case.

"They must have something planned for that psychic space rock," said Abberline. He uttered a giggle. "Blimey. Have you ever heard such a ridiculous phrase in your life? Psychic space rock."

He laughed again before taking another sip of brandy. The news that shoggoths may have waylaid some of his best men had relaxed his personal rule about drinking on duty.

"They obviously need that black mineral substance for something," said Burton. "I just wish I knew what. Perhaps it amplifies some dark power they innately possess, or wish to. They have certainly made a name for themselves among the city's occult community."

Abberline arched an eyebrow. "Bloody nuisance is more like it. I heard there was quite a row out front of the Theosophes meeting hall where Goforth and Swinburne have been holding court lately. There were some fisticuffs, and the head of the society and a few of his lieutenants were kicked out."

Burton scowled. "Truly?"

"Oh, yes. Now Swinburne, Goforth, and that actor chap Whiteside have taken it over, spouting some mumbo-jumbo about connecting with their past lives. Every one of those Theosophes have gone giddy for whatever they're sellin'."

"What of the other three? Nash, Greensmith, and Peacock?"

"Lit out of town," said Abberline. "Headed for Yorkshire, nearest we can tell. Mr. Holmes says he has some contacts out that way, but it will take days to learn anything."

"That's odd," said Burton. "I wonder why they left, and if they are coming back." He didn't like the thought of these entities traveling the country, maybe even the world, in their commandeered bodies, while the owners of those bodies remained trapped in some inaccessible limbo.

"Beats me. It means we've got a few less Awakened to worry about though, at least for the time being."

They drank and smoked in silence for a long time. Burton felt drowsy, but his nerves were too on edge for sleep. Besides, he wondered what strange new dreams would assail him once he closed his eyes. He remembered his hallucinations from the day before and shuddered inwardly, as from a damp breeze.

"What does Mycroft Holmes think of all this?" Burton asked.

"Oh, you know Mr. Holmes. Beneath his cool, calculating exterior, he's as confused as we are. That's extremely hard for a man who has to know absolutely bloody everything."

They sat in silence some more. Soon Abberline became acutely aware of the deepening shadows outside the study window. "I should go. There's paperwork to be done. Good evening, Captain Burton."

Burton nodded. He knew the real reason Abberline was hesitant to remain at Gloucester Place a moment longer and didn't think lesser of him for it. The growing shadows were the perfect hiding places for shoggoths.

"All right, then," said Burton, rising from behind his desk. He shook the policeman's hand. "Let me know what you find out, if anything. I feel as if something of great import is about to transpire."

"And that's what I'm afraid of," said Abberline. "My kingdom for an ordinary cutpurse." Abberline retrieved his bowler and disappeared down the stairs, where a police pantechnicon was waiting for him. Burton stared out the window as the two big drays pulling it clopped up the street, then stared at the cityscape stained pink with the setting sun.

He turned and looked at the shoggoth gun Challenger had constructed. He had set the professor to the task of building more, hoping that would give the man something to occupy his mind so he didn't go completely mad. And if what Burton feared was about to happen came to pass, they would need every flame-thrower Challenger could produce.

He tossed the remains of his cheroot into the fireplace and retired to his bedroom, removing his clothes and putting on a fresh *jebba*. Then he sat and meditated for a while, but he kept seeing the shoggoth bubble up out of the nothingness he tried to create within his mind, like Harvey Dunn's sack full of eyes.

Burton opened his eyes, sighed, and lay down on the bed, staring up at the cracked plaster ceiling. He let his mind wander, idly imagining that he was staring at an endless desert of ceaselessly waving dunes. He could almost feel the hot, dry air whipping the folds of his *jebba*. His eyes closed, and then—

—He was staring at an immense black pyramid rising out of the desert, his mount—a fine Arabian—reeling from the towering edifice emerging from the shifting sands. Burton pulled back hard on the reins, urging the horse as far away from the disturbance as he could. But the pyramid that rose before him was vast. It shone like polished onyx, and he knew no ancient Egyptian had built this. The monument had lain under the sands for far longer than any Egyptian—any human—civilization had existed. Every inch of its mirrored surface declared its vast antiquity, and when Burton looked hard enough he could discern faint, grotesque shapes inside it, like flies trapped in amber. Was this a tomb? No. It was a prison.

Burton spurred his horse to turn and sent it galloping away up a steep-angled dune, his heart hammering in his chest, sweat dotting his tan brow.

"Listen," said a voice coming from somewhere nearby. Burton stopped his horse's progress and turned about, looking for a source.

"Listen," it said again, and Burton realized it was coming from all around him. It was the wind. It was the soft pounding of his horse's hooves on the hot sand. It was the dry rattle of the pyramid as it shook itself loose of centuries of sand and time.

"Listen," the wind voice said a third time, and Burton listened.

"You are the key."

"What?" Burton heard his dream-self ask.

"The Dream Key," the voice answered. "The Key of Dreams."

Burton awoke sweating as Miss Angell came up with a tray of food and coffee.

"Are you going to sleep all day, Captain?" she said. "It's almost noon."

"Bismillah," Burton swore. He felt as if he had closed his eyes just moments before.

"Don't go using those heathen epithets around me. Now eat your breakfast before it gets cold." Miss Angell sat the tray on his lap and calmly left the room.

Burton stared down at it, blinking, the warm smells making him nauseous rather than hungry. He lifted the tray and set it on his bedside table. He couldn't think about food just now. The vestiges of the dream, if dream it had been, were still with him. He looked out the window, where a thick fog roiled. He imagined dark, inhuman shapes in it, feelers and tentacles reaching toward the glass. He shuddered as a terrible coldness settled somewhere deep within him. He felt unmoored from this life, his mind drifting away from his body. He squeezed his eyes shut and saw with his mind's eye the black pyramid rising from the shifting sands. The Dream Key. He was the Dream Key. What did that mean? Drifting in his vision now was a shining key. It was overly large and ornate, gleaming a bright, cold silver. He wrapped his right hand around it, and its cold seeped into his skin, down to his very finger bones. It did not grow warm to his touch. In it he felt pulsating energy. He heard a multitude of voices, not all of them human, issuing from it.

Next, he saw a pair of dark eyes burning through him, familiar. He realized with a start that they were his own, looking out at him from inside another face. Black jewels gleamed upon this Other's brow like spider's eyes.

When Burton opened his eyes, he was sitting up in his bed, right hand outstretched, fingers balled into a fist so tightly his knuckles were white. "Blast it all," he swore, releasing his grip. There was no key in his hand, but he could still feel its weight, its coldness there on his palm. He wiped his hand on the front of his *jebba* and doubted his sanity.

"I am the Dream Key. Bismillah. What does that mean?"

THERE WERE SHOGGOTHS IN MY BASEMENT

It had been seven days since the meteorite robbery, and no arrests had been made, by order of Mycroft Holmes. More police had gone missing, and there were reports of "odd, slithering slime moving of its own accord" reported all over the city. It seemed everyone had a sense of creeping dread that no one could explain, especially Captain Sir Richard Francis Burton, who seldom ventured out and only peeked occasionally from his study window just to make sure the city he knew was still there. Today he stared out on a decimated metropolis. The buildings and row houses opposite his home were utterly destroyed, the ruins leaning in toward one another like broken teeth. In the distance a large dome-shaped contraption walked carefully through the wreckage on long tripod legs, metallic tentacles flailing. The whole thing gleamed like brass in the sun.

"Time for tea," said Miss Angell as she entered the room with a silver tray laden with steaming tea and biscuits.

Burton sat and stared as his housekeeper began preparing his afternoon tea, oblivious to the nightmare tableau evident through the window.

"You really should get out and take in some fresh air," she said. "You haven't even visited your club in a week."

Burton said nothing as she dropped a sugar cube into his tea. "There you are," she said. "Drink up. It will do you some good. I know you're worried about your friend Mr. Swinburne, but he'll recover his wits."

She smiled at him and left the room. Burton watched her go, then turned back to the window, where a normal London afternoon once again presented itself. The buildings across the way were whole, and there was no sign of the tripod contraption. Burton sighed and sipped his tea, wondering what sanity-blasting new vista next awaited him. He had long since given up on his sanity and was now simply waiting for the men in white coats to come and seize him.

At night the dreams assailed him, strange visions with familiar faces in new roles. In one, he fought John Hanning Speke in a sword duel, the two of them dancing about an assemblage of vast basalt ruins, Burton parrying as Speke lunged for him around the black cyclopean masonry.

"The world is indeed comic, but the joke is on mankind," Speke said.

In another, he captained an airship under siege by some blasphemously hideous, winged creatures with long barbed tails and faceless heads capped with inward curving horns. "Night gaunts!" someone near him shouted as a series of shots rang out.

In yet another, he wasn't himself at all. He wasn't even human, but a massive insect-like creature enshrouded by a golden carapace. He and his kind chittered wordlessly, their many legs moving across smooth blocks that shown like polished hematite. Burton and the others surrounded a towering figure, vaguely humanoid in outline, covered in what looked like a burial shroud. It stood upright inside a great circle of green flame, and Burton and the others bowed toward it, as in supplication. Burton's mind wanted him to scream, but he dared not. He felt as if he were hiding inside this insect thing's body, and if he gave away his presence, the others would turn on him, devouring his chitinous flesh.

It went on that way, night after night, and Burton was no closer to figuring out what the mysterious yet familiar voice wanted him to do. He only got the sense that he was somehow important to whatever was about to take place regarding he Awakened, along with the unsettling feeling that he wasn't alone, that there were these mysterious Others watching him from afar. Not malevolent toward him, like the Elder Things that groped toward them with gruesome appendages from the Beyond, but not comforting either.

Burton attempted meditation to steady his mind, but these sessions too were interrupted by eerie sensations of being someone else and somewhere else. He felt once again the presence of some intrusive Other, much as the Lurker on the Threshold had haunted him during his last adventure, the other Burton from the stream of Time that had been disrupted by their journey into the past aboard Nemo's *Nautilus*. But this was different. Burton could not see him from the corner of his eye. This was not a feeling like things had fractured, but an intrusion from an entirely new plane of existence, and the rational part of Burton's mind wanted to run from it, to deny it and go about his business. But he could not, for when he closed his eyes the dreams assailed him with how solidified and real they felt. As tangible as the reality he journeyed through in his waking hours.

It was one of these troubling nights, during which he lay awake, that he heard a knock on his door.

"Bismillah," Burton swore, donning his dressing gown and slippers and heading downstairs before the persistent knocking awoke Miss Angell. He opened the door and found Professor Challenger and the Time Traveler on his doorstep. Herbert was hefting a glowing lantern, while Challenger held the shoggoth gun.

"We've found those Awakened scoundrels," boomed Challenger, a devious grin playing on his lips. "Your friend Swinburne is among them. We were hunting shoggoths."

"An unusual pastime," said young Herbert. "But one that has yielded positive results."

"What the deuce are you two talking about?" muttered Burton. "Come inside before you wake half the street. And turn off that flame on your shoggoth gun, if you please."

Professor Challenger twisted a nozzle on the side of the weapon and the flame spurting from the end of it went out. They stepped inside, and Burton poured them all brandies.

"Hunting shoggoths builds up a powerful thirst, eh Herbert?" said Challenger, taking a glass and draining it.

"I must ask you to please keep it down," said Burton. "My housekeeper is sleeping."

"I'm sorry to barge in like this," said Herbert. "The Professor insisted." He sipped his brandy leisurely. "I'm sorry we woke you."

Burton shook his head. "I wasn't sleeping. Tell me about the Awakened."

"They've taken over the Theosophical Society meeting hall," said Challenger. "Apparently it was quite the row. Split their organization in two. They brought most of the membership over to their cause with their talk of other worlds and ultimate knowledge."

"Inspector Abberline and I suspected as much," said Burton. "He said their leader and some of his lieutenants were ejected the other day. What are they doing now?"

"They're helping people tap into their past lives," said Challenger. "Pure bunk of course, but after all we've seen..." his voice trailed off. He poured himself another brandy and drained the glass.

"They have these glittering black jewels set into elaborate head-pieces," said Herbert. "Similar to the one we saw aboard Captain Nemo's *Nautilus*."

Burton felt a chill. "The crowns of the Deep Ones."

"The same," said Challenger. "I thought we had rid ourselves of those abysmal creatures."

"It never ends," said Herbert, sadly, draining his brandy. "Time on an infinite loop."

"The Deep Ones are not our primary concern," said Burton. "The Awakened are."

"Well, that's the beauty of it," said Challenger. "Call your Inspector Abberline. Have them arrested for the theft of the Wold-Newton fragments."

"I can't," said Burton. "Mycroft Holmes has ordered the police to leave them alone. We must learn what they are ultimately planning first. Besides, my friend Swinburne would be among them."

"Oh fiddlesticks," said Challenger. "I swear that pretentious fop causes more problems than he solves with that vast intellect of his. We could end this once and for all tonight."

"Perhaps it's the brandy talking," said Herbert, "but I agree."

Challenger laughed and clapped the young Time Traveler on the back so hard he almost spit out his latest sip of brandy.

"How did you get involved in all of this anyway, Herbert?" said Burton.

"It was quite horrifying. I awoke to a clamorous noise coming from my basement laboratory and found a pair of shoggoths studying my Time Machine!"

"Bismillah! You built another one? After I sent the last one hurtling unmanned into the future to keep Mycroft Holmes from getting his hands on it?"

Herbert shrugged. "I was only tinkering, really. More importantly, I had shoggoths in my basement. Apparently, they congealed under the basement door. I screamed, and next thing I knew Professor Challenger had kicked down the door and turned his flame-thrower on them."

"Searched round for the bloody things all evening," said Challenger. When I found signs of them in Kew Gardens, I knew they were up to something especially sinister. I tracked the ghastly blighters right to Herbert's doorstep. After convincing Herbert to join me, we tracked their spoor to the Theosophes, where Swinburne and the rest of that Awakened lot were holding their unholy court."

"Then we came to get you," Herbert added, his cheeks reddened. He had clearly had enough brandy.

"What did you do?" asked Burton, "Peek at them through a window?"

"Heavens no," said Challenger with a derisive snort. "I hid my flame-thrower behind a mail receptacle next to the building, and we walked right inside. The hour was late, but there were at least a hundred people in attendance, all wanting to know who or what they had been in a past life. The Awakened were quite convincing. By the time we left I wanted to get in line to have my fortune read."

"Was Swinburne there?" Burton asked.

"Yes, but not for long," said Challenger. "He appeared to be merely watching the proceedings, nodding his head approvingly. In the middle, he up and left. I'm sorry, Burton. I did not think to follow him, so enraptured were we by the rest of the Awakened's performance. But your friend appeared to be in charge."

"Tell him about the shoggoth we saw on the corner," Herbert said to Challenger, his face grim.

"Oh yes. As we neared Gloucester Place, another of the protoplasmic fiends showed itself. I destroyed it with my flame, but it appeared to be standing guard on your place."

"I had the feeling one of them was watching me," Burton said.

Challenger touched the tip of his bulbous nose with his right index finger. "Yes. Perhaps they've been watching all of us. But why?"

"Because of our connection to one another," said Burton, "and my connection to Swinburne. Perhaps they fear my interference. Perhaps Swinburne's mind, wherever it is, has told them about me and our work with the Shadow Council, though I told my friend very little. He never wanted the gory details."

"Whatever the reason, we have a way to stop them," said Challenger, picking up the flame-thrower and hefting it.

"They are going to catch onto that sooner or later," said Burton. "And we can't very well use it on the Awakened, now can we?"

"Why the bloody hell not?" shouted Challenger.

"Because they are human beings," Burton whispered. "Human beings in the grip of something beyond their control."

The sitting room door creaked open, and every head turned at the sound, half expecting a shoggoth to be sitting there. Instead, they found Miss Angell. "Captain Burton! Do you have any idea what time it is?"

"I do, Mother. I am very sorry we woke you. My friends were just leaving."

Burton's housekeeper nodded and left the room, mumbling "Worse than that Cannibal Club lot," under her breath as she departed.

Challenger chuckled. "Feisty woman. I think I rather like her."

"Let's convene this gathering for a more appropriate time," said

Burton. "The Inspector will be along in the morning. I suggest we meet here then."

"To do what?" asked Herbert.

"To draw out these Awakened once and for all," Burton declared.

"Oh, there was one other thing," said Herbert.

Burton arched an eyebrow. "Yes?"

"There was a large black stone in the center of the room. It looked incredibly ancient. They were lighting candles they had placed around it."

"A stone?" said Burton. "I wonder where they got it, and what use they have for it. Whatever it is, I don't like it. Meet me here tomorrow morning."

After seeing Challenger and the Time Traveler off, Burton trudged back upstairs to his bedroom, though sleep did not return to him for another hour. He kept thinking about his friend Swinburne, and what else might be lurking in the shadows along Gloucester Place, watching him through his bedroom window with myriad eyes.

THE STRANGE DEVICE

Burton, Challenger, and Herbert told Inspector Abberline what had transpired last night over a hearty breakfast of eggs and sausage. Abberline took it all in stride. He dabbed at his mouth with a linen napkin and said, "I wish we could go and arrest the whole lot of them this instant, but my orders are to continue watching them to determine what their ultimate plan is."

"Agreed," said Burton, happy to know that his friend Swinburne would not be clapped in irons this day. "We still don't know exactly who or what we are up against."

"It has something to do with those ghastly diadems, said Herbert. "They certainly seem to give off some strange vibration. I left that meeting with a headache, didn't you Professor?"

"I did indeed. Bloody hell. I thought it was just me. Though by the time we reached Gloucester Place it was gone, and I forgot to mention it."

"Perhaps they focus what powers, if any, the Awakened already possess," said Burton thoughtfully. He picked at his breakfast, and instead drank two cups of coffee in quick succession. "Perhaps they work to make the minds of the Theosophes more pliable, so that they can be manipulated."

"Something else occurred to me last night," said Burton after a long moment, "before I drifted off to sleep. Something else that might tie us all together."

"Do tell," said Abberline.

"Dreams," said Burton. "Dreams and visions of other times and places. You have experienced them yourself, Challenger."

The Professor seemed taken aback by the accusation, but he nodded slowly and uttered a deep sigh. Dabbing eggs from his beard, he said, "You are correct, Captain Burton. I thought I was going mad."

"If you are mad, then we all are," said the Time Traveler. "I too have suffered from strange dreams, around the time that the Awakened were first reported in the papers. I dreamed that my Time Machine carried me not into the past or future, but into alternate versions of our own present. Sidewise in Time, as it were, instead of forward or backward. It was very strange. It was our familiar London, but with sometimes remarkable, even ghastly differences."

"I have experienced the same," said Burton, "only much of it during waking hours."

"Hallucinations?" asked Herbert.

Burton nodded. "That's what I thought. At first. Now I'm not so sure. Remember the museum security guard's account of the robbery, Frederick? It was exactly like that."

"Blimey! You too? But you didn't say anything."

"I'm sorry, my friend. I needed to be sure I wasn't going insane."

"Well, while we're all sharing I suppose I should fess up too," said Abberline. "The other night I was out for a walk to clear my head. I turn a corner, and blimey, but I'm in a completely different locale. The buildings were of this strange pink brick, all glittery like, and it was broad daylight! And the people. You never seen such strange looking folks about. They wore these green cloaks, and had yellow, rheumy eyes."

"What did you do?" asked Herbert.

"What did I do? Why I turned and got out of there. I kept moving until things were familiar and dark again. Then I headed straight home."

"When was this?" asked Burton.

"A few nights ago."

"You think it's the Awakened playin' with them queer stones of theirs?" asked the Inspector.

"No. While I believe the Wold-Newton stones may give the Awakened this power, I think this is something or someone else," said Burton. "During one of my visions, a voice told me I am the Dream Key, whatever the bloody hell that is. It holds some special significance, but I don't know why. I was shown things. Different versions of myself. In one I wore an eye patch and commanded the *Nautilus*. We were at war with the Deep Ones, and losing. In another the *Nautilus* was attached to a huge canvas gasbag, like a dirigible, and we were flying over a vast desert, chasing a black pyramid that rose from the sand."

"Bloody hell!" Challenger swore.

"What do you think is happening, Captain?" asked Abberline. "I'm used to rounding up cutpurses. This is too much for an old copper like me."

"I think someone is trying to communicate with us," said Burton. "I think someone, or something, is trying to help us."

"That would be a refreshing change if true," said Challenger. "But for now we have no idea what this friendly force might be. But I think I know a method I can use to find out."

"Let's get started then," said Herbert.

"First we need to learn more about what the Awakened are up to. Though we must be careful. They have shoggoths protecting them and watching us."

Burton quickly explained to Abberline the events of the previous evening. The policeman's face turned the color of milk. "I need to inform Mr. Holmes."

"You do that," said Burton. "The rest of us are going to trail Swinburne and Goforth again. Professor, I need you to be our guard against the shoggoths. Can you do that?"

Challenger grinned. "It would be my honor and my pleasure, Captain."

~

An hour and a half later, Burton and Herbert were in heavy disguise, standing out front of Swinburne's home at 7 Chester Street, Grosvenor Place. Challenger was half a block away in a heavy coat large enough to conceal his shoggoth gun. No more police had been assigned to track the poet's movements since the last one had disappeared, and Burton was wary of any shoggoths that might be lurking about standing guard. Around nine o'clock Swinburne—or rather, the entity wearing his skin like a suit of clothes—exited the home and walked up the street toward Hyde Park, whistling an ethereal tune. He met up with Goforth in front of the entrance to Hyde Park, and the two hailed a hansom. Burton hailed another one, and he, Herbert and Challenger bade the driver follow the carriage for several miles before it stopped and deposited Swinburne and Goforth off at a familiar street.

"They're returning to the watchmaker's shop," Burton said after he paid the fare and they alighted from the cab. "Let's go. Keep your distance, but don't lose sight of them."

Sure enough, just as Burton had predicted, they went down the narrow maze of side streets to the watch and clock shop Burton had watched them enter before he had been waylaid by the shoggoth. Burton looked about fearfully for any signs of another of the foul creatures, but none presented itself. At any rate, they had the protection of Challenger's shoggoth gun this time. Perhaps the Professor's presence was keeping them at bay.

Burton and Herbert pretended to be interested in watching the candle maker practice his art through the window of his shop while Swinburne and Goforth conducted their business in the clock shop. When they exited, Swinburne held the door open for Goforth, who was carrying something covered in a piece of oilcloth. It was small but heavy, judging by the way Goforth hefted it in both hands. Burton and Herbert stayed where they were until Swinburne and Goforth passed, oblivious to their presence and chattering on in that alien tongue of theirs.

"What the devil do you think that could be?" Herbert muttered when they were out of earshot.

"No idea," said Burton. "Some clockwork contraption I should think. Let's go and ask the clockmaker."

"Good idea," said Herbert. "Before I became interested in optics, I was somewhat obsessed with the clockmaker's art."

"Splendid," said Burton. "You do the talking."

Burton turned as they entered the shop and found Professor Challenger crouched in a narrow alley between too buildings. He nodded to Burton. Sure that they would be safe from shoggoths, Burton followed Herbert into the shop.

A little bell hanging over the door announced their arrival. A little old man peeked up from behind the high glass counter. "May I help you?" He wore a threadbare tweed suit and a pair of thick spectacles perched atop the bridge of his beak-like nose.

"Hello there," said Herbert jovially, his mouth stretched into a friendly smile. "Those two men who were just in here. One of them is an old acquaintance of mine, though blast it if I can remember his name. I wanted to speak with him out in the lane earlier, but I was too embarrassed. Might you know his name?"

"Which gentleman are you talking about?" said the horologist.

"The red-haired gentleman."

"Oh yes. I believe he said his name was...what was it? Swinburt? Swanson? No. Swinburne! Yes. That's it. And his companion was a Mr. Goforth. How do you know these men?"

"Oh, they were old colleagues. I used to be somewhat of an amateur watchmaker, and the three of us enjoyed indulging in our mutual hobby together."

The old man arched an eyebrow. "Oh? I see. Well, I don't know about that. They told me they were psychic mediums. I never had much truck with that sort of thing, but they're the talk of the town. They requisitioned a most peculiar instrument from me. Not a clock, but I certainly had to use all of my skills as a clocksmith. It was good money too. My eyes aren't what they used to be, and I am not as adept at maintenance and repair as I used to be."

Herbert gave the man a sincere frown. "Oh you poor man. How dreadful. What did you make for them?"

The clockmaker stepped back from the counter. He glanced uneasily at Burton. "Why do you want to know?"

"Oh, I was just curious, that's all," Herbert said, glancing at Burton.

"My good man," said Burton, stepping forward and reaching into his coat. "I am Captain Sir Richard Francis Burton, and I am an agent of the Queen." He showed the man his card, given to him by Mycroft Holmes, showing his credentials and the Queen's official seal. The man stared at it through his thick glasses, transfixed. "Oh my," he said shakily. "Have I done something wrong?"

"Heavens no," said Burton, pocketing the card. "We just need to ask you some questions about those two men and the item they purchased from you. I apologize for our previous subterfuge. We must keep a low profile."

"Oh yes, I understand," said the old man, winking as if he understood very well. "The item doesn't have a name, at least as far as I know. They came in a few weeks ago and asked me to build it. They gave me these plans."

He puttered around a cluttered workbench behind the counter and hefted two sheets of paper. Drawn on them with almost machine precision was a set of plans. He passed them over the counter to Burton. He examined them with Herbert.

"They paid me an enormous sum," said the old clocksmith. "Five hundred pounds." He whispered this last, as if it were an obscenity he feared would be overheard.

"Remarkable," said Herbert.

The old man nodded. "They paid half then, and the other half just now."

"Do you know what this device is supposed to do?" asked Burton.

The old man threw up his hands. "No idea. I was just happy to have the work. Business has been slow of late. No one comes down to these shops anymore." He stared wistfully past Burton and Herbert toward the shop's front window and the empty street beyond.

"Well, I appreciate your cooperation," said Burton, rolling up the plans. "May we keep these?"

"Yes, I suppose. Mr. Swinburne and Goforth didn't care to have them back. So why not?"

"You've been most helpful," said Herbert, opening his wallet and handing over a twenty-pound note.

"Oh, no. I can't accept this," said the old man.

"Please, your time today was more than worth it."

The old man graciously accepted the proffered money, and Herbert and Burton turned and left the shop. Challenger greeted them in the street, the flame-thrower evident under his bulging coat.

"Well?" the Professor rumbled testily.

"They had the clocksmith make this," said Burton, showing him the papers. Challenger scowled over the schematics before eying Burton. "So? I'm a zoologist, not a bloody engineer. What the deuce is it?"

"We have no idea," said Burton. He glanced at Herbert. "I suppose you should hang on to these. The mechanical is your purview, and these plans might yet come in handy."

"If you say so, Captain." Herbert took them and folded them carefully before putting them in a pocket of his coat. "But it appears we are at somewhat of a dead end. We didn't even follow them to see where they went."

"Where they are going is no mystery," said Burton. "No doubt they are returning to the Theosophic Society meeting hall to hold another of their psychic sessions. And this time we are all going to be there."

CONFRONTING THE AWAKENED

The Theosophes meeting hall was filled almost to capacity by the time Burton, Herbert and Challenger arrived. Every seat was filled by expectant people hopeful for a glimpse into a past or even a future life. Challenger remained near the doors in the shadows, his shoggoth gun still hidden under his greatcoat, wary for any sign of the foul protoplasmic entities.

"Wait here," said Burton as he entered the crowded hall, where people in black robes muttered in hushed tones.

Herbert and Challenger started to protest, but Burton ignored them as he wedged himself into the crowd. He received a few vacant stares, but no one questioned his attendance. He watched Swinburne, Whiteside and Goforth enter a room at the far end of the central space, beyond the huge black stone standing at the room's center. A circle of candles sputtered around it, illuminating the garish glyphs carved into it so long ago they had almost worn away.

Burton entered the antechamber where Swinburne and the others were commiserating before their presentation. Swinburne looked up at the explorer and grinned. "Richard! So good of you to come."

"Might I have a word, Algy?"

Swinburne looked at Goforth and Whiteside, who exchanged wary glances, and nodded to them. The two other members of the Awakened left the room.

"What is it, Richard? Why so serious? Are you ready to explore new realities? I have learned so much since my awakening, as the papers are calling our shared experience."

Burton lunged for the poet, grabbing him by his lapels and slamming him against the wall. "No more games, whoever you are. I came here for answers. Who are you?"

Swinburne's expression hardened. "Now Captain Burton, is that any way to treat the body of one of your contemporaries? One of your closest friends? I'm not sure his diminutive frame can take much of a beating."

"You'd be surprised," said Burton. "Now what are you? What are you? Because one thing was immediately clear the minute you recovered. You are not Algernon Charles Swinburne."

Swinburne pushed Burton off of him with a strength the explorer didn't know the poet's tiny body could muster. "So the jig is up, eh?" He straightened his lapels. "I do enjoy the clever turns of phrase the naked apes of this time period employ. I suppose our ruse must fall apart sooner or later. So be it."

"Who are you?" Burton asked again.

"My name is unpronounceable to human lips, tongue and vocal chords," said Swinburne. "But my kind call themselves, with no small amount of hubris, the Great Race. We hail from a distant world we call Yith."

"How did you get here?" asked Burton. "And why are you here?"

"We are explorers much like yourself. We escaped cataclysm on our world by leaping through Time and into the bodies of beings that inhabited this world in the deep past. Using these new bodies, we built a wondrous library city on what you now call the continent of Australia."

"And what happens to the minds of those whose bodies you commandeer?"

The Swinburne-thing shrugged. "They switch places with us and inhabit our old bodies until we are ready to return to our own time."

"Bismillah! You switched places with Algy."

"Exactly," said the Swinburne-thing.

"So that's where Algy is now. In the deep past. Is he...safe?"

"Perfectly safe. And he has been gifted with sights few other human minds in history have ever seen, and through him our kind learn an inordinate amount about your species, as well as this marvelous time period."

"What do you want?" Burton asked. "Why here? Why now? Why not journey farther into the future? Surely there is a more technologically advanced time."

"We do not care about your pitiful technology. We have glimpsed wonders you soft pink apes couldn't dream of. Besides, greater sophistication leads to earlier detection of our activities. This age is still superstitious enough to believe in demonic possession. When the truth is far more mundane."

"It is funny what you consider mundane," said Burton. "Now release my friend."

"I'm afraid I can't do that. Our plan is not yet complete."

"And what is that plan?"

Swinburne uttered a screeching laugh. "Are you really that ridiculous to think that I will just lay out the particulars of our endeavors? Ho ho, Richard. I'm surprised at you. I'm afraid you'll just have to wait and see."

"What is that black stone for?"

"That? We dug that up in a field in Yorkshire. We knew right where to dig too, because in your year 1684 one of my compatriots, who now inhabits the body of your William Nash, buried it there."

"Why?"

"For safekeeping, of course. We had no use of it at the time, the stars were not right. And we couldn't risk its relocation or outright destruction."

"Ah," said Burton. "So timing is important to you, for some ritual you wish to complete, and you need that black rock, and the Wold-Newton stones, to help you do it."

The Swinburne-thing's body twitched spasmodically, and the creature wearing the poet's body had to steady himself, closing his eyes for a moment. "You are a clever, clever ape, Captain Burton," said the Swinburne-thing when he opened his eyes. "I must say I am quite fond of you, and of this period in your history. Not to mention this vessel I currently wear. I will tell you, however, that your friend Swinburne's body has a singular physiognomy. I am keeping open a tenuous telepathic link to his mind in the deep past—it helps us learn and thus assimilate to this time period faster—and I am receiving the strangest impulses from him." He shivered and shook again. "My hat!"

"Algy?" said Burton, rushing toward Swinburne's form once more, grabbing him and throwing him against the wall once more. Pinning Swinburne's arms with his elbows, Burton began a series of mesmeric touches on the poet's face and forehead.

"Stop it!" said the Swinburne-thing.

"Algy," Burton intoned. "If you can hear me, fight them. Fight them and come back to us."

"My Aunt Betty's bonnet," Swinburne squealed. "Richard? Is that you? I'd give my right arm for a drink. If I had any arms. Bloody hell."

The Swinburne-thing thrashed in his grip, uttering some vile epithet in his guttural, inhuman tongue. He kicked Burton in the shins, causing the explorer to release his grip and back away from the writhing figure. The Swinburne-thing said something else in that bizarre language and ceased his spasmodic twitching. "Do not do that again. I cannot guarantee the safety of your friend if you do. My kind can make of his stay a paradise or a hell. The choice is yours."

Nash and Goforth returned to the room. "It is time," said the Goforth-thing.

The Swinburne-thing nodded. "Very well. Let's proceed."

"What about him?" said the Nash-thing, pointing to Burton.

"He is free to stay or go as he wishes," said the Swinburne-thing. "He cannot harm us without harming those whose bodies we have usurped." The Swinburne-thing straightened his lapels as he walked past Burton toward the room's exit. "You are welcome to stay and usher in the coming of Yog-Sothoth. You strike me as the kind of man who prefers to see his doom coming toward him, rather than slinking up behind him in the night. Until then..."

The three Awakened left the room. Burton composed himself before following them out. He received a few stares from several of the Awakened's so-called acolytes, but no one tried to molest him as he left the crowded hall. Herbert and Professor Challenger awaited him out front.

"Thank heavens," said Herbert. "I was about to call the police."

"What did you hope to accomplish by going in there alone?" boomed Challenger. "I'm beginning to think you are as mad as I."

Burton smiled up at the zoologist. "I learned their plan. I also found a weakness."

THE EYES OF EL-YEZDI

Perhaps we should go to the police," said Herbert as they walked up the street and away from the former Theosophic meeting hall. Burton had just finished telling them all that had transpired with Swinburne in the back room. "Where's your friend Abberline?"

"I told you before we can't arrest them. That will only put a bandage on the wound," said Burton. "Staunching the flow of blood, when the wound must be sutured shut. The court could not hold them indefinitely, and as soon as they were released they'd continue with their plan."

"Or leap out of Swinburne and the others and into someone else," added Challenger sourly.

Burton nodded. "My point is, they have an eternity in which to scheme; we don't."

"This is madness," rumbled Challenger. I've never heard such rot. And yet I've seen enough to know our straits are indeed dire."

"It boggles the mind," said Herbert. "To think that our universe is not a single cog endlessly turning, but a multifaceted jewel. The implications are..." his voice trailed off.

"We've all seen it," said Burton. "In fact, I believe someone has shown us glimpses of these other facets for a reason."

"But who?" said Challenger.

"And how?" demanded Herbert.

"I don't know," said Burton. "But I think I know a way to find out. Come."

Burton hailed a carriage and gave the driver an address several blocks away.

They rode in nervous silence, Challenger the most nervous of all, casting a wary, bloodshot eye out the moving carriage at the passersby, his keen gaze no doubt looking for shoggoths.

Twenty minutes later they arrived at their destination. Challenger scowled when he saw the familiar brick storefront and the wooden sign emblazoned with the baleful all-seeing eye. "Bollocks. Not the Lady of the Eye again."

"Yes," said Burton. "She was of great help to me during our last adventure. Perhaps she can shed light on these strange visions we've all been having."

"Why not?" said Herbert as he alighted from the carriage. "It makes as much sense as anything else we've seen since getting caught up in each other's lives."

Herbert and Challenger followed Burton up the narrow path. Burton opened the door to the tinkling of a tiny bell set above the portal. The place was just as they had left it, dimly lit and smelling of incense. The proprietor floated toward them in loose-fitting, wine-colored robes. "Captain Burton. I knew you would return."

"Hello, Lady Helena. We need your help."

"Of course," she said, frowning. "Oh, you poor man. Your aura is in such disarray. Your spirit is fractured. I can sense other instances of you lashing out. Come, have a seat."

Burton caught Challenger and Herbert rolling their eyes at one another, but he ignored them. A year ago he would have joined them in their derision. But now, he wasn't so sure. Now, this was the only thing that made any sense.

"Give me your hand," said Lady Helena, examining Burton's palm closely. "Oh my. Your lifeline is fractured, branching off into tiny rivulets." She put his hand down and looked at him from across the little table. "But that is not why you are here."

"No," said Burton.

"You are here because someone is trying to contact you across a great distance."

"I believe so, yes," said the explorer. "Can you help me?"

Lady Helena glanced nervously at Herbert and Challenger before returning her gaze to the explorer. "I am not sure. Everything is in disarray today. There are dark forces drawing power."

"The Awakened," said Challenger. Lady Helena stared up at him.

"They are trying to summon some entity by the name of Yog," Burton began, scowling. "What was it? Yog? Yog?"

"Yog-Sothoth," said Lady Helena, slumping back in her seat. "I was afraid of this. No one should even know that name. To so much as speak it is to invite chaos."

"I was afraid of that," mused Herbert.

"These Awakened you've no doubt read of in the papers are not ordinary men," said Burton. "They are alien beings from another time."

Helena gasped. "That explains why the planes are in chaos. Both this one and the spirit realms."

"Well, I don't know about all of that," said Burton, "but I think I can stop them. If I can communicate with whoever is trying to help me."

She stared at Burton for a long moment. "The path will be difficult. These are not ordinary spirits or astral beings. But I believe I can help you reach a state where they can reach out to you."

"Burton nodded. "Let's do it."

Once more Helena led Burton to the couch, and the explorer lay upon it, closing his eyes. "You are a practitioner of Sufi meditation, yes?"

"I am," Burton said, nodding.

"Good. Begin."

Burton felt the weight of something heavy and cold resting on his forehead, and another on his chest. "You remember the crystals? They will help focus the energies at work around you. Things are in such chaos. This might not work."

"It has to work," Burton heard Challenger say as he began the meditation. He began by taking several deep breaths and relaxing his whole body. Then he cleared his mind of all thought. The only sound he heard was Helena's humming somewhere above him. At first nothing happened, and he thought this attempt would be a failure. Then he felt his body slowly drifting, untethered. He opened his eyes and saw himself lying on the couch, Herbert and Challenger standing by, hats in hand, while Helena stood waving her arms back and forth over his body. He saw glowing lines of force vibrating around his body, tangled like snakes. With each move of her hands the lines straightened, increasing in radiance. The scene below him faded from view then, and Burton found he was somewhere else, floating through an all-encompassing blackness. In this blackness he could hear strange voices, like whispers. A pinprick of light opened in front of him, growing larger and larger as he grew near it. It resolved itself into a hexagonal portal through which shifting golden dunes could be seen. Its desert heat blasted him as he stepped through.

Burton looked around, sinking into the desert sand as he scanned the area. He moved in a circle, taking everything in. There was nothing but limitless desert. Even the portal he had stepped through was gone. The heat was instantly oppressive. He began sweating immediately and removed his jacket as he decided what to do next. What direction should he go? What was he doing here? Was any of this real? He considered his options as a flash of movement caught his eye. It was a man wearing a flowing white *jebba* and turban, sitting astride a solid Arabian. The horse galloped toward him, kicking up puffs of sand beneath its pounding hooves as it closed the distance between them. Burton stood and waited for their arrival, his hand shielding his eyes from the sun. When the figure on horseback moved close enough to make out, Burton's knees almost buckled beneath him.

The horseman, on the other hand, did not seem that surprised. "Another one. Bismillah! I should have guessed."

Burton stared up at him. His face was tanned and hardened from the sun, his beard and mustache neatly trimmed. The long, Y-shaped scar across his left cheek left no doubt. He could easily pass for an Arab. But Burton knew who he was.

"You're me," said the explorer.

The horseman grinned. "Yes, and I am you. So it has been these last few days. Come with me, and all of your questions will be answered. Hopefully."

The horseman helped Burton onto the horse's back and turned the beast back in the direction he had come. He spurred the horse into a gallop.

"In my youth I dressed as you did," said Burton, "making the pilgrimage to Mecca incognito."

"As did I," said the horseman. "But after some time away I decided to return. People in these parts know me as Hadji Abdullah the Bushri. For simplicity's sake, you may refer to me by that moniker."

"And you can just call me Burton."

Abdullah the Bushri nodded. "As you wish."

They rode on in silence, Burton grinning at the feel of the powerful animal's graceful movements beneath him. He had ridden horses many times with Isabel at her family's country estate, but the experience hadn't been as exhilarating as this. This was like his time in Persia and his stint in the Army. They crested a dune and moved down toward a wide flat area. Several large tents had been erected in this spot, and Burton saw a figure tending to a horse near them. Abdullah slowed his steed as they entered the camp, and Burton saw that the figure tending the other horse was a woman. And not just any woman. She was thin and graceful, wearing a white flowing *jebba* with pants and boots. But it was clearly Isabel. A long thin scimitar hung from her belt, and she eyed Burton with intense curiosity.

"Yes, that is Isabel," said Abdullah, eying Burton. "*My* Isabel."

Burton nodded, understanding. The woman standing before him was a complete stranger. His Isabel was safe at her parents' home, awaiting word from him that it was safe to return to London. They got off the horse and Abdullah handed the reigns to a small boy before leading Burton into the main tent.

Inside, sitting at a long wooden folding table, was an assemblage of three other Burtons. The first wore a gray eye patch over his left eye. His beard was short but his hair was long, and he wore what appeared to be a Navy uniform of some kind. He scowled at Burton such that it made the explorer think this was his usual expression. The Burton sitting next to him gave the explorer a sneering smile. What was most notable about him was his right arm, which had been replaced by a complex, ornate mechanical appendage, a thing of gleaming brass inlaid with dark, polished wood, the metal fingers of which drummed on the table. At the far end of the table a thin, wizened, almost sickly version of Burton sat cross-legged in the chair, wearing only a white loin cloth and turban. Burton could see his ribs protruding through the man's parchment-like skin, which was covered in strange tattoos. His wrinkled forehead was encrusted with several of the black Wold-Newton fragments, and his deep, penetrating eyes appeared as if they were looking right through Burton. The explorer flinched under their intensity.

"You were right, as always," said Abdullah the Bushri to the thin man. "He was right where you said he'd be. Now what?"

"Now offer him a drink," said the wizened man with a thin smile. Abdullah motioned toward a wooden sideboard laden with clay decanters of wine.

"Help yourself," he said. "We're all friends here."

Burton poured himself a glass of rich dark wine and drank, recalling cherished memories of his own time in Persia. Then he turned and took a chair opposite the mechanical armed Burton.

"I suppose some form of introduction is in order," said Abdullah. "We can't very well call each other by our given names, now can we?" He went down the line, pointing at each of them in turn. "We call him the Captain," he said, pointing to the eye-patched Burton. "The fellow with the mechanical arm goes by the nom de guerre Ruffian Dick, and that mystical fellow on the end calls himself Abu El-Yezdi."

"Just call me Burton," said Burton. "I've seen some of you before. In my dreams."

"As have we," said Abdullah.

Burton addressed the Captain. "You command the *Nautilus*, yes?"

"Aye," said the Captain grimly. "After Nemo was killed battling the cursed Deep Ones. My world has been besieged by them. They held dominion over two-thirds of the planet for millennia, and now they almost have the final third in their grasp."

"I lost my bloody arm to John Hanning Speke," declared Ruffian Dick. "That mad blighter grew crazed when we happened upon a series of ruins near the Mountains of the Moon." He patted his mechanical arm. "This little beauty was a gift from Mycroft Holmes. A clever gentleman by the name of Daniel Gooch designed and built it for me." He balled its brass fingers into a formidable-looking fist. "It has its advantages, but it's just not the same."

"El-Yezdi brought us all together," said Abdullah. "Though we're still not exactly sure why." He brought out a pipe and lit it.

"The Man of Truth is beyond good and evil," El-Yezdi intoned. "The Man of Truth has ridden to All-Is-One. The Man of Truth has learned that Illusion is the One Reality, and that Substance is the Great Impostor."

Abdullah sucked on his pipe thoughtfully, nodding. Ruffian Dick rolled his eyes. "There he goes again."

"What's he talking about?" said Burton. "Bismillah, I have had enough of riddles. Especially from myself."

"We are all but aspects of the same Self," said El-Yezdi, "facets of the same Reality."

"But why have you brought me here?" asked Burton. "Why have you brought any of us here? And where the bloody hell is here?"

"That last one I can answer," said Abdullah. "We're in the Dream Realms that wind between realities."

"And as for the first question," said El-Yezdi, "because it is too late for us. And because you still have a chance to save your reality, your Earth."

"What do you mean?" asked the explorer.

The commander of the *Nautilus* said, "Eldritch forces have decimated us. Our civilizations are in ruin. Those that are left are slaves to those terrible star things. El-Yezdi reached out to us, pulled us through the First Gate, to the Dream Realms. To find and help you."

He looked at Burton with his remaining eye grimly. "He said you were the key."

"Yes," said Burton. "He told me that in my dreams. But what does it mean? What is the Dream Key?"

"You are," said El-Yezdi. You are our Facet in your reality. You anchor us and allow us to break through into your version of the All-is-One."

"That still doesn't make any bloody sense," said Burton.

"We escaped our realities, with El-Yezdi's help, through the Dreamlands," said Ruffian Dick. "The Australian aborigines call it the Dreamtime. But it's real. As real as my bloody brass arm. It's like a nexus between all the facets of reality."

The eye of every Burton turned toward him.

"What?" said Ruffian Dick. "I listen."

"So the visions I saw. That was you lot coming to get me." said Burton.

"Yes," said Abdullah. "This desert, all the things you saw in your dreams, just dream-vistas, flashes from us as we moved closer and closer toward your facet. El-Yezdi sent them to you."

"This boggles the mind," said Burton. "We grow accustomed to the world being a certain way. We think we understand it, and then a new understanding upends it. What can I do? The Awakened are many, and have a small army of acolytes. I am but one man."

El-Yezdi laughed then, a dry, almost ominous cackle.

"No," said Abdullah the Bushri, "you are five. We are all you, remember? And you are all of us."

"Bismillah!" Burton swore. "I didn't think of that. But what exactly are we to do about the Awakened? They have hijacked the bodies of innocent people, including my friend Algernon."

"Algy?" said Ruffian Dick. "I haven't seen him in ages. Not since the Deep Ones took Trafalgar Square. How the bloody hell is he?"

"Alive," said Burton, eying his doppelganger grimly. "And imprisoned in the deep past in the body of one of the Great Race."

"Do not fear," said El-Yezdi, "all shall be as it was. We have dealt with the Great Race of Yith before. We cannot kill them, but we can send them back to where and when they came before they complete their terrible ritual."

Burton arched an eyebrow. "How?"

"The Great Race's hold on your time is tenuous, and only moves easily in one direction." said the mystic. "To return to their bodies they must make use of a special device they have someone build in whatever time period they have invaded."

"Of course!" said Burton. "I've seen that device. My friends have the plans for its construction."

"Excellent," said El-Yezdi. "Truly you are the key."

Burton raked a hand through his beard. "They are anticipating returning to their own time and bodies should their mission fail, and this Yog-Sothoth refuses to grant them their wish."

"And what might that be?" asked Abdullah the Bushri. "And who or what is Yog-Sothoth?

"Yog-Sothoth is an outer god," said El-Yezdi. He is the progenitor of Yug and Neb, sires of Cthulhu. He is omniscient, locked outside of all Time and Space. Yog-Sothoth sees all and can access all."

"Why hasn't he done anything about the four of you?" asked Burton.

"He does not care. We are beneath his notice and too far from his center of influence. Would you care that an ant is carrying a bread-crumb a mile from your house? As for the Great Race, they wish to have access to the other facets of reality," said El-Yezdi. "That is why they summoned Yog-Sothoth in my facet. They have traveled ahead, far into the future, to the very death of your universe, to see how it all will end. They are ageless, timeless, but they cannot escape the end of Time itself. They will be torn apart by entropy just like everything else. Unless they can travel to another reality in which the universe is not yet in its death throes."

"And again and again," said Burton. "Through every possible reality. So how do we force them back to their own time preemptively, before they can summon Yog-Sothoth?"

"They must be in close proximity to the device when it is activated," said El-Yezdi. "Within mere inches."

"They are not going to go willingly," said the Captain. "We could hold them down."

"The device will be secreted away and heavily guarded," said Burton. "And they now have an army of acolytes who protect them."

"You'll never get close enough," said Ruffian Dick, tapping the fingers of his mechanical arm once more on the table.

Burton looked across the table at his double, his mouth widening into a smile. "Maybe we don't have to. My friends have the plans for this device. They are very clever. I'm sure they can build another one. A better one."

"By midnight your time?" said Captain Burton. "Ha!"

Burton arched an eyebrow. "We have to try. Besides, I know a way we might be able to get more time. But I must get back and tell my friends. There is much to do, and we are short on time."

He looked at the assembly of doppelgangers before saying, "Um, how do I get back?"

"I will help you," said El-Yezdi, his eyes once more burrowing into Burton's soul. "You have no doubt noticed the Wold-Newton fragments embedded in my forehead. They help me focus my mental powers. Through them I am able to traverse the different facets of reality, as the Great Race of your facet seek to do."

"Why haven't they succeeded?" asked Burton.

"Because they are minds without bodies. It takes both body and mind together, working in concert. They can shift reality only slightly, as well as increase their own ability to tell the future. To pierce the veil between realities, they need Yog-Sothoth."

Burton nodded. "They have used both talents to great effect. But how else can you help?"

"We can offer guidance, aspects of our being, but we cannot enter your facet. We are nothing but dream stuff. Only Yog-Sothoth could bring us through the Gate to your reality. And then there would be too many iterations of the Wold-Newton stones in a single facet. The resulting psychic resonance would kill the Awakened, as you call them, including your friend Swinburne. They would still exist, but their minds would be trapped in the past, in alien bodies, for the rest of the Great Race's natural lifespan."

"I understand. At least I think I understand. I thank you for your assistance. I am ready to return."

"Very well," said El-Yezdi. "Clear your mind. Begin the meditation that brought you here."

Burton closed his eyes and breathed deeply. Soon he felt himself drifting away.

THE COUNCIL OF BURTONS

Bismillah!"

Burton opened his eyes and sat bolt upright, knocking the crystals resting on his chest and forehead to the floor. Lady Helena ceased her ministrations and looked down at him, concerned. "Well, Captain Burton?"

"It worked." He glanced at Herbert and Challenger. "Bloody hell, it worked."

He then explained, as quickly and clearly as possible, all that he had seen and heard.

"Blimey!" thundered Challenger. "A whole council of Burtons, eh? Those Awakened won't know what hit them."

"We need to move quickly," said Burton. "We don't have much time." He glanced in Herbert's direction. "Or do we?"

The Time Traveler grinned. "There is always time. What we do with that time is the real issue."

"Bloody hell, Burton?" said Challenger. "What do you have in mind?"

"You still have the plans for that queer device?" Burton asked Herbert.

The Time Traveler patted his coat pocket.

"And your Time Machine is functional?"

"Of course," said Herbert, sounding offended. "Ready for another jaunt through Time, Professor?"

The big zoologist sighed. "Do I have a choice?"

"We just need a safe place in which to do our work undetected," said Herbert. "We must avoid meeting anyone who knows us, especially our past selves, if we are to avoid any chance of creating another paradox."

"I know just the place," said Burton.

They hired a couple of burly deliverymen with a carriage and a pair of sturdy horses to transport Herbert's brand-new Time Machine from his home in Kew Gardens to an old building at Covent Garden that belonged to Isabel's father's family. The place had been abandoned for years, and Mr. Arundell had given Burton the key for safekeeping. Burton knew that no one had been in the building at least during the last six months. Herbert and Challenger packed enough food and supplies for a week's worth of almost nonstop work, along with one of his shoggoth-guns just in case and, dragging the Time Machine into the building, they closed the heavy wooden doors and went back to a point one month in the past. After seeing them off, Burton went to find Inspector Abberline.

"Burton!" said Abberline, waving to him from a cordon of police standing outside the theosophic hall. "Where have you been? I've been looking all over for you!"

"And I you," said the explorer. The two men shook hands. "What's going on?"

"We're getting ready to move on these Awakened," said Abberline. "Mr. Holmes is done with their meddling. His man in Yorkshire said that Nash, Whiteside, and Greensmith dug up a large black stone from a field and brought it straight back here. Whatever they are doing in there, it stops tonight. We're preparing to turn off the gas and take a battering ram to those doors."

"You are right about that. It ends tonight. But not like this. Frederick, innocent people will be killed, including the men whose bodies the Awakened are inhabiting."

"I am sorry, Captain. My orders stand. Mr. Holmes believes keeping the city intact is more important than a few lives."

Burton glowered at Abberline for a long moment, then took a deep, relaxing breath. "I have a plan in place to stop them." He looked around self-consciously at the uniformed policemen standing around watching their exchange. "Can we speak in private?"

Abberline nodded and stepped away from the cordon. They moved a few feet away. "What are you planning? And perhaps more importantly, what are they up to in there?"

Burton explained things as best he could. "By Jove! I only wish that was the craziest thing I've ever heard, but we both know that isn't so."

"Burton nodded. "Their ritual will be completed by midnight, when this Yog-Sothoth will emerge into our world."

"And then they'll destroy everything."

"I believe that's their plan."

"And Herbert and Professor Challenger are building a device that can send them packing?"

Burton nodded.

"Without bloodshed."

"That is the idea, yes. If you send your policemen in there, innocent people are going to die, and I don't think Mycroft Holmes wants to explain to the papers exactly why that had to happen."

Abberline nodded. "All right. I agree with you. This whole business leaves a bad taste in my mouth. If we can stop this without violence, I'm all for it."

"Good man," said Burton, patting Abberline on the shoulder. "Now we just need to stall this ritual of theirs for as long as we can."

"And how do you intend to do that?"

Burton regarded the building. "I'm sure something will come to me. Let's go."

THE COMING OF YOG-SOTHOTH

The doors had been heavily bolted from the inside by the Awakened's acolytes, but Burton and Abberline moved around the building until they found an unsecured window. With some difficulty they managed to crawl through it into a small room cluttered with occult ephemera left behind by the Theosophes. "There are a few of those Theosophes outside as well," said Abberline. "Eager to get the use of their building back, I suspect."

Burton moved to the door, trying the knob. It opened a crack. "Come on. And be quiet."

Abberline drew his service revolver, and Burton wondered idly if he should have brought a weapon. He wanted this to have a peaceful resolution, and meant no physical harm to any of the Awakened, especially Swinburne. When all was made right, each of these men would no doubt feel no small amount of guilt for the actions of their commandeered bodies this night, and he didn't want them to also have spilled blood on their hands.

They moved into a dimly lit hall, through which chanting could be heard.

Yog-Sothoth knows the gate.

Yog-Sothoth is the gate. Yog-Sothoth is the key and the guardian of the gate.
Past, present, future, all are one in Yog-Sothoth.
He knows where the Old Ones broke through of old, and where They shall
break through again.
He knows where They have trod earth's fields, and where They still tread
them, and why no one can behold Them as They tread.

Abberline tightened his grip on his revolver. Burton, his nerves taught as piano wires, took a deep, steadying breath. The chanting grew closer, louder.

Yog-Sothoth, Scion of the Nameless Mist, hear us.
Open the Door we have prepared for thee, Beyond One.
For you are the Opener of the Way.
You are the All-in-One.
You are the One-in-All.

"This Yog-Sothoth must respond well to flattery," Abberline whispered.

"Shhh!" Burton scolded. They were at the end of the corridor now, which opened out into the wide central space crowded with black-robed acolytes, ordinary Londoners who had been taken in by the Awakened's feats of clairvoyance, and had no idea of the doom about to befall them. He scanned the room, picking out each member of the Awakened—Swinburne, Goforth, Nash, Peacock, Greensmith, and Whiteside—who were all standing in a circle around the immense black stone, their hands joined, their bodies swaying in supplication. The black jewels on the malformed headpieces they wore glinted darkly in the gaslights.

Burton stood ready to pounce, though to do exactly what he had no idea. Abberline placed a steadying hand on his shoulder. "Wait until they turn off the gas."

Burton nodded, noting Swinburne's position among the throng. If they could knock the malignant crowns from their heads, they would decrease the influence of the Wold-Newton stones, perhaps even disrupt the ritual enough that they would have to start it all over again. He felt the eyes of El-Yezdi upon him, could feel the presence of the other Burtons. His right arm felt strange, as if it was gone, and in its place was something heavy, a thing of brass and wood where blood and bone should be. He felt something covering his left eye, though he could still see. Felt the weight of a slim scimitar on his left hip. The others were here with him, guiding him, goading him forward.

The gaslights sputtered and died. The throng of huddled acolytes exchanged worried exasperations, but the Swinburne-thing urged them to keep going. Their chanting increased, and Burton thought he saw a strange electricity crackling along the rough-hewn edges of the stone.

They heard a thunderous noise coming from the main double doors into the hall. "Battering ram," said Abberline. "My boys are coming in." He moved around Burton, gun raised in the dark. "Metropolitan Police! You are all under arrest!"

"Poppycock!" he heard the Swinburne-thing screech. "Who dares interrupt the coming of Yog-Sothoth?"

"It's over, Algy," said Burton as he stepped up beside Abberline. "Or whoever you are."

A robed figure moved to confront him. Burton sent a fist into his face and the figure went down in a heap.

Lightning danced across the stone, blue claws arcing to the surrounding support pillars.

"How joyous!" said the Goforth-thing. "Look! Yog-Sothoth comes."

There was a tinge of ozone and something fetid as the hairs on Burton's neck stood at attention. A blast of cold air that whipped through his beard as he felt a vague sucking sensation, as of the sudden presence of a vacuum. He couldn't see well in the darkness, but as his eyes adjusted he got an impression of movement coming from the stone, long, ropey tendrils stretching out, wrapping themselves around the surrounding pillars. Interspersed along their length were large pale orbs.

The Awakened had backed away, and were the only ones still chanting, most of it in their bizarre guttural speech. But one phrase could still be clearly made out: *Yog-Sothoth. Yog-Sothoth. Yog-Sothoth.*

"Hear us, Opener of the Way!" someone near Abberline shouted.

So transfixed were the Great Race's thralls that no one tried to molest Abberline or Burton any further. They were all staring into the black void they all sensed rather than perceived was yawning open toward them. And through that limitless void something was coming.

Burton stood frozen, his heart hammering in his chest. In his mind's eye he could see El-Yezdi, could hear him whispering from across an immense distance.

The Man of Truth is beyond good and evil. The Man of Truth has ridden to All-Is-One. The Man of Truth has learned that Illusion is the One Reality, and that Substance is the Great Impostor. His forehead itched, and he reached up, feeling a series of cold lumps, the Wold-Newton stones embedded in the skin there.

Burton clenched his right fist, and found that it was made of brass. Afraid to break the illusion, he did not look down at it. He flexed the fingers, feeling the whir of tiny pneumatic pistons that could rend metal, crush rock.

We are with you, said Abdullah the Bushri, his whisper like a breath of hot desert wind. Burton clutched the handle of the gleaming scimitar with his left hand, the hilt cool and hard beneath his fingertips. The smell of Persian spices filled his nostrils, masking the fetid stench that came at them from the yawning opening.

He heard the sound of something wet sliding along stone, as if something very large was trying to fit through an opening much too small for its bulk. He sensed more of the pale orbs, and had the eerie feeling he was being watched by a million eyes, not unlike the sensation he got from being pursued by a shoggoth. But this was no shoggoth. Those loathsome creatures were nothing compared to the entity that was pulling itself into this world right in front of them. An army of shoggoths would cower in fear at this thing that loomed up before the assembly.

The pounding of the coppers attempting to batter down the door grew louder, more insistent.

"Yog-Sothoth," said the Swinburne-thing. "Scion of the Nameless Mist. Opener of the Way, Beyond One, hear our cries. We are of the Great Race of Yith, whom you have gifted with the ability to move through Time. We wish to join you through the Gate. We wish to leave behind our earthly shackles and move through the facets of reality as you do. Please help us, and this world is yours."

This world is but one facet of the All, and is already mine. The pitiful creatures who live within it are as base as the insects that grovel at your feet.

Burton and Abberline, along with everyone else in the room save the Awakened, clutched at their heads. The voice of Yog-Sothoth was deafening, and coming from inside their skulls. The entity was communicating with them through their minds, without words as Burton knew them.

He heard a high-pitched whine, and realized it was the stones the Awakened wore within their repugnant headpieces, humming in their mountings. Their ethereal vibrations made his back teeth ache.

"Beyond One," said the Swinburne-thing. "Father of Nug and Yeb. Grandfather of terrible Cthulhu. You survey all facets of reality, but powerful as you are, you are locked outside the universe. We wish to give you entry, to impart your will on this facet. We implore you. We retrieved a Doorway to receive your magnificence, and have obtained the ancient and holy psychic stones to focus your power in this realm. All we ask in return is to traverse the First Gate."

All who are deemed worthy may attempt passage through the First Gate. Let me through, and access to the All in One shall be yours.

"It's a bloody deal with the Devil," Abberline whispered beside Burton.

Burton considered the Inspector's words. This Yog-Sothoth was no ordinary devil as he knew the term. He was much bigger, much more powerful.

What is that infernal hammering? Said Yog-Sothoth as the sound of the police battering ram grew louder, every impact threatening to send the formidable double doors exploding into thousands of splinters.

"The humans of this facet attempt to stop us," said the Goforth-thing. "Even now they seek to sully this holy ritual with their presence."

They annoy me.

The sound ceased. Burton and Abberline looked at each other, a cold realization stealing upon Burton as he realized what must have happened. Yog-Sothoth, using but a modicum of his power, had stopped the police in their efforts to break down the doors. How this was achieved Burton didn't know, nor want to.

"Now see here!" Abberline shouted, an edge of fear in his voice. "Every bloody person in here is hereby under arrest. No more magic tr-"

Abberline seized and, panicking, dropped his pistol. Burton heard it clatter heavily to the floor as the police inspector fell against him, gripping Burton's shoulder. "What is it man?"

Abberline didn't say anything, but his panicking increased. He rubbed his face with his left hand, as if indicating the trouble sprang from that part of his anatomy. Burton squinted his eyes in the gloom, and in the pale light emanating from Yog-Sothoth's globes he saw a terrible sight. Inspector Abberline's mouth was gone. Not covered or obscured. *Gone.*

"These are the men who tried to stop us," said the Swinburne-thing, pointing at Burton and the frustrated Abberline. "They are the ones who tried to prevent us from becoming conduits for your perfect will."

Then they shall be the first to know what it means to bend to the will of Yog-Sothoth.

Burton felt his legs give beneath him, and he had the strange sensation that he was melting into the floor. Abberline looked at him askance, his expression frozen on a body that was now a mass of cubes. Burton reached for him with arms that were now giant lobster claws.

"Bismillah! Help me!"

As if in answer, the millions of cubes that now made up Abberline's body fell clattering to the floor.

THE MAN OF TRUTH

Burton wretched, but nothing came up. The assembled acolytes stared down at him with bulbous eyes on the ends of long, fleshy stalks. Burton wanted to scream. He squeezed his eyes shut instead.

The Man of Truth has learned that Illusion is the One Reality, and that Substance is the Great Impostor.

"El-Yezdi," Burton murmured. He was still there with him.

"What did you say?" asked the Swinburne-thing.

"El-Yezdi," Burton said again, flexing the fingers of his right hand, feeling the cold brass there once more, the solid and lethal scimitar hanging from his left hip.

The Man of Truth is beyond good and evil. The Man of Truth has ridden to All-Is-One.

They were all there with him. The Captain. Ruffian Dick. Abullah the Bushri. El-Yezdi. Especially El-Yezdi, whose eyes once more burned into Burton's soul.

"Something's wrong," said the Goforth-thing. "I don't like this."

"Nor do I," said the Whiteside-thing. "Something isn't right."

"Something else is here with Burton," said the Nash-thing.

"Wait, you dolts," said the Swinburne-thing. "Once Yog-Sothoth is through this will be over. We'll head for the Gate and leave these repulsive bodies."

So the ritual wasn't finished. Burton smiled, rising to his feet, which were no longer melting into the floor.

"No. It can't be," said the Nash-thing. "He subverts the will of Yog-Sothoth."

Burton stepped up to him, slashing out with Abdullah's scimitar, knocking the queer headpiece from his head. It clanged onto the floor and Burton stepped on it, rending the soft metal and dislodging the Wold-Newton stones from their fittings and crushing them to black dust beneath his boots.

"No!" cried Whiteside, lunging at the explorer. Burton slapped him aside with a brass hand that could dent steel plate, and the man fell to the floor in an unconscious heap. The rest of the Awakened moved toward Burton now, but they were no fighters, even in their normal lives. Burton dispatched them easily, careful not to wound them too severely as he dashed the obscene crowns containing the Wold-Newton stones from their heads.

"Keep chanting!" the Swinburne-thing screeched at his thralls. "We must complete the ritual!"

Burton came after him next, but the being from Yith ducked out of the explorer's reach. "Where did you get that sword? That arm?

Burton could see no scimitar in his hand, no brass and wood prosthetic where his right arm should be, though he could feel them. But he was glad Swinburne's impostor could see them. He grinned at the Swinburne-thing. "The Man of Truth knows that Illusion is the One Reality, and that Substance is the Great Impostor."

"Who told you that?"

He brought the scimitar up, its blade singing in time to the ethereal vibrations given off by the Wold-Newton stones. He brought it down in a sideways arc. The Swinburne-thing ducked, but the sword lodged between the combs of the elaborate, misshapen headpiece and pulled it from his head. Burton flicked his wrist, and the headpiece clattered to the marble floor.

"No!" said the Swinburne-thing, diving to the floor and grabbing it. "You don't know how many centuries we have prepared for this! You will not take this away from us, you repugnant pink ape!"

Burton placed the tip of his blade on the back of the Swinburne-thing's neck.

"Do it, Burton," the Swinburne-thing spat. "Go ahead. You will not kill me. I am Timeless. But the owner of this body, your dear friend the poet, will not be so fortunate."

In the distance the great bell of the Westminster clock tower struck the first chime of midnight.

"No!" the Goforth-thing cried. "The ritual!"

The tendrils of Yog-Sothoth that stretched out from the stone began to writhe and slink back within it, the tenuous foothold the eldritch entity had in this world slipping away.

"Come back, O Beyond One!" the Swinburne-thing cried, reaching for his master, heedless of the razor-sharp blade at his neck.

With the third chime, there was a sudden flash through the front windows from the direction of Westminster, and all of the Awakened went limp and senseless where they lay.

"Algy?" said Burton, leaning down to check his friend's pulse. His scimitar and mechanical arm, so solid and present mere moments before, were now gone. There was a blast of cold air from the stone, and a slight sucking sensation, then the essence of Yog-Sothoth was gone. The assembled acolytes moaned and held their heads, muttering questions to one another.

Burton looked behind him at the prostrate form of Inspector Abberline, who grumbled as he sat up. "Blimey. Where's my gun?"

"Over there," Burton pointed.

Abberline worked his jaw up and down, touched his hand to his mouth. "By Jove! My mouth is back! But where did it go?"

"I believe Yog-Sothoth was having some fun with us," said Burton. "An illusion."

"And you figured it out. But how?"

"The Man of Truth knows that Illusion is the One Reality, and that Substance is the Great Impostor."

Abberline squinted up at him. "And what the deuce does that mean?"

Burton chuckled, helping the inspector to his feet. "I have no idea. But it helped me dispatch the Great Race of Yith. We need to get the gaslights back on."

Abberline nodded, retrieved his gun, and headed for the double doors, where the policemen outside had begun striking it with their battering ram once more. In a few minutes the building was full of police carrying truncheons and lanterns, though they didn't have to make use of the former. The so-called acolytes were dazed and confused and had little recollection of how they had arrived there and the strange ritual in which they had taken part.

Once the gaslights were restored, Burton went to his friend, gently rolling him onto his back. He looked like a pale cherub in the sputtering gaslights and appeared as if he were only sleeping. Burton gently slapped at his cheeks. "Algy. Wake up."

The poet's eyes snapped open, and in his characteristic high-pitched voice screeched, "Oh, yes, Madam! Spank me! For I have been a very naughty boy!"

Swinburne sat bolt upright and looked around, his wild fiery hair in his face. Every eye in the room was on him thanks to his outburst. "Gadzooks! Where am I?"

Burton cleared his throat. "You are at the Theosophic meeting hall, Algy." Burton helped the poet to his feet as he looked around shakily.

Swinburne stood there a long moment, blinking at everyone standing or sitting around the large black stone. "My hat!" cried the poet. "Am I sober?"

"I'm afraid so, Algy."

Swinburne scowled up at him, hauling a thick lock of red hair out of his face. "A dreadful sensation which you must rectify immediately by buying me a pint. Or three."

"Very well, Algy," said Burton, glad to have his friend back. "Do you remember anything?"

"Why, no. One minute I was taking the lash, and the next moment, I'm standing here, stone sober and wondering what the bloody hell is going on."

"I'm afraid that will take some time to explain," said Burton. "I have some loose ends to attend to, but there's James Hunt. Let him examine you."

"My hat!" Swinburne squealed at the sight of their friend, walking in with a throng of police, his medical bag in hand. "James old son! Mind telling me, over a pint, what the devil is going on?"

"There's a good fellow," urged Burton as he turned to examine the black stone. It was twice as tall as him, standing within a circle made of candles. Its black surface was covered in strange, often grotesque sigils partially eroded away by time. He touched it, feeling the cold, rough stone beneath his fingertips.

"Burton!"

The explorer turned to see the rotund figure of Mycroft Holmes coming toward him, a couple of stiff and trim assistants bookending him.

"I take it this affair is concluded?"

Burton nodded. "It is. The Awakened have all recovered." He glanced at a couple of policemen helping Goforth and Whiteside to their feet. The old man looked a decade older as he wobbled in their grasp. "They seem to have no memory of what transpired and should not be found at fault for their actions."

Mycroft gave a derisive sniff. "And what of the Wold-Newton stones? The curator would like them returned."

"They are affixed to those ghastly crowns," said Burton, pointing. Mycroft Holmes ordered one of his assistants to retrieve them. The man held them close, causing Burton to suspect that the elder Holmes had no intention of returning them to the museum.

"And where are you associates?" asked Mycroft Holmes.

"Right here, Mr. Holmes sir," said Herbert as he and Challenger came striding in, their clothes grimy with grease. "Hello, Captain," he said, waving.

"You saved us all in the nick of time," said Burton with a grin.

"What is he talking about?" asked Mycroft Holmes.

"We constructed a device that sent that Great Race lot packing," rumbled Challenger. "And you're welcome."

"It is large enough to work anywhere in the city," said Herbert.

"Though we cannot be exactly sure of its range. It's in the clock tower, tucked up beneath Big Ben."

"What?" said Mycroft Holmes.

"Do not worry. It will not impede the normal operation of that venerable old timepiece," said Herbert. "And it's there in case it is needed again."

This seemed to placate Mycroft Holmes, and he focused his attentions on the great black stone in the center of the floor.

"The Awakened dug this up in a field in Yorkshire," said Burton. "One of them told me he and some associates buried it there in 1684 for later use. It functions as some sort of doorway for the deity they attempted to summon, this Yog-Sothoth."

"And were they successful?"

"Almost," said Burton.

Mycroft Holmes nodded. "You will be at the Tower at noon tomorrow for debriefing. I will make arrangements to get this stone removed."

Burton felt flushed with angry heat, but he said nothing. He didn't like the idea of someone like Mycroft Holmes taking custody of something that could be put to such malignant use, but there was nothing he could do about it. He wondered what other fiendish, esoteric items might be locked away in the Tower for "safekeeping."

"Mr. Holmes," said Abberline, stepping into view. "You'll be pleased to know that this entire lot can't remember a bloody thing."

"Wonderful," said Holmes almost casually as he turned to leave. "I trust you and your fellows to mop this up nice and tidy." He glared at Burton. "I'll see you tomorrow noon." He exited the hall with his assistants.

"My, but he's all business, isn't he?" Abberline remarked when Mycroft Holmes was safely out of earshot.

"In his line of work, he has to be," said Burton. To Herbert he said, "What took you so bloody long?"

"You said midnight," said the Time Traveler, looking hurt. "I wanted to avoid any possibility of a paradox, remember?"

Burton glanced across the room at Swinburne, who appeared his old self, if rather un-inebriated. He had been joined not only by James

Hunt, but Thomas Bendyshe, Charles Bradlaugh, and Richard Monkton Milnes, almost the full complement of Cannibals.

"I need a drink," said Burton. "Who's with me?"

"I'm with you in spirit," said Abberline. "But I have several more hours of work straightening things out here. Have a pint for me."

"Sounds bloody marvelous," said Challenger. He clapped the Time Traveler on the shoulder. "Herbert?"

"Not this time, I'm afraid. I must make arrangements for my Time Machine. And by that, I mean taking a wrench to it and dismantling the damn thing."

"Good man!" Burton exclaimed. "All right then. I'll leave things in your capable hands, Frederick. Do come around tomorrow and let's have a talk about it."

"Certainly, Captain. Good night. Er, good morning!"

Burton placed his arm around Swinburne's shoulders, and the group walked out of the Theosophic hall in search of the nearest pub. Burton smiled down at the diminutive poet, glad to have his friend back. He asked a few questions, which Burton tried to answer as best he could, but for the most part they spoke of other things, chiefly the poet's desire to get as drunk as possible. It felt good. It felt normal, though Burton wondered for how long that feeling would last. The world was no longer as simple as he once thought it was, but he also knew, whatever challenges lay ahead, he would never have to face them alone. For he was but one facet of a greater All.

PART IV
THE MAP OF TIME

"I was in the death struggle with self: God and Satan fought for my soul those three long hours. God conquered—now I have only one doubt left—which of the two was God?" —Aleister Crowley

"The past is but the beginning of a beginning, and all that is or has been is but the twilight of the dawn." —H.G. Wells, *The Discovery of the Future*

"It's no use going back to yesterday, because I was a different person then." —Lewis Carroll

Preserve us from our enemies;
    Thou who art Lord of suns and skies;
    Whose meat and drink is flesh in pies;
    And blood in bowls!
    Of thy sweet mercy, damn their eyes;
    And damn their souls! —The Cannibal Catechism, Algernon Charles Swinburne

802,701

The Time Traveler awoke, his mind reeling as he struggled to remember where—and when—he was. He was in the throes of the strangest dream. He had been running through a nighttime London street with two other souls, something monstrous chasing them, a thing like jelly, with many eyes. He shook off the vestiges of the nightmare and rolled over, finding Weena lying soft and warm beside him beneath the covers he had brought on one of his trips from home. He sat up with a grin when he realized his bedclothes were over eight hundred thousand years old.

He eased out of the bed—which had also been brought piecemeal from the past and assembled here in this strange future time—and stood by the windowless portal of the dome-shaped building on the hill they had taken for themselves. The Moon shone bright and clear over the green landscape, the eternally warm breeze tickling his naked flesh. Below him the glistening Thames, now purified and stretched miles from its original course, snaked languidly across the lush landscape. To the Time Traveler's right stood the great White Sphinx, a silent sentinel to a civilization now long dead, perhaps built by the last fully intelligent creatures on the face of the Earth.

"Herbert?"

Weena's voice trilled like a bird. The Time Traveler turned at the sound, like the soft tinkling of a bell. "It is all right, darling. Go back to sleep."

The tiny Eloi did as instructed, resting her small head back down on the pillow. She was asleep in seconds. The Time Traveler watched her for a long moment, smiling at the sound of his name that had come from her lips. He had accomplished much in six years working with Weena and the other Eloi. They could speak at least a little English, proving themselves to be much brighter than the livestock the awful Morlocks had bred them to be. It wasn't much, but it was a start. It would take centuries to remake what man in his foolishness had undone, but centuries the Time Traveler had in abundance. In just six short months he had freed the Eloi from the Morlocks and taught them how to fend for themselves. It went against their breeding, but mankind had once again shown itself to be an endlessly adaptable species. By day they toiled for their survival, and by night they gathered in the central area of their main gathering place while Herbert read Shakespeare and Aristotle to them. He knew they lacked the intellectual capacity to understand even a tenth of it, but they loved to hear the cadence of the King's English, and they parroted snippets of what they heard, adding it to their growing vocabulary. In another year, who knew? Perhaps they could put on one of the Bard's plays, performing the lines themselves. But that was a project for a much later date.

The Time Traveler donned his clothes and stepped out of the little dome-shaped structure. He felt safe and secure, even at night. There had been no sign of the Morlocks since he had set fire to their underground caverns and freed the Eloi—including Weena—from their clutches. His eyes followed the path of the Thames, which inevitably, even in this far distant time, led out to sea. He hoped to build a sailing ship someday, venturing across what was left of the English Channel to the Continent to see what time-ravaged remnants of humanity he would find there. Perhaps there were other pockets of docile Eloi who needed freeing from the cruel Morlocks. He would free them all, and they would be a great civilization once more. What the descendants of the Time Traveler's kind had wrought he would single-handedly undo. Even if it took the rest of his life.

He heard a slight rustle of the grass behind him and spun round, his heart hammering. Fearing a Morlock, he reached in his pocket for his pistol.

"Hello? Herbert? Is that you? Don't shoot. It's me. Burton."

"Who?" said Herbert, stepping around the hut and back into the moonlight. A figure stood there, tall and somewhat gaunt. As different from the short, pudgy form of the Morlocks as he was from the diminutive, lithe bodies of the Eloi.

"It's me, Burton," the figure said again.

The Time Traveler stared at the apparition, blinking. Could it be true? Or was it some Morlock trick? The man standing before the Time Traveler was older, wearing a dark greatcoat and top hat that, while right at home in the London of his time, was out of place and stifling in the humid hothouse the world had become over the succeeding millennia. What most easily identified the figure as Captain Sir Richard Francis Burton was the long, Y-shaped scar that ran down his left cheek, a souvenir from his army days. "Captain Burton! By Jove. I never expected to see you again. What in God's name are you doing here?" He stepped closer, extending his hand.

"Bismillah," said the figure, "you look a sight, man." They shook hands.

The Time Traveler raked his hand through his long beard. It was itchy at first, but he was getting used to it. "I suppose I do. But you are a sight for sore eyes. What brings you to the End of Time? And how did you arrive here?"

"The how is simple," said Burton, pulling his coat sleeve away from his right wrist. "I came here with the help of this." Attached to the explorer's wrist was some strange apparatus that glittered in the moonlight. Herbert turned Burton's wrist this way and that, examining the contraption. As his eyes adjusted to the moon glow glinting off brass, he made out more detail. A tiny brass disk gleamed atop what appeared to be an ordinary wristwatch housing. In place of the winding mechanism were two small nodes that protruded from the side of the device. A chill fled down the Time Traveler's spine.

"Good God. Is that what I think it is?"

"If you think it is a miniature, wrist-mounted version of your Time Machine, then yes," Burton said.

"But how? Who made this?"

"You did," said Burton. "After a fashion. It is based on your original design, constructed in the year 1945 or thereabouts." He pulled his sleeve back down, covering the device. "As for why I'm here, that will take a bit longer to explain."

"I'm afraid I don't understand," said the Time Traveler.

Burton smiled. "No, I don't suppose you do. Don't worry, old friend. I'll get you up to speed as best I can. Let's go inside your little hut there and have a drink."

"I'm sorry, I don't have any spirits."

"I suspected as much," said Burton with a grin. "That's why I brought my own."

He produced a small bottle of brandy from his back pocket and showed it to the Time Traveler. The amber liquid burned gold in the early morning sunlight that had just begun to peek over the horizon.

"Well, come inside, then," said the Time Traveler. "It appears you and I have much to discuss."

UNDER LONDON

T hank you for accompanying me, Captain Burton," said Detective Inspector Frederick George Abberline. "I know you are under no such compunction to do so. This isn't Shadow Council business."

"Think nothing of it, my friend," said the explorer as he held the lantern steady so the policeman could do his work. "When you said there was a cannibal on the loose, I couldn't resist. The grisly practice has long been an interest of mine."

Abberline ceased his labors and turned to glare askance at the explorer.

Burton laughed. "Not as a participant, old friend, but as an observer. Though now that I say that I suppose that doesn't sound much better."

"You have some strange hobbies, if you don't mind my sayin' so, Captain. But what do I know? I'm just a simple copper."

Abberline redoubled his efforts on the brickwork, inserting his pry bar into the small crevice and pulling the implement toward him. There was indeed a door here;.Abberline's unusual informant, the famous novelist and protege of Charles Dickens, Wilkie Collins, had reportedly escaped from what he described as an underground chamber of horrors presided over by monsters. The fact that Mr. Collins had been suffering from severe laudanum withdraw at the time did not make his story any less credible, as there had been similar tales of abduction, monsters in the sewers, and bodies found with signs of human predation.

Abberline gave a final grunt and the secret door opened, blasting them with a cold draft of air.

"What now?" said Burton, heart hammering at the prospect of encountering an actual cannibal. His one regret from his travels in Africa, morbid as it may have been, was that he had never gotten to witness the practice firsthand.

"Now we call my men. I'm not about to go in there just the two of us. You remember what happened the last time we did that."

Burton nodded, lowering the lantern. "Shoggoths."

"There are worse things in this world than shoggoths," said the detective, stepping around Burton and blowing on his whistle. Burton turned as a dozen lanterns bobbed up and down in the darkness as Abberline's best men lumbered up the hill of the cemetery toward the secret crypt. He looked at the hole, eager to see what was inside.

The whole thing had begun when a half-eaten torso was fished out of the Thames. The city's coroner examined the remains and determined that, however the poor fellow had died, his body had definitely been gnawed on by human teeth, though from a very small mouth and with strangely pronounced canines. When Wilkie Collins was found wandering the streets, naked and delirious, Abberline called Burton at once, knowing of his interest in cannibalism. Burton had never before seen the man so in his element. He was back to chasing monsters of the human variety, and it clearly suited him. Neither of them had heard anything from Mycroft Holmes in several weeks, and there had been no more shoggoth sightings since that night at the Theosophic Society. This suited Burton just as well, and he and Isabel were once again planning their long- postponed nuptials.

"All right, Captain," said Abberline. "We're ready. Just stay by me."

"Certainly, Frederick. Lead the way, please."

A dozen policemen, armed with truncheons and lanterns, flooded the opening. Abberline pulled the grate open with a rusty squeal and they entered the dark aperture. Burton had to duck low to keep from bumping his head as he walked hunched over through the tunnel of crumbling brick. The lanterns the coppers were holding swayed with their movements, throwing strange shadows. Burton imagined he was an explorer once again, journeying into a land as strange and exotic as any Persian oasis or African veldt. And it was underneath his feet every day.

The fetid stench of raw sewage reached them as they rounded a slight bend. One of the policemen retched, and Burton had to rush ahead, breathing shallow lest his gorge become buoyant. "Do we even know what we are looking for?" he whispered to Abberline.

"I heard from an anonymous source that people are living down here."

"Bismillah!" said the explorer. "Truly?"

"Yes. People who can't even afford to live in the Cauldron."

"That's deplorable."

"And what's more," continued the detective, "many of them have reportedly gone missing. But the really strange thing is what they say is taking these people."

Burton arched an eyebrow. "Do tell."

"Monsters."

They heard the sound of rushing water. "Must be one of the underground tributaries of the Thames," said Abberline. "It's getting louder."

Burton nodded. "Yes. Probably the Peck, or perhaps the Effra."

As they followed the sound, the tunnel opened wider. Up ahead, Burton noticed a vague phosphorescence that illuminated a vast open space. The smell of human waste was overpowering now, and Burton immediately saw why. Lined up along one side of the dark surging river was a row of large metal cages containing dozens of human beings, dirtied and befouled.

"Good Lord!" said Abberline. "Help them. Get them out."

He stayed back with Burton while the dozen policemen under his authority flooded the space, going to work on the cages as the people inside them called out for help.

"Who could have done this?" Burton grabbed a lantern from one of the policemen and moved it about, inspecting the space. It showed definite signs of habitation, littered with dirty blankets, the rat-chewed remains of food, and even children's toys. Tucked away in an alcove of moss-laden brick was something even more shocking.

"Frederick, come here, please."

"Yes, Captain?"

Abberline moved up beside him, his mouth opening in an O of surprise when he saw what was illuminated by Burton's lantern. A metal table stood there, piled with human remains. The desiccated skin had long ago been flayed open.

Abberline pressed a handkerchief to his face. "Bloody hell! What is this?"

"It looks like an autopsy," Burton murmured, his mouth suddenly dry. This looked all too familiar. He had been in a room like this, with cages and medical equipment, when he had traveled hundreds of thousands of years into the past aboard Captain Nemo's *Nautilus* and was a prisoner of the Elder Things.

"What monster could do this?" Abberline was saying. Burton snapped out of his reverie.

"Morlocks," said a hunched-over old woman recently freed from one of the cages. "Morlocks," she said again as if the word should mean something. Burton recalled seeing the word scrawled in one of the tunnels. He had heard the name before, from the fevered rantings of the Time Traveler, Herbert. The woman gave him a crooked-toothed sneer, pointing toward the far end of the opening. "Morlocks."

Burton understood what she meant. Holding up the lantern he peered into the distance. In a crack in the brickwork he saw what appeared to be a hunched figure. The thing had white hair, fungoid skin, and glowing yellow eyes. Burton didn't scare easily, but this apparition sent a chill fleeing up his spine. "There. Look!"

"Over there, gents," said Abberline. A dozen pairs of eyes locked on the frightful creature Burton had seen. It ducked back into the fracture and was gone. "Go get it!"

In the lantern light Burton saw several more of the small creatures in shadow, loping away. Something about the way they moved gave him an idea.

"They're afraid of the light!" he called. "We need more lights down here."

Gunshots rang out as a group of Abberline's policemen engaged with what must be the Morlocks, while another set dealt with their newly freed prisoners.

"Get them out of here!" Abberline barked, drawing his gun. "Get them to the surface."

The people were effusive in their thanks. Abberline nodded to them as they passed. Burton wished they could do something more, but he wondered how quickly they would be back down here, simply because they had nowhere else to go.

Another gunshot echoed in the distance. Burton wondered if any of the bullets found their targets, or if the Morlocks, if that is what they were, would just vanish like so much smoke. He vowed to have a long talk with Herbert when this was done.

"They're gone, sir!" one of the coppers called, running back toward them up the tunnel.

Burton flashed the lantern around. Beyond the cages, on the other side of the swirling tributary, there were other things. Brass glinted in the lantern light, and the steady green glow of the phosphorescent lichen picked out pieces of queer machinery. "How do we get over there?"

"What?" said Abberline.

"We need to get across." Burton pointed at the collection of machinery.

Abberline glanced around. "There." He pointed to a wide wooden plank spread across a narrow span of the underground river. Burton ran toward it, testing it with his right foot before putting his full weight upon it. He then bounded across it, followed closely by Abberline. The policeman stood holding a lantern high while Burton inspected the equipment.

"What is all this? Do you think those—those monsters built this?"

Burton's eyes caught on a framework of brass with two levers at the front and a hammered copper dish at the back. It was crude and looked as if it had been cobbled together from other, much older machinery, but the design was unmistakable.

"Frederick, what does this look like to you?"

The detective moved closer, shining his lantern down full upon the contraption. "Why, if I didn't know any better, I would say it's a bloody Time Machine."

"I was afraid of that."

The two men looked at each other, their faces heavy with the implications of what they had found.

"We must destroy this," said Burton. "Dismantle it."

"Are you sure?"

"Until we know exactly what we are dealing with, yes."

Abberline waved over three of his men and instructed them to dismantle the strange device. They went at the task with gusto, making short work of it with pry-bars and truncheons. Burton thought he heard something overhead. Expecting another Morlock, he looked up and saw a black-cloaked human figure staring down at them.

"Up there!" Burton shouted.

Every head lifted up. The black-garbed figure barked laughter and retreated into the shadows.

"Bloody hell!" said Abberline. "Who was that?"

Burton's eyes narrowed to slits. "I don't know. But I intend to find out."

SWINBURNE IN BEDLAM

The hansom carried Burton and Abberline through the gates of Bedlam and up to the high stone steps. "Are you sure you want to do this?" asked Abberline. "We had a long night."

The explorer looked at the policeman, a grim expression souring his already hard countenance. "I must, Frederick." He had returned home with the dawn to a letter brought earlier the previous evening by messenger from a Dr. Seward at Brightmoor Asylum. It said that his friend, the poet Algernon Charles Swinburne, a recent inmate of the dismal place, wanted to see him at once.

Abberline nodded, and the two got out. Burton paid the fare and the two men started up the steps to the tall oaken doors. Abberline stared up at the imposing edifice and shivered. "I've never liked this place," he muttered, as if he feared the building would hear him and take offense. Burton simply nodded and hauled open one of the oaken double doors. As he did so they heard a muffled wailing coming from somewhere inside, the cry of some tortured soul. Burton wrinkled his nose as they entered. The smell of antiseptic masking vomit and urine assaulted his nostrils. They moved to the front desk and rang the bell.

The biggest woman Burton had ever seen looked up at him impatiently. "Yes?"

"I'm here to see a patient of yours," said Burton. "Algernon Charles Swinburne."

"Sign your name here," she said, pointing to a ledger. Burton dipped a nib pen in ink and scrawled his name. The woman spun the ledger around and read it. "Oh, Captain Burton. Dr. Seward has been expecting you."

"Will you take me to him, please?"

"Follow me." The woman stepped through an adjoining door into the hallway and Burton and Abberline followed. They came to a row of doors and the woman knocked on one of them. They heard a muffled, "Come in," and she opened the door.

"Dr. Seward," she said. "Captain Burton is here to see Mr. Swinburne."

Burton heard the creak of a wooden chair and a man popped his head out the door, smiling at Burton.

"Hello," he said, stepping into the corridor. "I am Dr. John Seward." He extended his hand, and Burton took it, giving the man a brisk shake. "Who is your associate?"

"Detective Inspector Frederick Abberline," said the policeman, shaking hands with Seward as well.

"Splendid. Well, I know you want to see about your friend right away. His has been a most interesting case. When he began asking for you, I knew I must get word to you immediately."

"I'm glad you did," said Burton. "Are you sure my presence won't hinder his healing?"

"On the contrary," said Seward. "I believe seeing you may bring him back to himself. If you will follow me."

Taking a ring of ponderous keys from the nurse, Seward led Burton and Abberline through a veritable maze. The urine-and-vomit smell was stronger, and behind heavy doors they heard more sounds of human torment. Stopping in front of one of the doors, Seward inserted one of the heavy keys and unlocked it. "His is a most unusual case. Mr. Swinburne is quite a brilliant poet. I've been familiarizing myself with is work."

Burton and Abberline followed Seward into a padded cell. Swinburne huddled in the far corner of that room, tied in a straitjacket, drooling.

"Is this how you treat all of your patients?" said Burton, scowling.

"My apologies, Captain Burton. Mr. Swinburne tends to get over-wrought at times. He's been, uh, finding ways to hurt himself. For instance, goading the orderlies into thrashing him. He seems to, ah, enjoy it."

Burton nodded. "Yes. Algy's body interprets pain as pleasure."

"Ah," said Seward. "So he was like this... um before? Well, it's very interesting. But what I'm most interested in is his state of mind. He has shared with me some most outrageous things. Things I've never heard before from any of my other patients. His psychosis is very peculiar."

"Swinburne is a peculiar fellow," Abberline offered. Burton silenced him with a stare. *You'd be in a similar state if your mind had been imprisoned for weeks inside an alien body in the remote past*, Burton wanted to say to the policeman. But he had been forbidden by Mycroft Holmes from discussing the exact particulars of what happened to the poet, and at any rate, had he told anyone the truth he'd likely be tied in a straitjacket right next to Swinburne. "I assume that is what you wanted to see me about?"

"Yes," said Seward. Addressing Swinburne he said, "Algy, you have visitors. Captain Burton and Inspector Abberline."

Swinburne stared straight ahead, not looking at either of them, a glazed look in his eyes. His fiery red hair was flayed all about his head.

"Talk to him," Seward urged. "It may do some good. For you both." He stepped out of the way as Burton leaned toward his friend.

"Algy?"

"Richard? My hat! I need a drink."

"I know, old friend. I'm sorry."

At first Burton had thought his friend had suffered no ill effects from having his mind usurped by a member of the Time-traveling Great Race of Yith. But then, weeks later, he started to be tormented by strange dreams of his captivity in the deep past. Then other things began to assail him. Hallucinations. Foul moods. It got so bad that his parents had him committed.

"Bloody hell, Richard. The shoggoths."

"The shoggoths are all gone, Algy."

"No. Just sleeping," said the poet. "'That which is dead can eternal lie, but with strange eons even death may die.'"

"What?" said Burton. He had heard that sinister phrase before, uttered by the deceased John Hanning Speke in his own dreams. It sounded even worse coming from Swinburne's lips, more real and therefore more dangerous.

"Time out of joint," said Swinburne. "Captain Richard Francis Burton has come unstuck in Time. My Aunt Petunia's pretty lace bonnet. Unstuck. Captain bloody Richard Gloucester Place Burton."

"He's out of his bloomin' tree," Abberline mused. Burton ignored him.

"Algernon. What do you mean Time is out of joint? What do you mean I've come unstuck?"

"Time, Richard. It's off kilter. Mycroft knows. Mycroft bloody Holmes well knows. Look at the Sphinx!"

"Sphinx, Algy? In Egypt?"

"The White Sphinx," the poet corrected, shaking his head. "On the hill. The damned Morlocks. In the tunnels, Richard. Don't go in the tunnels!"

"Remarkable," said Seward, writing something on a notepad.

"Under London, Richard. Don't go under London."

"We've already been, Algy. Last night," Burton whispered, conscious of Seward listening in right behind him. He lowered his voice to a whisper. "We saw the Morlocks."

Swinburne stared wide-eyed, but said nothing.

"How long has he been this way?" Burton asked Seward.

"Since he was first brought to my attention," said the doctor. "I specialize in extreme cases such as his, and came all the way from Carfax to study—er—treat him."

"What seems to be the matter with him?" Abberline asked.

"I'm not sure," said Seward. "He's suffered some trauma which has greatly interfered with his sense of time. He talks about things that have already happened as if they haven't yet occurred, and current affairs as if they are old news."

"By the Fungi of Yuggoth," the poet screeched. "My hat, Richard. The bloody Morlocks are mucking about through Time."

"What do you mean, Algy?" said Burton leaning close and locking eyes with the poet. "What must I do?"

Swinburne returned the explorer's gaze for the first time since Burton had entered the padded cell. "You must go all the way to the end, then stop. You must stop Mycroft bloody know-it-all Holmes from getting the map."

"Map? What map?"

"The Map of Time."

"What the devil is he talking about?" said Abberline.

"I wish I knew," said Burton, standing and turning to face Seward.

"Listen," said the poet, "Richard Francis Burton has come unstuck in Time." He giggled, as if what he'd just uttered was the most fantastic joke, one of the bawdy tales he used to regale them with at the Cannibal Club. "Richard? Richard?"

Burton shuddered. "I'm right here, Algy. I haven't gone anywhere."

The poet giggled once more, his eyes wild.

"Did any of that make sense to you?" asked the doctor.

"Some," said the explorer.

"'We are not sure of sorrow, and joy was never sure; Today will die tomorrow, Time stoops to no man's lure,'" the poet muttered, giggling.

"That was a bit of his verse," explained Burton. He reached into his jacket and handed Seward his card. "You will contact me if his condition changes, for good or ill?"

"Of-of course," said Seward, taking the proffered card.

"Richard," said Swinburne as Burton turned to leave.

"Yes, Algy?"

"'At the door of life, by the gate of breath, There are worse things waiting for men than death.'"

More of the poet's verse. Burton nodded to his old friend. "Get some rest, Algy."

I must say, Captain," said Abberline as they walked down the steps of Bedlam. "That raised far more questions than it answered."

Burton said nothing as they exited the gate and walked slowly up the street. A mass of steel gray clouds had stacked up toward the east, giving the whole city a somber cast to match Burton's mood. "A few things are immediately clear," he offered as they moved away from the imposing insane asylum.

"Well, then would you kindly explain them to me?" said Abberline.

"I don't think Algy is mad, merely affected by what happened to him two months ago, as anyone naturally would be. And I think he was trying to tell me something."

"The shoggoths I understood," said Abberline. "All too well. But what was that other rot about sphinxes and so forth?"

"I don't know. Morlocks I have heard of, though, prior to our strange encounter beneath the streets last night." Burton whistled, and a hansom clopped to stop before them. "Kew Gardens, please," Burton told the driver as he and Abberline climbed inside.

"Yes?" said Abberline. "From whom?"

"Our mutual friend, the Time Traveler. I believe these Morlocks have something to do with his first journey through Time."

"But what about that other stuff?" said Abberline. "Mycroft Holmes knows? I don't like the sound of that at all. Things get down-right mad when he's involved."

"Nor do I," said Burton. "But I think Algy was trying to tell us something about consequences. The consequences of our actions."

"Consequences of Time travel," Abberline offered.

Burton nodded. "Perhaps. That's why I must interview Herbert at once."

They reached Kew Gardens within the hour, and Burton had the hansom's driver take them right to Herbert's doorstep. Paying the fare, they alighted and knocked loudly on the door. After almost a minute, Herbert's housekeeper, Mrs. Watchett, appeared, scowling up at Burton.

"You again," she said.

"Is your master at home?" said Burton. "I need to speak with him on an urgent matter."

"He's gone," she said. "Again. Went down to his basement laboratory three days ago and, poof! Gone. Him and that queer contraption of his."

"Did he given any indication of where he might have gone?" asked Abberline.

Ms. Watchett shrugged her hunched shoulders. "Probably to that future he's always blabbing about. Not healthy, you ask me. Man wasn't meant to go gallivantin' through Time. Ain't natural."

Burton gave her his card. "Will you please be sure he gets this when he returns?"

She stared at the card as if it were a venomous snake before finally taking it. "Yes, sir."

"Very good. Thank you," said Burton. "Have a nice—"

Before he could finish his sentence, the door slammed shut in his face.

"She's in a wee bit cross, isn't she?" said Abberline.

"So it would appear," said Burton. "Though based on our previous meeting I can't say I blame her."

"I suppose you're right, Captain. After all, you did punch the poor man in the face, and my fellow coppers confiscated his Time Machine. Under the direct order of Mycroft Holmes, of course, but still."

"Holmes," said Burton as they walked back toward the street. "Algy mentioned him."

"So?"

"So I've told him very little of Mycroft Holmes and my involvement with him and the Shadow Council," said Burton. "I didn't want to burden my fellow Cannibals with an overabundance of the strange. In any case it was all classified anyway."

"But your friend Mr. Swinburne sounded as if he knew Mr. Holmes quite well."

"Exactly. What if Algy's time as a prisoner of the Great Race has given him a modicum of their abilities? What if he can see things that have occurred that he did not personally witness, or things that have yet to transpire?"

"By Jove," said Abberline. "Are you saying he's a bloody oracle?"

"Perhaps. Perhaps not. It's just as likely he's gone mad, but for argument's sake, let's say he hasn't."

"He wasn't making much sense," offered Abberline.

"True. But perhaps he cannot make much sense of what he is seeing and experiencing. There were simply too many things he said that, while utter nonsense to anyone else, made perfect sense to us."

Abberline shook his head. "You are right, Captain. Oh, but that most of it *was* the ravings of a lunatic. But what do we do about it? How do we follow any of his instructions?"

"Hopefully when the time is right, we will know," said Burton. "In the meantime, I need an audience with Mycroft Holmes."

"He's been keeping us at arm's length since the Great Race affair," said Abberline. "I am afraid even I cannot get close to him. Though it's been nice returning to actual normal police work."

"That's all right, Algy. He'll see us. Or have his secrets published in the London Mail. Let's go to the Diogenes Club."

MYCROFT

Burton and Abberline found Mycroft Holmes in his usual place, the Diogenes Club's infamous Stranger's Room. The elder Holmes stared up at them from his morning paper, seemingly more annoyed than surprised at seeing them there.

"I had believed our working relationship had reached its end," he said, returning to the pages of *The Daily Caller* he was reading.

"So had I," said Burton. "But something has come up. Something we believe you are involved in."

"Oh?" Mycroft Holmes shook and folded the paper, placing it on a table beside him. "I am involved in so many things. Things to which the *hoi polloi* are not privy."

"Spare me your condescension, Mycroft," Burton countered. "I am in no mood for your foppery."

Mycroft Holmes looked taken aback. "You are forgetting yourself, sir."

"I forget nothing. At your urging, I have saved this city a myriad of times now. Therefore, it would behoove you to listen for once instead of turning up your nose and barking orders."

Mycroft Holmes shook inwardly. He was not the type to be rattled easily, and it made Burton proud that he was able to discomfit him so. "Fine," he said. "What do you want?"

Burton told him everything that had transpired in their meeting with Swinburne.

"It sounds as if your friend is quite mad," said Mycroft Holmes when Burton was finished. "For that I am truly sorry. But I don't see what it has to do with me."

"You don't?" Burton spat. "Well let me spell it out for you. Algy mentioned you by name. The two of you have never met, and I have never told him what I did on your behalf."

"He also mentioned the Morlocks, sir," added Abberline. "Those things we encountered in the tunnels just last night. How could he have known about that?"

Mycroft shrugged his shoulders. "They get newspapers in Bedlam, don't they?"

"He's been tied in a straitjacket and near catatonic," said Burton. "I believe his time among the Great Race of Yith has imbued him with a modicum of their abilities. I think he can see all the myriad strands of Time at once."

Mycroft Holmes shifted uncomfortably in his seat. "Do you have any evidence to support this hypothesis?"

"Only what Algy told me about you, these Morlocks, whatever they are, and other things he couldn't have otherwise known about."

Mycroft Holmes settled back into his seat. "Suppose for argument's sake you are correct. What would you have me do about it?"

"Take this seriously, for one," said Burton. "Let me investigate for another."

"And be honest with us, sir, about anything strange that comes to your attention," Abberline said. "Mr. Swinburne said Time was off kilter and that you knew about it."

Mycroft Holmes shook his head. "I have no idea what he's talking about. Everything seems to have gone back to normal, more or less, save for that strangeness in the sewers beneath Shoreditch. Morlocks, you say?"

"Yes," said Burton. "But it may be that what poor Algy warned us about hasn't happened yet. Time travel is a strange business. A business that I warned you not to meddle in."

Mycroft Holmes gave Burton a patronizing wave and a nod. "Talk to your associate the Time Traveler about the Morlocks."

"We called on him already," said Burton. "He wasn't home."

"Well, in that case, I'm afraid I can be of no further help. But if I find any evidence of Time being off kilter, according to your friend, I shall alert you immediately. Good enough?"

"I suppose," said Burton. "For now."

Mycroft Holmes snorted laughter. "When next we meet you shall keep your place, Captain Burton. And I won't have you bloody barging in here every time you feel like it. The Diogenes Club abides by certain rules."

"Stuff your rules," said Burton as he and Abberline left the room, one of the Club's attendants staring daggers at them all the way to the front door.

"Aye," said Abberline when they emerged from the darkened building. "He's even more cross than usual."

"He's hiding something," said Burton.

Abberline gave a derisive snort. "When is he not?"

"I mean about what I told him. He knows something. He was quick to dismiss Algy's words, but something about them resonated with him. I could tell by his expression."

"Bloody hell," said the detective. "You think Time really is off kilter somehow, and he knows about it?"

Burton shrugged. "It's possible. Bismillah! We must find Herbert!"

The explorer hailed a hansom. As it clopped up to the curb, Burton said, "Can you follow Mycroft Holmes for me? Without him discovering you?"

The inspector blinked at him. "I think so. But why?"

Burton glanced at the door of the Diogenes Club. "I believe he's up to something, and we must know what. I think Algy was trying to warn us about something involving our former employer."

Burton climbed into the carriage and gave the driver his address at Gloucester Place.

"Following the brother of the late Sherlock Holmes won't be easy," called Abberline. "But I've learned a thing or two running about with you, Captain." He tipped his bowler and gave Burton a playful wink.

"Good man." Burton sat back in the seat as the hansom started off.

MORLOCK NIGHT

On Wednesday, they hunted Morlocks.

At midnight on the dot, Captain Sir Richard Francis Burton, Inspector Abberline, and Burton's friend and fellow Cannibal Club member Richard Monckton Milnes met outside a sluice gate in Shoreditch. Milnes' lantern bobbed up and down before the gate, which was covered by a rusted iron casting. Dark, foul-smelling water trickled from the gate onto the ground between their feet.

"I was able to get the flow redirected," said Abberline. "But there's nothin' I can do about the smell. Sorry, gents."

"This had better be good, Dick," Milnes grumbled. "You and I should be firmly in our cups by now at the Cannibal Club, instead of traipsing through sewage."

Burton gave his friend a bemused grin, a wasted gesture in the dark. "Did I not promise you an adventure? This should be of great interest for you, given your penchant for the strange."

"It must be strange indeed," said Milnes, "to wander about in the sewers after midnight. Very well. Let's get this business done."

Abberline was fiddling with the padlock that held the casting secure. "My watch commander assured me this was the correct key," he said. "If you could hold the lantern steady, please."

Milnes stopped his lantern from swaying so much, and eventually Abberline had the hasp on the lock open. He pushed the casting open with a steady screech of rusted, wet hinges. "My study of the city's sewer system confirms this is the quickest route to that underground laboratory we found."

"Perfect," said Burton. "The less time we spend down here, the better."

Milnes handed the lantern to Abberline, who drew his pistol as he stepped up into the opening, followed closely by Burton and then Milnes. Burton was also armed, but he refrained from drawing his weapon as of yet.

They walked through smelly darkness for several minutes.

"Are we almost there?" Milnes whispered, his voice muffled by the silk handkerchief he held tightly over his nose and mouth.

"Not much farther, gents," Abberline said. Their voices echoed strangely up the large clay pipe, the lantern casting furtive shadows as it swung back and forth in Abberline's shaky left hand.

Soon, the pipe ended, and the three men found themselves in a high, open chasm. The rumble of rushing water surged somewhere off to their right.

"That should be the underground river we found last time," said Abberline. "And over here..."

He directed the lantern directly ahead. As their eyes adjusted to the gloom, Burton gasped. The police had collected almost everything into evidence, but the great iron cages still remained, as did the stainless-steel table someone had been using as part of a portable laboratory setup. They were back in the underground lair of the Morlocks.

"Cripes!" said Monckton Milnes. "Is this the place you were telling me about?"

"The same," said Burton as he looked around. "There's the laboratory. There's a pile of tattered garments from the poor retches the Morlocks kept prisoner."

"And what the bloody hell is that?" said Monckton Milnes, pointing toward the far corner.

Burton and Abberline looked in the direction Monckton Milnes indicated. There, crouching behind a crate, blinded by lantern light, was a Morlock. Its skin was pale white, like a mushroom, and it had long white hair that spilled onto its bare shoulders. Its only clothing was a tattered loincloth, and its beady eyes seemed to glow with their own yellowish green light. It shielded its eyes from the light, but Burton caught a glimpse of a huge mouth filled with crooked teeth. It gave them a wordless grunt, but remained where it was.

"They're real," said Burton. "I only caught a glimpse of them before, but this confirms it."

"But what is it?" said Abberline. "And where did the pitiful creature come from?"

"Yes," said Monckton Milnes. "What are they?"

"In the simplest terms," said Burton, "they are us."

A voice boomed from somewhere, echoing human laughter, and every head turned to look for its source. With the lantern light pointed elsewhere, the Morlock grunted and slunk quickly up a side tunnel and vanished.

"Who's there?' said Abberline, raising his pistol. "Show yourself."

"Do you want to know who I am?" said the voice. "Or do you want to shoot me? You can't have both."

"Who is that?" said Burton, scowling into the gloom. "Show yourself!"

"In due time, Captain. In due time. I see you've been admiring my Morlocks."

"*Your* Morlocks?" said Monckton Milnes. "You created them?"

The voice chuckled. "No. You hold that high honor. I merely brought them home."

A chill flew up Burton's spine. "You're a Time Traveler."

"Very good, Captain. Keep going."

"You brought them back here from the future. The year eight hundred and two thousand something."

"802,701," the voice corrected. "How much did Herbert tell you about them?"

"Only that he encountered them, and that he believes they are descended from our working classes."

"Precisely," said the voice. "That was my assessment as well. They are very clever. While sensitive to sunlight and thoroughly repulsive, they are highly intelligent and adept with machinery. The tunnels you stand in now will be their home roughly eight-hundred thousand years from now."

"Why did you bring them here to this time?" said Burton. "They don't belong here."

"To give them a head start, I suppose. But more than that, think of me as returning their favor. They were of great assistance to me, you see."

Off to their right, they heard steady, padding footsteps and saw more than a dozen pairs of glowing eyes loom up out of the darkness.

"Your little raid hurt my new friends, but they are patient," said the voice. "They can wait down here in the dark a veritable eternity."

"You're destroying their future," said Burton as he backed away from the slowly encroaching Morlocks. "This is not their proper time!"

"The fragility of the timestream is no concern of mine, Burton," said the voice.

"Then how can you possibly control it?"

The voice laughed. "I don't want to control Time! I know that every moment I change will simply create a new stream, the course of which cannot be charted ahead of time. No, I seek to upend it, to unravel its many threads one by one."

"Bismillah! But why, man?"

"Because I can! So long, Captain Burton. Enjoy your last few minutes of existence. I'm afraid there will be no laboratory study for you and your colleagues. My Morlocks are quite hungry after you denied them their previous meal." There was another laugh and hurried footfalls as the mysterious figure left through some hidden exit.

"Damnation!" said Monckton Milnes. "What do we do now?"

"We run," said Burton.

"They've cut off our exit," said Abberline.

"Then we go the long way round. Hurry!"

The three moved away from the enclosing semicircle of Morlocks and headed toward a familiar tunnel on the other side of the wide-open space, the one they had used days before when they raided the tunnel with the police. But as they reached it, they found more glowing eyes staring at them.

"It's a bloody invasion!" Abberline said as he swung his lantern around defensively. It did little good; the Morlocks only flinched momentarily before continuing their steady march toward the three men. Abberline aimed his gun at them, his hand shaking.

"That will do us no good, Frederick," said Burton. "We don't have enough shots in both our revolvers to take care of this lot. They have us outnumbered."

"This is madness!" exclaimed Monckton Milnes. "What nightmare have you dragged me into, Dick?"

"I'm sorry, old friend," said Burton. What else could he say? They'd had it. He thought of Isabel as the Morlocks closed in, their awful, subhuman hands reaching for them, the yeasty stink of their bodies combining with the sewer stench to assault the explorer's nostrils.

Then a brilliant light flooded the space, and the Morlocks squealed, shrinking back from it as if acid had been poured on them. They retreated to what shadows they could still find on the far edge of the brightness.

"Hurry," a woman's voice called. "The illumination won't last for long."

Burton looked up. The light was too bright even for his eyes, but he could just make out a crude rope ladder hanging down from the mouth of a pipe set high along the wall near their planned escape route. A lithe figure stood there, a dark shape against the light she held in her hand, a light brighter than a thousand gaslamps.

"Hurry!" she said again, and the three men got over their disorientation and made for the ladder. Monckton Milnes went first, shimmying up the awkward ladder like a sprinter. He was followed by Burton, then Abberline, who insisted on bringing up the rear.

The light shut off suddenly as Abberline hoisted himself up and over the lip of the tunnel.

Burton stared at their savior, but glowing orbs filled his vision, the aftereffects of the bright light. "Who are you?"

"Explanations later," said the woman as she grabbed up the ladder. "Running now."

She moved quickly up the tunnel, followed closely by Monckton Milnes. Burton helped Abberline to his feet and the four of them ran for their lives.

They followed the woman through a veritable maze of tunnels and pipes, until Burton felt like a blind, trapped rat, groping through darkness. After nearly an hour, the four rounded a bend and saw wan twilight coming from somewhere up ahead. In another few minutes they were out, slipping through a bend in the bars of a locked grate several miles from the tunnel they had entered through in Shoreditch.

"There," said the woman. "Everyone safe and accounted for?"

"I believe so," said Burton. He blinked, letting his eyes adjust to the gloom around them. "Now would you mind telling us who you are?"

"Yes," said the woman. "My apologies. There wasn't time back there for a proper introduction, and I'm sorry we had to meet under these circumstances. I'm a huge admirer of yours, Captain Sir Richard. Oh, this is a most momentous occasion! If you don't mind my saying so. I'm sure it seems very common to you."

"You can call me simply Captain Burton, if you must. And you are?"

"Oh, right. Sorry, Captain Burton. My name is Penelope Hemlock, and I am a Time Agent. Or, that is to say, I will be, from your vantage point. I haven't even been born yet, you see."

"She's off her bloody rocker," said Monckton Milnes.

Burton placed a hand on his shoulder. "Please, Richard. Let her explain."

"Yes, thank you." She glanced at Abberline. "You are, of course, Detective Inspector Frederick George Abberline. Everyone who knows London history knows who you are, what with the, uh, never mind. That dreadful affair hasn't happened yet."

She smiled at Monckton Milnes. "And you are Richard Monckton Milnes, 1st Baron Houghton. But not yet! Oh, sorry. I get my dates confused. Horrible thing for a Time Agent. But I'm just so excited. I do tend to prattle on so when I'm excited. My Da always used to say—"

"Baron?" said Monckton Milnes. "Bloody hell!"

"Calm yourself, Miss, please," said Burton. "And speak plain."

"Perhaps we should hear her explanation elsewhere," said Abberline, his eyes glancing warily about.

"I concur," said Monckton Milnes. "Preferably over a pint."

"My house, then," said Burton.

THE INDEFATIGABLE MISS HEMLOCK

They returned to Gloucester Place and went quietly up to Burton's study. Despite the late hour, Miss Hemlock was bubbly, bouncing around the room to admire Burton's library, his collection of swords, guns, and other weaponry he had picked up on his many travels, even his elephant's foot umbrella stand.

Monckton Milnes helped himself immediately to Burton's brandy, and after three glasses he finally stopped shaking. "This is pure madness, Dick. What the bloody hell are you involved in?"

"Mind your language, Richard!" admonished Burton. "We have a lady present."

"Don't mind me," said the woman as she scanned one of the explorer's bookshelves. "I've heard much worse from the soldiers, believe you me."

"Soldiers?" Monckton Milnes murmured.

Abberline sat by the fire, his bowler mounted atop his left knee.

"Frederick, you look positively done in," said Burton. "Why don't you go home?"

"No," said the policeman. "I'll be right as rain in a moment. Besides, I want to hear this."

Burton examined the woman as she bounced around his study

inspecting his spear collection. She was short and lithe, with close-cropped dark hair and inquisitive brown eyes. She wore a leather, American-style duster coat over a white shirt and brown pants and dark leather knee-high boots, like a man would wear. She wore no bonnet or hat, and her hair wasn't at all the current style. This, Burton knew, was a woman out of her place, and maybe even time. She spoke with a crisp, North London accent.

The woman slowly turned around as Burton, Monckton Milnes, and Abberline stared up at her. She blushed and smiled. "I'm sorry, gentlemen. Is everyone settled down? That was quite a row, wasn't it?"

Burton jammed a cheroot in his mouth and lit it, puffing aromatic smoke as he waited for her to get to the point.

"I can't believe I'm actually here," she said. "In the presence of such important men of your time. It's exciting, isn't it?"

"Perhaps if you tell us who and what you are we can share in your enthusiasm," said Monckton Milnes with a scowl.

"You're right. My apologizes. I do get overwrought sometimes. But it isn't every day you meet—never mind. As I was saying, I am a Time Agent. I come from the future, the year nineteen forty-five to be precise."

"Now I've heard everything," said Monckton Milnes. "Are we actually entertaining this, Richard?"

"Yes we are," Burton grumbled. "Now pipe down!"

Monckton Milnes harrumphed and helped himself to another brandy.

"It's true, Bar—uh, Mr. Monckton Milnes," said the woman. "I am a Time Traveler, as Captain Burton here has been."

Monckton Milnes stared at Burton.

"It's true," said Abberline. "On my sainted mother's grave, it's true."

"Since I'm not yet thoroughly in my cups," said Monckton Milnes, "then I must be mad." He took the entire decanter of brandy back to his seat behind Burton's other desk and sulked. "Yes, that must be it. I'm bound for Bedlam."

"Why are you here, Miss Hemlock?" asked Burton, ignoring his fellow Cannibal.

"I came here tracking a mysterious individual. No one knows who he is, but he's been a thorough thorn in our sides as of late."

"The man in the tunnel," said the explorer. "The one who brought the Morlocks back here."

"Exactly."

"But who would do such a horrible thing?" murmured Abberline. "And why? And how?"

"The how we know," said Miss Hemlock. "He has a Time Machine."

"But how is that possible?" said the detective. "I thought it destroyed."

"Herbert can build another one," said Burton. "He already has, once. But I assumed he had taken it to the far future with him and hasn't returned."

"That was our summation as well," said Miss Hemlock. "There is no further official historical record of him. He just up and vanished this year. There's no census information on him, no record of his death, nothing."

Burton nodded. "He has a fondness for far futurity," said Burton. "The year eight hundred and two thousand, seven-hundred and one, if I remember correctly."

"Good God!" Monckton Milnes, wiping brandy off his chin with a handkerchief.

"Yes, well, wherever he is, someone has gained his ability to travel through Time."

"Wait a minute," said the explorer. "You can travel through Time. Could he have absconded with one of your Time Machines?"

Miss Hemlock rolled up her sleeve. "No. All of our temporal transport units are accounted for." She extended her arm, stepping closer so that Burton could have a better look. Strapped to her wrist by a leather band was a brass contraption that resembled a wristwatch. She flicked a tiny lever, and the device clicked open to become a brass disk made to spin perpendicular to the inner surface of the device, which had some kind of rotating dial inside of it with a month, day and year. This month, day and year.

"Bismillah! It's a tiny Time Machine!"

"Yes. It allows one to travel through Time without a big, bulky conveyance that is difficult to hide or move around. I was also given to understand it's less bumpy than the original."

"But you miniaturized it?" said Burton. "How?"

Miss Hemlock smiled. "In the future, we will have miniaturization capabilities you couldn't imagine, or understand I'm afraid. It has few moving parts."

"You live in an age of wonders, Miss Hemlock," said Abberline.

"I wish that was the case. Such technologies have their downside. For every wondrous thing created, there are those who discern how to put them to terrible ends."

"That has always been the way of things, Miss Hemlock," said Burton. "Now, how can we help you? I assume you rescued us tonight for a reason."

She shrugged. "I had no idea you were going to be there. I was merely tracking our mutual enemy. I knew about the Morlocks, though, that's why I brought along my trusty electric torch."

She removed a large contraption from a clip on her belt beneath her voluminous duster. It was shiny yellow, with what appeared to be a large lens and a handle with a black cord depending from it.

"I picked this up in the late twentieth century," she said proudly. "It gives off ten thousand lumens."

"By Jove!" exclaimed Monckton Milnes. He followed this with a resounding hiccup.

"Where do you put the kerosene?" asked Abberline. "The candle?"

Miss Hemlock uttered a tinkling little laugh, like crystal. "It runs on electricity, stored in a battery. Unfortunately, the battery doesn't last very long, but I knew it would shine bright long enough to fend off a few Morlocks."

"Well, however it works," said Burton, "we are forever in your debt. We would like to help you apprehend this scoundrel."

"Good. I don't know exactly where he is, unfortunately, but I do know what he's doing here."

Burton arched an eyebrow. "Oh?"

"Yes. Sometime in the next week, a man named Mycroft Holmes is going to receive a very special document. A timeline of future events from now until the middle of the next century. A so-called Map of Time."

A knot tightened itself in Burton's stomach as he recalled Swinburne's words.

You must stop Mycroft know-it-all Holmes from getting the map. The Map of Time.

"You know of this," said Miss Hemlock, reading Burton's expression. It wasn't a question.

"I've heard of it, yes," said Burton. "I didn't know what it was before now."

"You think this mysterious Morlock wrangler is the one who gives this Map of Time to Mycroft Holmes?" asked Abberline.

"I do. Though what he is doing with these Morlocks, I can't fathom."

"How did you find out about this Map of Time?" Burton asked.

"That's probably going to sound like the strangest part of all of this," said Miss Hemlock. "From Mycroft Holmes himself, in the spring of nineteen forty-five."

"Bismillah! He'd be over a hundred and twenty years old. There's no way he could live that long."

"He doesn't, er, didn't," said Miss Hemlock. "Not exactly. He found a way to circumvent the aging process. After a fashion."

"Circumvent it?" said Abberline. "Goodness me, but how?"

"Through technology. Near the end of his life, Mycroft Holmes reportedly became interested in methods of prolonging life, through occult as well as materialist means. In nineteen forty-five, he is a being of pure mind, existing inside a complex analytical engine that is continually improved upon, and is currently—in my time—housed inside what once was the Westminster clock tower."

"Mercy me! Big Ben?" Abberline exclaimed. "And he told you all of this?"

"He did. He was doing a bit of bragging, and did not know that I was a Time Agent."

"What does he do up there in his tower?" Burton inquired.

Miss Hemlock uttered a deep sigh. "We are at war in my time, Captain. It has spread to consume the entire world, for the second time. Mycroft Holmes is known as The Thinker, and directs our war efforts as well as warns us of impending air raids."

"Air raids?" Monckton Milnes said. "My earlier assessment was correct. There isn't enough booze for this." He got up and went poking through Burton's liquor cabinet.

"Yes, air raids. I told you technology was a double-edged sword. We have machines that can fly, allowing people to traverse great distances in a matter of hours. But they have also been employed into dropping bombs. The Germans attack us almost nightly. The Thinker's predictions about where the bombs would land have been essential in saving lives."

"Bismillah! The conceited duffer has finally done it. He knows every major world event from now through the middle half of the next century. And he is alive—after a fashion—and in a place where he can direct these events to his benefit."

"He has all of human history in his hands," Abberline added. "We knew he was up to something! I followed him all of yesterday. He met with several prominent scientists and engineers. They must be building this analytic contraption you spoke of."

"Or an early prototype," added Miss Hemlock. "Parts are constantly being replaced and updated."

"But who is his mysterious benefactor? And why would he give this information to the likes of Mycroft Holmes when he could simply benefit from it himself?" Abberline worried his bowler again, turning it on his knee.

"He doesn't seek to benefit," said Burton. "He wants to completely unravel the threads of Time itself. He's obviously quite mad."

"Well, whatever his motives, we need to find him and stop him from giving Mr. Holmes that map, if he hasn't already acquired it." Miss Hemlock glanced at each man in turn. "Can I count on your assistance?"

"Of course," said Burton. "As I said, we are in your debt. Besides, someone is using Time as a weapon. We must stop him before everything we know ceases to be."

"You know I'm bloody well in," said Abberline. "What else can I do?"

Monckton Milnes hiccupped again, and regarded the woman with bloodshot eyes. "I'll be at the Cannibal Club, Dick. The next time you want to have a normal bloody conversation, stop by."

"I will, Richard," said Burton. "And for whatever it's worth, thank you."

Monckton Milnes harrumphed again and staggered out the door of Burton's study.

"I'm sure I don't have to tell you how dangerous this is," said the indefatigable Miss Hemlock. "I'm afraid I have diverged you from your current time streams. We are *tabula rasa* from this moment forth."

"We diverged long before you got here, Miss Hemlock. Whatever things come undone by this point, they are no fault of yours. We are all too familiar with the risks involved. In fact, you might be in even more danger than we are."

Miss Hemlock shivered and nodded. "You are right, of course. But I don't care what happens to me, so long as this unidentified miscreant isn't allowed to meddle with Time!"

WEAPONIZED TIME

T he late hour had become early morning, so Detective Inspector Abberline bid farewell and set off for home. Burton offered Miss Hemlock the use of his spare bedroom next to his study, and she took the offer.

Burton worried that people would start to talk about the mysterious woman who had taken up residence at Gloucester Place—and worse, tell Isabel—but Miss Hemlock assured the explorer she would be discrete, making use of the rear servants' entrance for her comings and goings. "I'm a Time Agent, Captain, Burton. We are trained to blend in." Burton didn't know how such a flamboyant woman could blend in, especially one in such unusual getup, but he nodded and bid her good night.

The next morning, Burton sat in his study wearing his *jebba* and ate a hearty breakfast of eggs, sausage and coffee brought up to him by Miss Angell, who stared at Burton's house guest crossly as she served them.

"Captain Burton," she said finally. "Will your guest be staying long?"

Miss Hemlock looked up at his landlady and housekeeper, a huge smile on her face. "Only a few days. I am so sorry for imposing, but Cousin Richard insisted."

Miss Angell fixed her with a flinty stare. "Cousin?"

"Distant," said Miss Hemlock. "I came here to see the city. I'm Penelope."

Unable to find fault with the ostensibly unseemly arrangement, Miss Angell's mood softened. "Oh. Well. That sounds quite nice. Eat up. You'll need your strength to keep up with the likes of him."

At that she left the room, closing the door behind her.

"Well done," said Burton.

Miss Hemlock giggled. "This isn't my first time."

"I'm sorry," said Burton. "She can be overbearing at times, but she means well."

"I like her. Though I wouldn't like to get on her bad side."

"That, my dear, makes two of us."

They ate in relative silence for a time, Miss Hemlock making gentle noises as she wolfed down her eggs and sausage.

"Would you like some more? Mother Angell insists on keeping me fat like a prized pig."

"No, no. This is plenty. In fact, it's a veritable feast. Because of the war, we subsist on rations. We hardly get any meat at all, and what eggs we have are powdered."

Burton arched an eyebrow. "Powdered?"

She smiled around a mouthful of eggs. "Please, don't ask. You don't want to know. It's all due to the war, of course."

Burton nodded. The war. The explorer had thought of little else since the Time Agent mentioned it the previous evening. What must it be like? No. He was better off not knowing. He couldn't do anything about it, and he wouldn't live to see it. There was that, at least. Still, he worried about those who would have to endure it. He had been a soldier, and knew the hardships involved. He doubted they had changed all that much. As he ate, he stared across the study at the wall of weaponry, mementos of death and destruction he had acquired during his travels. Guns, swords, spears. He had been stabbed in the face with a spear. What new methods of killing would man develop in the intervening eighty-one years? They already had flying vehicles that could drop bombs. He shuddered inwardly.

"So," said Burton when he had finished his breakfast. "What is the plan for today?"

"We need to find Mycroft Holmes and see if he has the Map." She wiped her small mouth with a linen napkin.

"You think he has already acquired it?" asked Burton.

The Time Agent nodded. "It's a possibility. Actually, I'd prefer it, because our mysterious figure will go on about his way thinking he has succeeded."

Burton nodded. "That way he won't try to stop us."

"Exactly. Now, you know the city at this moment in time, and you also know where Mycroft Holmes spends his days."

"Well, I don't know where he lives," said Burton, "but he spends most of his time at the Diogenes Club. He also has an office in the Tower of London."

Miss Hemlock nodded. "I thought as much. We'll need to be careful. He can't know who I am, and it would be best if he didn't see me at all. In my time, that photographic memory of his is legendary. I don't want him to recognize me when I interrogate him in his future, as he might not tell me what I need to know so that it is of use here."

"And thus come back here to prevent it," said Burton.

Miss Hemlock smiled. "Exactly. You *have* done this before, haven't you?"

"More than I would like. So, where should we head first?"

"The Diogenes Club," she said.

The explorer nodded. "We should round up Inspector Abberline. We might need his assistance."

"Very good," Miss Hemlock said, smiling.

"But how do we approach him?"

Miss Hemlock stood. "Leave that to me. Now, please exit your home as you normally would, and meet me down at the corner." She pointed out the study window. "The less people who see us together, the better. I need to keep as small a footprint in this time period as possible. My own future could depend on it."

343

"All right," said Burton. "Then we'll go find Frederick and get this Map of Time business attended to."

As instructed, Burton donned his coat and topper and left his home through the front door, then turned right and walked to the corner. He had waited several minutes for Miss Hemlock to join him when a familiar voice called to him from a carriage pulling pulled up to the curb. "Captain Burton."

He climbed into the carriage. "Where did you go?"

"This carriage was clopping by when I left through your servants' entrance," she said. "I hailed it and we went around the block. Oh, and I must apologize. I'm afraid you will have to pay the fare. I'm not carrying the proper coin of the realm, as it were." She blushed.

Burton smiled. "No problem at all, Miss Hemlock. A common occurrence in your line of work, I'm sure."

"Where to?" the driver called down.

"The Diogenes Club," said Burton. "Do you know it?"

"Aye sir. Indeed I do."

The driver urged his horse forward, and they started off.

"Were we not supposed to fetch Detective Abberline?" asked Miss Hemlock.

"If I know Frederick, he is already there waiting for us."

Twenty minutes later, they alighted in front of the infamous Diogenes Club to find Inspector Abberline leaning against the formidable brick building. "Captain, Miss Hemlock," he said cordially.

Burton paid the fare and shook Abberline's hand. "What are you doing out here?"

"Those ruffians threw me out! Me. An officer of the law!"

"What happened?" asked Miss Hemlock.

"I told the doorman I needed to see Mycroft Holmes at once." He glanced about the street before continuing, lowering his voice. "It's about those bloody Morlocks, you see. They're up to their old tricks again. More people have gone missing, this time somewhat closer to home."

Burton raked his fingers through his beard. "They're spreading outward."

Abberline nodded. "I thought Holmes would want to know, since defending the Crown against esoteric threats seems to be in his purview, but he didn't want to hear any of it. He had some of his bloody scoundrels throw me out, while he takes a meeting."

"With whom is he meeting?" Miss Hemlock asked eagerly.

"I don't know. Two men. I didn't recognize any of them."

"Wait," said Miss Hemlock, reaching into her coat. She produced a leather wallet and extracted from it two square pieces of paper. One by one she unfolded them and showed them to Abberline. "These people?"

Abberline studied the first one, a reproduction of an engraving depicting a man wearing a dark suit and long, bushy sideburns. "Yeah. That's him. Looks a bit younger in the flesh, but that's definitely him. I'd stake my badge on it."

Miss Hemlock glanced up at Burton. "Daniel Gooch, railway engineer."

She showed Abberline the next piece of paper, this time a reproduction of a photograph of an older man with a high forehead and receding hair. "That's the second man," declared Abberline.

"Charles Babbage," said Miss Hemlock.

"Yes, I've heard of Babbage," said Burton. "He invented something called a Difference Engine, said it would revolutionize industry. But he ran out of money before he could complete it. He's been begging for funds ever since."

Miss Hemlock returned the papers to her wallet and the wallet to her coat. "Then it seems I am too late."

"What do you mean?"

"What I had hoped to stop has already begun to transpire. Mr. Gooch and Mr. Babbage are two of the men responsible for creating the machine that Mycroft Holmes will one day transfer his consciousness into."

"You think Mycroft Holmes is already in possession of the Map of Time?" asked Burton.

"It is the only reason he would want to prolong his life," said the Time Agent. "So he can oversee and guide humanity through these major upcoming moments in our history."

"You haven't missed your chance," said Abberline.

Burton and Miss Hemlock stared at the policeman.

"You wanted to wait until your mysterious villain handed it off, right?" asked Abberline.

"Yes," said Miss Hemlock.

"Well, he's done so. Now you can get it."

"But I don't know where it is. I need to retrieve it without his knowledge."

"He's going to keep something like that close," said Burton. "We'd need to know the precise moment he acquires the document and see where he puts it."

"We can do that," said Miss Hemlock, "if I can get inside his—what is it called? Stranger's Room?"

"You certainly know your business, Miss Hemlock," said Abberline.

"I know my history," she corrected.

"But how can you spy on him when he's so close?" asked Abberline.

Miss Hemlock grinned. "As Mycroft's more famous younger brother would say, it's elementary. Captain Burton, you've traveled through Time. You know of its effects?"

"You mean the way Time moves around the traveler?" said Burton. "Yes. Like watching the whole world speed up or slow down around you, in either direction. Bismillah. You mean to—"

"Travel back in Time, in Mycroft's presence, until the moment he is given the Map. Then I'll zoom forward and look for a good opportunity to abscond with it."

"Bloody brilliant," said Abberline. "But there's just one problem. You can't get in to see him. No one can. Especially—and I beg your pardon—a woman. No one but a member can get inside the Diogenes Club without special invitation."

Miss Hemlock scowled. "You are right, of course. Besides, he is going to guard that map with his life. Whomever gave it to him must have warned him about attempts to retrieve it."

"Also, you must take into account that taking the Map in the past will alter the future, er, our present," Burton said. "One of Herbert's bloody paradoxes will ensue. Taking the Map then will eliminate our need to take it now."

"Bloody hell," barked Abberline. "Here we go again. All this Time travel rot is giving me a sore head."

"Not if we return to this precise moment," said Miss Hemlock, "and Mycroft Holmes doesn't learn of our deception until after I've returned with it."

Burton and Abberline mulled this over in silence for a long moment.

"I'm not saying it won't be dangerous," she continued. "Right now, there are too many variables to calculate our odds of success. But whatever damage we cause now is small potatoes compared to what Mycroft Holmes can do with the knowledge contained in that Map. We have to get it back, damn the consequences."

Abberline scowled disapprovingly at her epithet, but said nothing.

"What if I did it?" said Burton.

"What?" Miss Hemlock and Abberline said, almost in unison.

"I can get closer to him than you, a stranger and, forgive our backwards customs, a lady. We only need a distraction so that I can move through Time. One minute—one second—out of sync would make me invisible to him."

"It's very dangerous," said Miss Hemlock.

"I've traveled through Time before," said Burton. "Besides, what choice do we have?"

"All right," said Miss Hemlock, looking around. Spying an alley next to the Diogenes Club, she said, "Step into my office and I'll show you how my portable device works."

It was the work of a few minutes to familiarize the explorer with how to operate the wrist-mounted Time Machine. Despite its smaller size, it worked exactly like Herbert's original design. Once Burton had it secured to his wrist, he said, "I shall go back to earlier in the day and see if I can slip inside unseen. Then I shall locate Mycroft Holmes and go back further still."

"Wait," said Abberline. "How do we know this is where Mr. Holmes received the bloody Map of Time? The exchange could have been made anywhere."

"We must assume, for now, that he received it here," said the Time Agent. "His usual haunts aren't well known to history. Our mystery man would have also started here to look for the perfect time to pay him a visit."

Abberline nodded, and Burton took a step backward. "All right. Off I go. Once more into the bloody breach." He flicked open the device, carefully set the tiny dial back four hours, and set the machine in motion.

"You're a Time Agent now," said Miss Hemlock. "Do us proud."

THROUGH TIME AND SPACE WITH
DR. MOSES NEBOGIPFEL

T he tiny dish began to spin with a high-pitched whine, the vibration traveling up Burton's right arm. At first nothing happened. Then orbs of light began to dance before his eyes, and he felt himself receding. He saw Abberline, Miss Hemlock, and himself walk backward out of the alley and around the front of the building, watching as the traffic on the street in front of the building moved faster and faster in the opposite direction. The sun moved downward from its current position, back along its track until it was buried by the horizon and the tall buildings that fronted the opposite side of the street. Watching his destination appear in the dial, Burton slowed the miniature Time Machine to a stop—and promptly fell over, almost crashing into the side of the building.

"Bismillah!" he muttered. Regaining his footing, Burton looked around. The street was empty, the hour early. The sky was tinged pink with the early light of dawn.

Brushing himself off, Burton left the alley and went to the door of the Diogenes Club. The entrance was locked, so Burton knelt and produced a set of lock picks and got to work. Inside of a minute he had the door open and was inside, locking the door again behind him. It was dark, but just as posh as Burton remembered from his previous visits. He moved quietly past empty, richly appointed rooms, his boots sinking into the lush carpet as he hurried toward the building's far end, and the infamous Stranger's Room. Finding the room unlocked, Burton entered and looked around. Burton moved toward the far corner near the room's single window and set the miniature Time Machine in motion once more, this time moving forward.

Early morning sun leapt up and through the window, but Burton cast no shadow as he moved out of step with the normal course and speed of Time. His eyes moved from the dial of the device to the room beyond, waiting for any change that would signal he was nearing the point he needed.

Shadows danced across the sparse Stranger's Room, and Burton increased his forward march through Time just a bit. A strange flicker from the opposite corner of the room caught his eye. He thought it a trick of the light at first, a Time mirage. But it persisted, solidifying into a human figure.

"Bismillah!" Burton murmured, his voice taking on a strange echo. "The other Time Traveler!"

Thinking this is the mysterious figure Miss Hemlock tracked here from the future, Burton continued to watch, hoping his presence was masked by his own movement through Time. Indeed, it appeared both men were out of sync, not only with each other, but the inexorably slow, one second per second course of Time. But now the figure started to move, flickering from one place to another, bounding across the room and directly toward Burton in an instant.

The explorer raised his arms in a defensive posture, still moving forward through Time. The door to the Stranger's Room silently opened, and Mycroft Holmes entered with an attendant. With a speed impossible for any human being, Holmes zipped behind his desk and began reading a newspaper. But Burton had other things to worry about at present.

The face of the other Time Traveler flickered before him. He was a dark man with sour features and a neatly trimmed black beard. He leered at Burton, reaching for him but never laying hands on him because they were still out of sync with each other. Still, Burton shrank back from him reflexively, a wave of dizziness moving through him. He teetered and almost fell over. That's when the cold hands of his opponent seized him.

They were traveling at the same speed now, their bodies hurtling in sync into the future. Afternoon and evening came and went as Burton grappled with his foe. If he could halt the Time Machine's forward motion, he would fall out of step with his assailant and escape his grasp.

The explorer twisted his left arm free and reached for the device before his attacker could grab him again. He flicked the tiny lever, slowing his progress, and felt himself falling away from his assailant, who reached for him once more, only to pass through him like a ghost.

Burton fell into darkness, landing with a thud. It was evening. The Stranger's Room was dark. A pale moon shown through the single window. He had gone hours into the future. He'd have to start all over, this time in reverse.

He heard the creak of a floorboard, and snapped to attention, rising swiftly to his feet. Surrounding him was a trio of Morlocks. They were wearing goggles with smoked lenses over their eyes, and they reached for him with pale, fungoid, subhuman hands. On one of their wrists was another miniature Time Machine.

They overpowered the explorer, their small stature masking their brute strength. Burton managed to punch one of them hard in the stomach, but his comrades redoubled their efforts, grabbing his arms and stretching them apart as the one he had punched wrenched the tiny Time Machine from his wrist. Then, with a mighty swipe of its pale arm, the Morlock rendered Burton senseless.

Richard Francis Burton opened his eyes. He was lying on something cold and hard. Around him stood a group of Morlocks, black goggles strapped tightly around their misshapen heads. They looked down at him, muttering in their incomprehensible tongue.

"Ah," said a voice behind them. "At last you rejoin us. I feared my associate was a bit overzealous in his attack."

With a groan, Burton staggered to his feet. "Who are you?"

"I call myself Dr. Moses Nebogipfel," said the man. He was still obscured by the Morlocks clustered around him. They appeared to be standing in some sort of vehicle, and Burton felt the sensation of forward movement. The front of the compartment was covered in thick windows that reminded Burton of the portholes aboard the *Nautilus*. Through them, he saw gray clouds. Or was it fog?

"Where the bloody hell am I?"

"You are aboard my craft. I haven't chosen a name for it yet. Do you like it?"

"What manner of craft is it?"

"In a general sense it is a dirigible. But in practice it is much more."

"You mean I am standing in a bloody balloon?"

The Morlocks parted, and the man he had grappled with earlier stepped toward him. "No, you are standing in the gondola of a bloody balloon. Welcome to my Time Machine, Captain Burton. Or is it Captain Sir Richard? I get confused."

"Captain Burton is sufficient, if you must address me at all. What sort of name is Nebogipfel?"

The man smiled, clapping his hands together. "I love the sound of nonsensical words, don't you? So alliterative, so poetic. Are you familiar with the work of Charles Lutwidge Dodgson? He writes under the *nom de plume* Lewis Carroll, an anagram of his real name. Wonderfully outlandish work. 'Twas brillig, and the slithey toves did gyre and gimble in the wabe. All mimsy were the borogoves, And the mome raths outgrabe.' Magnificent."

Burton eyed the stranger, finding a hint of the familiar about him. He was shorter than Burton, wearing a dark, tailored suit and affecting a dark, neatly-trimmed black beard. But there was something about the eyes.

"Why did you bring me here? Why not have your Morlocks eat me and be done with it?"

His captor uttered dark laughter. "My dear Captain Burton, the answer should be obvious. I would much rather have you alive. You are too important to history. I brought you here to give you something."

The other Time Traveler began to pace around Burton, the Morlocks giving him an ever widening berth as he did so. "Journeying through Time is a terrible gift. I want you to see it as I do, all the myriad strands of Time. I want you to see how they bend and fold, how easily they snap and break."

"I already know how fragile Time is," said Burton. "Now who are you? And why did you bring the Morlocks here?"

"The answer to your first question will take some time. The answer to your second question, however, is this: I think they should have their place in the sun again. They are our cousins. Humanity's discarded."

"But their time is not yet!" Burton declared. "Why must you meddle with the natural course of Time?"

Nebogipfel leered at the explorer. "Because I can."

"You're using Mycroft Holmes for that purpose, aren't you?"

"He's just the meddlesome sort for the job, isn't he? The empire he will build and oversee will last untold centuries. I've already seen it. The last human army ever to do battle upon this beleaguered old Earth will march under his banner. And the machines, Burton! You've never seen such machines. Machines that can plumb the deepest ocean, dominate the sky and even break the bonds of this planet to explore the heavens."

"Machines of war," said Burton with a scowl.

"Man is a warlike species. I was once naive enough to think that would not always be the case. I found out better. As a wise man once told me, the greatest desire of a slave isn't freedom, but a slave of his own. War, not hope, springs eternal in the human breast."

A realization sunk in his chest like a stone. The wise man Nebogipfel spoke of was Burton himself, over a year ago in the belly of the *Nautilus*. "Bismillah! It *is* you. I was uncertain at first, but... Herbert? Is that really you?"

Nebogipfel gave a courtly bow. "At your service, Captain Burton. But more precisely, I *was* Herbert, until our lives diverged."

"Diverged? How?"

Nebogipfel ran a hand through his short, dark beard. "When we traveled into the dim past aboard Nemo's *Nautilus*, Herbert had trouble coping with the madness that surrounded him.

Burton nodded. "I remember. Poor fellow was almost catatonic for most of the journey."

"Yes, well, being shown such antediluvian horrors will tend to warp one's personality. It certainly did poor Herbert's. That is when I first came into being, when the schism between us first occurred. Perhaps it was a way for Herbert's mind to heal itself, to deal with everything that was happening. Whatever the cause, I was born, quietly at first. I felt trapped inside the mind of this amorphous other. I accessed Herbert's memories and figured out what was happening. What Herbert found frightening about his situation, I found fascinating. What filled him with terror filled me with curiosity, and I saw before me the vast sweep of Time!

"Upon our return to the present, Herbert recovered most of his wits, but I remained, a silent passenger within his fractured psyche. After unloading his Time Machine, with the help of some of Captain Nemo's swarthy sailors, and returning to his home in Kew Gardens, the man you call the Time Traveler hopped onto his contraption and went hurtling into the future, to the year 806,701, arriving at nearly the same moment he left on some errand before he was waylaid by the lovely Miss Marsh. I don't have to tell you, Burton. The journey was exhilarating! It was then that I knew I must take control. But he was calm there. Happy. The happiest he had ever been, and I should know, for I was him, and he was me. It wasn't until he returned and met up with your friends again, and you dragged him off on another ghastly adventure being chased by those repulsive shoggoths, that the stress that created me began to swell within Herbert's mind and body once more.

"After that last horrid affair reached its conclusion, he fell into such a torpor as I have never seen. But through it I saw my escape. I tried moving him. Subtly at first; a finger, a toe. Until I had him upright. I could see through his eyes and talk through his mouth and, bidding his utterly perplexed housekeeper adieu, grabbed coat and hat and set off into the nighttime London streets, looking for a way out of my fleshy prison."

"And what did you find?" Burton asked.

"Exactly what I sought. I am loathe to admit it now, but I first sought fleshly pleasures in the Cauldron, and it was there that I found my salvation. There was a big, brutish sort prowling the East End called Edward Hyde. One night, in a brothel, I heard him bragging about an elixir that had freed him of his every inhibition. I found this most curious, since this man had no inhibitions whatsoever as far as I could tell. He came and went as he pleased, drank to excess, and roughed up the girls when they refused his aggressive advances. So I cornered him as he was leaving the place, and asked him about this miracle elixir. He said a man called Dr. Henry Jekyll had invented it. Curious, and still not at all entirely sure if this disagreeable brute was telling me the truth, I offered to buy the bottle from him. I handed him a ten-pound note in return for what was left in the bottle, and made my way out of Whitechapel, returning to Kew Gardens with the dawn.

"Still unsure what was in the bottle, I did not drink it, instead getting out Herbert's old chemistry set. Before he turned to the study of optics, you see, our Herbert was obsessed with chemistry. That knowledge was still inside him, and I could access it. I studied the elixir's chemical makeup and was able to successfully reproduce it, in any quantity I wanted. Its efficacy wears off with time, you see. The next time Herbert sank into a malaise, I came to the fore and tested it. It tasted bloody awful, but it did the trick, allowing me full control of his body when he was unconscious, and suppressing him. It was as if our consciousnesses swapped places within Herbert's brain."

"Your personalities diverged fully," Burton said, remembering what had happened to his friend Swinburne and the others when the beings from the far future swapped minds with them. "Bismillah."

Nebogipfel smiled, nodding. "Indeed. More than that. The elixir alters my very appearance. This beard of mine grows in minutes! But it had a positive effect on our Herbert as well. Freed from his darker impulses, our dear Time Traveler was able to once more concentrate on his work. But at night, I came to the fore, and began asking questions of nature that Herbert wouldn't dare give thought to. I studied Herbert's work closely, learning how his Time Machine was constructed so that I might do the same, perhaps even improve upon his original design. I also began thinking about the full implications of what he had built."

"Bismillah! Why not erase Herbert permanently and be done with it? A stronger version of the elixir or something."

"Because I knew Herbert was onto something. I knew what power the Time Machine would represent. But I also knew I could never reach such lofty heights on my own, without his base intellect."

He returned to his position at the dirigible's sparkling brass controls. "Besides, I need Herbert. Just as he needs me. We are two sides of the same coin. One cannot possibly exist without the other." Something about his tone suggested to Burton that he didn't entirely believe this.

"But how do you maintain this dichotomy?" asked the explorer. "The human body needs rest. How does Herbert get any with you hopping about whilst he sleeps?"

"You're still not thinking fourth-dimensionally," said Nebogipfel. "With the Time Machine, I can remain gone days, weeks, get plenty of rest and come back to the precise moment I left, without Herbert knowing anything has transpired."

"So what do you want?" asked Burton.

Nebogipfel tapped his chin. "As I watched the Time Machine in action, I began to wonder, what if the Time Machine could move through Space as well? Think of the possibilities. What good does it do to travel to some distant time, only to find that the really interesting stuff is taking place thousands of miles hence? Like standing before Nelson's Column and trying to travel back through Time to see Alexander the Great destroy Tyre. Now, imagine a conveyance that has no limits in Time or Space, like the Time Machine when it was connected to Nemo's wondrous *Nautilus*. Imagine a craft that could travel to distant Mars and move back through Time billions of years to when that cold, red world possibly teemed with life? Or visiting distant locales on this world at any point in history?"

"So you built this dirigible," said Burton.

"With the help of the Morlocks, yes. I took pity on them, you see. My counterpart has been quite cruel to them, so I went back to the moment when the Morlocks briefly absconded with his Time Machine, in the year 802,701. It took a bit of work to ingratiate myself to them, but once they warmed up to me I found them amiable enough. They are astounding tinkerers, and have a real knack for machines. They learned how the Time Machine worked by taking it apart and putting it back together, with such precision that Herbert couldn't tell it had ever been tampered with at all."

"Why are they so friendly toward you?" asked Burton.

"Because I am their savior. Herbert tried to burn them out of their subterranean den. I rescued them, bringing them aboard my bloody balloon, as you called it. And the rest, as they say, is history."

"I think you've meddled quite enough," said Burton.

"And I say I'm just getting started," said Nebogipfel, twirling a finger in the air.

On this signal, rough hands seized Burton.

"What are you doing?"

"Giving you the gift I mentioned earlier." Nebogipfel stepped toward Burton, holding a familiar-looking brass device attached to a leather strap. He secured it onto Burton's wrist.

"This is a Time Machine similar to Miss Hemlock's," he said. "But with one difference. Only I can control it."

"You mean to strand me somewhere in Time?"

"Heavens, no. Your history is already written. I have seen your death, friend Burton, years hence and many miles from England's shores. No, I mean to show you something. You'll move through Space as well as Time, via a mechanism too complex to explain."

Burton glared at the device, flexing his hand.

"But I must warn you, Burton. "Do not attempt to remove it or alter its workings, or you shall become unstuck in Time, drifting either forward or backward forever, and not even I can locate you and effect a rescue. Good journeys, Captain Burton."

"Do I have a bloody choice?"

Nebogipfel nodded, and the Morlocks released him, stepping back from the explorer in a widening circle. Nebogipfel stepped once more

357

to the dirigible's controls and flicked a crystalline lever. "While you're gone, I am going to go back and deliver the Map of Time, as you call it, to Mycroft Holmes. You interrupted my first attempt."

Burton saw orbs of light once more flicker before his eyes, and the scene aboard the dirigible began to pull away from him, growing indistinct. He felt ghost-like, his feet passing through the inlaid brass floor of the Time Balloon as he sank into indigo mists.

THE RATIOCINATOR

Captain Sir Richard Frances Burton emerged from indigo mists to the sound of a blaring horn and a large, wheeled vehicle careening towards him.

The explorer, eyes wide, dived out of the way just in time, landing in the mouth of a refuse-strewn alley. The contraption belched smoke from a pipe jutting from its rear, its driver yelling a string of incomprehensible curses as the craft swerved around a corner and disappeared.

Burton stood, brushing himself off, Nebogipfel's Time Machine heavy on his wrist.

"Blimey," said a young voice from the alley. "Are you all right, gov? You almost got creamed by that lorry."

"Creamed," Burton murmured. He looked into the alley and saw a small boy, about twelve years old. He was rail-thin, and dressed in threadbare clothes. He clutched a bundle of newspapers under one arm.

"Uh, yes," said Burton. "I suppose I nearly was. Say, can you tell me the date?"

"April first," said the boy.

Burton eyed his collection of newspapers. "Can I see one of those?"

The boy backed away. "Gotta pay for it first."

Burton nodded. "Of course. How much?"

"Five pence."

Burton almost balked, then realized things probably cost more in the future and, in a functioning economy, must do so. He reached into his pocket and fumbled around until he had the five pence. He placed this in the boy's hand.

"Blimey!" he said, staring at his open palm. "These are old coins. My Da collects 'em. For these, you can have my whole bloomin' stack."

Burton chuckled. "That won't be necessary, my good fellow. Just one is enough, and you can keep the money."

The boy pocketed the coins and handed Burton a paper, his eyes growing wide when he saw the Time Machine strapped to Burton's wrist.

"Is that a Ratiocinator? Looks different."

"A what?"

"You know. A Thinker." The boy pulled up his right sleeve and showed Burton a smaller brass device secured to his wrist by a worn leather strap. Its face had a sickly green orb for a dial with a tiny grille underneath. It reminded Burton of a smirking cyclops.

"It tells us when there's trouble," said the boy.

As if to demonstrate, the dial began to glow and a tinny voice issued from the strange device.

"Air raid tonight. Stay indoors from 8 p.m. to midnight. Greater threat levels in Greenwich, Covent Garden, and West End."

"What was that?" asked Burton.

"That's The Thinker. It operates out of old Big Ben. Where have you been?"

Burton smiled at the boy and nodded, unfolding his paper. The newsie shrugged and, clutching his antique coins, ran away up the street, dropping the rest of his bundle, heedless of any lost revenue they might represent. The explorer looked up from his paper to watch the boy go, shaking his head before returning his attention to the newspaper.

There, under the masthead, was the information he sought: Tuesday, April 1st, 1945. The Time Traveler's doppelganger had stranded him in the future. But for what purpose?

Burton turned and stepped from the alley's mouth. He had always been an explorer at heart; and would be again. Concealing the Time Machine as best he could under his coat, the accidental Time Traveler merged into the throng and let it carry him away up the street.

The city had grown more crowded and clamorous in the intervening eighty-five years, the streets filled with more of the machines like the kind that had almost run him over. It seemed they had completely replaced the horse and buggy as the preferred means of transport. People dressed strangely and, Burton was pleased to see, a bit less formally. Gone were the tight corsets and voluminous bustles for the women, and beards and top hats seemed to have gone out of style for the men. The only formal dress Burton saw were among the soldiers, young lads decked out in crisp, dark green, with gleaming gold epaulets and symbols of rank that Burton found comfortingly familiar. But everyone had one item in common: the queer Thinkers, like the one the newspaper boy wore, strapped firmly to their wrists.

The air smelled just as foul as the London he remembered, only instead of coal smoke and refuse, it was something else, possibly the fuel they burned in their calamitous auto carriages. It was a wonder they all didn't suffocate and die where they stood. Burton needed a plan. The sooner he saw whatever it was Nebogipfel wanted him to see, the sooner he could be gone from this abysmal future time. Besides, he wasn't about to wander aimlessly around this familiar yet alien city like a bloody lost tourist. Looking around to get his bearings, Burton spied the familiar Nelson's Column, the poor fellow looking dingy and much the worse for wear. This put him at Trafalgar Square.

He moved east, threading his way through the throng of people and vehicles, with no clear idea of where he was going. Until he saw the sign. It read Occult Ministry, and was fastened to the front of a tall, imposing brick building onto which esoteric symbols—possibly ones of protection—had been painted. Burton found it odd that such a department not only existed, but that they would announce their presence so boldly. Burton surmised that in this future time, the existence of the occult was common knowledge, and a shudder ran through him. It meant that his—and the Shadow Council's—efforts to keep such things secret were all for naught. He stepped up to a set of heavy wooden doors, turned one of the knobs and walked inside.

He found himself standing in a dim and cavernous hallway. People moved about, heedless of Burton's presence. On either side of the hall were open doors leading into various offices, from which Burton heard a strange rhythmic clacking and, from the far end of the building, an insistent, shrill bell that rang loudly at random intervals.

A young man in a pale blue suit came around a corner, his arms laden with thick, ancient leather-bound volumes, and almost slammed into Burton. The explorer backed away, apologizing. Taking a chance, he said, "Can you tell me where I can find Miss Penelope Hemlock?" Burton knew she wasn't likely a part of the Occult Ministry, but she was the only person he knew in this time.

"Down the hall on your right," said the man, and hurried off.

Burton tipped his hat in thanks, but the man had already disappeared into one of the offices to put down his burden. Burton walked in the direction indicated, wondering if he was altering Time even further. If this was a time before Miss Hemlock left to go back to Burton's London, he would be adding an additional paradox onto an already fractured timeline. He muttered all of this to himself, longing for the bygone days when all he had to worry about was malaria and bloodthirsty natives.

At the end of the hall was a wooden door affixed with a brass plate that read Operation Chronos. Burton smiled and knocked. When no one acknowledged him, he turned and knob and entered.

Operation Chronos consisted of a single narrow room, both walls lined with shelves filled almost to bursting with papers and books. At the far end was a desk with a pentagram emblazoned on its front. A tall, slender man sat on the edge of it perusing through a thick volume, a black cigarette holder jutting from his mouth, his head wreathed in acrid smoke. He looked at Burton, slamming the volume closed.

"I'm sorry," said the explorer. "I was looking for Miss Hemlock. Is she in?"

"She just stepped out," said the man, looking Burton up and down disapprovingly. "Mission. Are you one of the wizards? You're supposed to report to Simon Iff. He's upstairs."

"I'm not a wizard," said Burton. "I'm—this is going to sound terribly strange. I'm Richard Francis Burton."

The man jumped from the desk and moved toward the explorer, eying him. He had a high forehead and dark hair giving way to silver. "By Jove, man. You bloody well are. How marvelous to meet you. But what are you doing here?"

They shook hands. "It's quite a a long story," said Burton. "It seems I have run afoul of the man Miss Hemlock has been chasing through Time."

The man's mouth opened so wide he almost dropped his cigarette holder. "Bloody hell! I told her not to go traipsing off after that madman. Which means she's absconded with our chronos unit. That impudent girl. I'm sorry she's dragged you into this. You shouldn't be here!"

"It is not her fault I am here," said Burton. "It was the man you've been chasing. I thought you knew Miss Hemlock had traveled back through Time to stop him."

The man scowled. "Good heavens! No. I'm afraid Miss Hemlock has a mind of her own."

"I don't understand," said Burton. "She told me she was a Time Agent."

The other man snatched his cigarette holder from his mouth and uttered dry laughter. "Time Agent? I'm sorry, Captain Burton. The fool girl misrepresented herself. I shall give her a stern talking to once she returns. *If* she returns."

He tamped out his cigarette in a silver ashtray and set another in its place, lighting it with a match before taking a deep drag from it. "I'm forgetting my manners. I am Ian Fleming, late of the Naval Department, now assigned to the Occult Ministry as assistant to Aleister Crowley."

Burton arched an eyebrow. "And who is he?"

"He runs the whole Ministry. He's a ceremonial magician who warned us of what Germany was doing on the esoteric plane. He helps us counter their magic with some of our own. Well, he and the Thinker, of course."

"Yes, I know of the Thinker," said Burton darkly.

"Yes, well, I'm sure our Miss Hemlock told you of the war."

"She did. So you don't have any so-called Time Agents running about trying to counter Germany's war efforts?"

"Goodness, no. Bad stuff, Time travel. We only had the one working prototype, which I unwisely gave to Miss Hemlock for safekeeping. I hope she hasn't been too much trouble for you back in your time."

"No," said Burton. "On the contrary. She's quite formidable. In fact, she saved my life."

Fleming chuckled. "Well, that's something at least. But if she isn't here with you, how did you arrive here?"

Burton showed Fleming the device Nebogipfel had strapped to his wrist. "The villain Miss Hemlock chased back to my time put this on me and sent me here. He said he wants me to see something. I don't know what."

"Good heavens," said Fleming. "It's similar to the one our scientists built, based on the mysterious Time Traveler's original design, as left to us in the files of Mycroft Holmes."

"Yes," said Burton. "Similar, but not the same. He controls it. If I attempt to remove it, I will be lost in Time forever."

"So why are you here now?" asked Fleming.

"I'm not sure. Our mutual devil insists on teaching me something about the nature of Time. But I know who he is."

Fleming arched an eyebrow. "Oh?"

"It is hard to explain, but he represents the darker impulses of the Time Machine's original inventor."

Fleming puffed on his cigarette and stared at Burton. "You mean he is the mysterious Time Traveler?"

"Yes," said Burton. "A version of the man, prone to mischief and evil. But now that I think about it, I believe he sent me here to stop something, something he himself set in motion back in my time. The thing Miss Hemlock went back to stop."

"What do you mean?"

Burton moved upwind of Fleming's cigarette smoke. "Tell me more about Aleister Crowley."

Fleming nodded. "He's our Occult Minister. A new post, he's the first of his kind. When Germany was just getting started flexing its military muscles, I was working for the Navy. Crowley came to me with an unusual request. He wanted to fight Hitler using magical means. I, along with nearly everyone else, thought the man insane. Then a village in Poland was stamped out of existence by a giant, invisible foot. We employed Crowley's help immediately, and I became his right hand."

"Where is he now?"

"The old man is all over the place these days," said Fleming, sucking his cigarette down to the filter. "He's working on something big he says will change the tide of the war in our favor, something called the Babalon Working. He spends a lot of time with the Thinker. He's there now, completing his final preparations."

"Yes," said Burton. "I know of this as well. Your Ratiocinator. It's actually the mind of Mycroft Holmes installed with the aid of the Wold-Newton stones into a difference engine."

"You are well-informed," said Fleming. "No one is supposed to know that. I shall need to have a few words with Miss Hemlock upon her return."

"She told me what she thought I must know," said Burton. "Mycroft Holmes is still alive inside that machine in the clock tower because of a Map of Time, a list of future events that the Time Traveler's doppelganger gave him in the past."

Fleming's mouth opened in surprise, almost losing its cigarette holder. "Are you saying our current state of affairs is all due to his meddling?"

"I'm afraid so," said the explorer. "Miss Hemlock traveled back to my time in an attempt to steal the Map of Time from Mycroft Holmes after Nebogipfel gives it to him."

Fleming scowled. "Who?"

"Moses Nebogipfel. That is what the scoundrel calls himself."

"Oh hell," said Fleming. "This Time travel is a ghastly business. I rue the day Prime Minister Churchill had the bloody thing constructed."

"You don't know the half of it," said Burton. "Now, I think that the only way to stop Nebogipfel in my time is to stop this Crowley fellow from carrying out his magic spell in yours."

Fleming dashed out his cigarette and prepared himself another. "Why on earth would you want to do that?"

"Because it will end badly!" Burton declared. "Crowley is meddling with forces he cannot possibly understand. I've seen this before. There are things beyond the veil that are neither god nor devil but worse than either! Whatever Crowley is trying to bring into this world is better left where it is."

"Even if that were true," said Fleming, blowing a ring of blue smoke, "We cannot possibly disturb him now. His working is at a crucial juncture, and the balance of the war is at stake. We're getting hammered, Captain Burton. And the Yanks just got into things. It could go badly for us before they're able to make a dent in Germany's war machine."

"I can't tell you how to end this war," said Burton. "All I can tell you is that what Crowley is up to is very dangerous. The entities he is trying to summon will destroy you all. Humanity is a nuisance at best to them, and a bloody pestilence at worst."

Fleming tapped his right foot on the carpeted floor. "I don't know..."

"At least let me speak with Mycroft Holmes. Whatever is left of him. Perhaps he will give me a clue to the Map's whereabouts back in my time. If I can convince him what a fool's errand this has all been, maybe he'll help me undo it."

"Tell me this," said Fleming. "What happens to me when this is undone? What happens to everything?"

"I do not know," said Burton. "The moments of your life will rearrange themselves into their original course, with you none the wiser. Beyond that...I don't know."

Fleming shrugged. "That is enough, I suppose. I miss my work with the Navy. I'm tired of this bloody war. You go and have your chat with the Thinker, not that it will do you much good, I'm afraid." He glanced at the door before continuing. "Holmes, what's left of him, is blinking mad."

"Thank you," said Burton as he turned to leave.

"Good luck, Captain Burton," said Fleming.

Burton paused at the door and nodded once toward the other man before exiting the room.

~

It was an hour's walk to the Westminster Clock Tower. Burton looked up at it to see that it had been altered. No longer did a clock face on all four sides of the tower greet his eyes, but an enormous green sphere like a huge leering eye looked down on fog-shrouded London.

"Bismillah!" Burton swore and went inside. He was surprised to see no attendants, no guards, as he walked up the flight of steps that led into the clockwork heart of the tower the world at large mistakenly called Big Ben. When he reached the top, Burton was surprised once more. The interior of the structure had been gutted of clockwork. In its place were banks of dusty metal components with large glass tubes jutting from them. An old man with parchment-like skin huddled over a large tome in the far corner, muttering to himself.

"Richard. Francis. Burton."

The explorer looked around. The voice, which sounded like air being forced through a gigantic bellows, seemed to come from all around him.

The old man, whom Burton surmised to be Aleister Crowley, scowled in his direction. "No visitors!" he said. "I told Fleming on no uncertain terms, no bloody visitors. I am at a crucial juncture."

"I need to converse with the Thinker," Burton said. "He and I are old friends."

Crowley scowled at him some more, then stepped around the wooden dais which held the book from which he was reading. "It can't be! Oh, but it is. Explain this, Mycroft."

"It. Is. Captain. Sir. Richard. Francis. Burton," the machine intoned. "He. Traveled. Here. Through. Time. Just. As. I. Was. Told. He. Would."

Crowley laughed, which came out as a phlegmy cackle. He rubbed his bald head with talon-like fingers. "This is an auspicious occasion. The signs are in our favor. I am a great admirer of yours, Burton. It is an honor to meet you."

Burton nodded. "What are you doing, Mr. Crowley?"

"That's *Minister* Crowley, if you please. And I am opening the veil. Summoning the elements. Putting the balance in our favor. This damnable war ends tonight."

"You are mad," said Burton. "You must stop what you are doing. You are inviting entities into this world that only want our destruction."

"They will destroy our enemies."

"They will destroy everyone," the explorer corrected.

Crowley gave him a dismissive wave. "I haven't the time to deal with this just now. Speak your peace with Mycroft the Thinker and begone. You do not belong here." The old man hobbled back to the dais and began his arcane muttering once more.

"What. Do. You. Want?" the machine said.

"I'd just like to know," said Burton, "was it worth it?"

"Was. What. Worth. It?"

Burton gestured to the machinery around them. He smelled dust and ozone. "All of this. Losing your humanity to become a difference engine, a calculation machine."

"That. Is. Not. Why. You. Came. Here."

Burton realized then that he was hearing Mycroft Holmes' actual voice, but reedy and thin. "How are you speaking with me?"

"Wax. Cylinders. I. Recorded. My. Voice. Long. Ago. Common. Phrases. Numbers. The. Alphabet. I. Use. Them. To. Speak."

"Bismillah," said Burton.

"You. Came. Here. Because. Of. The. Map. Of. Time."

"That is correct. I need to know where it is, Mycroft. Nebogipfel used you as a pawn to change history. You're not some overseer of Time. Every moment you influenced changed Time's original course. You're barely staying ahead of any of it, are you?"

"I. Am. Timeless. Burton. I. See. All."

"For what purpose? You're bodiless. You're wax cylinders and clockwork. You sit here helpless while Crowley is about to destroy you all."

"You. Are. Tiresome. I. Don't. Owe. You. An. Explanation. But. You. Are. Correct. I. Have. Grown. Weary. I. Have. Saved. Lives. But. History. Is. Vastly. Different. Than. The. Map. Originally. Revealed. Constant. Corrections. Are. Needed."

"And they're still not enough, are they?" said Burton.

The machine rumbled. "No."

"Nebogipfel has played you for a fool. Help me stop him. You have the gift of hindsight. Tell me where I can find the Map of Time after he gave it to you, and I can put an end to this nightmare history."

"It. Is. Too. Late."

"No, it isn't. Time is malleable. Time is mutable."

"I. Thought. So. Too. Once. Too. Unpredictable. You. Would. Make. My. Same. Mistake?"

Burton raked a hand through his beard. This much history had already been rewritten. Who was he to untangle its thread? But who was Mycroft Holmes to do so? Who was Moses Nebogipfel?

"I have to try to put things back as they were, even if we won't ever know the difference."

The machine that was once a man named Mycroft Holmes hummed. The machine rumbled. The machine clacked. Registers clicked throughout its bulk as it thought.

"I. Grow. Weary. Of. This. Existence."

"Stop talking like that," barked Crowley. "I can barely hear myself invoke."

"And. I. Grow. Tired. Of. Your. Ministrations. Wizard. Burton. Is. Right. You. Are. Unleashing. Forces. That. Will. Doom. Us. All. I. Have. Seen. These. Forces."

"Why are you doing your bloody ritual up here?" Burton asked the old man. Then he realized the answer. "Of course. The remaining Wold-Newton stones. They are part of your bulk, am I right, Mycroft?"

"You. Are. Correct."

"Their ethereal vibrations will help pierce the veil," said Crowley with a sneer. "What of it?"

"Where?" Burton asked the machine.

"Above. You."

Richard Francis Burton began to climb.

"What are you doing?" Crowley shouted from below. "Stop, damn your eyes!"

Burton ignored the old man, hauling himself up on wooden rafters and metal framework to a matrix high above. In the space where the great bell once hung suspended was a crystalline structure, like a giant snowflake. Inside this was six black stones that glinted in the milky light coming in through gaps in the top of the clock tower.

"Stop!" Crowley croaked. "My working will not be interrupted!"

Burton ignored him. "Tell me where the Map of Time is hidden," said Burton to the machine.

The bellows wheezed. The cylinders of wax turned on their great spindles. "I. Kept. It. On. My. Person. At. All. Times," the machine said. "Safest. Place."

"Blast!" said the explorer. How would he get it from him now?

He reached the top of the tower, and the Wold-Newton stones. Crowley seethed below him with wheezy, inchoate rage. "Blast you, Burton! I need those stones intact."

Burton went to where they were secured in the crystalline lattice. The way they caught the light reminded him of the crystalline control levers of the Time Machine. The explorer removed a penknife from his pocket and went to work, prying the first stone free. It was big as a marble, and cut into facets like a diamond. He stared into it and thought he could see universes. The faces of the other Burtons he had met danced within each facet. He held it between thumb and forefinger, then tossed it into the whirring mechanism below. It caught in the teeth of two cogs and was ground into dust.

He went to work on the other stones, freeing all six of them and dashing them to powder while Crowley fumed helplessly. At some point he had called for assistance; Burton could hear many booted feet running up the stairs that led into the top of the tower.

"Thank. You," said the Thinker. Without the Wold-Newton stones, there was nothing else pinning his soul to the machine. With a puff of smoke and the smell of burnt wiring, Mycroft Holmes was no more.

Burton felt a wave of dizziness smash into him, sensed this undone causality collapsing in upon itself, and he fell from the rafters and down into clockwork and wires and components he did not have names for. One name escaped his lips.

"Isabel."

THINGS TO COME

Burton opened his eyes and found himself lying on the deck of Nebogipfel's strange craft once more. Herbert's doppelganger helped the explorer to his feet.

"How did you enjoy your jaunt through things to come?" Nebogipfel asked with a sneer.

"I could have done without it," Burton declared, removing the Time Machine from his wrist and dashing it to the floor. "Why did you send me into the future?"

"To show you what is possible," said Nebogipfel. "To show you what my glorious work in your time has wrought. Splendid, isn't it? A Britain ruled by a mad magician and a clockwork mind! An empire that will reshape the world in numerous and untold ways. And it's all my doing."

Burton sat up. Nebogipfel hadn't been watching him. He didn't know what he had done. "You're insane. Time is not clay that you can mold however you like, only to smash it all and start again."

"Oh, but it is," said Nebogipfel. "I've just proven it to you. I am the God of Time." Nebogipfel spun in a circle, arms outstretched. The Morlocks watched him impassively through their smoked goggles.

"Poor Herbert never really understood what his invention repre-

372

sents. He journeyed through Time as one on a sight-seeing trip, a passive observer, a voyeur who acted as if all that he was witnessing couldn't be altered, as if the future in which he found himself couldn't be changed for the better. Or worse."

"But he did change it," observed Burton. "He freed the gentle Eloi from the cruel Morlocks." He stared at Nebogipfel's companions self-consciously as he said this.

"But not at the source, when it could have done some good," said Nebogipfel. "And he chose the wrong side; the descendants of the aristocracy and landed gentry he has always inwardly railed against, rather than the poor Morlocks, children of the poor, put-upon working class. I seek to correct that error."

"You're taking one error and adding to it a thousand-fold," said Burton. "Herbert sought to learn from Time. You seek only to control it."

"No. That's not it at all. Don't you see from your own wanderings? You can't control it. Whatever we touch is irrevocably altered in ways we cannot foresee. That is the beautiful and terrible nature of Time."

While Nebogipfel was dancing about, Burton moved closer to the raised control panel where Miss Hemlock's wrist-mounted Time Machine lay. Now he was close enough to touch it. He reached for it, elbowing a Morlock in the nose who tried to stop him.

"No!" Nebogipfel exclaimed, reaching for the explorer. But it was too late. Burton gripped the miniature Time Machine tightly, thumbing its tiny lever. Nebogipfel and his tableau of Morlocks faded from view.

~

The sun was climbing high overhead as Burton completed his tale and finished off the brandy. Herbert stared at him, blinking. Weena was in the next room, singing softly and arranging unusual flowers in a vase, heedless of the explorer's presence.

"Where did you get the brandy?" asked the Time Traveler.

Burton looked down at the empty bottle. "Oh. On the way here I stopped by my home and grabbed a bottle. I needed a drink, and figured you could as well, given all I had to tell you. And here we are."

"Yes," said Herbert, arching an eyebrow. "Here we are. I still can't believe I have a mischievous doppelganger who has befriended the bloody Morlocks."

"Neither can I. But I've seen them with my own eyes. What horrors this future holds."

"Horrors that are now spreading," said Herbert. "But what can be done about it? I'm sorry I ever built that bloody thing." He pointed. In a far corner of the hut was the Time Machine, its crystalline levers removed.

"I was hoping you might have some idea how to stop him. After all, Nebogipfel is you."

Herbert sat on the edge of his bed, cradling his head in his hands. "Bloody hell, Captain Burton. This is all so confusing. And frustrating. To think that I have an evil twin who has been mucking about through Time with those bloody awful Morlocks. And all because I came here in the first place."

"I know it's a lot to take in," said Burton. "I know how confusing it must be. But you might be our only hope in stopping all this."

The Time Traveler nodded and stood. "Care to take a walk with me?"

Herbert whispered something to Weena and gave her a peck on the cheek. Then the explorer and the Time Traveler walked down the gently sloping green hill toward the plain where the Palace of Green Porcelain and the White Sphinx stood. "Nebogipfel won't come here," Herbert said.

"How do you know that?" asked Burton.

"Because he can't risk my discovering him. And because I am always at peace here. More peace than I have ever felt at any other time or place in my life."

"But what does it matter that he doesn't come here? He's got all of Time and Space to play with."

"His ability to move about isn't the issue," said Herbert. "The issue is with me. He thinks of this far future time as my complacent prison, one in which I am content to remain while he plays about causing trouble."

Burton shrugged. "So?"

"So," said the Time Traveler. "What is the one thing this self-described God of Time wants? What's the one thing that his mastery over all of Time and Space can't give him? He gave you a hint when he repeated some of your first words to me, when we met aboard Nemo's *Nautilus*."

Burton froze in his tracks. "Bismillah! He wants his freedom."

"Precisely. He can never truly be free until he is rid of me."

"But he can't kill you," said Burton. "He can't kill you. He would cease to exist as well. Good God!"

The Time Traveler grinned. Exactly. He wants to use the Wold-Newton stones to split us off."

They stopped near the White Sphinx, Herbert looking up at Burton in the shadow of the great statue. "He wants our schism to be permanent, but to do that he must bifurcate the timeline so that there will be two of us. One, here in this dead future, with only the docile Eloi for company, and one free to rove about all of Time and Space, seeding Morlocks everywhere. And who has the Wold-Newton stones?"

"Mycroft Holmes," Burton murmured.

"Exactly. And what better way to get hold of them, or at least find out where they are so he can steal them, than to offer Mycroft a gift that arrogant, manipulative sot could not possibly refuse?"

"Bismillah!" said Burton. "Can Nebogipfel even do such a thing?"

Herbert shrugged. "Perhaps. You told me of the stones' power to make contact with other realities, in which you met alternative versions of yourself. He may seek to enter one of these realities. Who knows? All I know is that, given what you have told me, that is what I would do if I were him. He cannot risk anything happening to me, or he will cease to exist. I'm too far away from the turbulence he is causing to be that much affected."

"What do you mean?" said Burton. "Every alteration of an event causes ripple effects that can be felt years, decades, centuries hence."

Herbert put his arm around Burton's shoulder. "Look around you, Captain. This is a dead world, save for the Eloi and whatever Morlocks might be left, of course. But everything our kind created is gone. There are only our degenerate children, living in the shadow of what we built. Everything we accomplished, every piece of knowledge we acquired, has long since turned to dust. But gone too is every sign of our wars, our saber-rattling, our ignorance. Whatever we make of ourselves, for good or ill, this shall be the end result. Man had his time in the sun."

He began walking again, and Burton followed. "And even should a race of creatures with some semblance of ourselves reach out to toil among the stars, those same stars shall eventually grow dim and die, either by exploding violently or collapsing in upon themselves, until the entire Universe follows suit. Every last possible chemical reaction will have long since occurred, and all will be nothingness. Neither our greatest triumphs nor our worst mistakes will change that. I know this all sounds morbid and dour, but I find it strangely comforting. Everything, you see, works out exactly as it is supposed to in the end."

"I think I understand what you mean," said Burton. "In the grand scheme of things, one paltry human life doesn't seem like much. But when that paltry human life is your own, you want to do your utmost to protect it."

"And protect it we shall," said Herbert. "We are going to put an end to Nebogipfel's foolishness once and for all. I will help you."

"Thank you, old friend," Burton said, craning his neck to stare up at the White Sphinx. "Say, has your Sphinx always looked like that?"

"What do you mean?" asked Herbert, following the explorer's gaze up the base of the statue to the stern countenance staring out across the Thames valley. "Yes. It's exactly how I remember it."

"Bismillah!" said Burton. "That's Mycroft Holmes. He made his mark on history after all."

"I don't remember it looking any other way," said Herbert. "Perhaps the White Sphinx was destined to wear his countenance."

"Perhaps," Burton mused, stroking his beard. "Do you know of the people who built it?"

"No," said the Time Traveler. "Only that they were more advanced than the Eloi and Morlocks. I thought about moving my Time

Machine next to it and going back through Time to watch its dismantling and then construction, find out who built it, but I knew I'd be
tempted to stop and meet them, and that would cause further paradoxes for me in *this* time."

Burton nodded. "It's of no matter. We must get the Map away from
Holmes."

"Agreed," said Herbert. "All we need is a plan."

Burton shook his head. "I don't have one. Your doppelganger can
foresee every contingency. Or, failing that, go back in Time and
undo it."

"Perhaps not," said Herbert. "Let's go and have a talk with the
fellow. He won't be expecting me. It might throw him off his game
enough for us to gain the upper hand."

Burton shrugged. "It's worth a try."

The two men walked back up the hill toward the hut-like structure
the Time Traveler shared with Weena. Burton was sweating. "I'll say
one thing, your London has better weather."

"Yes, this region, perhaps even the entire planet, has warmed
greatly since our time. A shame our kind are no longer here to
enjoy it."

Herbert took Burton's wrist, reading the tiny dial on the miniature
Time Machine, then went to his own machine and set the destination
dial accordingly. "I'm glad I added slots for the hours and minutes," he
said, patting the dial. Burton inspected it, noticing the difference.

"An alteration I made in this latest incarnation of my Time
Machine," he said with a grin. He went to Weena. "I must go, my dear.
But I will return soon, in mere moments from your perspective."

"Oh, all right," she cooed and went back to making a crown from a
handful of freshly picked flowers.

Herbert mounted the machine. "When you're ready, Captain.
When we arrive at the appointed day and time, we shall be in my back
garden. I do hope my Time Machine doesn't flatten the hydrangeas."

"That will be satisfactory," Burton said. He flicked the tiny lever,
feeling a spinning vibration from somewhere inside the minute
device. Herbert jerked at his levers, and the two of them were gone,
careening through Time in concert.

INVASION OF THE MORLOCKS

Mycroft Holmes sat by the window in the Stranger's Room, reading that morning's edition of *The London Mail*. He wasn't surprised as he looked up to see Dr. Moses Nebogipfel standing there, his hands clasped in front of him.

"I trust you found the Map's first prediction satisfactory," said Nebogipfel.

Mycroft Holmes arched an eyebrow. "More than satisfactory. It was accurate in every detail. And the event was so mundane. A horse frightened by a policeman's whistle and overturning its master's apple cart at precisely half past seven, and that I would see this occur as I was returning home."

"Good," said Nebogipfel. "Then I assume you are confident about the accuracy of the rest of the events in this timeline."

Mycroft Holmes nodded.

"Then I expect my payment. The remaining Wold-Newton stones, as we agreed."

"I appreciate this glimpse into the future you have afforded me," said Mycroft Holmes. "Though I will not live to see all of them, I am already setting into motion procedures that will allow us to weather the coming storms, and even benefit and profit from them. I am also looking into ways to prolong my life, so that I may witness these future events firsthand and can guide them to this nation's benefit personally."

"You are as resourceful as legend says," replied Nebogipfel with a smile.

Mycroft Holmes folded the newspaper and rested it on his lap. "But I cannot in good conscience give up any of the Wold-Newton stones. Their propensity for mischief is just too great."

"Then let me assure you I mean no mischief. No harm will come to you or anyone else in London, or all of Britain, through my use of them. I seek to use them in a personal manner, and wish no one else any harm. In fact, I am going to return them to you, so that you may make use of them in the future for your, uh, longevity plans, the successful completion of which I have already witnessed."

"You may not wish us harm," said Holmes. "But harm may still be the end result. I'm sorry, good sir. But I cannot have someone running about through Time with such a powerful set of artifacts. Good day to you."

Leaning back in his chair, the elder Holmes took up his paper again.

Nebogipfel scowled down at him. "I am sorry you feel that way. It is my own fault for dealing with such an unsavory, untrustworthy sort."

Mycroft glared up at him. "Unsavory? You forget yourself, Time Traveler."

Nebogipfel arched an eyebrow.

"Yes, I recognize you, Herbert, or whatever you call yourself. My own brother, master of disguise that he is, cannot fool me, and he has tried much harder than you. Now materialize elsewhere, before I have you thrown out bodily."

"You mean like this?" Nebogipfel clapped his hands, and the door to the Stranger's Room opened. In loped three hunched figures in black greatcoats and top hats. They wore glasses or goggles with smoked lenses and sidelights. These disguises failed to hide their bluish-white skin, long white hair, or hideous countenances. The

Morlocks moved to stand beside Nebogipfel, staring down at Mycroft Holmes through goggled eyes.

"What is the meaning of this?" Holmes stammered. "What are these hideous creatures?"

"Mankind's destiny," said Nebogipfel. "And now your doom. I did not give you the precise date of every important future world event for the next two centuries out of the kindness of my heart. I expected something in return. Now I will simply take the Wold-Newton stones and leave my friends here to devour you all. Starting with you."

"These are the cannibals from the sewers?"

Nebogipfel nodded. "The same. Enjoy your feast, my friends. Goodbye, Mycroft Holmes. I can see why Captain Burton dislikes you so."

Nebogipfel touched a device on his wrist, flickered, and vanished.

~

F ive minutes after Burton vanished through Time, Miss Hemlock and Inspector Abberline emerged from the alley to find that something was not quite right. They heard a woman scream, glancing up the street to see her being chased by a pair of loping, fungus-colored figures with long, stringy white hair.

"I've got a bad feeling about this," Miss Hemlock muttered.

"Blimey!" said Abberline. "It's those bleedin' Morlocks. What are they doing out in broad daylight? I thought the sun hurt their eyes."

"They're wearing goggles," said Miss Hemlock. "And protective clothing. It appears this was our mystery villain's endgame after all. Come. We must find a way to stop them."

Miss Hemlock ran toward the entrance of the Diogenes Club and opened the door. It was unlocked and unguarded. Abberline joined her as she ran inside. The place was deserted, which was just as well. The Club's clientele would not approve of a woman wandering their infamous halls.

"Where is the Stranger's room?" she asked.

"This way." Abberline led her through the plush maze to the infamous abode of Mycroft Holmes. Abberline kicked the door open to find Mycroft Holmes tangled in Morlocks.

"Get them off of me," the elder Holmes managed, uttering a choked cry as the Morlocks sought to haul him from his chair and presumably carry him away.

Abberline drew his revolver and fired into their midst, striking a Morlock in the right shoulder. It cried out, staggering back from the group, clutching its arm. The concussion of the weapon was deafening in the small room. Abberline had to be careful. He did not want to hit Mycroft Holmes.

Miss Hemlock could not hope to overpower the beast-men, but she sought to cripple them as much as she could, kicking their legs out from under them in an impressive show of martial prowess. Abberline fired his pistol at the ceiling, the noise causing the Morlocks to retreat behind Mycroft's chair, giving the large man a chance to get up.

"He wanted the Wold-Newton stones," said Mycroft Holmes. "When I refused to give them up, he sent these creatures after me."

"They're running all over London," said Miss Hemlock. "I fear that was his plan all along. Where are the stones now?"

"Safe," said Mycroft Holmes. "And who in blazes are you? Women are not allowed in the Diogenes Club!"

Miss Hemlock laughed. "I daresay neither are Morlocks, and you see how well that turned out. Perhaps you should install a placard."

Mycroft Holmes harrumphed.

"At any rate, my name is Penelope Hemlock, but I'm afraid we don't have time for introductions at the moment. Now where are the stones?"

"In the Tower of London," said Mycroft Holmes. "Where he can't get them."

"He has a Time Machine," said Miss Hemlock. "I assure you, he can. He probably has them already. We must hurry."

"Who is this confounded woman?" Mycroft Holmes asked as he let himself be herded from the Stranger's Room and into the hall.

"It would take too long to explain, Mr. Holmes," said Abberline. "Suffice it to say she is a Time Traveler. From the future."

"Bloody hell," said Mycroft Holmes. "Is there no end to this temporal nonsense?"

"You should know. You were the one who caused it."

Mycroft Holmes glared at Abberline, who returned his gaze. The elder Holmes said nothing as he let himself be ushered down the hall.

"You get Mr. Holmes to safety," said Miss Hemlock.

"And what are you going to do?" asked Abberline.

"I've got to get to the Tower of London and stop Nebogipfel."

"But you said so yourself. He's a Time Traveler. He probably has the bloody Wold-Newton stones already."

Miss Hemlock gave him a playful grin. "So am I."

"But there are Morlocks out there."

Miss Hemlock glanced toward the front door of the Diogenes Club, then back at Abberline and Mycroft Holmes. "I have to try. I'll think of something. I always do."

Mycroft Holmes peeked through a lace-curtained window at the chaos erupting outside. "Where the hell is Burton? He's usually right in the thick of such things."

"We don't know, sir," said Abberline. "It was our hope that you had encountered him earlier today."

"I've been in the Stranger's Room all day," said Mycroft, arching an eyebrow. "You sent him on some errand through Time, didn't you? To retrieve the list of future events?"

"Precisely," said Miss Hemlock. "And while we're on the subject, how about handing it over."

"What?" said the elder Holmes. "I will do no such thing. The time-line is state property."

"Hand it over, Mr. Holmes, or I'll hand you over to the Morlocks me bloody self."

Mycroft Holmes glared at him. "You wouldn't dare."

"Try me," said Abberline.

Mycroft stared into the policeman's eyes and found nothing but cold resolve, nothing to indicate the policeman was bluffing. He sighed and reached into the breast pocket of his tailored suit coat. "Very well." He extracted a piece of paper and handed it to Abberline, who in turn handed it off to Miss Hemlock.

"Thank you," she said. "Now, I get to the Tower immediately."

Abberline reloaded his revolver. "Stay inside, Mr. Holmes. Don't open this door for man or Morlock."

"Are you giving me orders, Inspector?"

Abberline looked him up and down. "Why yes, I bloody well am. Now stand back and let me do my job."

For once in his life, Mycroft Holmes did as he was told. He stepped back from the portal, allowing Detective Inspector Abberline and the mysterious Miss Hemlock to exit the Diogenes Club. Then he closed the door behind them and bolted it.

From all over the city the Morlocks emerged, stepping out of dim alleyways, crawling out of sewer grates. People ran from them, screaming. Spooked horses bolted, turning over the carts and carriages they hauled, spilling out cargo inanimate and human alike. People fought off the Morlocks as best they could, with walking sticks, umbrellas and bare fists. Under the direction of Inspector Abberline, the London Metropolitan Police showed up in short order, forming a cordon around the area near the Diogenes Club, which was where the largest group of Morlocks seemed to be converging.

Miss Hemlock looked about for a way to reach the Tower of London and catch Nebogipfel before he could abscond with the Wold-Newton stones, if he hadn't already. She knew the chances were great that he already had, but she would deal with that when the time came.

As she ran up the street, she was accosted by a Morlock, the pale brute grabbing her from behind. She screamed, twisting around to get her hand on its goggles. She yanked them off, exposing the creature to the bright midday sun. It howled in pain, shrinking back from her. She gave it a swift kick between the legs for good measure. The Morlock mewled like a wounded animal as she ran up the street away from it, reaching for her Time Machine. If she couldn't navigate through the chaos she would move around it through the fourth dimension. She was about to activate it when a familiar voice called her name.

"Miss Hemlock!"

She looked up to see a carriage driven by none other than Captain

Burton. He slowed the horses to a stop beside her. Inside the carriage was a man who looked strangely familiar, like Nebogipfel, only without the dark beard.

"What are you doing here?"

"We don't have time to explain," said Burton. "Where's Nebogipfel now?"

"He is going to the Tower of London to retrieve the Wold-Newton stones."

"Get in!" said Burton. "Herbert will explain everything on the way."

"I will?" said the Time Traveler.

"Hurry!"

Herbert opened the carriage door and helped Miss Hemlock inside. No sooner had she climbed in than the carriage started off, Captain Burton spurring the horses into a gallop. The carriage bounced so that she feared the entire carriage would come apart at the next bend in the road.

Getting herself seated, she said, "What is going on? Why is Captain Burton with you?"

"He came to see me in the future," said the Time Traveler. "I'm Herbert, by the way."

"So I gathered."

"I'm afraid my doppelganger has been running amok."

Miss Hemlock stared at him for a long moment. "Your what?"

Herbert explained things as best he could as Burton drove them through a sea of marauding Morlocks. Outside the carriage, a few more of the fungoid beasts had been relieved of their goggles, and were being held back people brandishing burning sticks of wood.

"Heavens," said Herbert, staring out one of the carriage windows. "The Morlocks have never had to work so hard for their supper. They bred the Eloi to come to them."

Miss Hemlock didn't have the foggiest idea what the man was talking about, and didn't want to. One thing she had learned from traveling through Time was that it was possible to know too much. Herbert's doppelganger had certainly used that knowledge for ill intent. She knew one thing: none of this was supposed to happen. There was no historical record of Morlocks invading London, and no way to keep such a large-scale event a secret. This was yet another paradox atop an assemblage of paradoxes, and she didn't think she would be able to untangle them.

"This is all my fault," said Herbert. "I never should have built my Time Machine."

"No," said Miss Hemlock. "It's mine. I should have stopped this from happening. Your doppelganger, or whomever he is, should never have been able to come back here. He stole a Time Unit from my offices."

"You did everything you could," said Herbert. "He also went into the future, and brought an army of Morlocks back through Time with him, right under my nose. I should have seen it. He's me, for God's sake!"

"We shouldn't be beating ourselves up," said Miss Hemlock. "There is one person to blame here, and that is this Nebogipfel fellow. We need to find him and put an end to this nonsense once and for all."

"You're bloody well right, of course," said Herbert. "But how? He's been ten steps ahead of us this entire time!"

Miss Hemlock tapped her chin with an index finger. "What does he want with the Wold-Newton stones?"

"He wants to remove himself from this timeline," said Herbert. "This version of Earth."

"What? Can he do that?"

Herbert shrugged. "He thinks he can. Captain Burton has had some experiences that seem to suggest it's possible."

Miss Hemlock arched an eyebrow. "Experiences?"

"He met versions of himself from an alternate timeline," said Herbert. "It was quite fascinating. One of these other Burtons was some sort of mystic who actually had pieces of the Wold-Newton stones embedded in his forehead. By focusing his mental energy, he seemed to be able to move himself and the other versions of himself through different universes. By Jove. I suppose it isn't a universe anymore, is it? Perhaps a multiverse..."

"That is fascinating," said Miss Hemlock, interrupting him. "And it gives me an idea."

ALL THE MYRIAD STRANDS OF TIME

Captain Sir Richard Francis Burton, the Time Traveler, and Miss Hemlock arrived at the Tower of London to discover it overrun with Morlocks. They heard screams and gunfire as they drove beneath the large archway that curved toward the main entrance. Burton urged the wary animals to a stop near the tall steps that led into the ancient structure. The explorer smelled gunpowder and blood as he hopped down from the driver's box and opened the carriage door.

"What is this plan of yours?" asked the Time Traveler

"It's simple enough," said Miss Hemlock, stepping out of the stolen carriage. "We let Nebogipfel win."

"What?" protested Herbert. "That's the opposite of what we should do." But as he alighted from the carriage, his mouth stretched into a devious grin. "By Jove! No, Miss Hemlock is right. We must let him win. It's the only way to stop him."

"I'm afraid I don't follow," said Burton.

"I'll explain on the way," said Miss Hemlock. "Come. We must hurry."

"If we are to let him win," said the explorer, running after her, "why not let him take the Wold-Newton stones and be gone?"

"Because then he wins," said Miss Hemlock as they went up the steps. A Morlock lay upon them, bleeding, its smoked goggles yanked half off its misshapen head.

"This ill-advised daylight invasion isn't going to end well for the Morlocks," Burton said.

"My doppelganger is using them as a distraction," said Herbert. "With half the city fighting the Morlocks he can get at the Wold-Newton stones. Besides, I think he intends to leave them here, giving them a head start on eating humanity. We're nothing but Proto Eloi, as it were."

"Do you have any idea what he's talking about?" asked Miss Hemlock.

Burton nodded. "I'm afraid so, my dear." He produced a revolver from his pocket. Herbert was similarly armed. Miss Hemlock gasped in surprise.

"We stopped by Gloucester Place to procure weaponry," Burton explained. "I'm afraid I was unsuccessful in absconding with the Map of Time. I was waylaid by Herbert's evil doppelganger."

"No worries," said Miss Hemlock, holding up a sheaf of papers. "I got it. He had it on his person."

Burton grinned. "I know. He told me so in the future. I should have known he'd want to keep something that important close at hand at all times. He probably planned to sleep with it under his bloody pillow."

Miss Hemlock stared at him. "You traveled into the future? My future?"

Burton waved the question away. "Yes. Nebogipfel sent me there to gloat. I'll explain later."

"Ah, yes. Well. As for the weapons, let's hope we don't need them," Miss Hemlock said. "Remember, whatever harm befalls Nebogipfel will be visited upon poor Herbert as well. The two are the same person."

"Right," said Burton. "Enough chin-wagging. Let's get this nonsense over with."

The trio of Time Travelers found Nebogipfel easily enough. They simply followed the carnage into the deepest recesses of the Tower of

London, where all of Mycroft Holmes' best secrets were kept. The hallways were littered with bodies, both human and Morlock, and more screams could be heard down dim corridors and at the bottom of curving stone staircases.

Herbert's dark doppelganger leered at them as they entered a large, high-ceilinged room empty save for a complex apparatus of wood and metal that stretched high into the air. A chill flew up Burton's spine as he recognized it as a crude version of the machinery that housed—would house—the consciousness of Mycroft Holmes in the year 1945.

"Herbert!" Nebogipfel exclaimed when he saw the Time Traveler. "So good to see you, old boy. I'm sure this must come as a shock to you."

"Not really," said Herbert. "Captain Burton explained everything to me."

He glared icily at Burton. "How wonderful. You're just in time—pun intended—to witness my latest triumph." He turned, busying himself with fitting the Wold-Newton stones into a wire housing at the center of the mass of wood scaffolding, copper wiring, and brass fittings. Burton noted the wire framework he inserted the stones into looked too much like a human brain.

"Go right ahead," said Miss Hemlock. "We have no intention of stopping you."

Nebogipfel laughed. "Splendid! Then it appears I have over-prepared."

"Your Morlock invasion was entirely unnecessary," said Herbert.

Nebogipfel shrugged. "Live and learn. Ah. There now. All is ready."

"This was your endgame all along," said Burton. "You exploited Mycroft's obsession with prolonging his influence on the world so that you would have the means to separate yourself from Herbert."

"You figured it out! You were always the clever one. History will honor that cleverness, Captain Burton, I assure you. I've seen it with my own eyes. But Mycroft Holmes gets what he wants too. I'm not a monster. I never expected the mountebank to renege on our deal."

"You mean you never made sure he'd go through with it?" asked Miss Hemlock.

Nebogipfel turned to face them, shaking his head. "No. I never went forward through Time again to see if he kept his end of the bargain. He will use this technology to prolong his existence, after a fashion. Of that much I am certain. Isn't that right, Captain Burton?"

The explorer nodded. "That's true. I've seen it. Mycroft's mind will exist in a future version of this contraption, half mad, while an old man mutters incantations."

"Crowley," said Nebogipfel. "And do you know the true purpose of that incantation?"

"I do!" blurted Miss Hemlock. "It's for your benefit, isn't it? Some kind of temporal resonance?"

"Very good, my dear. And I thought Captain Burton was the clever one."

"Temporal resonance?" Burton murmured.

"Of course!" exclaimed Herbert. "By Jove! He intends to set up a harmonic and temporal resonance between these stones and the ones in the future. The ones that contain Mycroft's consciousness."

"Great minds think alike," said Nebogipfel with a smile, tapping his right temple. "Or is that like minds think greatly?"

"Crowley's incantation, then," said Miss Hemlock, "is intended to help you cross out of this timestream."

"Right again," said Nebogipfel, dancing. "The doddering old fool thinks it will summon a supernatural champion to whip the Germans into surrender."

"You're being flippant about a serious matter," said Burton. "This void to which you seek access is far from empty. I've been there. There are *things*, entities, that live within it, and you will only call attention to yourself."

"I know where the monsters lurk, Burton, and I can't wait to make their acquaintance. Perhaps I shall befriend them like I did the Morlocks."

"You would doom us all? Doom me? Just to escape?" said Herbert. His voice was soft, almost pleading.

"I would do anything to be free of you, Time Traveler, with your grand, socialist visions and your naive outlook. Every place—every

389

time—man plants his foot turns to dust. You will be nothing without me, but I will be everything without you."

"But where will you go?" asked Herbert. "What will you do?"

"Why, whatever I want," said Nebogipfel. "Whenever I please. Maybe I'll go back to the start of it all, the dawn of human civilization. You went to humanity's end to try to fix things, poor fellow. I will start at its beginning. With my hand to guide them they may just get it right this time."

Nebogipfel leapt from the platform, staring at his outstretched hands. "It's starting! I can feel it."

"I feel something too," said Herbert. "The hairs on the back of my neck are standing up. It's—"

Herbert doubled over and fell to his knees. Burton flew to his side.

Nebogipfel became translucent. Burton could see through the top of his head to the throbbing Wold-Newton stones vibrating in their wire framework behind him.

"Yes. It's working!" Nebogipfel declared. "Oh, it's wonderful. I can see the Void, Captain Burton. And the Gate beyond."

The room filled with Morlocks, sidling in silently behind the three as they watched Nebogipfel flicker from ghostly translucence to stark solidity and back again. A few of them removed their goggles, but they made no move to assault Burton and the others.

"My children," Nebogipfel said to them. "It is almost time for us to go."

"It will be too late once he is split from Herbert," Burton whispered to Miss Hemlock. "His Morlocks will easily overpower us."

"So much for my plan," she said.

"Maybe not. Nebogipfel showed me the point in the future he is currently in resonance with, and I changed the outcome."

Miss Hemlock stared at him. "What?"

Burton grinned. "I stopped Crowley's ritual and, per Mycroft's request, destroyed his consciousness by grinding the Wold-Newton stones to dust."

"Oh my," said Miss Hemlock. "And Nebogipfel doesn't know?"

"Apparently not. He wanted me to see what he has wrought in

order to gloat. I didn't tell him what transpired when he put me there."

"Then it appears we have an ace up our sleeve after all."

Herbert shuddered. Nebogipfel screamed, falling to the floor. He was solid again.

"What's happening?" he said. "Something's wrong. It isn't working."

"I forgot to mention," said Burton, "when you sent me to your warped future, I destroyed what was left of Mycroft Holmes and stopped Crowley from completing his ritual."

"What? No! The Wold-Newton stones?"

"Destroyed," said the explorer. "They no longer resonate with the versions of themselves here in our time. It's over, Nebogipfel."

The Time Traveler's doppelganger climbed to his feet. "No! I am the Master of Time! It is never over. I shall simply have to go back and try again. Find another iteration of the Wold-Newton stones. I can outlast empires, Burton. Watch the sun blaze to life and die, all in the same afternoon. I am Chronos incarnate, God of Time."

"No," said a syrupy voice behind Burton. The explorer turned as one of the Morlocks, this one still dressed in modern finery, approached, passing Burton, Herbert, and Miss Hemlock and addressing Nebogipfel. "It is over."

"You can speak?" said Nebogipfel.

"Of course," the Morlock said. "We could always speak. We just didn't know your language. Until now. We just needed time, which you provided via your wondrous and terrible machine. You have shown us much. We wish to be more than toilers in the dark, feeding off the gentle Eloi. We want what you offered us. A chance to begin again. To be something more. The Time Ship is waiting."

"But he tricked you," said Miss Hemlock. "Used you. All of you. And you want to take him with you?"

The Morlock turned to her. "He is broken. Like all of us. We will fix each other. Nebogipfel and we Morlocks have much in common. We are tinkerers at heart."

"Wait," said Herbert, rising to his feet, the fugue that had overcome him abating. "What of me? Nebogipfel and I are still the same person."

"No," said the Morlock. "The timestream Nebogipfel comes from no longer exists." It climbed up the scaffold and wrenched the Wold-Newton stones from their wire housing, dashing all but one to the floor before climbing back down. Burton took it upon himself to smash these to dust beneath his boots.

The Morlock glanced at what Burton had done and nodded. "Now they will not exist in 1945," he explained to the Time Traveler. "You last drank your elixir after sending Burton to see the version of 1945 you created through your meddling here. Since that future has now been undone, you are cut off from the path that would have allowed you to wake up as Herbert when the elixir wore off, in the far future, which means the two of you now exist as separate entities."

"No!" cried Nebogipfel. "It can't end this way! Not like this. Not when I was so close."

"But you got what you wanted," said the Time Traveler. "You are free of me." He sounded hurt.

"Yes," said Nebogipfel. "But at the cost of the glorious, chaotic future Mycroft Holmes and I would create together."

"Bismillah!" Burton swore. "The eldritch things Crowley attempted to summon would have destroyed that future. Like everyone else who has dabbled in such things, he failed to realize the true nature of the entities he was asking for help. They do not do man's bidding."

"Not only that," said Miss Hemlock, "but Mycroft Holmes cannot remain in power behind the scenes, or give Crowley the incantation to put the stones in resonance back here. Why didn't I think of that?"

"Because you are now cut off from that timestream as well," said the Morlock.

Miss Hemlock opened her mouth to say something, but no words came out. Finally, she said, "Bloody hell. You're right. My version of 1945 no longer exists. Why, I might not even exist there at all."

"Unlikely," said Herbert. "You're still here with us, after all. Your life might be very different, I grant you that."

"But I can't go back," she said tearfully. "Where I came from no longer exists. My Time Device doesn't have a point to return to."

"Time will return to its original track from this point forward," said Burton. "Without Mycroft's meddling, Aleister Crowley will never become Occult Minister and never attempt to summon eldritch horrors to assist with the war effort and doom mankind as a result."

Miss Hemlock activated her miniature Time Machine. The tiny components whirred, and she appeared to flicker for a moment before returning to full solidity. "I'm stuck. I can't return to the moment I left, because that precise moment no longer exists. Even if I could go back, I'd be a stranger. No family. No birth records. I'd be a temporal ghost. Or, perhaps even worse, there would be two of me. That would certainly be hard to explain to my—our—parents."

"Be not disheartened," said the Morlock, handing her the last Wold Newton stone. "You have a greater purpose."

"What am I supposed to do with this?" She held the glittering black stone between her thumb and index finger, its natural facets catching the light.

"The stone is compatible with your Time Machine apparatus," said the Morlock. "Please. Allow me."

The creature helped Miss Hemlock remove the leather gauntlet from her wrist and open the Time Machine's casing, exposing the device's internal mechanism. His long, hairy fingers were surprisingly adept at working with the minute components of the mechanism, and in a moment he had affixed the remaining Wold-Newton stone to the interior of the device. He secured everything back together and returned the Time Machine to Miss Hemlock.

"You must fix the damage Nebogipfel has wrought," the Morlock said.

Miss Hemlock glanced from Burton and Herbert to the Morlock, a pleading look on her face. "But I don't know how. I don't know where he's been."

"The stone knows," the Morlock said. "It will show you the way. You also have the document Nebogipfel created."

"The Map of Time!" Miss Hemlock pulled the sheaf of notes from her pocket. "I almost forgot." She fastened the Time Machine back onto her wrist. "I still haven't the foggiest idea of how to go about all this."

"You must, my dear," said Burton. "There are certain of the Old

Ones who can take advantage of tears in the fabric of Time to seek access to this world. We're counting on you."

Miss Hemlock considered the explorer's words, taking a deep, steadying breath to steel herself. "That sounds like a noble cause, but I still don't have a home to return to," she said.

"All of Time is your home," said the Morlock. "You will thrive between the ticks of a second. Past and Future shall live within you, from the birth pangs of creation to the final heat death of the universe."

"I am envious, my dear," said Herbert. "You have a front row seat for all of human history, and beyond."

Miss Hemlock gave the Time Traveler a thin smile as tears rolled down her cheeks. "Well, I hope I live up to everyone's expectations. Time Travel is not something to take lightly."

"Which is why we feel you are best suited for it," said the Morlock.

"And what of you?" asked Burton, pointing at the Morlock. "What happens now?"

A group of Morlocks appeared, entering the room and taking Nebogipfel gently by the arms and moving with him toward the room's entrance. He was silently muttering something, seemingly oblivious to his surroundings. Burton wondered if the madness he first developed on the lost continent of R'lyeh in the deep past had at last taken its final toll.

"We are going into the far future, where our presence will not disturb the current timestream. We have much exploring to do, in Space rather than Time. Nebogipfel will be safe with us, and will never again be allowed to travel through Time."

"In that case," said Herbert, "farewell. I hope you find whatever it is you seek. We are no longer enemies."

The Morlock nodded to the Time Traveler and turned to leave, the whole, hairy mass of them—including a captive, catatonic Nebogipfel —flickering out of existence.

"Well, that's quite a mess your doppelganger and the Morlocks left behind," said Burton, glancing around. "We'll have a devil of a time explaining this to Mycroft Holmes and the authorities."

"Then I suppose I'd best be off," said Miss Hemlock. She leaned in and gave Burton and Herbert a quick kiss on the cheek.

"I don't suppose we'll ever see you again," said Burton.

Miss Hemlock shook her head. "Not if I do my job right. It was an honor meeting you, gentlemen."

"And you as well, Miss Hemlock," said Burton.

"Godspeed," said the Time Traveler.

Miss Hemlock flicked the switch on her miniature Time Machine and was gone.

"Well," said Herbert. "That's that. With the Wold-Newton stones gone, Mycroft Holmes won't be able to rule the roost from now till Judgment."

"Hey," a familiar voice called from the doorway. "There you are. I've been looking all over the bloody city for you two!"

"Frederick!" Burton called. "Good to see you, old man."

Detective Inspector Abberline stumbled in the door and looked around at the strange apparatus erected along the room's far wall. "What the devil is going on? All the bloody Morlocks just up and vanished. Even the dead ones! I never thought I'd miss tangling with the bloody shoggoths. Where's your blasted doppelganger, Mr. Herbert?"

Burton and the Time Traveler exchanged bemused glances. "Everything is all tidied up here, Frederick," said the explorer. "But I'll explain everything as best as I can, over drinks at my club."

"Does this explanation involve a lot of that time travel rot?"

"I'm afraid so," said the explorer.

"Then I'm going to need a lot of drinks."

When they arrived at Bartolini's dining rooms on Fleet Street an hour and a half later, Burton realized that Miss Hemlock's tidying up of the timestream had already begun.

"Richard!" said Algernon Charles Swinburne, hiccuping as he gestured to the explorer. Sitting nearby were Charles Bradlaugh, Richard Monckton Milnes, and Dr. James Hunt.

"Where have you been?" asked the poet. "We were just about to recite the Cannibal Catechism. There were bloody creatures running rampant through the streets moments ago. I figured you were on some daft errand for that arrogant foozler Mycroft Holmes."

"Just finished, Algy," said Burton. He blinked at the diminutive poet. "Algy? Is that really you?"

Swinburne laughed, hiccupping again. He swiped a shock of his curly red hair from his eyes. "My Aunt Petunia's pretty lace bonnet! Of course it's me? Who bloody else?"

Burton and Abberline exchanged wary glances. "And you're...all right?"

"Of course! Why wouldn't I be? I'm in my cups, surrounded by good meat and drink. Especially drink." He drained a glass down his neck. "My hat, Richard. You look like you've seen a bloody apparition. It's that gibface Holmes chap, isn't it? Poor fellow. Come, sit and regale us of your latest tale of derring-do. And while you're at it, tell us how we may hire the elder Holmes' younger brother, so we may solve the mystery of why Mycroft is such a bloody fop. Hey hey!"

That got a laugh out of everyone, including Burton, who didn't have the heart to tell Swinburne that the younger Holmes was dead, and who for the moment gave silent thanks to Miss Hemlock for restoring his friend, and for wrangling all the myriad strands of Time. For the first time in a long while, Richard Francis Burton looked forward to his future. A wide open future that was, for the moment, blissfully unknown.

The Time Traveler watched the sun come up over the Palace of Green Porcelain. Behind him in their hut, Weena moaned softly. He turned to watch her, noticing the swollen curve of her belly as she slept.

"Hello, Herbert."

The Time Traveler spun around, heart leaping into his throat. "Bloody hell, Captain Burton! Must you keep doing that?"

"I'm sorry. I can't judge distances between future landmarks."

"It's all right. What can I do for you?"

"Just checking," said the explorer, removing his topper and mopping sweat from his brow with a silk handkerchief. "Seeing how things turned out."

"Well, I can only assume they are much the same," said the Time Traveler. "It doesn't look like all of our mucking about through Time saved humanity, if that's what you're wondering."

"As a wise man once told me, humanity has had its time in the sun," mused Burton with a grin. "No, I was just making sure everything had been put to right again."

"The Sphinx?"

"The Sphinx," said Burton.

The two men walked down the sloping hill, lush grass of a kind Burton had never seen crunching under his booted feet. The day was young and it was already getting hot. "I hope you know what you're doing here," said the explorer. "No one appointed you humanity's savior, you know. Or its martyr."

The Time Traveler chuckled. "Whatever are you talking about, Captain?"

"Aren't you trying to restart humanity?"

His chuckle became a full-blown guffaw. "Oh no, Captain. Nothing quite so grandiose. I am merely making sure Weena and her people are safe. That and, uh…" His voice trailed off.

The explorer arched an eyebrow. "Yes?"

"Weena. I've taken a liking to her. And, well…she's with child."

Burton smiled. "I see. So you are trying to restart humanity."

The Time Traveler laughed, shaking his head. "I don't know what I'm doing. I had the best of intentions."

"As do we all," said Burton. "History is paved with good intentions."

"What of you?" asked the Time Traveler. "What will you do upon your return to our time?"

"I'm going to throw this miniaturized Time Machine into the bloody Thames," said the explorer. "Then I'm going to marry my Isabel, take a boring diplomatic post, and write. In other words, live the rest of my life, as I intended before it was interrupted by submarines and Time travel and monsters and Mycroft bloody Holmes. As history intended."

They neared the Sphinx, its soft white body glowing with reflected early morning sunlight. They walked around the base to peer up at the face carved there.

"By Jove!" said the Time Traveler. "It's a woman this time."

They stared at it for a long time, Burton's mouth stretching into a long smile.

"You know her?" asked the Time Traveler.

"Why, yes," said Captain Sir Richard Francis Burton. "Yes, I believe I do."

THE END

ACKNOWLEDGMENTS

No book springs fully formed from the writer's brow like some mythical god. I'd like to thank everyone who had a hand in this book's creation. John Hartness for giving me a chance; everyone who edited these books, whipped my turgid prose into something presentable, and helped me remember how to spell *Cthulhu fhtagn*; Melissa McArthur for creating such amazing covers for each of these volumes, and everyone who has read and enjoyed them. I never could have imagined a single crazy, one-off idea could have turned into all of this, and to everyone who helped me get there, thank you.

ABOUT THE AUTHOR

James is an award-nominated writer of science fiction and pulp adventure. He is the author of the space opera novels *Star Swarm* and *Ix Incursion*, as well as four novellas in the Shadow Council Archives series from Falstaff Books: *The Depths of Time*, *Shadows Over London*, *The Dream Key*, and *The Map of Time*. James is also the editor and co-creator of the shared world, Cold War giant monster anthology series *Monster Earth*. A recovering comic book addict, James lives in the wilds of Northeast Georgia with his wife and daughter, three dogs, and a metric crap-ton of books. For more of his shenanigans, and to get a free e-book of space opera stories, visit www.jamespalmer-books.net.

FRIENDS OF FALSTAFF

The following people graciously support the work we do at Falstaff Books in bringing you the best of genre fiction's Misfit Toys.

Dino Hicks
Samuel Montgomery-Blinn
Scott Norris
Sheryl R. Hayes
Staci-Leigh Santore

You can join them by signing up as a patron at
www.patreon.com/falstaffbooks.